Infrastructure in Dystopian and Post-apocalyptic Film, 1968–2021

Infrastructure in Dystopian and Post-apocalyptic Film, 1968–2021

Christian B. Long

Bristol, UK / Chicago, USA

First published in the UK in 2024 by
Intellect, The Mill, Parnall Road, Fishponds, Bristol, BS16 3JG, UK

First published in the USA in 2024 by
Intellect, The University of Chicago Press, 1427 E. 60th Street,
Chicago, IL 60637, USA

A catalogue record for this book is available from
the British Library.

Copy editor: MPS Limited
Cover designer: Tanya Montefusco
Cover images: Bridge. Credit: Denis Torkhov;
Broken buildings. Credit: Bulgac.
Production manager: Rosie Stewart,
Westchester Publishing Services UK
Typesetter: MPS Limited

Print ISBN 978-1-83595-003-6
ePDF ISBN 978-1-83595-005-0
ePUB ISBN 978-1-83595-004-3

To find out about all our publications, please visit our website.
There you can subscribe to our e-newsletter, browse or download our current
catalogue and buy any titles that are in print.

www.intellectbooks.com

This is a peer-reviewed publication.

Contents

Figures

Acknowledgements

I wrote this book where the apocalypse already happened: in Meanjin Brisbane, on Yagerra and Turrbal land, where sovereignty was never ceded.

I was lucky that while I assembled ideas, notes, drafts, revisions, a manuscript, and a revised manuscript about the end of the world, a lot of people made my life more pleasant.

Thanks to my fellow office drones: Christie Viggers, Kaitlin Blockey, Marie Morcom, Simone Magnabosco, Natalie Cowley, Lauren Cunningham, Kathryn O'Halloran, Susan Ben Dekhil, Christian Romuss, and Ongelle Rice. Thanks to the other side of the office's drones too: Diana Marsh, Harry Goswami, Angie Kahler, Lindsay Muller, Kirstin Woodward, Alison Pike, Alexandra Hutchinson, and Sally Goodwin.

All the people in university administration who pay ridiculous fees to consulting firms that always recommend cutting jobs and making those who remain precarious deserve nothing but scorn. It's with mixed feelings that I acknowledge they'll never read this book and see this sentence: *You are scum and I hate you all.* True story: Indiana University Press cancelled our agreement because I 'sent a curt message showing disdain for [their] payment system'. This message was about tax forms a year before even submitting a manuscript.

On a more positive note, football is a source of great joy. Thanks to my teammates at Southside Eagles Football Club over the past few years: Aaron, Ari, Ben, Blake, Brad, Dimitri, Edreece, Geoff, Henry, Juil, Kristian, Lachlan, Marsh, Max, Nick, Ryan, Sam, Som, Tait, Tom L, Tom S, Wanlin, and Ed Butcher, who keeps putting my name on the team sheet. Thanks as well to Dr Rasha Al-Tameemi, the staff at the Princess Alexandra Hospital's (PAH) kidney clinic, and the staff at the PAH's audiology clinic.

In the United States: J. D. Connor wrote extensive and detailed feedback on the introduction that increased its quality considerably; Jeff Menne offered some key insights on an early analysis of *The Postman*.

In Canada: Derek Nystrom provided key suggestions on structure, and Tom Ue helped with ideas about *Ready Player One*.

In Germany: Jenny Stümer offered extensive, thorough, and incredibly helpful feedback on my work that made this book better.

In Aotearoa New Zealand: Lloyd Carpenter was always available to read a paragraph in trouble.

In Australia: Alex Bevan was a welcome in-person source of production culture research insight and feedback; Angie Kahler delivered two absolutely key sentences when she read a near-final draft of the manuscript revision; Lisa Bode was key in making my proposal better; and Alastair Blanshard not only snuck me in to teach a class on utopian and dystopian worlds but also made a great sounding board for wild ideas. Thanks as well to Suzanna Fay, Barbara Hanna, Rob Pensalfini, and Paco Perales.

Thanks to the Käte Hamburger Centre for Apocalyptic and Post-Apocalyptic Studies at the Universität Heidelberg for their 2022 conference, which provided an excellent audience to spur revisions. In addition, two anonymous readers of the Centre's journal *Apocalyptica* offered generous feedback on what became the food chapter. I presented parts of the chapter on waste at the *2022 Fantastische Geographien 2022* conference held at the Technische Universität Dortmund and parts of the chapter on transportation at the *2022 Disaster Discourse: Representations of Catastrophe* conference held at Universitatea din București. In both cases, audience members' questions proved useful to getting the chapters into better shape. Parts of the article 'The postman and renewable energy after the apocalypse', originally published in *Peephole Journal* issue 12 (2019), appear in the introduction and the energy chapter. Parts of the introduction, as well as parts of the chapters on energy, transportation, and water, appear in a different form in the chapter 'The infrastructure of the planets of the apes', in *Worlds Ending. Ending Worlds: Understanding Apocalyptic Transformation*, edited by Jenny Stümer, Michael Dunn, and David Eisler. DeGruyter has kindly allowed me to use that material here.

Thanks to Julia Brockley, Jessica Lovett, Helen Gannon, Jelena Stanovnik, and the gang at Intellect, who were a dream to work with a second time. Thanks to Rosie Stewart for shepherding the book from manuscript to final version.

I'm lucky to have friends around the world like Mark Maguire, John Foersterling, Chris Simich, Rob Garcia, Sophie Abel, Karyn Gonano, and Steve Malley. Thanks to Sleep, SUNN O))), Philip Glass, and Mogwai, the soundtrack to my writing. Thanks to Archie and Ozzie, you two monsters.

I miss seeing my sisters Colleen, Killian, and Megan, and the rest of the family: Dad, Piper, Wren, Rachel, Grace, Dave, Matt, and Max. I come from a stereotypical loud working-class ethnic family; the Clements are a stereotypical reserved Yankee farm family. Bruce and Ellen; Becca and Clayton and Thea; Matt and Kate and Luke and Madison are a wonderful family to have joined, mysterious as we are to each other. I wish Vincent Giallombardo, Frank Ward, Geraldine Long, and Paula Giallombardo could see this book.

As if living through a global pandemic and another few natural disasters wasn't enough, Jennifer Clement had to spend most of that time stuck in the house with me as I talked through my ideas about the end of the world and football. Jennifer's critical comments on the too-long drafts I share with her always make me look smarter than I am. There's not enough space in the acknowledgements to begin to say all that she means to me. In brief: everything. This book is for her.

Introduction: Infrastructure in Dystopian and Post-apocalyptic Film, 1968–2021

Using a working flush toilet is one of the most ordinary, taken-for-granted late twentieth- and early twenty-first-century activities. Simple acts like turning on the lights or getting a glass of water or taking a shower, driving down the road or taking transit to the shops, as well as cooking and eating which in turn lead back to the toilet and the sewer system, all require infrastructure. However, as many have noted, infrastructure, when it works, is invisible. This means that the material basis for much of contemporary life is somewhat mystified. That is, the material foundation of everyday life appears as though it has always been there when in fact someone – many someones – must design, build, and maintain our infrastructure. I begin with using the toilet and move to sewers and human waste not simply to be scatological, but rather to make present a part of everyday life that is more often rendered invisible, the infrastructure of everyday life. The ending of *I Am Legend* (Naomi Shoan and David Lazan 2007) presents a similar fictional lacuna.[1] With this in mind, I want briefly to consider three shots from the first twenty minutes of *I Am Legend*, as well as its last shot. A short analysis of the literal construction and function of a number of these shots' elements will show how cinematic imaginings of life after the apocalypse can help expand what appears to be possible in making a better, liveable world.

I will take the images out of narrative order to concentrate on a sequence of infrastructural changes after the apocalypse. When Neville (Will Smith) explores Manhattan a little more than twenty minutes into the movie, he stops at a Mobil station to pick up fuel for the generators at his brownstone fortress (Figure I.1). A low angle shot places Neville in the foreground of the frame, and the Mobil sign is visible in the background. The price of gas is $6.63 per gallon, much higher than the 2007 New York average of $2.53–3.38; such a steep increase in cost, a combination of price gouging and creeping peak oil, is a logical consequence of capitalism facing a natural disaster (US Energy Information Administration 2020: n.pag.). In the moment of apocalypse, the market will bear a

FIGURE I.1: *I Am Legend* gasoline prices.

FIGURE I.2: *I Am Legend* subway pumps fail.

significant price for fuel, as it is an essential component to potential survival: cars to escape and generators to survive use gasoline and/or diesel. Fuel also plays a key role soon after the apocalyptic moment. In the film's first image of the post-apocalypse (Figure I.2), an overhead shot shows a flooded street coming out of a tunnel, the water deep enough to cover city buses. The title says, 'three years later', but tunnels would fill with water in short order, as they require pumps to keep them dry, and those pumps require fuel to operate continually. Alan Weisman explains tunnel flooding, in his case subway flooding, as possible in even tame inclement weather:

> In an abandoned city, there would be no one [...] to race from station to flooded station whenever more than two inches of rain falls – as happens with disturbing

> frequency – sometimes snaking hoses up stairways to pump to a sewer down the street.

Weisman interviews a Metropolitan Transportation Authority Maintenance Supervisor, Peter Briffa, who says that '[a] flood in one zone would push water into the others. Within 36 hours, the whole thing could fill' (2005: 25). An above-ground tunnel like the one in *I Am Legend* would likely take more than the subway's 36 hours, but the danger would still be inescapable. Without pumping, a tunnel will flood.

Changes to infrastructure after the apocalypse on a slightly longer time scale appear in a long shot shortly after the shot of the flooded street and tunnel. We see Neville driving his sports car down a New York City street overgrown by weeds, or at least overgrown by the standards of twenty-first-century affluent Manhattan streets (Figure I.3). A half dozen clumps and lines of plants grow out of the street, and green streaks the grey concrete. Like a flooded tunnel mouth, a Manhattan street with large clumps of ankle-high weeds shows how much effort goes into maintaining roads to keep them smooth and usable. With the New York City Department of Transportation no longer resurfacing and reconstructing the streets, freezing winters and hot summers would soon create cracks in the road. Seeds would get into those cracks and start to grow. The plants would set down roots and spread out, cracking the road open further. As the documentary *Life After People* (de Vries 2009) explains in its tour through the people-free future, '[f]ive years after people, the roads of the world are disappearing beneath a green mat that spreads like some relentless monster'. *I Am Legend* may in fact be frugal in its plant cover and optimistic about its streets' drivability.

FIGURE I.3: *I Am Legend* urban prairie.

FIGURE I.4: *I Am Legend* sheep and cows.

I Am Legend's last shot (Figure I.4) shows a concrete wall that encircles a compound for escapees from the zombified city. This fictional compound is not a medieval-style walled city, but rather a sliver of a New England town ringed by a wall. The shot of Elena driving up to the compound's entry door shows the wall to be nearly ten feet high. As she walks into the compound, the wall appears to be about ten feet thick at its base, narrowing as it goes up. On average the wall could be as much as five feet thick. The length of the wall depends on how much land would they need for the number of sheep and cows they plan to keep. In the final overhead shot there appear to be around 60 sheep and 20 cows. Without going too far into the weeds of pasturing sheep and cattle, the compound, including greenhouses, roads, and forest covers 100 acres, which would be enough for the sheep and cattle to graze on with careful pasture management. One hundred acres is 484,000 square yards. This would require a wall about 8,900 feet in perimeter. A wall 8,904 feet by 10 feet by 60 inches would require a minimum of 16,489 cubic yards of concrete. To build a wall of the size seen in *I Am Legend* would require work on a slightly larger scale than a trip to Home Depot; one 40-pound bag of concrete provides .011 cubic yards of concrete. At a slightly greater scale, a standard cement truck capacity is 8 cubic yards, which means that the wall would have required a minimum of 2,011 trips between the work site and a nearby concrete plant. It probably would take closer to 3,000 trips on unmaintained roads in rural Vermont, not exactly the home to dozens of gas stations to fuel the trucks, as well as the skilled labour to build the wall and to operate and maintain the vehicles and machinery. Assuming a concrete plant within 30-minute drive and enough materials to supply the entire wall construction, working continuously,

3,000 repetitions of concrete mixing, transporting, pouring, levelling, and curing would take at least 50 days, probably closer to 75 given the toll it would take on the workers. A walled compound is indeed a very smart approach to keeping the zombie hordes at bay, but building the wall for that compound in Vermont would pose significant logistical problems.

Second, the compound has a massive excess of renewable energy generation: three horizontal-axis wind turbines, two vertical-access wind turbines, and solar panels on all its greenhouses. Even if we assume that the solar panels will produce power for the agricultural work in the greenhouses, the walled compound will produce much, much more energy than it needs – with nowhere for it to store or sell its excess. An average onshore wind turbine with a capacity of 2.5–3 MW can produce more than 6 million kWh in a year – enough to supply 1,500 average EU households with electricity. I use EU electricity use because the average EU use is substantially lower, and it stands to reason that a post-apocalyptic United States would require less energy use than its current wasteful standards demand. Looking at the housing available in the compound, there appear to be about a dozen houses along the main road, with a larger house to the far left of the frame. Even given a large-scale biomedical production line in the compound, turbines producing at half capacity would produce more energy than could possibly be used. The survivors be better off using one turbine for production and the others for parts when maintenance becomes necessary.

Finally, while the survivors will clearly have something to eat – lamb, mutton, beef, veal, milk, cheese, whatever vegetables they grow in the fields and greenhouses, and maple syrup – less clear is how much water they will have to drink and to use for bathing, as well as for agricultural purposes and the small-scale industry the settlement would need, including small-scale repairs and cleaning the lab in which they would make the zombie-cure vaccine. No irrigation system is evident in the farm areas of the compound, which is to be expected, as Vermont has a low level of irrigation use in its agriculture (US Geological Survey 2020: n.pag.). Depending on rainfall appears to be the plan, as there is no river or creek running through the compound. Given the apparent age of the town centre in the compound, it stands to reason that at least one well has been drilled within the compound's walls. However, this would likely make the collection and distribution of water into domestic spaces an ongoing chore for the residents. Given the compound's rural setting, toilet facilities would likely take the form of septic tanks and, when those fill up, outhouses or the woods.

On the one hand, my analysis sounds like a pedantic killjoy making far too much out of a CGI-augmented shot of a New England village and wondering how people use the toilet in a movie. On the other hand, these images highlight that *I Am Legend*'s hopeful ending depends on the imagination of a particular kind of utopian space that simultaneously roots salvation in some forms of infrastructure while glossing over the practical matter of the construction and maintenance infrastructure requires. A walled compound powered by renewable energy, with a sustainable farm and plentiful well water would be a nice place to live for a short time, while waiting for the dark seekers to die. But it would be a little less nice over the long term since a small village still needs infrastructure and maintenance. Where is the concrete for patching the wall? The oil to lubricate the turbines? The seed vault to keep the greenhouse growing? The septic tank service plan? The end of *I Am Legend* is only a happy ending if we believe that an effective vaccine can be mass produced at the compound. That is to say, it will be a happy ending if people can eventually leave the compound and live elsewhere. The lack of infrastructure and potential for what little there is to fail shows how tenuous the survivors' grasp on civilization will be in the interim, calling that happy ending into question.

My analysis of the infrastructure of *I Am Legend* is meant to show the kinds of concerns and questions that animate this book. As I examine a wide range of films, I ask: what do filmic imaginings of dystopian/post-apocalyptic worlds' infrastructure look like and do? What does the infrastructure in the 'better world' the film offers look like and do? How do these films organize both dystopias and post-apocalyptic worlds, politically and socially, as well as their improved versions? Production designers oversee art directors and set designers who are tasked with building dystopian and post-apocalyptic film worlds, gathering ideas from existing technologies, futurists, catastrophe management consultants, engineers, and engineers of various stripes. In front of the camera, Eli (Denzel Washington) renders a cat for fat in *The Book of Eli* (Gae S. Buckley 2010); behind the camera, the set designer Patrick Cassidy has ensured that the spaces Denzel Washington occupies look weathered enough to make the need for cat fat moisturizer appear logical. Sometimes the worlds work, as in *The Book of Eli*, but sometimes they are flimsy mock-ups, as in *Fortress* (David Copping 1992). Whether they work or fail, in this book I take the films I analyse at their word. That is to say, I take their production design literally, treating sets and locations – and the connections created between places through editing – as actual literal places and networks in which people live and die. In this approach I treat the visual evidence on screen (and sometimes the evidence of dialog and off-screen sound) as a working fictional world undergirded by an infrastructural network that peeks through the *mise en scène*.

In this book I will seek out these moments of infrastructure, both at the centre and the edge of the frame, using simultaneous close-textual nuance and wider generalization first to identify moments where infrastructure appears as part of the diegesis and also as part of the production design, both in use and in the background. Second, I identify how infrastructure offers dystopian and post-apocalyptic movies a basis – a grounding – for both for imagined bad worlds and their hoped-for regeneration. My analysis of the infrastructure of dystopian and post-apocalyptic film worlds will trace the outlines of the thinkable form of a world that either functions too efficiently in the direction of tyranny or must be jerry-rigged to function at all, to offer a glimmer of something beyond bare life. In recognizing these outlines and filling in the first few lines of shading, I hope to create something like what Hans Robert Jauss would call the horizon of expectations for the foundations of practical everyday life in dystopian and post-apocalyptic worlds on film. In cultural terms, I want to develop a clearer understanding of the social imaginary of infrastructure and its roles in practical everyday life. In *Modern Social Imaginaries*, Charles Taylor defines the social imaginary as 'the ways people imagine their social existence, how they fit together with others, how things go on between them and their fellows, the expectations that are normally met, and the deeper normative notions and images that underlie these expectations' (2004: 23). He elaborates further with three points that make mass audience dystopian and post-apocalyptic films particularly apt texts for study. 'I adopt the term imaginary', he writes,

> (i) because my focus is on the way ordinary people 'imagine' their social surroundings, and this is often not expressed in theoretical terms, but is carried in images, stories, and legends. It is also the case that (ii) theory is often the possession of a small minority, whereas what is interesting in the social imaginary is that it is shared by large groups of people, if not the whole society. Which leads to a third difference: (iii) the social imaginary is that common understanding that makes possible common practices and a widely shared sense of legitimacy.
>
> (Taylor 2004: 23)

This is why Hollywood films – as well as mass audience films from the United Kingdom, Australia, and Aotearoa New Zealand – constitute the basis of the study. I concentrate on films from the rich anglophone countries for their unselfconscious world-bestriding nature. Put another way, the end of the world looks different from the top of the heap. As JD Connor puts it, '[f]iguring out Hollywood amounts to figuring out culture as a whole – not because culture begins and ends with Hollywood, but because the *whole* of the equation of pictures prompts us to investigate both culture's capacities and its limits' (2018: 10). Post-apocalyptic and dystopian films have shown a broad appeal: huge commercial successes like *The Hunger Games* (Phillip Messina 2012), some like *Soylent Green* (Edward C. Carfagno and George W. Davis AD 1973) have become part of everyday speech (Soylent Green is people!), cult and academic favourites, many of which were box office failures like *Blade Runner* (Lawrence G. Paull 1982), family-friendly films like *WALL-E* (Ralph Eggleston 2008), young adult films like *Divergent* (Ralph Eggleston 2008), sombre near-horror films like *The Road* (Chris Kennedy 2009), and even comedies like *Zombieland* (Mahar Ahmad 2009). Almost every film I analyse in this book comes from a major studio or from an exploitation tradition, with an clear eye toward box office returns; they create images, stories, and legends for the mass audience of 'ordinary people'. I try to balance three concerns in my selection of films: films a lot of people saw (hits), critically acclaimed films (prestige), and, finally, noble failures, often in the form of box office flops like *The Postman* (Ida Random 1997) or films that feature interesting ideas and/or production design like *The Quiet Earth* (Josephine Ford 1985) (author's choice). For this reason, I did not include 'art house' films with a dystopian tinge like Michael Haneke's *Time of the Wolf/Le Temps du Loup* (Christoph Kanter 2003) and Yorgos Lanthimos's *The Lobster* (Jacqueline Abrahams 2015). This book covers infrastructure on film from 1968 to 2021. The first film, chronologically, is *Planet of the Apes* (Jack Martin Smith and William Creber AD 1968) because, to begin with, it was a critically well-received box office success. The film has also had incredible staying power, not only as a going box office concern – the Music Box Theatre in Chicago played it in 2023, 55 years after its release – but also as a source of culturally significant images and lines – the Statue of Liberty buried up to the neck, 'it's a mad house!' – as well as a film with a production design that informs its ideas about US race and class relations. The films I analyse in this book address a large group of people (if for no other reason than to give themselves a chance to recoup their production costs, as dystopian and post-apocalyptic films tend to require sizable budgets) and in doing so form a common basis for understanding possible common practices in possible dystopian and post-apocalyptic futures.

'Mad Max' describes not only a film series, but also one broadly recognized version of post-apocalyptic life. In this book, I expand our film-derived shorthand vocabulary to include the infrastructural foundations of both dystopian/post-apocalyptic and contemporary life. I will range across about one hundred dystopian and post-apocalyptic movies, from yesterday's visions of tomorrow's apocalypse in *Planet of the Apes* to *Gattaca*'s (Jan Roelfs 1997) eugenic dystopia to *The Purge* series' (2013–21) fascist-eliminationist dystopias to *The Matrix*'s (Owen Paterson 1999) tech apocalypse and more. I do not intend to offer definitive answers. Rather I propose a number of practical/infrastructural options that might make the rapidly approaching end of the world more liveable if we take mass audience dystopian and post-apocalyptic movies as a starting point for our plans.

Infrastructure, dystopia, post-apocalypse

In his book *Eaarth*, environmental activist Bill McKibben writes:

> Begin with the most boring word in the political lexicon: *infrastructure* [...] infrastructure – our physical stuff, our housing stock and our roads and our rail lines and our ports and our fibre-optic cables and our pipelines – is what defines us as an advanced economy.
>
> (2010: 59)

The litany of what constitutes infrastructure appears throughout the literature in anthropology, geography, history, and urbanism, as well as in film and literary studies. In an early article on the anthropology of infrastructure, Susan Leigh Star offers an accessible list with which to start thinking about what infrastructure includes: 'People commonly envision infrastructure as a system of substrates – railroad lines, pipes and plumbing, electrical power plants, and wires' (1999: 380). In an article in the *Journal of Urban Technology*, Michael Neuman notes that infrastructure is not always what we can see, as it 'first referred to facilities built below the Earth's surface: water, sewer, steam, and drainage systems installed under streets' (2006: 10–11). This sense of the hidden facilities undergirding life above appears in Patricia Yaeger's 'Dreaming of infrastructure', in which she writes, '[*i*]*nfra* means beneath, below, or inferior to, while *infrastructure* represents the equipment, facilities, services, and supporting structures needed for a city's or region's functioning. Airports; communication systems; computer grids; highways; gas, electric, and water systems; sewers; streets; waste management' (2007: 15). Recognizing infrastructure, which is sometimes above ground, visible, and familiar, but at other times underground and hidden, or unfamiliar and opaque, requires some experience or training. Brian Hayes's *Infrastructure: The Book of Everything for the Industrial Landscape* offers its readers

> a guide to the common sights of the built environment [...] that we pass by every day and yet seldom really notice [...] places that most of us never see close up; many of us would go out of our way to *avoid* seeing them.
>
> (2005: 1)

Hayes closes the introduction with '[m]y hope is that this book will cultivate greater awareness of all the miscellaneous hardware that goes into making a civilization' (2005: 5). In other words, training our eyes to see what we pass over – the miscellaneous hardware of our surroundings – will reveal what undergirds civilization, what enables us to, for example, go out for a dinner and movie or to stream a movie at home.

It seems, based on just the short paragraph above, that it would be difficult to miss infrastructure, so long and varied is the list. For Brian Larkin infrastructure 'refers to this totality of both technical and cultural systems that create institutionalized structures whereby goods of all sorts circulate, connecting and binding people into collectivities' (2008: 5–6). Infrastructure connects and creates communities, making it essential to surviving a dystopian world and recreating civilization after the apocalypse. Many writers on infrastructure note that the only time it enters the public consciousness is when it breaks. The phone call drops out. The pothole makes the road impassable or gives you a flat. The sewer backs up. Infrastructure, what Pierre Belanger calls '*the basic system of essential services that support a city, a region, or a nation*' (2016: 96, original emphasis), can determine the shape of everyday life. The invisibility of this infrastructure, combined with its everydayness, makes it vulnerable. As McKibben's starting point indicates, 'infrastructure is supposed to be boring, practically by definition' (Rubenstein et al. 2015: 576). In practical and political terms, boring infrastructure means it is relegated to trade publications rather than the front page of the *New York Times* and falls under local government body control – and the low voter turnouts that come with such offices – rather than a high-profile state or federal office.

In film formal terms, boring means infrastructure frequently appears, metaphorically speaking, at the edge of the frame, peripheral to the *mise en scène*, and as non-essential to the narrative's main interests, which tend to be more psychological and problem-solving and goal-oriented. As Alexander Sergeant describes this phenomenon, '[w]hen we see, for example, a close-up of a character, or a single shot of a location, we do not imagine that the bodies or settings we see merely stop at the end of the frame' (2021: 139). The familiarity of infrastructure renders it *almost* invisible: a street scene can feature paved roads, sewer grates, rubbish bins, and so on, that pass almost without notice until a pothole causes a car to throw up a splash of water, or an important object falls to the ground and rolls through the sewer grate. The edge of the frame offers a starting point to think beyond the plot problems found in the film and to consider the physical basis for solving not only the large-scale problems that drive film narratives, but also the everyday getting-through-the-day problems – the taken-for-granted eating, drinking, travelling, power-and-toilet using that often lands on the cutting room floor – that fictional worlds (and their audiences) take as their baseline.

In this book I use the term dystopia in the same sense that Tom Moylan describes it, 'a detailed and pessimistic presentation of the very worst of social alternatives' (2000: 147). In dystopian literature,

> the material force of the economy and the state apparatus controls the social order and keeps it running; but discursive power, exercised in the reproduction of meaning

> and interpellation of subjects, is a complementary and necessary force. Language is a key weapon for the reigning dystopian power structure. Therefore, the dystopian protagonist's resistance often begins with a verbal confrontation and the reappropriation of language.
>
> (Baccolini and Moylan 2003: 5–6)

In dystopian film, while language retains its power, the brute physical surroundings of a film mean that the appropriation of space, even in unremarked moments, occupies an important position in the resistance to the controlling social order. Accordingly, I will concentrate my analysis on the spatial and material contours of the imposition and reorienting of social order. I will use post-apocalypse and post-apocalyptic in their more informal use, not in their religious sense. Accordingly, I will consider post-apocalyptic to mean a world after 'widespread and catastrophic destruction' (Peebles 2017: n.pag.). Thus the what-comes-before of the films I analyse will have 'the character of an apocalypse or world-consuming holocaust', 'a catastrophe that, in its sublime horror, reveals and *collapses* the past, present, and future' (Baldick 2015: 21; Mantoan 2018: 163) as their starting point. The body of the film will find its characters living in the aftermath of not just a collapse of past, present, and future, but also in a world where the infrastructure has, to some degree or other, collapsed in a literal sense.

I will also engage with the cultural and ideological implications of dystopian and post-apocalyptic narratives in a manner common to film, literary, and cultural studies. As Rafaella Baccolini and Tom Moylan put it in *Dark Horizons: Science Fiction and the Dystopian Imagination*,

> the dystopian imagination has served as a prophetic vehicle, the canary in a cage, for writers with an ethical and political concern for warning us of terrible socio-political tendencies that could, if continued, turn our contemporary world into the iron cages portrayed in the realm of utopia's underside.
>
> (2003: 1–2)

Post-apocalyptic narratives differ slightly from dystopian ones; as Cuddon defines the term, 'prophetic or quasi-prophetic writings [...] tend to present doom-laden visions of the world and sombre and minatory predictions of mankind's destiny' and 'apocalyptic writing is usually concerned with the coming end of the world, seen in terms of a visionary scheme of history' (Cuddon 1998: 48; Baldick 2015: 21). I will situate my analyses of post-apocalyptic films in the material context of their production in a very literal sense. I want to look at infrastructure as the key to the political contestations in dystopian and post-apocalyptic worlds, and as one of the primary means to understand both the anti-utopian and utopian impulses of anglophone, mostly Hollywood/American, culture (Wegner 2003: 170). Understanding how fictional post-apocalyptic worlds imagine rebuilding their infrastructure diagnoses the essential functions to return to civilization and can show us how heading off the apocalypse might take infrastructural form.

Infrastructuralism

In an end of the world narrative, Gary Wolfe writes:

> [T]here are commonly five large stages of action: (1) the experience or discovery of the cataclysm; (2) the journey through the wasteland created by the cataclysm; (3) the settlement and establishment of a new community; (4) the re-emergence of the wilderness as antagonist; and (5) a final, decisive battle or struggle to determine which values shall prevail in the new world.
>
> (2011: 106)

All five stages of action are interesting in their own way, but in this book I will analyse moments when infrastructure supports not just exciting, spectacular action, but also some of the basic functions of everyday life – the settlement and establishment of new communities, in other words. This means that, while I am interested in the plots and events of these films, I am equally interested in what happens at the edge of the frame, the sorts of things that establish the extra-diegetic reality of the fictional dystopian and post-apocalyptic worlds. To pursue this line of inquiry, I will investigate ways that transportation infrastructure (roads and rail/transit in particular), electricity generation and use, water use and provision, food creation and consumption, and waste disposal including recycling and sewerage, operate as concrete objects and processes in dystopian and post-apocalyptic films. In other words, how do these films imagine life going on from day to day, not so much to solve the problems of the films' plots but to make possible a credible, coherent world in which more quotidian problems might be solved? How do their worlds support everyday life so that the extraordinary can be foregrounded?

Infrastructure is a real thing, and it is also a metaphor. In his foundational essay 'The politics and poetics of infrastructure', Brian Larkin writes that '[r]oads and railways are not just technical objects then but also operate on the level of fantasy and desire. They encode the dreams of individuals and societies and are the vehicles whereby those fantasies are transmitted and made emotionally real' (2013: 333). Infrastructure gives form to the abstractions of fantasy, desire, dreams, emotions, and more. In a more avowedly political vein, Adam Rothstein writes in *Rhizome* that, infrastructure is 'the underground, the conduited, the containerized, the concreted, the shielded, the buried, the built up, the broadcast, the palletized, the addressed, the routed. It is the underneath, the chassis, the network, the hidden system, the combine, the conspiracy' (2015: n.pag.). Infrastructure mediates the concrete economic processes Rothstein describes, most tellingly in being kept out of sight. In a historical vein Chris Otter links infrastructural maintenance to social reproduction: 'The civil city is always a work in progress. It is never assembled; it is always being maintained, inspected, improved. This laborious process of upkeep is easily forgotten' (2002: 14).

It is possible to fuse the literal/physical and the metaphorical/abstract in the form of infrastructure. As Hanna Appel, Nikhil Anand, and Akhil Gupta write,

> The temporality of infrastructure, therefore, matters a great deal in the creation of spatial patterns of living, working, and entertainment; it influences the direction and degree of spatial extension; and it has profound social and political impacts. Like metros and rail lines, highways, cable networks, and even wireless communication all extend spatially over time, and it is this temporality that in turn produces variegated forms of spatiality and particular patterns of sociality.
>
> (2018: 17)

One pattern of sociality and its political impacts that infrastructure mediates is access to clean drinking water. As Appel, Anand and Gupta put it, 'through everyday connections and disconnections, pipes, roads or electricity wires form populations that are unevenly governed and left aside […] To govern infrastructure […] is to govern the politics of life, with all its inequalities' (2018: 21). The state of Michigan, for example, is home to Gross Pointe – average 2018 household income $108,083 – and Flint – average 2018 household income $27,717 (US Census Bureau 2022a: n.pag., 2022b: n.pag.). The unevenly governed nature of the state appears not just in the massive income disparity between Grosse Pointe and Flint, but also in the connection of some water pipes and the disconnection – or dangerous functioning – of others. The absence, malfunction, and even composition of water pipes in Flint, as opposed to the water pipes in Grosse Pointe, clearly show that the physical aspect of infrastructure has tangible effects – increased mortality rates, for example – and affective ones as well. In 'The infrastructure of intimacy', Ara Wilson argues that

> relationships take place in environments comprised of these material and immaterial, functional or failing networks. Understanding how infrastructures enable or hinder intimacy is a conduit to understanding the concrete force of abstract fields of power by allowing us to identify actually existing systems rather than a priori structures.
>
> (2016: 2)

When President Barack Obama visited Flint in May 2016, he said:

> Because if there's a child who feels neglected on the north side of Flint, or a family on the east side of this city who wonders whether they should give up on their hometown and move away, or an immigrant who wonders whether America means what we say about being a place where we take care of our own. That matters to all of us – not just in Flint, not just in Michigan, but all across America. Flint's recovery is everybody's responsibility. And I'm going to make sure that responsibility is met.
> (Reilly 2016: n.pag.)

The intimacy here is the President's inclusion of Flint in the category of 'Americans', as a group that takes care of its own. The conditions for everyday life – safe water, in this case – are a failed collective responsibility, and it is possible to read that failure as an index of the value of the people the system failed. But the ongoing infrastructural failure in Flint causing continued boil orders makes plain that maintaining or rebuilding a national identity depends on concrete infrastructure to support daily life and to create the possible conditions for the formation of abstractions such as a shared discourse around national belonging.

This discourse has a textual form. I engage with three authors to arrive at a point in literary-cultural studies that I will use in this book in my own analyses: infrastructuralism. Sophia Beal's *Brazil under Construction: Fiction and Public Works* argues that twentieth-century Brazilian writers successfully engaged the role of infrastructure in shaping perceptions of Brazil, and that by 'analysing portrayals of public works in literature, we can better understand the conflicting conceptions of the nation that grew up alongside these public works' (2013: 2, 10). Like Beal, Michael Rubenstein connects nation and infrastructure: 'works of art and public works [...] are imaginatively linked in Irish literature of the [Modernist] period for reasons having to do with the birth of the postcolonial Irish state' (2010: 2). And also like Beal, Rubenstein's analysis of Irish Modernism looks to public works, a kind of infrastructure. Bruce Robbins speculates on why projects such as Beal's and Rubenstein's were among the first to investigate infrastructure in literary and cultural studies: 'Public utilities drop off the radar because they seem to constitute a minimum threshold, an Earth-bound zone in which the large irresolutions of politics can for once be ignored and decisions safely left to the technocrats' (2007: 31). Robbins concludes his piece making the case for infrastructure as a key sociocultural diagnostic:

> Infrastructure needs to be made visible, of course, in order to see how our present landscape is the product of past projects, past struggles, past corruption [...] But we also need to make infrastructure visible as a guide to the struggles of the present.
> (2007: 32)

In this book I direct my attention towards what Dominic Davies calls 'the more conventional side of the infrastructural coin [...] the occurrence of a certain type of infrastructure *in*' the text (2017: 18, original emphasis). This means I will first concentrate on the appearance and function of infrastructure in films. As my examples in this introduction have already shown, because dystopian and post-apocalyptic films take place in physical locations, they cannot help but have infrastructure in them. However, I hope that this book, conventional though its approach may be, will be more than a catalogue, more than just 'representations of infrastructure in dystopian and post-apocalyptic films, 1968–2021'. As Adam Rothstein argues, '[t] here is always a danger of myopia in infrastructural work. In the bright light of a revealed world we are dazzled by the mystery of scale, the techno-capitalist sublime, and we might forget the lived realities we are dealing with' (2015: n.pag.).

A brief example can make clear how easy it can be to stop with the appearance of the representation of infrastructure; often it is at a physical scale that requires long shots and extreme long shots, and such shots can shrink the humans who use the infrastructure into insignificance. In *The Road*, the man (Viggo Mortensen) and the boy (Kodi Smit-McPhee) stop on a highway overpass, spending the night in a crashed tractor trailer. Before going to sleep, the boy tells his father that he wishes he was with his mother. 'You mean you wish you were dead', the man says. 'You mustn't say that. It's a bad thing to say [...] You have to stop thinking about her. Go to bed.' In a sequence filled with golden light, the man dreams of playing piano with the boy's mother. He awakes and remembers – without the golden light – breaking up furniture for fuel. Crying, he gets out of the trailer cab, and we see a long shot from below the overpass, creating an abstract composition of light and dark, with no human presence in the frame at first. A tiny dot appears, the man's head, and a cut takes us to a high angle overhead shot of the man looking down from the overpass. In a straight-on medium shot, he takes out his wallet and looks at a photo of his smiling wife (Charlize Theron). A cut to a longer low angle shot of the overpass shows the little dot releasing the wallet from his hand. After another cut to a high angle shot above the man, a couple of medium shots show the man taking off his wedding ring, and then a close-up shows him pushing the ring across concrete with his finger. He pushes the ring along a crack in the concrete and pauses with the ring at the very edge of the concrete. He remembers, again without golden light, his wife walking out of the house – going out to meet her own death – for the last time, telling him to head south before winter. Returning from the flashback, the man's voice-over of the memory finishes, '[t]here is no other tale to tell', and a cut shows an even longer extreme low angle long shot of the overpass, again without a human form present.

One of infrastructuralism's main aims is 'to be attentive to the difference between the "planned violence" of infrastructures of control and coercion, often imposed from above in the interests of power, and the infrastructures of provision and entitlement, often demanded from below' (Rubenstein et al. 2015: 581). *The Road* shows a massive sweeping highway overpass designed for fast travel and the consumer culture of post-war suburbanization. But after the apocalypse these uses are long gone, as are suburban domesticity and consumerism. The man and boy's shopping cart is filled with scavenged items essential to survival – water tanks, tarps – not indulgent purchases. They walk south for bare survival. Balancing the from-above and from-below means balancing not only the representation of infrastructure but also the ways in which that infrastructure is put to use. Sometimes this will be explicit in the narrative, as with the man, his wedding ring, and the overpass. Other times, it will be implicit and part of the film's imagination of a fictional world, in establishing shots, in moments when characters take infrastructure for granted by just going about their dystopian or post-apocalyptic business, crossing the country and using overpasses along the way.

Treating the infrastructure *in* the text as background that speaks builds on Caroline Levine's perceptive claim that, 'to accept the status quo requires a dampening of perception' (2015: 590). To see more of the frame, including the nearly invisible infrastructure in it, serves not only the aims of film studies but also those of cultural criticism. In *Corridor: Media Architectures in American Fiction*, Kate Marshall similarly notes how attention to what she calls corridors helps us to see the cultural organizational logic behind texts:

> Visible infrastructure brings structure to the surface, but not as a superstructure, which would imply that something remains beneath, propping it all up. Infrastructure as a description and concept has come to signify organization in its physical and abstract senses: it can refer to the bureaucratic structures composing the modern state; public works such as mass transit systems, roadways, and power and sewage utilities, technical communication media and their networks, and the organization underlying social formations and modern business.
>
> (2013: 83–84)

Strange as it seems, dystopian and post-apocalyptic movies usually conclude with optimism, with a window into what is possible in the face of social dysfunction (and worse). The infrastructure that peeks through at the edges of the frame surfaces some of the concrete ways in which dystopian and post-apocalyptic survivors have made do with their damaged and destroyed worlds. If the happy endings so common to Hollywood and mass audience films do not provide an all-encompassing vision of a better world, the presence of infrastructure, whether old or retrofitted or new, offers a starting point for the continued work of building toward the future. Changes to infrastructure, both in its narratively key functions and in its ambient presence at the edge of the frame, allow us to see imagined worlds better, to understand how they retain desirable and essential infrastructure, imagine changes to imperfect infrastructure, and lose sight of what might be essential infrastructure on which to build the new post-dystopian and post-apocalyptic communities.

Production design as infrastructure

To specify exactly how I will be approaching infrastructure as film form: I balance my attention between the people and narratives in the films I analyse, and the worlds that they build and recover as well as the material foundations of those worlds, which often operate as the structural preconditions for life in those fictional worlds (rather than the more limited concern of the film narrative). Such an approach pays attention to how films explicitly and implicitly 'encode the dreams of individuals and societies' in infrastructure (Larkin 2008: 33). Thus, an infrastructuralist approach to film needs to place production design in its sights to understand the power of infrastructure in the maintenance, creation, and supersession of the fictional worlds of dystopian and post-apocalyptic films. Production designers synthesize their preproduction research into the film infrastructure that sometimes occupies the centre, sometimes the edge of the frame, the ambient surroundings of dystopian and post-apocalyptic worlds.

Two books in particular offer a critical foundation to analysing how production design builds the infrastructure of movies and of their fictional worlds: Charles and Mirella Jona Affron's *Sets in Motion: Art Direction and Film Narrative* and C. S. Tashiro's *Pretty Pictures: Production Design and the History of Film*. Both describe the workings of art direction and production design as well as critique particular manifestations. Films are attributed to directors, producers, studios, and sometimes stars, but not often to their set director or art director, with science fiction, fantasy, and post-apocalyptic films offering exceptions to the rule. Movie starts and directors appear on red carpets, and make the promotional rounds. When was the last time a production designer was a guest on a late-night talk show? Though a junior or broadly under-recognized partner in the collaborative art of filmmaking in the general public discourse on film,

> [t]he success of the individual art director in imposing his or her vision on the interpretation of the script, in designing sets that control the mise-en-scène, can constitute an emphatic narrative intervention. Self-effacing craftsperson, expert technician, accomplished artist, the set designer moves variously through a system

> that generally demands only innocuous backgrounds but sometimes [...] allows for decors of significant narrative power.
>
> (Affron and Affron 1995: 5)

The push and pull of production design is apparent: on the one hand, the obvious cinema of mass audience entertainment pictures demands an innocuous, unobtrusive background for its goal-oriented, problem-solving narratives, lest it distract from the plot and performers. On the other hand, sometimes a set or location – dressed and designed to serve its fictional world – can contribute significantly to its extravagance. In this way the work of production design has narrative and extra-narrative power, serving the narrative and also creating a world in which narrative events and consequences are made possible and consequential.

Laurence Buell notes that, in the 1970s, '[d]epictions of future societies in the midst of perpetual environmental meltdown multiplied as sexy backgrounds for new kinds of excitement; environmental crisis in full bloom was recruited as an only nominally dystopian background against which thrilling high-tech adventures might unfold' (2003: 197). While spectacular sets are easy to recognize and remember, setting as unobtrusive space is more common. In the introduction to *British Film Design: A History*, Laurie Ede describes the unobtrusive set in terms that resemble how infrastructure is defined: 'This book is about some of the things that we take for granted, in films and elsewhere', adding later that

> the normal function of the designer is to flow with the mood of the story, to support the aims of the production and to ensure that the sets don't disrupt the illusion [...] good film décor will always have something to tell us; it colours our understanding of characters and their verisimilitudinous screen worlds.
>
> (2010: 1, 5)

Along similar lines, in *What an Art Director Does: An Introduction to Motion Picture Production*, which aims to demystify the process, Ward Preston preaches humility on the part of an art director. Recounting his first day as set designer, Preston asks his boss, the art director, what an art director does: 'After what I presume to be reflective thought, he replies proudly: "The art director is responsible for everything you see on the screen", he pauses to consider the modifying clause: "that doesn't move" then, searching for a further amendment, wistfully adds: "and is usually out of focus"' (1994: x). Preston later offers a way to evaluate a set designer's work that matches Ede's claims:

> The real test of a [set] designer's work is the story the sets and locations tell. Let's hope that it's the same story that's emerging from the dialog, the action, the editing, and the

> score. And like the editing, the camera work, and the score, the sets are most effective when they don't call attention to themselves or overpower the story.
>
> (1994: 75)

Here we can see Ede and Preston treating the set and art direction as a kind of infrastructure, only visible when it breaks down or ceases to function in its expected narrative-prioritizing way. Clearly, production design in a movie and the infrastructure that makes our everyday lives possible are not the same thing. Finding a set impressive or indicative of a dystopian world is not the same as Texans freezing because of a failed power grid or people in Jackson, Mississippi not having clean water. But there is a clear similarity, and it makes sense to use the same techniques of analysis in both cases.

These visions of set and art direction as a kind of infrastructure that can vary in form and function call out for a typology, and Affron and Affron offer the most useful. Their framework describes what they classify as the five levels of a set. The first, Level One: Set as Denotation, offers no more than transparent decorative intervention and appears in 'narratives determined to depict the familiar through the Verisimilitudinous' (Affron and Affron 1995: 37, 38). At the simplest level of appearance, this would take the form of a ranch house in the suburbs having electric-powered lights and running water in the kitchen sink. Level Two: Set as Punctuation, appears in 'moments of emphasis, [when] décor enters into a dynamic with narrative that establishes not time, place, and mood alone, but time, place, and mood as these center on the specificities of class, gender, race, and ethnicity' (Affron and Affron 1995: 38). That is to say, 'the punctuative set aspires to be expressive. By defamiliarizing the quotidian and the verisimilitudinous, it replaces conventional codes of art direction with design strategies that advance the film's narrative propositions' (Affron and Affron 1995: 38). An expressive infrastructural set appears on a small scale in Malcolm's (Jason Clarke) place in *Dawn of the Planet of the Apes* (James Chinlund 2014). His room has a high ceiling, and a red tube snakes down from the ceiling, across the room, into a large white plastic barrel. Malcolm collects rainwater on the roof and has rigged a system to deliver it to his living space, testament to his ingenuity in the face of post-apocalyptic deprivation. Moving slightly further away from the verisimilar nature of Level One, Level Three: Set as Embellishment offers

> powerful images that serve either to organize the narrative or as analogies to aspects of the narrative [...] At the punctuative level the exceptional set can, in a certain sense, continue to be perceived as essentially denotative by the viewer; at the level of embellishment the viewer cannot fail to read the design as a specific necessity of the narrative [...] [T]hey may propose immense, spectacular sets [...] they may lavish

> attention on elaborate constructions so as better to demolish them during extended scenes of disaster and de(con)struction.
>
> (Affron and Affron 1995: 39)

The mountain-sized reactor at the end of *Total Recall* (William Sandell 1990), with its alien hand starting mechanism, heating rods hundreds of feet long, and huge exhaust pipes leading to the surface of Mars, all indicate that it would indeed be possible to create a breathable atmosphere out of the glacier, such is the size of the reactor. Big action films are partial to Level Three sets, as they reward the massive explosions in the third act. Level Four: Set as Artifice sets 'privilege their own artificiality [...] The décor of artifice is, in fact, a primary focus of the narrative, challenging the force of plot and character [...] Here, décor has the privilege to create new realities' (Affron and Affron 1995: 39). A film like *Dredd* (Mark Digby 2012) revels in the potential to show a fascist future written all over the walled Mega City 'rationally' laid out in a grid of massive multilevel highways pierced by massive concrete block towers. Lastly, Level Five: Set as Narrative, describes 'those unusual films in which the field of reading is composed of a single locale' (Affron and Affron 1995: 39), which do not appear in any of the films I analyse in this book.

All these descriptions and schemas of set direction and art direction place décor at the service of the film narrative, encouraging not the sexy background but the stolid grounding of narrative-serving invisibility. However, as JD Connor points out, '[o]ne difficulty with this model is that it presumes a rather overweening primacy of narrative' (2015a: 121). Tashiro makes much the same claim, noting that

> just as narrative directs attention to parts of the image at the expense of others, assuming that narrative has this capability has channeled discussion of the image *toward its narrative function*, regardless of whether or not such a discussion reflects the experience of a film.
>
> (1998: xv)

In broad terms, establishing shots offer a view of infrastructure in a broader context, which we might call landscape. In 'Between setting and landscape in the cinema', Martin Lefebvre asks:

> [W]hat about landscape in narrative fiction films that focus on events and action? We are familiar with the accepted golden rule of classical cinema: everything must be subordinated to the narrative. In principle, each element of the film ought to be able to be integrated into the narrative process. This is especially true for the setting (including exteriors) which situates the action and events related by the film.
>
> (2006: 28)

Alexa Weik von Mossner writes that 'Lefebvre differentiates between "setting", "landscape", and "territory", arguing that film landscape emerges in the moments when a natural space becomes "autonomous" from the narrative' (2012: 43). In these moments of autonomy, landscape takes primacy over narrative and 'rather than on the story, or viewers themselves shift their attention away from the narrative and towards the "background"' (Weik von Mossner 2012: 43). I am certainly interested in the showy moments of landscape, but not to the exclusion of the 'hidden in the background' moments of landscape/background/setting – the world that emerged from decades of higgledy-piggledy infrastructural development. That is to say, when it comes to production design I too am less interested in the primacy of narrative and narrative functions than I am in the imagination of a functioning world behind and beyond the film narrative.

Infrastructure that not only appears but also – as a concrete thing – reveals the workings of the fictional world will serve as the film-form basis for my analyses. As Eva Horn describes the process,

> This is not a matter of plumbing the elements of this world for their symbolic or metaphorical meaning but rather of accepting them as diegetic realities – only in order to marvel at them all the more. To 'enter' a diegesis, a fictional universe, is to tap into its context, just as we explore unfamiliar worlds in our everyday lives – not, that is, to understand them as signs or symbols that in turn refer to something outside of this world (in the abstract realms of literary history, philosophy, theology, and so on). To comprehend the scenario of a potential world is not merely to illuminate it with historical knowledge but *also* to do so with a sort of heuristic naivety that is oriented toward descriptions, literal meanings, and 'basic' understandings.
>
> (2018: 19)

To use Affron and Affron's schema, level one's denotation of the quotidian, level two's defamiliarization of the quotidian, level three's spectacular constructions, and level four's new realities will appear in my analyses (level five will not appear at all). I will somewhat counterintuitively operate as if all these levels are in fact level one denotations of the quotidian to analyse how production design imagines a kind of verisimilar everyday life in dystopian and post-apocalyptic fictional worlds – if not always their plots – by imagining how infrastructure appears, functions, and sustains life for the people in those worlds. For all the narrative spectacle that levels two, three, and four offer, such sets and the worlds they present also take as given that characters *live* in those settings. And everyday life depends – to varying degrees, on infrastructure. If it can be imagined to work in fiction, it might be worth trying in the real world before everything falls apart completely.

Establishing dystopian and post-apocalyptic worlds

Treating dystopian and post-apocalyptic worlds as diagnostic texts takes seriously two aspects of their worldbuilding. The first concerns the way in which creators give rise to extensible settings, what we might call the infrastructure of narrative coherence. The second concerns the ways production design can solve problems on set and in the real world as well, a kind of method-acting of solutionism (thanks to JD Connor for this phrase). While it is important to create 'imaginary worlds with coherent geographic, social, cultural, and other features', fictional worlds, as Umberto Eco pointed out, are largely incomplete by their very nature (von Stackelberg and McDowell 2015: 25; Bertetti 2017: 49). But just how incomplete is an open question, especially given the early twenty-first-century predilection for IP-driven franchises that return the same world across multiple movies (and television/streaming series) such as *The Hunger Games* and the updated *Planet of the Apes* (Rick Heinrichs 2001). Such '[r]ich storyworlds – the "universes" within which stories are set – provide detailed contextual rule-sets that develop a larger reality that extends beyond a single story, while potentially providing a deeper understanding of the underlying systems that drive these worlds' (von Stackelberg and McDowell 2015: 25–26). These systems can be ideological – *The Hunger Games*'s fascist President Snow – and/or infrastructural – the underground rail system that serves the Capitol. But even in stand-alone films, 'there may be a wealth of details and events (or mere mentions of them) which do not advance the story but which provide background richness and verisimilitude to the imaginary world' (Wolf 2012: 2).

Escape from New York (Joe Alves 1981) describes its fictional world as a dystopia on one side of the wall and a post-apocalyptic world on the other with the opening voice-over narration: 'The United States police force, like an army, is encamped around the island. There are no guards inside the prison. Only prisoners and the worlds they have made.' Other dystopias may not be as on the nose as Carpenter's, but they often introduce their imagined worlds early and in terms of the violence that people face on a day-to-day basis. *The Hunger Games* cuts from the glitz of blue-haired Caesar Flickerman interviewing intricately bearded Gamemaster Seneca Crane to a long shot of a holler, with the title District 12 in the bottom right corner (Figure I.5). The colourful gloss and glitz of the interview disappears, replaced with the washed-out grey drabness of District 12, joined by the sound bridge of a child screaming. The alarmingly unpleasant imaginary world here erupts in the terrified scream, and the iron cage of the economically depressed grey road contrasted with the flashy TV studio interview shows, through what Affron and Affron would call a denotative design, how the dystopian underside of District 12, with its line of power poles receding into

FIGURE I.5: *The Hunger Games* District 12 establishing shot.

the distance and a broken-down rusted cart in the foreground, makes possible the spectacular comforts of the Capitol. District 12 has electricity, but their transportation infrastructure obviously lags behind the Capitol.

Strange Days (Lilly Kilvert 1995), imagines an intensification of contemporary Los Angeles in a two-minute-and-thirty-four-second sequence that uses a talkback radio segment to establish societal breakdown in 1999 Los Angeles. Three years after grainy home video footage of the Rodney King beating showed how the police operated as a kind of terror and execution squad, the same kind of city – but more so – appears in the film. The radio callers express a range of reactions to the millennium cut against imagery of violence, especially in the form of the militarization of the police. In addition to the calls, the cutaways from Lenny during the scene further flesh out a dystopian Los Angeles. During the first call a biker gang rolls past a car on fire in the middle of the street. Another series of cutaways show two people chasing Santa with ironic choral music playing on soundtrack. We see riot cops frisking people, two people brandishing automatic weapons outside a store, a cop frisking a person in an alley while another holds gun on 'suspect', a police helicopter overhead and its search light sweeping over an apartment building, a police roadblock, cops with machine guns patrolling on foot, a motorcycle cop, more riot police, and two cops pushing a sex worker into a car. All of this is to say that *Strange Days* shows the alarmingly unpleasant parts of Los Angeles, including the punctuation of the iron cages of the city of dream's underside. This dystopia-establishing scene shows that

> *Strange Days* is a sci-fi mystery that doubles as an extended meditation on the Rodney King riots. The film imagines what would happen if the LA riots never entirely ended

> but survived indefinitely as a low-simmering form of never-ending social unrest (which is in fact what happened).
>
> (Rabin 2007: n.pag.)

If the dystopias such as *Escape from New York*, *The Hunger Games*, and *Strange Days*, with their distrust of militarized policing, look all too familiar to contemporary audiences, that's because dystopias are often not far from the world from which they emerge. The post-apocalyptic *Waterworld* (Dennis Gassner 1995) is also quite close to the world from which it emerges, despite taking place well into the future. *Waterworld* begins with a corporate logo, as nearly all films do; in this case the Universal Pictures logo, 'Universal Pictures' in gold letters in front of a turning globe, North and South America facing out. Then, in what JD Connor calls an 'elaborate and narratively crucial' logo bleed from corporate logo to film world, the Universal globe logo begins to change as the camera swoops down towards it, with the white ice of the Arctic disappearing, turning the globe into a monochrome watery blue orb (2015b: 22). A narrator (well-known voice-over performer Hal Douglas) portentously explains, 'the future. The polar ice caps have melted, covering the Earth with water. Those who survive have adapted to a new world.' The film title comes up on the screen. Now within the film world, a second sequence shows one such adaptation: a hand-cranked contraption that turns urine into drinkable water. The two sequences – the first to set the world and the second to show someone living in it – take up less than three minutes of screen time. Later, the Mariner (Kevin Costner) arrives at an elaborately bricolaged atoll that had to be built twice, as the first version of it sank in a storm. As Affron and Affron note, the atoll, even if we don't know the production history, functions both as denotation – people have built a floating settlement – and as embellishment that places *Waterworld*'s massive budget on the screen and offers a guarantee of spectacular action.

While the future apocalypse in *Waterworld* is the result of climate change, spreading responsibility across most of the developed world at the time of the film's release, *I Am Legend* identifies a different cause for the apocalypse: not a fossil fuel-based economy, but good medical intentions in the here and now. The film opens in a television screen ratio, with a newscaster interviewing Doctor Alice Krippin, who has redesigned the measles virus to cure cancer. Unfortunately, the next shot, in widescreen format, shows dozens of cars underwater on a flooded street next to a tunnel, with the title 'Three years later' at the bottom of the screen. The shot tilts up to show the New York skyline. A few specific locations: the Flatiron Building, the UN Building, the Union Square subway stop, empty streets. In every shot, no human presence, only buildings, abandoned cars, and the sounds of birds tweeting. Then, in an overhead shot of the city, a single red object moves, and the sound of a car engine replaces the sounds of birds. The driver of the car is Neville, the last survivor in post-apocalyptic Manhattan, with his dog Sam. They drive through flocks of birds, past roadblocks of military vehicles and buildings with scaffolding still up. A herd of deer cross their path, and Neville hunts them, clearly hoping to take home some meat for dinner. In much the same way Alex Bevan asks, '[w]hat stories to coffee tables and wallpaper tell?' (2019: 1), I want to ask what stories Pyrex beakers turned water purification system and streets-turned-grasslands tell. The narrative legibility of the Mariner recycling his urine and Neville using the empty city streets as a personal hunting ground economically establishes the changed state of the world in quotidian, infrastructural terms.

Escape from New York images the apocalypse as the result of a militarized police state that offshores a prison-based return to a war of all against all. *Waterworld* imagines the apocalypse as the result of climate change. *I Am Legend* imagines the apocalypse as the result of biomedical research gone wrong. *Resident Evil: The Final Chapter* (Edward Thomas 2016), the sixth film in the original series, imagines the apocalypse coming through religiously informed biological warfare instigated by a corporation. In a meeting before the zombie apocalypse, Dr Isaacs pitches his plans for the future of the company and the globe:

> I propose that we end the world, but on our terms. An orchestrated apocalypse. One that will cleanse the Earth of its population but leave its infrastructure and resources intact. It's been done once before with great success. The chosen few will ride out the storm not in an ark as in the Book of Genesis, but in safety underground. And when it's over, we will emerge onto a cleansed Earth, one that we can then re-boot in our image.

Isaacs's proposition fuses corporate dominance, fascism, an ecologically coloured eliminationism, and religion. In his one-minute-and-twenty-five-second speech there are 60 cuts, often not to other characters sharing the board room space, but rather to stock footage imagery. The stock footage gives form to the basis for Dr Isaacs's orchestrated apocalypse: a microscopic view of cells/viruses, a low angle shot of cooling towers, a long shot of a refinery, a heat intensity map of population, an overhead flying shot of corn field followed by a rotted corn cob. When he tells his audience '[i]t's been done before with great success', a cut takes us to a close-up of a Bible. The images abstract the problems, and the Bible presents the answer for the very real people in the board room with him.

All of these examples adhere to Hollywood's usual approach of goal-oriented characters in narrative-driven films. Each example also features something else so common that it usually goes unremarked, although *Resident Evil: Final Chapter* puts the word in the villain's mouth: infrastructure. In a dystopia infrastructure appears as supporting a working society, sometimes authoritarian, sometimes tenuous. For example, *The Hunger Games* dystopia-establishing shot features beat up roads and power lines in District 12, as well as an implicit power grid that makes the television broadcast possible as a level one, verisimilar world of infrastructure. Similarly, *Strange Days* finds Lenny driving through violence and madness on heavily policed roads, in a Los Angeles where the power is still on; a kind of level two set as punctuation. In a post-apocalyptic world, the remnants of the old infrastructure appear, but in slightly new forms. *Waterworld* reimagines waste handling and water provision as a kind of level three spectacular set of an ad hoc atoll made of scavenged materials. *I Am Legend* goes further when it shows a mostly destroyed but still functioning transport system of roads, and a lack of power as evidenced by the flooded tunnel, and a spectacular city-set destroyed in service of the film's scene setting.

Though there are some exceptions, dystopian films establish their boundaries to make one of the goals to escape and/or redraw those boundaries, to remake the world as something more liveable. On the other hand, post-apocalyptic films establish how the world ended to create a world that the survivors must then *live within*. To come to terms with the world, you might say. In either case, infrastructure plays a key role in maintaining, exceeding, and even escaping the boundaries imposed by these imagined worlds.

The end of the world has been coming for a long time, and mass audience movies appear to be getting ready for it, and getting the mass audience ready for it, in terms of infrastructure, the transportation, water, waste, and food systems that make civilization possible and possible to restart. *Escape from New York*'s engagement with the crumbling infrastructure of power generation gives form to the deteriorating world of the film and its possible escape from disaster. Snake Plissken (Kurt Russell) gets sent into the prison not only to rescue the president, but also to secure the secret of nuclear fusion. The mission, as Hauk puts it, is essential to 'the survival of the human race, Plissken. Something you don't give a shit about.' *Escape from New York* ends with Snake showing he indeed does not give a shit about the survival of the human race; he destroys the tape with the secret to nuclear fusion, effectively erasing the boundaries of the future by plunging the entire map into darkness (in the sequel, *Escape from LA* (Lawrence G. Paull 1996), Snake is no more altruistic). New York was on the upswing in the early twenty-first century, but energy once again presented a key obstacle in *I Am Legend*. The only electricity in Manhattan after the apocalypse comes what Neville runs from his generators, on diesel fuel. But unlike the grim gas crisis 1970s, *I Am Legend*'s conclusion shows a sense of optimism based not only on antibodies-rich blood, but also on the wind and solar generation that will make producing a cure based on that blood possible. Hope in dystopian and post-apocalyptic movies is often individualized, as with Neville's research and blood, but civilization appears in shared form, as power generation, transportation, water, waste, and food systems. I will investigate each form in turn, somewhat distinct from the others in the chapters that follow.

The films I analyse come from 1968 through 2021, and 1968 comes at the end of the Federal-Aid Highway Act 1956's original funding – bringing to an end the largest public works investment of the twentieth century. While federal and state and local highway and road construction has continued, as have other infrastructural projects, since the 1960s, the US federal government has not prioritized infrastructure investment, leading to a slow drift toward a less functional infrastructural system and the social breakdown that accompanies it. As Representative John Yarmuth put it in a 2019 House Committee Report, 'transportation and water infrastructure spending as a share of GDP represents the lowest level in more than 60 years (spending peaked at about three percent in the late 1950s)' (2019: n.pag.). An early and successful instance of the federal government investing in infrastructure is the Rural Electrification Administration, begun by executive order in 1935. Between 1936 and 1960, the country went from 90 per cent of farms not having electricity to 90 per cent of farms having electricity. In the post-1945 era, the Federal Highway Act of 1956, also known as the National Interstate and Defense Highways Act created the basis for the construction of almost 41,000 miles of highway between cities of more than 50,000 people (the system grew to almost 47,000 miles). Rather than making all the highways toll roads, the Highway Revenue Act of 1956 used a three cents per gallon fuel tax (and a number of other user fees) to finance highway building and maintenance. In 2020 the fuel tax rate on gasoline was up to 18.40/gallon, plus an average of 29.86/gallon in state taxes (US Energy Information Administration 2021: n.pag.). However, the federal rate has not been increased since the early 1990s, furthering the problems caused by the underfunding of infrastructure. Matthew Wills writes that since at least the mid-1980s, in American political rhetoric 'infrastructure has become a permanent crisis, highlighted by highway collapses, levee failures, and hospitals and morgues utterly overwhelmed by pandemic' (2021: n.pag.). The crisis emerges out of what Elizabeth Drew calls

> the near-total failure of our political institutions to invest for the future, eschewing what doesn't yield the quick payoff, political and physical, has left us with hopelessly clogged traffic, at risk of being on a bridge that collapses, or on a train that flies off defective rails, or with rusted pipes carrying our drinking water.
>
> (2016: n.pag.)

Any attempt to address the crisis seems to follow the same trajectory: '[E]very presidential administration wants to fix America's "crumbling infrastructure" until they discover the business interests profiting from disrepair' (Baker 2022: n.pag.).

The turn to short-termism Drew identifies largely matches the periodization found in works such as Giovanni Arrighi's *The Long Twentieth Century: Money, Power and the Origins of Our Times* and Ernst Mandel's *Long Waves of Capitalist Development: The Marxist Interpretation.* The expansionist wave that came in the wake of The Second World War was followed by a depressive long wave, in which

> it is no longer possible to assure full employment, to eradicate poverty, to extend social security, to assure a steady (if modest) increase in real income for the wage earners. At that point the fight to restore the rate of profit through a strong upswing in the rate of surplus value (i.e. the rate of exploitation of the working class) becomes the top priority.
>
> (Mandel 1980: 100)

That is to say, the pivot in the long wave of United States-led accumulation toward financialization appears around the end of the 1960s when, as Arrighi describes it,

> the dynamic of world capitalism has not only changed over time but has made the financial expansion of the late twentieth century anomalous in key respects. A critical anomaly is the unprecedented bifurcation of financial and military power, which, I argued, could develop in one of three directions: the formation of a world empire; the formation of a non-capitalist world economy; or a situation of endless systemic chaos.
>
> (2010: 372)

The films I analyse in this book frequently represent the depressive long wave generating a specific form of systemic chaos that retains the privileges of the elites while increasing poverty, eliminating social security, and the hyper exploitation of the working class along the lines of company towns, serfdom, and even slavery. Crumbling infrastructure offers a concrete experience of those on the short end of the financialization stick in the last quarter of the twentieth century; similar changes in infrastructure – quite often crumbling for the many and privately servicing the few – embed the indignities and struggles dystopian and post-apocalyptic worlds pose to everyday life.

As the United States pivoted away from public works infrastructures in the last quarter of the twentieth century, one form of infrastructure enjoyed significant funding: media infrastructures. Perhaps unsurprisingly, ARPANET packet-switch network and remote access, among other 1960s projects, originated in the Department of Defense, leading to the first computers being connected in 1969. Through the 1970s the network expanded, and in the early 1980s supercomputing came to universities, expanding the network and its capabilities. The 1990s End of History economic boom was in part driven by this investment in media infrastructure: The first transoceanic fibreoptic cable was established in 1988, leading to more than a decade of one kind of infrastructural investment. As Nicole Starosielski notes in *The Undersea Network: Sign, Storage, Transmission*, 'in the early 2000s, toward the end of the fibreoptic cable boom – a period of intense infrastructure building coincided with the emergence of the Internet' (2015: x). On the back of decades of public research, investment, and installation, what we now know as the internet was outside of public infrastructure and in private hands soon after the internet had the infrastructural capacity to be truly global in reach. And for all the defence-driven investment in ARPANET, 'a large and close-to-monotonic decline in the size of infrastructure as a percent of GDP beginning around 1970, for most categories of infrastructure, both defense and nondefense' appears (Fair 2021: 1). While the funding of ARPANET was partially motivated by the need to maintain enormous funding for defence in the face of a falling rate of profit, it wasn't entirely determined by that need. That is to say, alternative pathways were available, even in the Cold War, for infrastructure investment. We still see those in dystopian and post-apocalyptic films – often in the form of computer surveillance systems – but more often their absence registers: there's no internet in or on *The Road*.

Moving into the third decade of the twenty-first century, 'on average, European countries spend the equivalent of 5 percent of GDP on building and maintaining their infrastructure, while the United States spends 2.4 percent' and China spends about 8 per cent of its GDP on infrastructure (McBride and Moss 2020: n.pag.). Writing in Bloomberg's *CityLab*, Laura Bliss notes that

> with a few exceptions, Congress has also done little to tackle U.S. infrastructure needs. Transportation, emergency resilience and energy bills proposed by both Senate and House members have largely languished, including the $1.5 trillion Moving Forward Act, an infrastructure package passed by the House in July. A second pandemic relief package – which many expected to include funding and jobs for infrastructure – also has yet to pass. Inaction by Congress predates the current president. But in 2020 its consequences were stark.
>
> (2020: n.pag.)

The consequences of underinvestment since the 1960s continue to build. Writing for the more progressive-minded think tank Center on Budget and Policy Priorities, Elizabeth McNichol argues that the pattern of states neglecting their part in infrastructure investment 'has serious consequences for the nation's growth and quality of life as roads crumble, school buildings become obsolete, and outdated facilities jeopardize public health [...] Falling federal spending on infrastructure is exacerbating the problem' (2019: n.pag.). But pushing for greater infrastructure investment is not the sole province of centre-left groups. In addition to Bloomberg, noted above, McKinsey, Council on Foreign Relations, and Milford Asset, which in no way resemble centre-left, much less social democratic, groups, are also making similar critical claims about the kind of damage a sub-3 per cent of GDP investment in infrastructure can do (McBride and Moss 2020: n.pag.; Johnston 2017: n.pag.; Woetzel 2016: n.pag.). There is consensus around the problems infrastructure can solve and that its neglect creates. There has not been, however, much concrete action. Dystopian and post-apocalyptic movies imagine the potential worlds created by continuing to ignore, or being unable to address, or facing up to these problems.

In each of the chapters that follow, I balance two goals: on the one hand, I take an encyclopaedic approach that seeks to identify consistent trends across dystopian and post-apocalyptic films; on the other, I offer case studies that, by more thoroughly contextualizing and formally analysing films, offer an ideological reading of infrastructure in dystopian and post-apocalyptic film. Each chapter stands on its own, but the chapters when taken together make a larger argument about the physical construction of worlds that have gone wrong, have been destroyed, and have been provisionally rebuilt.

Chapter 1 provides an overview of energy production and consumption. After an overview of fossil fuel extraction, production, and use; nuclear power generation and use; weaponized energy; and renewable production and use, I turn to a more detailed engagement with energy production and use in *Dawn of the Planet of the Apes*, *War for the Planet of the Apes* (James Chinlund 2017), and *The Quiet Earth*. The chapter shows that post-1973 oil crisis dystopian and post-apocalyptic films show how rebuilding a world worth living in needs locally controlled power production. In search of a liveable future, renewable energy sources replace fossil fuels to make communities self-sufficient and more able to self-manage. While large-scale electricity production operates from the top down, creating the potential for large-scale abuse, locally produced electricity creates a potential for small-scale democratic societies that can create *post*-dystopian and *post*-apocalyptic societies worth living in.

Chapter 2 considers how road and rail systems present often-ambivalent paths, both literal and metaphorical, out of dystopias and towards post-apocalyptic communities. I pay particular attention to not just the everyday use of the transportation infrastructure but also its maintenance – not just getting from point A to point B but continuing to get there. I first provide an overview of the practical and ideological construction of the transportation system in the United States and Australia; the role of mass transportation infrastructure in films; and how genre conventions interact with the mass transportation infrastructure in chase sequences. I then examine the breakdown and maintenance of paved highways and unpaved roads and how mobility registers relative levels social breakdown and danger. Maintenance and the people to perform maintenance labour rarely appear in dystopian and post-apocalyptic films, showing more than the continuing breakdown and danger to dystopian and post-apocalyptic worlds. My readings of *Dawn of the Planet of the Apes*, *Mad Max* (John Dowding AD 1979), and *Never Let Me Go* (Mark Digby 2010), to name a few examples, show that post-Second World War car-centric development paired with a valorization of innovating our way out of problems misses the ways maintenance of the transportation infrastructure – whether under terrible circumstances, as in dystopias, or the worst of circumstances, as in post-apocalyptic worlds – remains essential to fulfilling a key role of the transportation system: connecting people across distances both small and large.

It is possible to make do without a railroad or paved street; electricity is a new addition to everyday life, all things considered. Water, on the other hand, is essential. Chapter 3 concentrates on films made in the 1990s and after, an era in which the privatization of water was a priority for governments and transnational institutions. The logic of competition and individualism inherent to privatization and marketization means that the logic of public provision – cooperation and community – loses out. At best this is anti-social. At worst, as dystopian and post-apocalyptic films show, it can enable oppression. With extended attention to *Mad Max: Fury Road* (Colin Gibson 2015), *V for Vendetta* (Owen Paterson 2005), and especially *Tank Girl* (Catherine Hardwicke 1995), I argue that dystopian and post-apocalyptic films consistently identify the necessity of water not just to sustain life, but the necessity of water as the essential shared public good that must be present to create a better world.

The physical infrastructure makes possible larger social systems, such as the food system. In Chapter 4 I present an analysis of how food systems link the energy, transportation, water, and waste infrastructures to create a world towards which to strive. I show that food itself – meat or grains or fruit or vegetables or candy – comes a close second to public provision of water in creating a liveable future. And, like water, whether food comes from scavenging, hunting, or horticulture/agriculture a bottom-up, more democratic and local food system seems essential to the best food system's organization. In addition to cataloguing the importance of canteens to dystopias and canned food to post-apocalyptic worlds, I also give more sustained attention to the *Divergent* series, especially *Divergent and Insurgent* (Alec Hammond 2014). Though the major set pieces tend to occur in the city of Chicago and the wastelands that surround it, the *Divergent* series also finds time and space for an extensive food system that undergirds both its dystopian post-apocalyptic world of control and its imagination of a better world. In particular, the frequently imagined future that uses the necessity of clustering together for safety to make room for urban agriculture. This motion towards a more self-sustaining community offers these settlements something like food sovereignty. In this manner a full belly and clean water to drink makes the creation of a better world more possible.

I then consider the forms waste and waste disposal take, starting with the aesthetics of garbage and moving towards the social relations that waste and recycling put on view. If the transportation infrastructure in its forward motion gestures to the future, waste points to the past. But waste also offers some direction to the future. After discussing how waste as a thing and as an idea can be used to exclude and to draw a public–private distinction, I sketch the aesthetic of trash in dystopian and post-apocalyptic film. I provide an overview of solid waste, sewers and wastewater, and recycling and e-waste disposal. I provide a series of close readings of *WALL-E*, *Isle of Dogs* (Paul Harrod and Adam Stockhausen 2018), *Ready Player One* (Adam Stockhausen 2018), *Demolition Man* (David L. Snyder 1993), and *Blade Runner 2049* (Dennis Gassner 2017) to analyse how waste and waste disposal create and maintain boundaries, and reveal the spatial character of social relations in those films and the cultural moments from which they emerge. If we attend to waste disposal and recycling, we can see what David Harvey calls the spatial fix of capitalism in action. Future trash and recycling/reuse reveal the essentially spatial character of the future dystopian and post-apocalyptic movies see, where rich countries like the United States, the United Kingdom, and Australia experience the wages of their downturn in the form of having to deal with the waste of industrial and post-industrial society. Sites of waste disposal and recycling help to identify what might have been correctly discarded and what might be made to work once again to escape a dystopia or secure a *post*-apocalyptic life.

In the concluding chapter I first analyse two recent films set in the ecological, economic, and racial dystopia of early twenty-first-century America: *First Reformed* (Grace Yun 2017) and *Sorry to Bother You* (Jason Kivarday 2018). Both films propose infrastructurally based actions that might allow the world to reverse course away from apocalypse. Toxic waste sits at the heart of *First Reformed*, and the physical and spiritual pollution it represents can be cured not by Superfund clean-up, but the cleansing fire of the righteous person's direct action of killing corporate executives. By contrast, *Sorry to Bother You* a vision sees the enemy as institutional, identifying sidewalk space as a key infrastructural site for change. During the film's strike sequences, among others, the use of sidewalks plots a path to a better world that starts not from the top down, but from the ground up, making the sidewalk a shared (and celebratory) public space under democratic control leading to a better future. I then offer a brief analysis of the US-Rwandan film *Neptune Frost* (Cedric Mizero and Antoine Nshimiyimana 2021) as a contrast to the mass audience blockbusters that make up the majority of the films I analyse in the book. Any project to imagine a post-dystopian or post-apocalyptic vision would necessarily need to contend with the vision of more than Hollywood movies. An Afrofuturist film, *Neptune Frost* offers a distinct visual vocabulary and mental framework, including in its consideration of how infrastructure functions and might function in remaking the world for not just the lucky ones in the Global North, but worldwide.

Planet of the Apes was in theatres in 1968, when massive protests and strikes across the United States, Europe, Mexico, and South America did not dislodge the most powerful from their positions at the top of the heap. Capitalists stayed in power, and continued uneven development – neocolonialism rather than colonialism – caused an ever-accelerating form of fossil fuel-driven multinational capitalism that has fuelled the escalating dystopian nature of life, an increasingly unequal global order rushing towards social and environmental apocalypse. In a 2017 review of *War for the Planet of the Apes*, Dan Hassler-Forest argues persuasively that in the early twenty-first century we are

> in dire need of revolutionary narratives. As part of the fabric that makes up our pop-cultural vocabulary, we need accessible and appealing tales that reject the utter nihilism of *Game of Thrones*–era neoliberal culture. More specifically: The left needs stories that foreground political organization in the face of exploitation and oppression. It needs popular myths that revive solidarity and compassion as crucial components of progressive political struggle. It needs casts of characters that are radically inclusive, fully embracing the fundamental intersections between feminism, anti-racism, and anti-capitalism. And it needs grand utopian horizons that don't shy away from the promise of a future that is better – or, at the very least, *different*.
>
> (2017: n.pag.)

In this book I connect the idealist – tracing the boundaries of our collective imagination – with the materialist – the practical concrete foundation of such worlds and lives as we can imagine. To escape the current escalating apocalypse of our own making, the boundaries of our imagination need to expand along the lines of our fellow humans and to become more fantastic along the lines of what we as humans might organize and produce together. But this will only be possible if our imagination becomes much more mechanically mundane at the same time. In *The German Ideology*, Marx places critique next to more prosaic, everyday work in some future communist society,

> where nobody has one exclusive sphere of activity but each can become accomplished in any branch he wishes, society regulates the general production and thus makes it possible for me to do one thing today and another tomorrow, to hunt in the morning,

> fish in the afternoon, rear cattle in the evening, criticise after dinner, just as I have a mind, without ever becoming hunter, fisherman, herdsman or critic.
>
> (1845: n.pag.)

What I hope this book will show is that the future better world will need much the same combination, and we can look to dystopian and post-apocalyptic movies for a sense of where we might begin. To build castles in the sky worth fighting for will require ideas. It will also require infrastructure.

NOTE

1. To accentuate the importance of production design to my project, I will be noting the production designer for films at their first appearance in the text rather than the director. If no production designer appears in the film's credits, I will name either the set designer (SD) or art director (AD).

1

Energy: Power Is Power, Renewable or Not

The generation and control of energy in most dystopian and post-apocalyptic movies follow a predictable path. A world that still uses fossil fuel or nuclear power tends to be oppressive. Whether controlled by the oligarchs in *Blade Runner*, *The Island* (Nigel Phelps 2005), *Elysium* (Phillip Ivey 2013), or *Chappie* (Jules Cook 2015) or the faceless bureaucracy of *Brazil* (Norman Garwood 1985), or the quasi-feudalist oligarchy of *The Hunger Games* series, fossil fuel by its very nature – coal and oil are found and extracted and processed and stored in places that can be owned and defended through guard labour – makes oppression possible and likely. Nuclear power offers similar spatial advantages to oppressive structures. Fascists in *V for Vendetta*; kleptocrats in *Babylon AD* (Paul Cross and Sonja Klaus 2008); faceless pleasure-killers in *THX 1138* (Al Locatelli 1971); corporate religious fanatics in *Resident Evil: Apocalypse* (Paul Denham Austerberry 2004). Renewable energy, when controlled from the top down, makes improving dystopian and post-apocalyptic worlds more difficult, as in *Escape from New York*, *Soylent Green*, *Oblivion*, *WALL-E*, *Dawn of the Planet of the Apes* , the *Divergent* series, the *Matrix* series, *Blade Runner 2049*, the *Hunger Games* series, *Book of Eli*, *Mad Max Beyond Thunderdome*, and *Mad Max: Fury Road*. However, renewable energy appears as a desirable path away from dystopia and apocalypse in *Ready Player One*, *The Hunger Games*, *The Matrix Reloaded*, *Zombieland*, *Zombieland Double Tap*, *Waterworld*, and *The Postman*.

Writing about the rise of dystopian and post-apocalyptic films in the first decades of the twenty-first century, Christopher Schmidt makes two observations on electricity – one theoretical point in some detail, one practical point in passing. As part of his answer to the headline 'Why are dystopian films on the rise again?', Schmidt notes that films tend not to appear in dystopian movies:

> The post-apocalyptic film thus functions something like an *apotropaion*, a totem warding off bad fortune by containing the catastrophe it represents. The hidden logic

> of spectatorship is this: if I possess the freedom and technological resources to enjoy such a film, then I cannot live in the dystopia depicted within it.
>
> (2014: n.pag.)

Movies in dystopian movies tend to serve nefarious purposes – surveillance and control, propaganda, even no movies at all – but that's the best-case scenario. But two sentences later, Schmidt notes in a parenthetical aside, 'rare is the post-apocalyptic world in which the electrical power grid survives intact' (2014: n.pag.). In the worst of dystopias and the post-apocalypse, there is no culture. In even the best post-apocalyptic world, there probably won't be electricity to run a film projector, Blu-ray player, or computer for streaming. Culture would have to return to earlier, non-electronic media: theatre, books, acoustic music. These cultural events would, of necessity, be smaller (as will be shown in some examples that follow) and more hand-made in their form and aesthetic. Post-1973 oil crisis dystopian and post-apocalyptic films show how electricity is a tool and a weapon, both culturally and literally, and that rebuilding to create a world worth living in is almost uniformly accomplished with locally controlled power production.

In this chapter, after a brief overview of energy generation and transmission, I will analyse four important ways energy appears in dystopian and post-apocalyptic movies: as fossil fuel extraction, production, and use; as nuclear power generation and use; as something portable, usually a weapon; and as renewable production and use. As one of the apes says in *Dawn of the Planet of the Apes*, 'power is power'. Electricity produced on a large scale creates the conditions for oppression from the top down, whereas electricity produced locally often creates space for democratic rebirth and a path out of dystopian and post-apocalyptic worlds. Rebuilding dystopian and post-apocalyptic worlds to create a new world worth living in is almost uniformly accomplished with locally controlled power production that moves from fossil fuel to renewable fuel sources. The smaller scale of human settlements and a distrust of what a centralized authority would look like in a dystopian or post-apocalyptic setting means that what makes energy production desirable in dystopian and post-apocalyptic films is its local generation and use. When communities can be self-sufficient and self-manage, the world is not so dystopian, and a path to a liveable post-apocalypse can be navigated.

Power generation: Electricity or social relation?

The word power appears frequently in film and literary criticism, but not as the thing that runs the machines with and by which those articles and books were written and printed. Power, in much film and literary criticism, appears as an abstraction (a discourse) or as a social relation. For example, in Tudor Balinisteau's article on *Tank Girl*, 'Goddess cults in techno-worlds: Tank girl and the borg queen', every mention of 'power' is an expression of a social relation. But *Tank Girl* is, in fact, incredibly didactic about how power as a social relation is materially grounded. I will return to Balinisteau's analysis of *Tank Girl* later, in the chapter on water, but I bring up the article and its use of power here to turn the sequence of the expression of power back to front, at least in terms of how it often appears in film studies. As Brian Larkin puts it, '[w]e often see computers not cables, light not electricity' (2013: 329). I want to take literally the appearance of power as an infrastructural effect, as the production of electricity for domestic and sometimes industrial use within film worlds. But first I turn to how electricity production, distribution, and use express power as a social relation. For clarity's sake, I use 'electricity' or 'energy' when I refer to power as a concrete thing, and power when I refer to the social relation.

Starting at the beginning of the electricity generation process, John Perkins identifies 'nine sources of heat or electromotive force [that] comprise the primary energy resources: coal, oil, gas, uranium, falling water, solar radiation, wind, biomass, and geothermal heat' (2018: 169). Eight of these sources will appear, to varying degrees, in this chapter (geothermal heat will not), as they represent the primary energy sources used in the United States, the United Kingdom, Australia, and Aotearoa New Zealand. Because 'previous investments leave a legacy of infrastructure, customs, and human relationships, which shape future decision-making', the appearance of different energy sources in oppressive and/or rebuilding worlds offers a window into the horizon of possibility, a sense of what is thinkable and achievable if human society is to flourish (Perkins 2018: 170). Since English capitalists chose to take coal out of the ground and use it to produce steam power at the start of the Industrial Revolution, a specific infrastructure of electrical production has developed and grown, and this legacy of fossil fuel-driven industry and growth has led, as Andreas Malm (2016), among others, argues, to our current historical moment and physical world.

Two broadly recognized physical expressions of electricity generation are the cooling tower (often associated with nuclear plants) and power lines because a physical infrastructure to generate and transmit electricity is necessary. On a large scale, the transmission of electricity requires transmission line towers, the transmission lines themselves, the copper and aluminium conductors that actually carry the electricity, the substations that reduce voltage to make transmission easier and safer, and the transformers that step the voltage down for local distribution or step voltage up for long-distance distribution (Hayes 2005: 230–52). Electricity distribution requires pole-mounted transformers and/or transformers in boxes on the ground to step up and step-down voltage as needed and power lines strung between wood poles and concrete poles (Hayes 2005: 263–75). Utility poles can carry much more than electricity. In addition to primary and secondary electric power distribution lines, a pole can feature switches, fuses, transformers, street lighting fixtures, traffic signals, cable television feeders, telephone cables, a grounding lead, and sometimes a temporary cell site (Hayes 2005: 266). The electricity infrastructure, when given the names above, can seem unfamiliar, but most filmgoers would find 'that grey box on the power pole' in a film's set design to be quite familiar indeed.

In the United States, with universal access to electricity, the sight of power lines is so common as to be nearly invisible, and the consistent functioning of electricity is so taken for granted that its disappearance represents something terrifying, as many horror movies at some point demonstrate. The three key questions to energy geography – production of energy, transportation of energy, and consumption of energy – converge in the form of a power pole. A film made in the United States after the Second World War – the films I analyse in this book – will almost without fail feature power poles and power lines in the background. These pieces of set decoration are for the most part unobtrusive, but they nevertheless register, in their presence-functioning and/or their absence-non-functioning, the essential nature of electricity to contemporary everyday life. Gerald Manners, writing in the late 1960s, notes that 'there is a high degree of positive correlation between the consumption of energy and the standard of living in a country' (1966: 16). Manners here echoes the thinking that undergirded the Rural Electrification Administration in the United States, which between its founding in 1935 and 1960 brought electricity to 90 per cent of the country's farms, not only stimulating the economy but also creating greater equity between urban and rural Americans. Similarly, a decade earlier, Lenin's concise equation of Communism = Soviet power + electrification of the whole country led to the rapid electrification of the Soviet Union, which went from a feudal to an industrial state with a significantly higher standard of living within decades. If, in the first half of the century, electricity made the Good Life of being part of the industrialized world possible, in the second half of the century and the twenty-first century, electricity made Life Itself possible. Electricity thus clearly functions as a concrete expression that both reflects and forms social relations. Electricity is power.

Fossil fuel

For as important as coal has been to the growth of global capitalism, it does not find a large place in dystopian and post-apocalyptic movies. Coal as a cultural signifier plays a major role in the *Hunger Games* series, but it is less clear how coal as an energy source operates in the series. *The Hunger Games* novel identifies District 12 as a place once called Appalachia. In the film, the men of District 12 appear as a mass of grey-clad miners coming up the elevator after their shift ends, and the women, including Katniss Everdean (Jennifer Lawrence), her sister, and her mother, all appear in grey homespun. On the one hand, coal and Appalachia are shorthand for impoverishment and a place exploited for its natural resources. But more practically speaking, why are they still using coal? If we place District 12 in West Virginia, that means the coal would have to travel almost 1400 miles to reach the capital in the Rocky Mountains. As Manners puts it,

> the geographical disposition of coalfields in relation to their markets is such that water transport frequently is not available; and, as a result, railways – historically speaking and neglecting the pipeline, the next cheapest form of transport – are used to move considerable quantities of coal throughout the world.
>
> (1966: 88)

Even if there were high-speed freight rail, there seems to be no reason to transport coal from Appalachia to the Rockies, especially since the rich districts are shown to have their own hydropower generation. This would imply closer, local coal-fired plants, and the grey sky and evident poor health of District 12's people offer evidence of environmental health deficits. But no fossil fuel-burning plants appear in the *Hunger Games* films, rendering coal mining a punctuation set, a visual shorthand for the Capitol's make-drudgery programme for the most dystopian of Panem's single-biome districts.

In a post-apocalyptic setting, as prison warden Hauk suggests, the prisoners in *Escape from New York* have rigged up a set-as-embellishment power plant to run on oil drilled on Manhattan Island, and they have also retrofitted car engines to steam power, perhaps using coal. More traditional use of fossil fuel appears in *Day of the Dead* (Lawrence G. Paull 1985) in the natural gas piping outside of the military's underground bunker; in *Land of the Dead* (Arvinder Greywal 2005), a natural gas bottle, first seen in its intended use of fuelling a grill to enable cooking in the city's slums, reappears later as a bomb. The voice-over narration to the opening sequence to *The Road Warrior* (Graham 'Grace' Walker 1981) speaks of 'another time where the world was powered by black fuel and the deserts sprouted great cities of pipe and steel', and the last remnants of these cities appear in the fortified village with an oil pump at its centre where the film's showdown with Humungus takes place. Off land, oil fuels the Smokers in *Waterworld*. In particular, they take their oil from the set-as-embellishment Exxon Valdez, the tanker that ran aground and represents the carelessness of late twentieth-century fossil fuel dependence and the danger it represents.

Whereas coal is mined for uncertain reasons in the *Hunger Games* films, evidence that petroleum is extracted and used to fuel the city appears in *Blade Runner*'s *mise en scène*. During the film's opening sequence, as cars fly through Los Angeles's night sky, flare stacks light the night, offering evidence of oil drilling, refinery activity, and gas processing. The gas flares range from flicks of flame against the black background to large explosions, at once beautiful and violent. The opening sequence not only establishes the film's overall aesthetic approach but also makes clear the practical basis for the neon-infused world at street level. Electricity from fossil fuels has created a polluted, ruined world; off-world colonization for those who can afford it becomes desirable. The early history of this environmental degradation appears in *Death Race 2000* (B. B. Neel and Robinson Royce AD), during a scene in which Frankenstein talks with his navigator as hundreds of oil rigs – the in-place, denotative industrial landscape of southern California – flash past in the background. Another southern California-set film shows the importance of fossil fuel to California during a chase sequence. *The Island*'s major car chase shows parts of the refinery and fuel storage infrastructure at the Port of Long Beach. Outside of the United States, a number of extreme long shots in *Mad Max* place refineries in the background, an ambient reminder of what fuels the vehicular mayhem (Figure 1.1).

Fossil fuel takes on much higher stakes in post-apocalyptic narratives, as gasoline represents the potential for mobility and escape from the dangers the end of the world presents. Post-apocalyptic survivors must chase after not only fuel for themselves (as I will show in Chapter 4 on food) but also fuel for their vehicles. Fuel running out, or even the potential for it to run out, makes refineries particularly important to post-apocalyptic life. During the panic-buying/scavenging moment

FIGURE 1.1: *Mad Max* refinery in the distance.

as the outbreak spreads in *World War Z* (Nigel Phelps 2013), Gerry and his family drive past an industrial landscape that includes refineries. In this regard, New Jersey offers something New York does not, as New York has no refineries of its own, but rather depends on other neighbouring states for its petroleum refineries. To take another example, between *Mad Max* and *The Road Warrior*, the apocalypse came, making a small oil well and the potential to refine that oil a very desirable location. Max (Mel Gibson) first spies it from afar, inside a fortified ring, then as a cluster of small fires at night, not unlike the gas flares in *Blade Runner*, and then finally from inside the ring, helping to defend it against Humungus and his gang. A refinery also appears in *Mad Max: Fury Road* in a manner that echoes the first film in the series. As Furiosa leaves the Citadel in hopes of acquiring more guzzeline, an extreme longshot shows a massive black cloud of pollution over a prickly set of spires, both from a high-angle shot and from a shot taken from bumper level along the highway.

To operate a refinery requires specialized labour and a measure of security, making already-refined gasoline and/or diesel a priority to post-apocalyptic mobility. The main targets in the search for fuel is a leftover from the pre-apocalyptic world: the gas station and the gas tankers that bring the gas. In the morning after the world-erasing Project Flashlight event, Zac Hobson of *The Quiet Earth* fills his car up at the servo. A bit later in the post-apocalypse, Columbus stops off at a gas station in Garland, Texas in *Zombieland*. Both George Romero's and Zack Snyder's *Dawn of the Dead* (Josie Caruso and Barbara Lifsher SD 1978; Andrew Neskoromny 2004) feature a gas pump that presents the potential to fuel up and escape to more human-friendly climes. Later after the apocalypse, Fiddler's Green, the gated community for the elites of *Land of the Dead*, keeps a working gas pump in its parking garage, should its residents need to escape the lumpenproletariat and/or zombies at some point. I have already noted that the mass evacuation of New York leaves gas at Neville's disposal, even three years after the apocalypse, in *I Am Legend*. *Dawn of the Planet of the Apes* shows a gas station reclaimed by the forest, with a horse in what was once the service area to accentuate how much transport has changed. Finally, well into the post-apocalyptic world of *The Road*, when the man encounters a gas station, he reflexively checks to see if it works. Similarly, when motorcycle-riding Alice pulls up at a gas station in *Resident Evil: Extinction* (Eugenio Caballero 2007), she checks the pumps just in case.

A gas station stores its fuel underground, which means the visual evidence of gasoline takes the form of checking the pump and a stream of liquid. A gas tanker, on the other hand, represents fuel availability above ground. A tanker truck, depending on its size, can carry between 3000 and 11,000 gallons, which could make a lot of travel through the wasteland possible. The ersatz family piled into Frank's black cab siphons gas out of a tanker as they make their way north out of London in *28 Days Later* (Mark Tildesley 2002). In *Resident Evil: Extinction*, the convoy of survivors completes chores such as checking the level of gas remaining in the tanker that makes up part of their convoy and fuels its various vehicles, including a school bus. A similar moving fuel storage and living quarters appear in *Waterworld*, in which the Smokers live in, travel, and use the fuel of the Exxon Valdez. Probably the most thorough-going use of fuel tanker trucks appears in the *Mad Max* series. In the first, dystopian, film in the series, crims stalk a tanker to steal fuel for their cars. In *The Road Warrior*, Max agrees to drive the tanker that ends up being a decoy, filled with dirt rather than fuel. Imperator Furiosa owes her reputation to her ability to drive her tanker across the wasteland to trade guzzeline, a currency matched only by water.

On a smaller scale, maintaining access to some sort of energy-producing materials makes survival more likely in dystopian and post-apocalyptic worlds. Dystopian settings show a more limited access to stored energy. Outside of the portable batteries strapped to jet skis in *Waterworld*, the non-portable tanks of oil and gasoline and natural gas remain under the control of the authorities. The fuel for vehicles in *Land of the Dead* sits behind barbed-wire fences; tanks of propane are stored at rebel military bases in *The Hunger Games: Mockingjay, Part 2* (Phillip Messina 2015); the port area features massive gas storage in *The Island*; and the factory where Max (Matt Damon) works in *Elysium* maintains its own fuel storage tanks. When they're not finding ways to retain their humanity by engaging with art, post-apocalyptic survivors in *The Omega Man* (Arthur Loel and Walter M. Simonds 1971), *Day of the Dead*, *Road Warrior*, *The Road*, and *Resident Evil: The Final Chapter* all carry jerry cans filled with fuel to ensure their survival. In *The Omega Man*'s opening sequence, Neville (Charlton Heston) remembers to take his jerry can out of the back seat of a wrecked car, and its importance is underlined when Neville walks away from an armoured car with gold bars and dollar bills falling out of it. In a world without exchange value, the jerry can represents true use value. With this small-scale personal access, survivors can patrol slightly farther than their vehicle's tanks allow and expand their resource base. Even better, in a pinch the jerry can might quickly create a weapon, about which more later.

Nuclear power

Although the familiar hyperboloid style of cooling tower is not exclusive to nuclear plants, the equation of the two occurs across most dystopian and post-apocalyptic movies. For instance, in *Chappie*, Ninja and Yo-Landi live with Chappie in a set as denotation: an abandoned industrial building with graffitied cooling towers in the waste space next to it. Rather than a nuclear plant, the towers would be more likely to have served the industrial plant, burning fossil fuel. A more likely appearance of nuclear plant cooling towers appears as Toorop (Vin Diesel) travels across the high-radiation zone in *Babylon AD*, where smokestacks and sets of hyperboloid towers flank the road. Unlike the mucky exterior shot of *Babylon AD* revealing cooling towers, a small nuclear symbol pasted to a white wall, just above a bench where THX and SEN sit, stands out in *THX 1138*'s austere *mise en scène*. *THX 1138* goes further in its distrust of nuclear power, showing a partial meltdown caused by human error.

V for Vendetta's V has a different view on nuclear power. As dangerous as a nuclear accident is, a virus is a biological version of a neutron bomb. 'Nuclear power is meaningless', V explains, 'in a world where a virus can kill an entire population and leave wealth intact'. *V for Vendetta* (the film, not Alan Moore's comic) conjures a disaster out of a nuclear power plant *not* being attacked to cause a meltdown. In this film, the instigating action did not need to be an attack on a nuclear plant, with all the social and ecological *and financial* dangers that come with it. Instead, attacks on other parts of the infrastructure – which I analyse in other chapters – are visible in the physical monuments of cages and prisons for migrants; the abstract and rhetorical ideas take the form of fascism, an exclusionary 'greater good' without a dangerous Geiger counter reading. The promise of moving beyond nuclear power appears in *Escape from New York*, which finds Snake Plissken tracking down the kidnapped president so that the secrets to nuclear fusion might bring peace to the world. Hauk describes the point of the mission to Snake as 'the survival of the human race, Plissken. Something you don't give a shit about'. By placing his bet on the future on nuclear fusion, Hauk, a prison warden, takes a social disorganization theory approach to crime: the decay evident in *Escape from New York*'s fictional world can be reversed, it seems, with cheap, abundant energy. Such a position makes sense in a film that comes at the end of a decade that saw an oil/energy crisis. Nuclear energy and the dangers it entails accentuate the dystopian, whereas the fantasy of nuclear fusion offers the hope of a better way to generate electricity and escape the dystopian.

Dawn of the Dead shows how nuclear power allows civilization to shamble on while the dead walk the earth. Landing on the helipad on the mall roof, the band of survivors investigates the building as a potential place to hide. After peering through some skylights, Peter pauses in front of some humming air-conditioning units. He meets up with his colleague Roger and delivers a key piece of infrastructural dialog: 'Guess the power's not off in this area. Could be nuclear.' Noting that there is a nuclear plant nearby not only reinforces the apocalyptic nature of things even *before* zombies arrived – the film came out before Three Mile Island, but nuclear was not a universally embraced power source – but also explains the practical matter of the lights being on. Nuclear meltdowns and dystopian/post-apocalyptic narratives inform each other quite obviously, with fictional disasters revealing anxieties over the safety of nuclear power. *Dawn of the Dead* understands nuclear power as a zombie-like: no one is working at the plant, but the nuclear material still creates electricity; the Three Mile Island incident in 1979 shows the danger of nuclear energy creation, even with trained hands at the controls.

Eliminating people eliminates expertise, and the damage of the monkey virus, when combined with the nuclear fallout and damage of nuclear plant meltdowns, hastens the end of human civilization in the 2011–17 *Planet of the Apes* series. The virus that spreads across the globe in the credits sequence to *Dawn of the Planet of the Apes* affects energy production as well: one piece of voice-over in the sequence features a power plant spokesperson saying: 'The reactor is overheating. We can't stop the meltdown.' The scavengers in *Oblivion* (Darren Gilford 2013) plan to repurpose an alien reactor as a weapon that Jack Harper (Tom Cruise) can use against the aliens, showing, on the one hand, the danger of nuclear energy, but, on the other hand, given the blasted state of the earth that the scavengers live on, it looks like nuclear winter has already come. A similar sense of a blasted world making the destruction of a nuclear plant a less undesirable option appears in *The Matrix Reloaded* (Owen Paterson 2003). The decisions in *Oblivion* and *The Matrix Reloaded* are made by victims of the apocalypse, but in *Resident Evil: Apocalypse* (Paul Denham Austerberry 2004), the decision to use the worst possible outcome of nuclear energy as an explanation for exterminations appears first as theory, then as practice. As Alice (Milla Jovovich) and her small group of comrades hide out in a bus, they wonder how the Umbrella Corporation will explain the destruction of all of Raccoon City. 'Cover up's already prepared', Alice explains. 'A meltdown at the nuclear power plant. A tragic accident'. Soon after, a news report shows the chyron 'Reactor Meltdown', with footage of a cooling tower crumbling and falling, and a voice-over calling it 'the worst disaster since the Russian Chernobyl incident in 1986'. Then a nuclear weapon is dropped, wiping the city and evidence of the corporation's crimes off the earth.

Energy as a weapon

Nuclear energy as a weapon, as seen in *Resident Evil: Apocalypse* and *Oblivion*, represents a power of destruction on a massive, even global scale. Energy sources such as gasoline, biodiesel, natural gas, and electricity offer smaller but still powerful weapons for the weak against the forces who control dystopian worlds or who seek to make post-apocalyptic worlds even more oppressive. In a summary of Mohamad Ali Kadavir's research, James Stout writes that

> in recent decades citizens fighting against the state have been more likely to democratise their countries by taking mass unarmed actions against property, rather than taking to the mountains with Kalashnikovs. From the Winter War to the Arab spring, there has been a rudimentary tool in the hands of people undertaking this approach to fighting government oppression: the Molotov cocktail.
>
> (2020: n.pag.)

The Molotov cocktail features in both *Escape from New York* and *Escape from LA* as a weapon that can secure a getaway, as when Cabbie tosses one at Snake's pursuers. Some variation of a fuel source as a weapon appears in a number of other forms: as gas pumped through a windshield, turning a car into a flaming death box in *Land of the Dead*; as a gas tanker turned into a flaming weapon in *The Terminator* (George Costello and Maria Caso AD 1984); as barrel bombs dropped from above in *Resident Evil: The Final Chapter* (gasoline) and *Zombieland Double Tap* (Martin Whist 2019) (biodiesel). Cholo creates an IED by rolling a natural gas bottle into a fire in *Land of the Dead*. Both Zac Hobson in *The Quiet Earth* and Alice in *Resident Evil: Apocalypse* use a combination of accumulating natural gas in an enclosed space and flame to create an explosion to escape from where they are trapped. These non-traditional incendiary moments of self-defence and/or necessary violence emerge from the potential to improvise a weapon out of some form of gas and flame.

Slightly more controllable than a Molotov cocktail, electricity can be used as a weapon, both in its presence and absence. In *28 Days Later* when Selena (Naomie Harris) and Mark catch Jim (Cillian Murphy) up on what happened when he was in a coma, Mark tells Jim, 'there's no government, no police, no army. No TV, no radio, no electricity'. Lack of electricity takes away the familiar – TV, radio, light – creating an advantage for those suffering from the rage virus, even if they don't know it. The rage zombies aren't the only ones who weaponize electricity. *28 Days Later* shows that the question of who is in power when electricity returns matters a great deal. Selena and Jim and Hannah (Megan Burns) return to what appears to be civilization when they make it to the north. The army's secure house has electricity, as well as water and food. But the mad Major Henry West (Christopher Eccleston), in addition to being heavily armed, also controls the electric lights that make it possible to monitor encroaching zombies, giving him an even greater measure of power over his 'guests'.

The rarity of electricity after the apocalypse makes a weapon of both its presence and absence. Dystopias have electricity, and the rulers of dystopias frequently find it necessary to make a weapon of electricity, lest their subjects do the same. The state using electricity provision as a control measure appears as a joke in *Judge Dredd* (Nigel Phelps 1995). After Dredd (Sylvester Stallone) and Fergie

(Rob Schneider) are sent to prison and survive the crash of their transport plane, they are captured by a gang of cannibals. They fight off most of the cannibals, the last of which is the cyborg Mean Machine. Mean Machine misses a punch, lodging his arm in a pillar. Even though he's no longer a judge, Dredd informs Mean Machine he's in violation of 'Code 4722, illegal use of city electricity', playing the regime's use of restricted electricity access – in the bureaucratic language of Code 4722 – for laughs. Dredd's judgement, however, is a real weapon, as he jams an electric cable onto Mean Machine's exoskeleton to electrocute him. I have already noted a few ways energy functions in the dystopian *Hunger Games* series, and electricity plays a determinative role in the second film of the series as the game arena – in its planning, execution, and surveillance – depends on electricity. The destruction of the game arena in *The Hunger Games: Catching Fire* (Phillip Messina 2013) similarly depends on electricity. Katniss shoots an arrow connected to the 'five billion joules of energy' created when the like-clockwork lightning strikes the tree in the middle of the game arena to destroy the roof of the arena and put an end to the Hunger Games. The games end not with a sole survivor but with cooperation. A top-down dystopian system that uses electricity for an oppressive spectacle is no match for a bottom-up, cooperative approach to harnessing electricity.

Almost all the examples of energy as a weapon in these films contain a liberatory aspect: the user often, but not always, fights against an oppressive system with an everyday part of the infrastructure. Even when it is an arrow carrying a lightning bolt, the scale of an energy source, or an energy source harnessed as electricity as a weapon, tends to be personal or concentrated in a small area. The electromagnetic pulses (EMP) that appear as weapons in *The Matrix*, *Resident Evil* (Richard Bridgland 2002), and *Escape from LA* have a much greater range. An EMP is a non-lethal weapon, in that the pulse itself does not kill you. But that does not mean an EMP is not dangerous. The EMP is a simple weapon to create, which makes it a good tool for fear mongering and for *deus ex machina* work in fiction. In the wake of a North Korean nuclear test in 2017, *Popular Mechanics* ran a piece on EMPs. 'What would an actual North Korean attack look like?', it asked. 'Chances are, it's not what you're thinking. Instead of unleashing the traditional nuclear nightmare, North Korea could go another route – an EMP. An electromagnetic pulse could take down an electrical power grid, causing economic chaos rather than human casualties' (Hambling 2017: n.pag.). Simple to create with the potential to take away the United States' main advantage – its economic standing – the EMP seems a nightmare.

The current and voltage surges caused by an EMP's huge amounts of radio energy would destroy not just electronic objects themselves but also how they relate to and undergird each other's functioning. A world without electricity would resemble much of what appears in *The Postman*, *The Road*, and *Waterworld*: a muscle- and wind-powered world; 'the meek, that is things made of valves, wood and flesh-and-blood will inherit the earth. Horse and bikes would still work' (Kruszelnicki 2001: n.pag.). Doomsday preppers have an interest in EMPs, as they show the wisdom of the self-sufficient rural living frequently espoused by their community. As one anonymous prepper website describes a post-EMP world, 'the electrical power grid also powers the other utilities we take for granted, such as our mains water supply, sewage systems, gas supply, phone and internet; also banking, refrigeration, petrol pumps, and so on' (Anon. 2017: n.pag.). A successful EMP attack would literally put its victims in the dark, cut off from the last century-plus of technological innovations that are now considered indispensable. Thus, to use an EMP against an adversary would make anarcho-primitivism the end point of the engagement. David Hambling admits that in such a situation, '[w]hat happens after that is speculation. The most extreme suggestion is that, pushed back to 19th century technology, America would starve, but likely it (*sic*) the situation wouldn't be quite so dire' (2017: n.pag.). A country accustomed to industrialized, mechanized agriculture that employs about 1 per cent of the population would certainly find the sudden adjustment – the step 'back in time' – difficult.

In other words, to use an EMP would be apocalyptic in the sense that it would reveal the truth about the society against which it was used. Three films hinge on the use of an EMP. The first, *Resident Evil*, uses something close to an EMP – 'a massive electrical charge' – against the Umbrella Corporation's artificial intelligence slash defence system. In traditional movie-computer style, this 'forces the mainframe to reboot', saving Alice and her comrades. An EMP functions similarly in *The Matrix*, in which the *Nebuchadnezzar*'s EMP weapon disables the sentinels that chase Neo (Keanu Reeves), Trinity (Carrie-Anne Moss), and Morpheus (Laurence Fishburne) and their comrades. Both *Resident Evil* and *The Matrix* feature more targeted EMP-type weapons, directed at immediate enemies. *Escape from LA*, on the other hand, imagines far more, aiming the weapon against a dystopian United States as well as the rest of the world. The scientific expert Test Tube explains the weapon in terms that could be taken out of the material cited earlier:

> The instruction disk hooks you right into the sword of Damocles, the ultimate defensive weapon system. You see that? There's a ring of satellites encircling the earth. Attached to each satellite is a mega neutron bomb. When detonated, each satellite unleashes an intense electromagnetic pulse, but EMP doesn't harm a living thing. What it does do is shut down every known power source, all electrical devices, cars airplanes, toasters, computers, everything, even batteries. But this makes this an aiming device that gives the user incredible accuracy. You can pinpoint precisely what you want to shut down. A taxi cab in Buenos Aires. The entire country of Spain. Amazing. Brilliant. Hell, you could key in all the satellites and shut down the whole planet, send it right back to the Dark Ages.

Both *Resident Evil* and *The Matrix* take place in worlds that are already in the Dark Ages: either zombie hordes or sentient machines chase the few remaining humans as prey. *Escape from LA*'s religious dictatorship that deports 'all people found undesirable or unfit to live in the new moral America' to Los Angeles Island, an 'island of the damned', offers a larger, continent-sized target.

The scale and type of destruction an EMP can cause organizes *Escape from LA*'s final showdown between the hero, Snake Plissken, and the villains, the US president, and US police force commander Malloy. As Plissken holds the controls for the satellites that can unleash the EMP, the president asks: 'Us or them?' Snake muses aloud, 'shut down the Third World, they lose, you win. Shut down America, you lose, they win. The more things change, the more they stay the same'. When the president asks, 'so what are you going to do?' Snake tells him 'disappear' and begins to input the code that will EMP-attack the entire world. Trying to forestall the attack, Malloy reminds Snake, 'you push that button, everything we've accomplished for the past 500 years will be finished. Our technology. Our way of life. Our entire history. We'll have to start all over again. For God's sakes don't do it Snake!' Repeating his catchphrase, Snake reminds Malloy, 'the name's Plissken' and keys in 6-6-6. Everything goes black. Kendall Phillips argues that *Escape from LA* fits within director John Carpenter's auteurist signature as relates to the frontier, meaning that

> [t]he decision is obvious: to complete the reversal of the frontier-myth and with the push of one button return everything to the primordial state in which endless possibilities stretch out into an uncertain future.
>
> (2012: 164–65)

Carpenter's no-fuss, even obvious style provides clear evidence for a second part of Phillips's argument. Phillips claims that

> [e]ven Snake Plissken, one of the most cynical of Carpenter's drifter-heroes, reveals his optimism in the end. His destruction of modern, technological civilization is done in the hopes of a return of the human and American spirit – a spirit that might be freed from the overwhelming strictures of modern life and once again take on the endless possibilities of the uncertain frontier.
>
> (2012: 164–65)

After unleashing the EMP, Snake finds a pack of American Spirit cigs, shown in an insert closeup, and lights up. He takes a long look at the match's flame, then looks into the camera. He blows out the match and the image goes to black, echoing the EMP attack. Snake's voice then says: 'Welcome to the human race.'

The EMP removes any technological advantages the United States may have, but Snake savours the American Spirit he finds in the aftermath. Michael Ryan and Douglas Kellner write that

> future films on the Right dramatise contemporary conservative fears of 'terrorism', or socialism, or liberalism as in *Logan's Run* or *Escape from New York*. Left films (*Outland, Blade Runner*) take advantage of the rhetorical mode of temporal displacement to criticise the current inequalities of capitalism. These films display what we have called the American quandary.
>
> (2004: 53)

In terms of a frontier, the EMP reopens the globe as a frontier for the United States to conquer, making *Escape from LA*, on its surface, a political successor to *Escape from New York*'s status on the right. However, this misses that Commander Malloy invokes 500 years of technology that must be retained, even if that means propping up a theocracy. Snake consigning these technological advantages to the dustbin of history would be, in Ryan and Kellner's account, a criticism of the current inequalities of capitalism. Evan Calder Williams' account of *Escape from New York* applies equally well to *Escape from LA*: 'Snake's refusal to play along [...] is a knowing rejection not of the world as such but of the first world's claim to be the only world' (2011: 237). Whether from the right or left, the EMP that plunges the world into a pre-electrical 'Dark Age' demonstrates the essential nature of electricity not only to dystopian rulers but also to the ruled. Sometimes the only response is to pull the plug and start again.

Renewable energy production

However, not everyone wants to start from scratch. Rather than restart entirely, a number of dystopian and post-apocalyptic movies imagine versions of renewable energy production as a path out of dystopia and towards a stable post-apocalyptic society. After the 1973 energy crisis and in light of the increasing damage of climate change, solar, wind, hydro, and other forms of renewable energy production provide the backbone for the creation of a more optimistic horizon of expectations for a liveable future. In addition to the existing fuel options – fossil fuel (petroleum, natural gas), nuclear, wood, coal – described earlier, technological change presents a few more options for energy. Bright-green environmental options including hydrogen, algae fuel, and carbon extraction from the air and water offer a technological fix to the carbon economy and its damage. However, these fuel sources do not appear in mass-audience dystopian and post-apocalyptic films.

The imagination of alternative fuels looks not to algae or ocean vents, but rather to muscle power. For instance, in *Soylent Green*'s (Edward C. Carfagno and George W. Davis AD 1973) dystopian New York City, Sol (Edward G. Robinson) pedals a bicycle to generate electricity for the apartment he shares with Thorn (Charlton Heston); the same setup appears, with an extensive array of batteries, in Martha Philip's much more extravagant multi-room apartment. In the post-apocalyptic world of *Mad Max: Fury Road*, Immortan Joe commands a massive army not only of war boys but also of energy production boys, who turn a massive metal treadmill that does jobs that would normally require electricity, such as lowering and raising the platforms used by the settlement's vehicles. The energy produced by human muscle power is renewable so long as the human remains fed and fit, no small trick in a dystopian – to say nothing of a post-apocalyptic – setting.

The machines that rule the world in *The Matrix* solved this problem by taking the muscle out of muscle power. At first, the machines were solar-powered, but soon the energy source changed. As Morpheus explains it to Neo:

> The human body generates more bioelectricity than a 120-volt battery. And over 25,000 BTUs of body heat. Combined with a form of fusion, the machines had found all the energy they would ever need. There are fields, Neo, endless fields, where human beings are no longer born. We are grown. For the longest time I wouldn't believe it. And then I saw the fields with my own eyes, watched them liquify the dead, so they could be fed intravenously to the living.

As Joshua Clover puts it, the industrialized use of humans for energy, and the coincidental industrial farming of humans to feed that energy production (in a practice not unlike the use of rendered bovine-origin proteins in cow feed that led to mad cow disease), 'is not the *plot* of the movie; it's the circumstance of the world in which the story unfolds, and the engine of the narrative' (2008: 59, original emphasis). The images that accompany Morpheus's speech – pink pods filled with human bodies, stretched out to the horizon, giraffe-like machines attending the pods, a baby pierced with tubes that recycle humans back into further energy production – are followed by Neo's rebirth, emerging out of his pod in a stack of pods that resembles Bertrand Goldberg's Marina Towers apartment building in the Wachowskis' hometown of Chicago. In opposition to the gooey, human-powered energy system for the machines, the world of *The Matrix* imagines something else entirely for the humans, something more mysterious. One night, unable to sleep, Neo talks with Counsellor Hamman in Zion City's 'Engineering level'. Looking out over the level, Hamann describes a post-apocalyptic relationship to infrastructure that Brian Larkin, as I quoted in the introduction, would recognize (emphasis added):

> Almost no one comes down here, unless of course there's a problem. That's how it is with people, nobody cares *how* it works as long as it works. I like it down here. I like to be reminded this city survives because of these machines. These machines are keeping us alive while other machines are coming to kill us. Interesting, isn't it? The power to give life and the power to end it.

Hamann and Neo then discuss what it means to be in control when the machines control the work done on the engineering level.

NEO:	But we control these machines. They don't control us.
COUNSELLOR:	Course not. How could they? The idea is pure nonsense, but it does make one wonder just, what is control?
NEO:	If we wanted, we could shut these machines down.
COUNSELLOR:	Of course. That's it. You hit. That's control, isn't it? If we wanted, we could smash them to bits. Although if we did, we'd have to consider what happens to our lights, our heat, our air.

There's a bit of a mystery how Zion gets its power, making the digital image of the engineering level a kind of set as artifice that creates a new, possible reality. The power plant coded as nuclear I mentioned above exists inside the matrix, whereas Zion exists in the Real World. But Hamann never describes what kind of energy source Zion uses, and the film offers no clues as to the fuel source. The scene at the engineering level hints at some kind of renewable means, but nothing so simple as the stationary bicycle Sol cranks to generate electricity. This mystery accentuates Hamann's point that caring about *how* the lights stay on begins, for most people, only when the lights go out.

A civilization that doesn't want the lights to go out confers a great deal of power on whoever controls the electricity switch. Master-Blaster (Angelo Rossitto and Paul Larsson) loves to teach this lesson to the people of Bartertown, especially its leader Auntie Entity (Tina Turner), in *Mad Max Beyond Thunderdome* (Graham 'Grace' Walker 1985). Some of the motive force in Bartertown is muscle power, as when very muscular men turn a wheel that lifts the elevator to Auntie Entity's headquarters. Jim Poe writes that 'Aunty Entity controls Bartertown from an airy, elevated dwelling, while workers and convict slaves (a nod to Australia's colonial history) refine methane from pig shit in the gloomy Underworld' (2021: n.pag.). Auntie Entity may have a couple of buff guys, but Master Blaster has hundreds of pigs, all their shit, dozens of slaves, and a processing plant. Auntie Entity may provide the security force, but everyday life needs more. The methane plant provides electricity for Bartertown, turning fans and powering lights, which means that Master Blaster has a claim to run Bartertown that might even trump Aunty Entity's.

He asserts his claim when he decides to withhold energy from the city, and only after Aunty Entity publicly admits that 'Master Blaster runs Bartertown' does the electricity return. We might say that Master Blaster provides the bread of everyday electricity production, while Auntie Entity provides Bartertown's people with the circus of Thunderdome. Her revenge against Master Blaster is to place Blaster – the hulking muscle who carries the small technical expert – in Thunderdome with Max (Mel Gibson). Max fights Blaster out of necessity, but refuses to kill him and then sides with Master to escape Bartertown. In short, a warlord like Aunty Entity is less useful to rebuilding after the apocalypse than a person who knows how to turn pig shit into electricity.

Solar and wind

Raymond Malewitz writes about the presence of renewable energy sources in literature as a product of their novelty:

> Solar and wind farms, for example, are now far more visible within and beyond literary settings than their equally artificial predecessors – coal power plants, irrigation canals, and so on – simply because they are new; older infrastructural technologies, on the other hand, disappear from view because we have grown accustomed to seeing them and they no longer exert a hold on our imaginations.
>
> (2015: 719)

A solar panel doesn't appear accidentally in a novel or poem. It can appear in a set as punctuation-like manner, entering into a 'dynamic with narrative that establishes not time, place, and mood alone, but time, place, and mood as these center on the specificities of class, gender, race, and ethnicity' (Affron and Affron 1995: 38). In other words, the sort of person who has rooftop solar in Australia in 2000 would differ in class position (or at least income level) from the person who has rooftop solar in 2008, after the federal government put tax credits in place for installation costs, increasing the reach of solar generation. Broadly speaking, solar production on a large scale in a dystopian or post-apocalyptic movie tends to speak of bad news. The army of machines in *The Matrix*, Morpheus explains, originally ran on solar, 'but we know that it was us that scorched the sky. They were dependent on solar power, and it was believed that they would be unable to survive without an energy source as abundant as the sun'. As noted above, human bodies solved that little problem. A similar failing of large-scale solar appears in *Blade Runner 2049*. In the film's opening sequence, K (Ryan Gosling) flies over what look like miles of solar arrays that must be the source for the electricity that makes all the neon and holograms in Los Angeles possible. Large-scale wind production only appears once in the movies I analyse in this book: in *WALL-E*, wind turbines line the tops of garbage mountains, taking advantage of the increased wind at higher elevations (*28 Days Later* features a striking aestheticized shot of turbines). But all that massive investment in renewable energy was too little too late; the earth's ecosystem still collapsed.

Contrariwise, solar and wind on a small, local scale can promise an improved situation. The smaller scale of human settlements and a distrust of a possible centralized authority in a dystopian or post-apocalyptic setting informs this valorization of local energy production. Solar panels appear as level-one or level-two set decorations, the background of everyday life in dystopian and post-apocalyptic cities. For instance, as Wade walks through the streets of The Stacks in *Ready Player One*, he passes solar panels mounted on signal poles and the frames that support The Stacks. Higher up in The Stacks themselves, small wind turbines offer another means to generate electricity to power trips to OASIS. The walled city of *Warm Bodies* (Martin Whist 2013) similarly deploys solar panels to generate electricity for streetlights and even an iPod charger. In *The Postman*, the village of Pineview generates some of its electricity through wind power: what looks like a wind speed gauge stands next to the village post office. This little spinning turbine might explain how the social event of the season – the dance The Postman (Kevin Costner) attends – can have multicoloured fairy-light decorations: a wind gauge repurposed. The *Divergent* series places solar panels on the sides of large vehicles, and in *Insurgent*, the solar panel also doubles as a video screen, allowing Jeanine (Kate Winslet) to address the people of Chicago on a self-powering screen. The Waste Allocation Load Lifter Earth Class machine, WALL-E, is also self-powered by solar, allowing it to continue to work through the mountains of trash left on earth.

Further out into the country, Alice drives a solar-powered car, allowing her to drive through the *Resident Evil: The Final Chapter*'s wasteland without worrying about where the next tank of gas will come from. Beyond Alice's solar-powered Toyota, there are the steam-powered cars of Manhattan Island's prison and electric cars in *The Island*, but otherwise the internal combustion engine retains such a purchase on the imagination that standard fuel-burning cars remain a feature of most films. Another form of wind power – sailing – powers *Waterworld* in the form of the Mariner's catamaran and a number of other boats. But the wind does more than move boats. The atoll where Mariner stops has a large windmill, and Old Gregor wears a wind-powered miner's helmet lantern to see during the night.

Finally, rural settings offer space for both solar and wind to power small settlements, whether in the form of the walled compound at the end of *I Am Legend*, or Jack's set as a punctuation cabin in the post-apocalyptic woods in *Oblivion*.

Granted, small-scale solar generation is put to oppressive use in the *Divergent* series, and the solar use in *WALL-E* is, like *Blade Runner 2049*, too little too late. A similarly ambivalent appearance of renewable production appears in *Interstellar*'s (Nathan Crowley 2014) drone chase sequence, which begins at Cooper's farm and ends at the edge of the reservoir. While the focus at the sequence's end is on the drone and its hardware, in the distance, more than a dozen wind turbines occupy the background of the image, a reminder of one sort of adjustment to the climate change that defeated human ingenuity. But the solar-powered car that helps Alice to escape Washington, DC, the hideaways in *Oblivion* and *I Am Legend*, and home use for both need and entertainment in *Ready Player One* show that solar and wind, when in the hands of those who use it themselves, rather than in the hands of those who control people through the medium of energy, offer a path to a more liveable and survivable dystopian and post-apocalyptic world.

This is not to say that only small-scale energy production can be good and that any large-scale energy production will automatically lead to oppressive measures. As Raymond Malewitz argues, 'new infrastructure projects operate as metonyms for the monumental changes that are taking place within US communities and around the globe' (2015: 719). Parallel to the massive urbanization of world populations, we can see a movement of energy production away from those urban centres. After all, the optimal locations for wind farms are those where it is windiest; naturally, many of those places are far from where people live. Because wind and solar farms/technologies are placed in rural areas, not cosmopolitan cities, 'this inversion renders the peripheries of American culture more modern, in a sense, than their metropolitan counterparts' (Malewitz 2015: 720). The same metropolitan–periphery inversion holds true for the United Kingdom, as shown in *28 Days Later*. About 40 onshore wind farms were installed in England in the decade before *28 Days Later* was filmed, a significant change in energy production from the wake of the role coal played in the 1980s. Jim, Selena, Frank, and Hannah drive past one of these farms on their way north, the massive turbines looming over their black cab. Nearly every UK wind farm established in the 1990s is outside of southeast England, the monied urban heart of the United Kingdom. Instead, wind production happens in Cornwall, Cumbria, Lancashire, Northumberland, North Yorkshire, South Yorkshire, and West Yorkshire, as well as Northern Ireland, Scotland, and Wales. In the present, this wind production allows London to leach the rest of the island even further. In the future, as the survivors' flight in *28 Days Later* shows, not London but the north of England, in particular, represents the more liveable future. If there is to be a future in London, according to *The Girl with All the Gifts* (Kristian Milstead 2016), it must be at a very small, solar-powered scale. The post-post-apocalyptic ending of *The Girl with All the Gifts* shows zombie children lining up for lessons outside of a solar-powered lab that sustains the non-zombie schoolteacher

FIGURE 1.2: *Warm Bodies* resources from beyond the wall.

Helen Justineau. Similarly, the post-apocalyptic walled city in *Warm Bodies* rigs up a solar-powered communications system so that the city's leader, Grigio (John Malkovich), can address the young people going out to forage medical supplies from beyond the walls (Figure 1.2). That same solar generation makes it possible for young people to listen to iPods. It is not clear where the power comes from in the statue-dedicating scene that closes *The Postman*, but it is not too much of a leap to say that the camera runs on a battery charged by wind or hydropower, which have already appeared throughout the film. Renewable energy in the set design, both on a small and grand scale, creates a sense of society planning, of making a conscious return to civilization, providing an undercurrent of comfort for the mass audience: post-apocalyptic life will be uncomfortable, but also with the potential to be pretty much like what we have now.

Hydro: The durability of Hoover Dam's power provision

Zombieland Double Tap explains the presence of working electricity with a throw-away line of dialog that echoes the one given in *Dawn of the Dead*, only in a world of dependable, renewable hydrogeneration: 'It's amazing. As long as it rains the dams give us power'. More than explaining the presence of electricity, the line offers a practical explanation for the way in which the zombie apocalypse managed not to change a number of aspects of early twenty-first-century life, like the appeal of shopping for scented candles. You could probably shop for a long time if hydro powered what was left of the world. The Hoover Dam, 726 feet high, 1244 feet long, and 45 feet wide, isn't one of the twenty largest dams in the world by height, reservoir created, area flooded, installed capacity, or annual production; however, it still may well survive for 10,000 years. If people were no longer to occupy the control room, it could continue to produce power for weeks, months, perhaps even years if invasive species do not clog the pipes and conduits feeding water through the system. Such a monument to its builders seems appropriate to a nascent empire like the 1930s United States. As David Nye puts it in *American Technological Sublime*, 'during the 1920s and 1930s hydroelectric dams became symbols of both technological progress and economic prosperity [...] The public did not understand the dams on the Tennessee and Colorado in merely utilitarian terms' (1999: 137). The dams were sublime artistic expressions. An unshared prosperity makes the dams a target in the dystopian Panem of the *Hunger Games* series. A dam frequently appears in establishing shots of Capitol City, and a larger dam features in *The Hunger Games: Mockingjay, Part 1* (Phillip Messina 2014), when rebels stage a critical infrastructure attack, planting bombs in a large hydroelectric dam in District 5, causing all of the lights to go out in Capitol City. Ending the brute utilitarianism of energy production shows how the dam produces more than electricity. It produces power. As I noted above, it seems strange that District 12 mines coal when there is a less-polluting energy source and a district to produce it right there in Panem. But the key to my point here is the central control the Capitol exerts over the dam's energy production; the destruction of the dam speaks of the fragility of President Snow's power.

In the post-apocalypse, the ability of hydroelectric dams to produce – and to continue to produce – electricity offers a path back to civilization. *The Postman* links hydrogeneration to rebirth. Before the film's climactic battle, The Postman arrives in Bridge City, a settlement on top of a dam, where they use the electricity generated by the dam for their needs, creating a small and peaceful community. After the battle, a more literal equation of hydrogeneration and rebirth appears. Returning to Bridge City, The Postman reunites with Abby, who has just had a baby. In one almost twenty-second shot, The Postman occupies the foreground, cradling a baby, with the cascading water of the dam in the image's background, with a slow zoom occupying the shot's last five or so seconds (Figure 1.3). A dissolve to 30 years later shows a woman – the baby all grown up – dedicating a statue to The Postman, a monument to the new society that emerged from the hydro (and wind) generation of the communities to whom he delivered mail.

Whereas *The Postman*'s hydrogeneration makes community and rebirth possible, the opposite is true in *Oblivion*. The hydrorigs, a level-three set design of spectacular quasi-natural monumental structures, have to be destroyed to save the already-depopulated earth. The alien hydrorigs turn ocean water on earth into a resource to extract, making *Oblivion* a story about the end of fossil fuels told through 'renewable energy' exhaustion imposed from the outside.

FIGURE 1.3: *The Postman* hydroelectric and new life.

Energy on The Quiet Earth

In *The Quiet Earth*, the mysterious Project Flashlight causes the apocalypse, and Zac Hobson (Bruno Lawrence) does a lot before the electrical grid finally stops working. He breaks into a house, walks through the wreckage of a plane crash, plays saxophone in a downpour, drives a train, and takes a moa statue home with him from the mall. Zac also records and broadcasts a radio message, plays with a model train set, plays snooker, watches a videotape on television, and delivers a speech/confession to an audience of cardboard cutouts of famous people and the moa statue. Zac needs electricity to do all of this. Stuart Murray writes that

> the fears surrounding the nuclear debate are central to Geoff Murphy's *The Quiet Earth* (1985), which opens with a giant sunrise over the sea that, as the sun is about to break the horizon, suddenly seems to take the form of a vivid mushroom cloud produced by a nuclear explosion. In the film, a mystery scientific 'effect' that is controlled by the US, but which has a physical base in New Zealand, has seemingly destroyed nearly all of humanity, and it is clear that the analogy is with nuclear devastation.
>
> (2008: 171–72)

That is to say, Aotearoa New Zealand's policy forbidding nuclear-powered or nuclear-armed vessels from entering its waters in this use entails nuclear *weaponry*, a key context for the film. The New Zealand Nuclear-Free Zone, Disarmament, and Arms Control Act 1987 began with the election of David Lange's government in the year before *The Quiet Earth*'s release. But *The Quiet Earth*, though it certainly speaks to the moment of its release, is based on a novel published in 1981, in the middle of Robert Muldoon's nine years as prime minister, and was filmed in the winter of 1984, at the same time as the election. Considering how much electricity Zac uses in the first third of the film, Aotearoa New Zealand's domestic policy on energy production and industry seems to be of at least as much significance as its policies on disarmament and arms control.

The Quiet Earth begins with Zac waking up and not encountering a single living person in Hamilton or Auckland. Zac listens to a Dictaphone recording of his own voice describing Project Flashlight and its 'phenomenal destructive potential'. He updates his situation on the Dictaphone: 'One, there has been a malfunction in Project Flashlight, with devastating results. Two, it seems I am the only person left on earth.' Two weeks after every person seems to disappear from Aotearoa New Zealand, if not the earth, Zac watches a videotape, shotgun in hand. A man with an American accent says that it is essential for New Zealand to take part in technological research to 'maintain the balance of power that exists in the world today'. Zac shoots the television, screaming 'what are you trying to do? Destroy us all?' Then he whispers, 'I'm taking over'. Taking over requires electricity. He sets up a line of four reel-to-reel tape players that he controls with a remote control. He strings an extension cord through a hole in the exterior wall into the front garden, where he plugs the cord into an amplifier. He stacks plug adapters into surge suppressors. He turns on a set of bright lights on the house exterior. He piles still more adapters into the surge suppressors; he plugs in a couple more cords. He turns on more lights on the house's exterior. In a high-angle shot, Zac walks onto the second-floor balcony to horn fanfare and the sound of a cheering crowd coming from the reel-to-reel players. A cutaway shot shows a cardboard cutout of Bob Marley in the right foreground, with a cutout of Alfred Hitchcock in the middle distance left, and a mannequin plus cutouts of Elvis Presley, Charlie Chaplin, Fred Astaire, and Benito Mussolini in the background. Another cutaway shot shows a two shot of cutouts of Pope John Paul II and Queen Elizabeth II. A cut to a medium closeup of Zac is followed by a slow pullaway from Zac, who begins to speak, clicking the remote when he desires the sound of applause or music:

> I have dedicated all my scientific knowledge and skill to projects which I knew could be put to evil purposes. 'For the common good!' they said. How easy to believe in the common good. When that belief is rewarded with status, wealth, and power! How hard to believe in the common good when every fibre of my being tells me that the awesome forces I have helped to create have been put into the hands of madmen! And became, by the product of my own corruption! Is it not fitting then that I be president of this quiet earth?

He finishes his speech muttering to himself: 'I've been condemned to live.' A medium closeup shot of Zac cuts to a shot of the four reel-to-reels playing the diegetic cacophony of drums, trumpets, cheers, and sieg heils. The sound on the tapes slows, becomes garbled, and then stops. The lights at the house go off. A long shot of a high-rise at night shows all of its windows go from lit up to dark. A shot of the Auckland skyline shows it going dark. A neon sign flickers off. A cut to a closeup of Zac shows the lights go off, leaving him in almost total darkness, the tears on his face reflecting what little light there is. A high-angle long shot of the house shows the balcony is dark. The shot cranes down, and a dissolve takes the shot to morning, with Zac walking on the field at Eden Park. So goes the first third of *The Quiet Earth*. After two weeks without any human interaction, Zac Hobson goes a little mad. And now there's no electricity.

The audience to Zac's balcony address makes clear how important the domestic Aotearoa New Zealand context is to *The Quiet Earth*'s imagination of infrastructure after the apocalypse. Dictators Benito Mussolini and Adolph Hitler not only frequently addressed crowds from balconies but also undertook large infrastructural projects to write their signatures on the nation. Aotearoa New Zealand's longstanding colonial relationship appears in Queen Elizabeth II and Winston Churchill. The potential for a new geopolitical/imperial power appears as Richard Nixon. Cultural imperialism takes the form of figures such as Alfred Hitchcock, Elvis Presley, Charlie Chaplin, and Fred Astaire. Two postcolonial figures, Mahatma Gandhi and Bob Marley, offer an alternative path, both politically and culturally (Marley played a show in Auckland in 1979 to a great deal of public interest). And then there's the moa taken from the mall, the only other kiwi, if you will, that Zac encounters in the immediate aftermath of the end-of-the-world event (Figure 1.4). Later in the film, Zac will meet Api and Joanne, and Murray argues that the way *The Quiet Earth* 'brings together its trio of effect survivors – Pakeha man, Māori man, Pakeha woman – projects much of its rumination on ideas of the end of the world in a specifically New Zealand context' (2008: 172). But neither the Māori man nor pākehā woman is present at Zac's speech. As the only member of Zac's audience actually shown to be loaded into his vehicle, the moa occupies a position slightly apart from the other inanimate audience members, the only audience member endemic and exclusive to Aotearoa.

After the 1973 oil crisis, dystopian and post-apocalyptic films like *The Quiet Earth* show how energy generation and even electricity itself can function as a weapon, and that rebuilding to create a world worth living in is almost uniformly accomplished with locally controlled power production. Electricity produced on a large scale undergirds bad use, whereas electricity

FIGURE 1.4: *The Quiet Earth* address to dignitaries.

produced locally for local use is usually a better sign. The smaller scale of human settlements and a distrust of what a centralized authority would look like in a dystopian or post-apocalyptic setting inform this sensibility. In an analysis of a number of rural energy projects in western Europe, Laure Dobigny observes that

> within the majority of these towns, it is a succession of renewable energy projects, on a fairly variable time scale, from 4 to 20 years, which has, in the end, led to this autonomy. It is not self-sufficiency which was sought, but instead a certain autonomy (whether decision making, economic and political).
>
> (2019: 193)

In these projects, technical skill and knowledge about energy production emerge as a key point. For all his faults, Robert Muldoon recognized the importance of energy to Aotearoa New Zealand, though his prescription for greater fossil fuel investigations was short-sighted. Seen this way, *The Quiet Earth* fits in post-1973 oil crisis narratives quite clearly. The 1973 energy crisis made the energy infrastructure visible through its failures – lines for gas, power outages – and it became clear that control of energy could be weaponized. Energy in the form of oil, gasoline, electricity, and power generation became something people in the industrialized world had to think about rather than take for granted. In Aotearoa

New Zealand, this meant expanding how the nation produced its energy. As the Ministry for Culture and Heritage's Te Ara site puts it:

> 'Think Big' was a government programme of energy-related projects designed to reduce New Zealand's dependence on imported oil, and to broaden the basis of exports. It focused on using offshore Taranaki gas reserves for industrial development, and building the Clyde dam in Central Otago for power generation. Several of these projects were hastened through the approvals process by the National Development Act 1979, which allowed the acceleration of projects believed to be in the national interest.
>
> (Pawson 2010: n.pag.)

Robert Muldoon, the prime minister and minister of finance from 1975 to 1984, hoped the Taranaki gas fields would be

> a new bonanza. This was in keeping with New Zealand experience of periodic rescue from depression or doldrums by a leap in technology [...] In the 1980s an expected electricity and gas 'surplus' was to be turned into industrial production generating directly and indirectly a total of 410,000 jobs over the next decade or so.
>
> (James 1992: 62)

The causes of the Think Big approach's failure are multiple: the public's decreasing trust in Muldoon and the rise of environmental sensibility across the populace, to name a couple. But the source of the Think Big approach is clear: the importance of energy, energy production, and energy security to secure a prosperous national future.

In this context of energy scarcity, the film's framing of Zac's address functions as a sort of confession, and the end of the address, when the power goes out, offers a clue about how Zac might have served Aotearoa New Zealand better instead of following his own corrupt interests. To understand how the end of the world came about, to power computers to analyse data, Zac Hobson needs small-scale local power production. His solution is to fire up a generator and run extension cords up the side of a building into the labs he needs. As *The Quiet Earth* takes place soon after the event that eliminates almost every person, fossil fuel is still available, and it is all Zac uses. The rudimentary number 8 wire system of extension cords and surge suppressors that Zac creates on his own allows him to address a set of cardboard cutouts that stand in for a global audience. That is to say, electricity creates a communications network that connects Aotearoa New Zealand to the rest of the world, ending the tyranny of distance, but at the potential cost of its independence and the end of life on earth.

Conclusion

In *The Quiet Earth*, no authority remains to control electricity, only Zac and later Api and Joanne. In the *Mad Max* movies, small settlements and survivors live in fear of warlords like Humungus and Auntie Entity and Immortan Joe. The *Mad Max* movies repeatedly show the near end of life of earth in terms of a strongman or strongwoman appearing to control electricity through force, making life in the post-apocalypse survivable but unbearable. This top-down control of electricity appears throughout the more pessimistic of dystopian and post-apocalyptic movies. Neither has a particularly optimistic vision for the future on earth. The perpetual war over fuel/guzzeline in the *Mad Max* series maps the post-apocalyptic world's independent outposts in terms of the maximum travelable distance one tank allows between autonomous settlements.

Snake destroys the secret to nuclear fusion in *Escape from New York* because an oppressive government would still control it; he plunges the world into a new Dark Ages without electricity in *Escape from LA* for much the same reason. A dictator exerts total control over Panem in the *Hunger Games* series, but at least the energy infrastructure mega-projects provide work to maintain a quiescent population. In *Blade Runner 2049*, an oligarch controls electricity, and in *WALL-E*, a mega-corporation does. Warlords assert power through energy generation in *The Book of Eli*, *The Road Warrior*, *Mad Max Beyond Thunderdome*, and *Mad Max: Fury Road*. Bureaucratized warlords, a group of experimenters, control Chicago's infrastructure in the *Divergent* series, not the five faction groups that live there. And sometimes the control is not even human: In *The Matrix*, sentient machines completely control the human world and its electricity production, which amounts to the same thing, and aliens with far superior firepower control the electricity of their clone-human servants in *Oblivion*.

More optimistic dystopian and post-apocalyptic movies put locally produced energy in the hands, which is to say in the decision-making, of the people who make and use it. The solar and wind energy in *Ready Player One*'s Stacks allows its residents to enter the virtual reality where they might find some meaning in their life. Sol gets in some exercise and powers the lights in the apartment he shares with Thorn in *Soylent Green*, which when paired with his research for Thorn shows that love and solidarity still exist in dystopian New York. While machines control energy production above ground, the people of Zion in *The Matrix Reloaded* live in what appears to be a self-sufficient enclave where they produce their own energy. There may not be much electricity in *Waterworld*, but from batteries to run winches on catamarans to batteries on ancient jet skis to a windmill that provides power to a peaceful atoll community, locally made and used energy keeps the watery globe liveable. In *The Postman*, locally made and used energy in the Pacific Northwest is key to the establishment of the Restored United States. In *Oblivion*, Jack uses old technology to make an old world to escape back to, linking the power of renewables to the rugged outdoorsman myth, an individualized vision for renewable energy production. Even the wasted earth in *WALL-E* shows a failed hopeful vision: the wind turbines turn the garbage piles into natural formations, showing that amidst consumerist waste there was enough power to create a hyper-technologized society of destructive, fully automated luxury capitalism rather than a more sustainable (if perhaps fantastic) fully automated luxury communism.

This finally brings us to the hydro dam in *Dawn of the Planet of the Apes*. The small band of survivors in northern California need to get the dam back up and running to maintain their civilization and to communicate with any other survivors who may be out there. Driving through the forest, the apes' territory, the humans find the abandoned dam. Twice the importance of electricity generation gets explained. First by Dreyfus (Gary Oldman), who tells the remaining people of San Francisco,

> we're almost out of fuel. Which means no more power. Which means we could slip back to the way things were. That dam up there was the answer [...] That power, it's not just about keeping the lights on. It's about giving us the tools to reconnect to the rest of the world. To find out who else is out there. So that we can start to rebuild. And reclaim the world we lost.

Then Malcom explains to Caesar and a number of other apes the energy history of the ten years after the virus wiped out much of human civilization.

> This is what we used to call small hydro, but we've been working to reroute the power lines to city because the city used to run off nuclear power, but that ran out years ago. So we've been using diesel generators and gasifiers. But if we can just get the dam working, then we have a shot at restoring limited power.

This will provide, as Caesar says, lights. And while the nuclear plant continued to work for a while, as in *Dawn of the Dead*, generators and a limited fuel supply soon came into play, as in *The Quiet Earth* and *The Omega Man*. But eventually the region's remaining fossil fuel stores would run out, leaving hydro the best option. And, as I noted earlier, a hydrogeneration plant would likely have stopped working because of clogged water pipes and conduits. As the apes destroy the small number of guns the hydro dam-restoring humans brought with them – part of the agreement to work on the dam – Koba tells Caesar, 'if they get power, they'll be more dangerous'. After Malcolm and his team get the plant working, a massive celebration happens in the corner of San Francisco where the humans have made their settlement. But Dreyfus, who prefers war to coexistence with the apes, controls the energy, not the more conciliatory Malcom. In *Dawn of the Planet of the Apes* and, after it, *War for the Planet of the Apes*, the return of electricity means the return of oppression. Apes may not need electricity or lights, but Koba nevertheless recognizes that when it comes to electricity generation in dystopian and post-apocalyptic worlds, energy is power.

2

Transportation: Filling Potholes at the End of Humanity's Road

The most dangerous thing most people do on any given day is get in a car. George Miller, the writer and director of the *Mad Max* series, was an emergency department doctor; he knew how dangerous cars could be. Even when they work 'properly', highways are dystopian. In Australia, 'external causes of injury' such as car accidents account for about half of deaths for people under 45. In 1970, when Miller was about to begin his brief career as a medical doctor, the car accident death rates were '49 and 18 deaths per 100,000 population for males and females respectively' (Australian Institute of Health and Welfare 2006: 72). After three decades of changes to public health policies, the car accident death rates fell to fourteen (males) and six (females) per 100,000 (Australian Institute of Health and Welfare 2006: 72). In addition to restrictions on acceptable blood alcohol level, mandating seat belt use, and lowering the speed limit, two that seem to be more questions of engineering rather than public health stand out: safer car design and better roads. The effects of the car accidents he saw in the hospital informed the vehicular mayhem – and its results – in the *Mad Max* films. *Mad Max*'s Toecutter drives like an absolute madman, and he does so on an unsafe road. Dystopian and especially post-apocalyptic movies are filled with such unsafe roads. In many cases, unsafe desert roads that cross the wide-open spaces caused by nuclear fallout or the desiccation of formerly irrigated farmland or unspecified global changes. Almost three-quarters of Australian land is arid, with 30 per cent of the country desert. In addition, more than 80 per cent of the population lives along the coasts, leaving the middle of the country – the desert/arid parts – with a population density less than 0.1 people per square kilometre. In other words, a sparsely populated, desert landscape, which describes not only the *Mad Max* series settings, but also the worlds of *The Book of Eli* and *The Road*, as well as parts of *Blade Runner 2049*, *Judge Dredd*, the *Resident Evil* series, and the *Divergent* series to name a few. Roads and the vehicles that use them are common in both dystopian and post-apocalyptic worlds, but mass transit is not. As there is no centralized government or even a sizable population in a post-apocalyptic world, there's not much call for a subway or a bus system. But in a dystopian world, mass transit, often in the form of some kind of rail transport, serves as a significant means of transportation for people and for goods.

To understand the importance of the transportation infrastructure to dystopian and post-apocalyptic film worlds, I want to investigate not only the everyday use of it, but also its maintenance. That is to say, I want to combine public policy style uses of infrastructure such as the speed and the way people travel with the engineering style uses of road and rail upkeep. Brian Larkin combines the sociological and the engineering aspects of transportation in 'The politics and poetics of infrastructure', writing that 'roads and railways are not just technical objects then but also operate on the level of fantasy and desire. They encode the dreams of individuals and societies and are the vehicles whereby those fantasies are transmitted and made emotionally real' (2013: 333). Roads and rail stetch across landscapes, as paths across a decayed social fabric and as decaying physical objects. Both literally and metaphorically, road and rail systems present an often-ambivalent path forward – and backward – to civilization for those who remain.

In this chapter I begin with a brief overview of the construction of the road system (the highways) in the United States and Australia, and the rail systems of the United States, describing their practical and ideological functions. The second section analyses the role of mass transportation infrastructure in films, in particular how a working system and a broken system differ in their importance, and how genre puts even a non-functioning mass transportation infrastructure to work in chase sequences. The third section examines the breakdown of road systems, starting with one of the most common establishing shots in dystopian and post-apocalyptic movies, a street or overpass or rail line in disrepair, then searching for examples of maintenance and its effects on the everyday life of people in dystopian and post-apocalyptic worlds. The fourth section considers two main types of still-functioning roads, paved highways and unpaved roads (both in urban areas and in more sparsely populated remote areas), and how the mobility those roads offer provides one of the most recognizable indices of societal breakdown and personal danger. I conclude the chapter by asking how adjustments to dystopian and post-apocalyptic life are expressed in transportation choices.

One literal problem that dystopian and post-apocalyptic societies pose, either by force or by circumstance, is physical disconnection. The questions '*where* do we go' and '*who* else is out there?' imply '*how* do we get there? *how* do we find them?' By car, by train, by boat, or by starship? A transportation infrastructure can address the problems posed by disconnection, but to do so requires a lot of collaboration. I look at the endings of the films I analyse throughout the chapter to scan the horizon of what better world of transportation might be possible to imagine. Whether it's the rigid control of trains running on time or a crumbling road system that makes connections across settlements difficult and dangerous, the transportation infrastructure is essential not only to literal movement as travel, but also to the forward motion of dystopian and post-apocalyptic societies. The transportation infrastructure gives concrete form to a belief in a particularly linear kind of future common to mass audience films: of progress, of things getting better. However, a transportation infrastructure that continues to function requires maintenance. What is particularly important to dystopian and post-apocalyptic worlds is the degree to which (and perhaps also the pace at which) maintenance of the transportation infrastructure is at least possible. To put it simply, potholes need to be filled to continue moving forward, to advance human civilization, even after the apocalypse. How else can someone like Max Rockatansky keep moving deeper into the desert of post-apocalyptic Australia, in search of gasoline, food, and maybe home? Andrew Russell and Lee Vinsel argue that rather than innovation, maintenance and repair 'has more impact on people's daily lives than the vast majority of technological innovations' (2016: n.pag.). Russell and Vinsel continue, making the modest but essential claim that fixing potholes keeps the world going: 'We can think of labour that goes into maintenance and repair as the work of *the maintainers*, those individuals whose work keeps ordinary existence going rather than introducing novel things' (2016: n.pag.). However, such maintenance plans and the people to perform the labour on behalf of others rarely appear on film; dystopian and post-apocalyptic films in search of a better world either leave terrestrial travel behind – taking to the water or resorting to the wishful thinking of space travel – or pessimistically hold on to the crumbling remnants of the post-war infrastructure. The physical form of the transportation infrastructure – its rails and roads and paths – fights against the decay caused by conscious destruction, neglect both benign and malign, and apocalyptic damage. Dystopian and post-apocalyptic movies show that the twentieth- and twenty-first-century valorization of innovating our way out of transportation problems with maglevs or flying cars might too quickly skip over the ways in which the unheralded but necessary work of long-term maintenance remains key to retaining the local and regional connections necessary to sustain a liveable future.

Road and rail

Roads and rail lines have a practical use, and that practical use in turn expresses the politics of their world. The ease of getting from one place to the next is a given in contemporary western life. The power of car culture in the United States,

Australia, and Aotearoa New Zealand (as well as the United Kingdom, to a lesser degree) means that drastically reduced mobility is the underappreciated result of the apocalypse. In addition to mobility and the technical questions of road and rail building, the oppressive nature of this limited mobility, in a dystopia, and the world-shrinking result of it in the post-apocalypse, reveals an infrastructural substrate to the imperial English and settler-colonial cultures from which the movies come. A world without the kind of road and rail systems that allows almost uniformly white, heterosexual, able-bodied people to live the life they expect, places them in the position of the people who were displaced and oppressed by the infrastructures that created the cultures and systems that existed before the dystopian/post-apocalyptic world arrived. Our current world, in other words.

In *The Accumulation of Capital*, Rosa Luxemburg identifies the importance of the transportation infrastructure to the exploiter class. 'In districts where natural economy formerly prevailed', she writes:

> [T]he introduction of means of transport – railways, navigation, canals – is vital for the spreading of commodity economy, a further hopeful sign. The triumphant march of commodity economy thus begins in most cases with magnificent constructions of modern transport, such as railway lines which cross primeval forests and tunnel through the mountains, telegraph wires which bridge the deserts, and ocean liners which call at the most outlying ports. But it is a mere illusion that these are peaceful changes.
>
> (1951: 386)

The more abstract concepts of the commodity economy and exploitation in its many senses, as well as the illusion of peace, are given a specific form and geographic setting in Walter Rodney's *How Europe Underdeveloped Africa*. 'The combination of being oppressed, being exploited, and being disregarded is best illustrated', he explains,

> by the pattern of the economic infrastructure of African colonies: notably, their roads and railways. These had a clear geographical distribution according to the extent to which particular regions needed to be opened up to import-export activities. Where exports were not available, roads and railways had no place. The only slight exception is that certain roads and railways were built to move troops and make conquest and oppression easier.
>
> (2018: 250–51)

What Rodney describes is a dystopia. The natural wealth of the land is taken out, and an occupying force moves freely in and through the territory, all thanks to a transportation infrastructure imposed from without. The result of Europe's imperial exploitation of Africa means that 'the roads in Africa led to the seaports and the sea lanes led to Western Europe and North America. That kind of lopsidedness is today part of the pattern of underdevelopment and dependence' (Rodney 2018: 280). The lopsidedness of the dystopian and post-apocalyptic life on film is perhaps most clearly visible in the *Hunger Games* series, in which each district exists to send raw materials to the capital as a kind of internal colony. To put the world back into balance, to undo the dystopia, to make it through the post-apocalypse, requires a reimagining of the transportation infrastructure. Food and raw materials will still be required, people will still travel, but as dystopian and post-apocalyptic roads and rail lines demonstrate, if a better world is to be built, the transportation infrastructure must be maintained as a physical object and refurbished as an expression of civilization and rebuilt accordingly. In what follows I offer an overview of how transit and roads appear and function in dystopian and post-apocalyptic worlds. I then consider the role that maintenance plays in making dystopian and post-apocalyptic worlds more or less liveable. Building on this, I then turn to how the imagined dystopian and post-apocalyptic transportation infrastructure and its everyday use can take us somewhere worth going.

Transit

Few things are easier to register in dystopian and post-apocalyptic movies than the way mass transit breaks down hand in hand with civilization. However, the two are not uniformly linked. In dystopian movies, the replacement of individualized everyday activities such as car travel with mass transit travel would seem to be a simple way to register the presence of top-down control, as it does with food, a topic I discuss in a later chapter. Strangely, this vision of top-down, transit-only control of mobility seems not to be the case. The bus system still seems to work in the *Purge* movies, as when buses are shown leaving Staten Island before sundown. Buses represent the potential for cooperative and in the United States, heavily classed action, and the rabidly individualist and capitalist/exploiter-driven Purge Night itself makes buses fair game for arson and violence against their passengers, as in *The Purge: Anarchy* (Brad Ricker 2014). Buses still run in *Children of Men* (Jim Clay and Geoffrey Kirkland 2006) too, both as quotidian local service (good or at least neutral) and dystopian refugee relocation (bad).

The presence and functioning of mass transit registers when life as we know it turns into something more dangerous, sometimes capturing the exact moment of change. For instance, Zac's wander around Auckland in the opening of *The Quiet Earth* shows how quickly Project Flashlight changed the world: a bus takes up an intersection, halfway through a never-completed left-hand turn. The opening credit sequence to *World War Z* shows the generically standard vision of everyday life before the apocalypse: people go to work, some of them boarding the subway that then moves on to its next, predictable stop. But later, a zombie horde swarms over a bus, killing the passengers and putting an end to the normal functioning of what seemed to be a 'safe' walled city. The predictability of transit disappears, replaced with the predictability of danger. The presence of apes riding on top of San Francisco's cable cars in *Rise of the Planet of the Apes* (Claude Paré 2011) indicates that the world has fallen out of balance, the apes are literally on top of what was once a shared human enterprise. In *Blindness* (Matthew Davis and Tula Peak 2008) the mass transit ceases to function without anyone to drive the trains; people find moving beyond their immediate surroundings dangerous.

For all the importance of a ragtag band of brothers and sisters in dystopian and post-apocalyptic movies, the individual is still the most important part of a Hollywood film, especially for the director Zack Snyder. Early in *Dawn of the Dead*, Snyder establishes the world pitching into apocalypse with a misanthropic and anti-communitarian shot through the rear window of a Milwaukee bus. He turns the people who would normally ride the bus, the predominantly non-White working class and poor, into dangerous zombies. The cruel touch is that while a group of zombies tear a person apart as Ana (Sarah Polley) watches from her car, Snyder and art director Arvinder Greywal place on the outside of the bus what appears inside the bus in *Children of Men*: propaganda. A bumper sticker in the lower left of the bus's rear window uses the word 'transit' twice. But while *Children of Men* offers an ironic vision of the nationalism of a dead empire within the film narrative, *Dawn of the Dead* appears to flatter those who would be driving behind the bus, filled as it is with dangerous monsters. If you can read this, you're one of the elect driving, and not one of the abject inside the bus. In *Shaun of the Dead* (Marcus Rowland 2004) Margaret Thatcher's perhaps-apocryphal quip 'a man who, beyond the age of 26, finds himself on a bus can count himself a failure' applies to Shaun, who rides the bus to and from his frustrating service sector job. Access to cars – his flatmate Pete's, his stepfather's – makes Shaun's heroism possible. In advance of the Umbrella Corporation dropping a nuclear bomb on Raccoon City, as I discussed in the chapter on energy, *Resident Evil: Apocalypse* Alice and her crew hide out in a bus, the very picture of abjection, aware that they are disposable and discussing what form their eradication will take. These examples show the last working moments of mass transit and then the tilt into something much worse, making transit spaces expressive sets-as-punctuation. Most also communicate the relative lack of social importance of the people who would use that mass transit, and their fitness for the new world ahead.

Heavy intercity rail appears frequently in dystopian movies, often as a token of a measure of the success in which the oppressed cannot share. In *The Island*, for instance, Amtrak now offers quite posh high-speed travel, a significant change from the 2005 of its release. Similarly, the *Hunger Games* series features high-speed luxury rail that connects districts and carries Katniss and her entourage from District 12 to the Capitol. Within and under Capitol City the underground system seen in *The Hunger Games: Mockingjay, Part 2* seems to offer a way to move goods across the city. Though *Mad Max* is full of car chases, the gang arrive on motorbikes to collect the Night Rider's coffin, which arrives by train. The small town's train station is a well-kept early twentieth-century building, unlike the mid-century Halls of Justice that has already fallen into disrepair; the train, like the roads, connects remote Australia to urban Australia and its hoon trouble. The train station in *1984* (Allan Cameron 1984) isn't nearly as nice as *Mad Max*'s, nor is the train itself as luxurious as those in *The Island* or the *Hunger Games* series. In its Blitz-coded dilapidation, the train station functions as an elaborate set as embellishment. Winston's train trip takes him from a nearly destroyed train station in the city to the countryside, and the train on which he makes the trip looks as though it is almost entirely decayed and falling apart. But the tracks remain and make it possible for Winston to leave the city.

Even after the apocalypse, train lines remain useful. After discovering he's the only person left in Auckland, *The Quiet Earth*'s Zac drives a train in what looks like a childhood dream come true (he also plays with a model train set). Trains don't run in *The Postman*'s world, but the rails function as a road that a horse-based transportation system can still use. The Postman follows an old rail line across the Pacific Northwest, and finds Bridge City, a peaceful refuge from the militaristic Holnerists. They still have cars in the post-apocalypse of *Mad Max Beyond Thunderdome*, and non-car travel tends to be by foot (sometimes gyrocopter). But a train line still runs out of Bartertown, allowing Max to attempt an escape. The train in *Snowpiercer* (Ondrej Nekvasi 2013) is life itself, running in an infinite loop around the globe. The Chicago of the *Divergent* series retains an at-grade freight rail system that brings raw materials from Amity settlements into the city, and city's elevated line continues to function as well. The empty Tube lines offer a path for Jim and Selena to follow in *28 Days Later*; parts of the Tube are back in operation in *28 Weeks Later* (Mark Tildesley 2007), taking repatriated people from the airport into London's Green Zone. Almost all these cases, even in the post-apocalypse, depend on functioning mass transit systems, or at the very least systems that retain the bus fleet and driveable roads, rolling stock and/or the rail system, though it is unclear how the rails (to say nothing of the buses and trains) are maintained.

Moments in which transit appears as punctuation and as spectacular sets create a horizon of expectation for the film audience. To repeat the definition, the 'punctuative set aspires to be expressive. By defamiliarizing the quotidian and the verisimilitudinous, it replaces conventional codes of art direction with design strategies that advance the film's narrative propositions' (Affron and Affron 1995: 38). The Dauntless of the *Divergent* series shows that they belong in the faction and prove their bravery by jumping from the moving train, showing their disregard for established stations. In *Code 46* (Mark Tildesley 2003) Maria rides in an empty subway car after her lover William leaves town. The likelihood of the Shanghai subway, with a daily ridership of 10 million, offering an empty car at any hour turns the empty car into an expression of her loneliness. Her loneliness in this moment contrasts with other moments in the subway, in which she moves through the crowded subway system without connecting to other people, in another version of loneliness, offering a more human kind of set as punctuation when compared to *Dawn of the Dead*'s anti-transit sensibility. The subway track and empty platform along which Johnny (Keanu Reeves) and Jane (Dina Meyer) walk in *Johnny Mnemonic* (Nilo Rodis Jamero 1995) express the enforced emptiness of Johnny's head and his desire to return to an identity that makes connections.

The survivors walk along rail lines in *28 Days Later* because those routes would be familiar to them from their use as Tube rides. The rage virus remakes the world, turning every street corner dangerous, but the vision of London a transit-rider carries in their head makes city travel safe again. Although the schematic Tube Map by Harry Beck condenses some distances and warps aboveground London, it is still possible to navigate the city, which their walk along the empty rail lines to relative safety demonstrates. In the opening sequences of *Isle of Dogs*, the voice-over narrator explains that 'dog flu threatens to cross the species threshold'. Here there is a symmetrical shot of a subway car, the back of a sitting dog's head in the centre of the image, with people seated in the seats on the left and right of the image. The narrator continues, '[a]nd enter the human gene pool'. With this line of narration, a second shot makes one change: the dog now looks into the camera with its teeth bared and tongue out, it has yellow gunk under one eye. Though it is less obvious after the Covid pandemic, all the humans on the car wear masks. What at first appears to be a dog simply riding the subway turns menacing set as punctuation: a disease vector on the subway. An even more politically charged transit-based punctuative set appears in *Children of Men*'s buses, as Londoners ride on buses outfitted with steel cage windows, with screens overhead blaring 'Only Britain Soldiers On'. These propaganda-filled caged buses for the 'free people' of London offer a different version of imprisonment, something of an echo of the buses that ship away refugees. As Marcus O'Donnell points out, 'the constant physical presence of apocalyptic structures such as caged refuges who line the sides of railway stations and streets' places societal decay and increasing carceralism in everyday spaces of travel (2015: 26). Spaces of public transport thus reflect not just characters' conflicted internal states, as in *Code 46*, but also locate the societal dangers that dystopian worlds impose.

Three films show how the 'elaborate constructions' of sets as embellishment often – but not always – set the stage for scenes of destruction. In *Resident Evil*, an underground train line and loading area in the Hive provides the setting for the final action sequence. A mutant creature tears apart the moving train car, and Alice triumphs in their fight by forcing him through the floor of the car, where he catches fire from the electrified rail, ending the fight in an exploding ball of fire. To look beyond massive sets that exist to be destroyed, *I, Robot* (Patrick Tatopoulos 2004), *I Am Legend*, and *Beneath the Planet of the Apes* (William Creber and Jack Martin Smith AD 1970) all present an elaborate vision of spaces of mass transit and how it can function as an index for a world worth living in. *I, Robot*'s futuristic Chicago retains the city's El, updating it from boxy cars to sleek, ovoid cars that glide along next to highways and above city streets. This vision of a future quasi-utopian city built on the back of robot labour resembles the present, only glossed up, an improvement over the 2004 of the film's release. The subway again registers the future's liveability in *I Am Legend*. In addition to the scene of flooded car tunnels, a brief shot of the aboveground entrance to the Union Square stop shows that while some parts of New York look close to the same, the absence of people renders public spaces dead. The death of public space appears in *Beneath the Planet of the Apes* in terms of the subway as well. Not only does Grand Central Station remain a key location in New York, but the decay of the world is evident in the ruined station Brent encounters when he walks along abandoned tracks. He finds a mosaic wall that identifies the platform where he stands as the former Queensboro Plaza station; the suburbs have fallen. If a multi-lane highway packed with abandoned cars registers the end of the suburban way of life, then a destroyed subway or subway station registers the end of a highly urbanized society in the form of a set as embellishment.

Rail lines frequently appear in the service of generic requirements to action movies, as part of a chase sequence. For instance, subways play a key role in chases in both real-world locations, as in *Minority Report* (Alex McDowell 2002) (DC Metro) *The Purge: Anarchy* and *Strange Days* (Los Angeles subway), as well as in fictionalized or virtual locations, as in *The Hunger Games: Mockingjay, Part 2*'s Capitol City underground and *Ready Player One*'s virtual New York City subway. The danger the subway poses to John Anderton (Tom Cruise) comes not from the physical transit infrastructure nor from his fellow passengers, but from 'the interactive marketing activated through retinal scanning [...] *Minority Report*'s utopian environment suddenly becomes another pursuer' (Hanson 2004: 93). *Strange Days* uses the ticking clock of the regularity of subway train departures to generate tension – will the pursued woman be able to escape her pursuers via a departing train? – and to render the violence of the Los Angeles police quotidian. The chases in both *The Purge: Anarchy* and *The Hunger Games: Mockingjay, Part 2* find groups using subway lines and platforms to avoid their pursuers, with all the running and darkness-fighting that entails. The dystopian *Ready Player One*, dystopian/post-apocalyptic *Aeon Flux* (Andrew McAlpine 2005) and the post-apocalyptic *28 Weeks Later* stage chases in a similar manner, using the confined spaces of tunnels and set routes to drive the chase. With zombies chasing them in *28 Weeks Later*, Scarlet and Doyle must flee along the Tube lines because the military in the Green Zone do not act to help them. Similarly, in *Minority Report*, *The Purge: Anarchy*, *Strange Days*, *The Hunger Games: Mockingjay, Part 2*, and *Aeon Flux*, the enforcers of the current order create danger in the subways, not fellow passengers. That is to say, as Althusser would have it, if the buses with their native propaganda create space for ideological state apparatuses to work on film audiences, the enclosed space of subway lines, as seen in chase sequences, creates an ideal setting for the operation of repressive state apparatuses against those who would seek to change the functioning of a dystopian or emerging post-apocalyptic society within the films. These two approaches to transit in dystopian and post-apocalyptic movies foreclose a number of potential avenues for escape, but tellingly leave open the potential for cooperation amongst transit passengers. All the while, the skilled workers who might keep the trains running stay off screen, showing how public transit when it appears takes for granted the presence of not only the train driver but also the train maintenance crew.

Streets

One of the most common and easily identifiable images in a post-apocalyptic movie is the establishing shot of a street covered in litter and dotted with abandoned cars. Cars jammed together represent a mass panic that caused people to flee, unsuccessfully; the garbage testifies to the societal decay of no one collecting the trash after the panic. The *ne plus ultra* such establishing shot appears in the opening images of *WALL-E*, where mountains of trash cascade down over highways, dooming *WALL-E* to a Sisyphean eternity of trash compaction to clear the highways for the return of humans to Earth. The destroyed street establishing shot can represent the intensity of the apocalypse. For instance, *Zombieland* shows the extent of the destruction of the United States in the background of a number of images. When Columbus (Jesse Eisenberg) explains 'Rule #7 Travel Light', he occupies the centre of the image filmed from knee level, with the title a lighter-coloured silver against dark roller suitcase. As the camera rises, Columbus walks between two lines of cars at the left and right of the image, creating a tunnel effect of dark at the edges of the frame. The camera continues to rise, showing that Columbus is walking into the rear of frame that shows dozens of cars, many with the doors open as if their drivers had just jumped out, crashed together on the highway. A different use of the image background appears in Tallahassee's (Woody Harrelson) entrance. When Tallahassee emerges from his up-armoured SUV, he looks towards the camera, and a cut shows Columbus shaking with fear. Another cut takes us back to Tallahassee from about 45 degrees to Tallahassee's left. The backgrounds to the two shots of Tallahassee show the two sides of the highway. In the first, the lanes going in the direction Tallahassee is driving, a massive car pileup occupies the horizon of the image, with the vehicle's driver side window creating a second frame within the frame. In the second, a fire truck and ambulance occupy the rear of the image, with the SUV's window creating a second frame that draws attention to an empty gurney still on the road.

The constant background of life on the post-apocalyptic road consists of this kind of evidence of multi-car pileups and injury/death, the result of the people in cities (and suburbs) attempting to escape urban areas. The urban chaos these drivers seek to escape appears at the end of the first *Resident Evil*. After surviving the zombies inside the Umbrella Corporation's headquarters, Alice emerges onto the street of Raccoon City, where she sees a newspaper with the headline 'THE DEAD WALK!' An overhead shot watches as Alice tries to get into a police car, and then an extended crane pull away shot shows the extent of the damage: an entire city street, bordered by skyscrapers, crammed with abandoned cars, some on fire, and trash. This film-closing, franchise-establishing shot reveals the scale of destruction beyond the confines of the underground headquarters where the outbreak began. A similar film-ending, franchise-establishing use of a damaged city streets appears in *Rise of the Planet of the Apes*: the battle between ape and human leaves the Golden Gate Bridge filled with cars and debris, with humans doomed to a global viral outbreak and the apes set to take up residence in Muir Woods Park. In these cases, the street surface registers danger, but the street itself registers little to no damage: no potholes, no sinkholes, not even sizable cracks in the pavement.

Highways

Roads can represent continuity as much as they can represent decay, sometimes simultaneously. In both *Judge Dredd* and *Dredd*, the massive highways in Mega City continue the car-based development of post-1945 anglophone nations. While establishing shots of highways often offer a sense of physical scale, the artifice of the mega-highways that cut through Mega City in rigid grids also shows the scale of social domination. The first two *Mad Max* films, *Mad Max* and *The Road Warrior*, show a well-maintained set of roads in remote Australia, but the emptiness of the Outback means that social control is more difficult to achieve. The latter two films in the series, *Mad Max Beyond Thunderdome* and *Mad Max: Fury Road*, move off road with greater frequency, from the chase in *Mad Max Beyond Thunderdome* that takes place, for the most part, on a train track and the unpaved right of way on either side of it, to the two-lane blacktop and open desert chase of *Mad Max: Fury Road*. In both Australia and the United States, roads cut through arid/desert areas that appear to be both endless and uninhabited (though they are not). The extreme long shot as Furiosa begins her journey shows the Gastown refinery spewing black smoke at the distant rear of the frame, with the narrow black strip of highway cutting through the red-orange desert. Why is Gastown located out in the desert and not closer to Immortan Joe's fortress that at least has a supply of water? In his preface to *Infrastructure: A Field Guide to the Industrial Landscape*, Brian Hayes asks much the same question of a collection of gas tanks on the outskirts of Gallup, New Mexico, right next to beautiful natural red sandstone buttes:

> Why did they have to build it *here*? Couldn't the gasworks have been put somewhere less conspicuous? There is an answer. The propane plant was put below the buttes because that's where the pipeline runs, carrying petroleum products from Texas to California. And the pipeline takes that path because it follows the highway and the railroad. And before the highway and railroad were built, a stagecoach line followed the same route. And before that, there was a trail used by the native peoples who have maintained an urban culture in this region for at least a millennium. In other words, this is a landscape that has been put to human use for a very long time.
>
> (2005: 3)

From a pre-industrial trail to industrial-era mass-use highway to a post-apocalyptic near-single-use road, the highway between the fortress and Gastown, Furiosa's drive continues the process that Hayes describes. The rarity of its use and its desert setting means that the main problem the road faces is being covered in sand rather than decaying into gravel. The desert roads remain driveable for formal reasons: driving stunts are dangerous enough as it is. But rather than the road itself, the *Mad Max* films return repeatedly to the importance of gasoline – wars and violence are about resources, after all. Society has decayed under Immortan Joe, but at least there's still a road that makes shipping possible; in Mega City the millions of residents drive under the central control of a 'rationally planned' street system. In this way, *Judge Dredd* and *Dredd* show how an intensification of an approach to transportation infrastructure can facilitate fascist power, while *Mad Max: Fury Road* registers the same by imagining a world that retains one tenuous infrastructural connection to the pre-apocalyptic world.

Roads can also disappear in post-apocalyptic movies, which leads to a change in transportation modes. In the *Mad Max* movies, this usually means tricked out dune buggy-like vehicles re-engineered to work on sand. But in a number of other cases, the end of reliably paved roads (and reliable gasoline supply) leads to the end of the car and its internal combustion engine as the preferred mode of transport. The survivors of both the recent apocalypse, *The Postman* and *War for the Planet of the Apes*, and the more distant apocalypse, in both the 1968 and 2001 *Planet of the Apes*, travel trails under animal power. The Postman walks and sometimes rides his donkey across the Great Salt Flats, and the apes both ride horses and use humans as pack animals. Areas outside of settlements, lacking the skilled labour to create road construction materials and to maintain roads, see the transportation infrastructure change from concrete and asphalt to dirt trails with wagon ruts, moving back in transportation time to retain connections across even relatively short distances.

Suburban streets

In a dystopia, more often than not, the suburbs survive as a place for the elites, and their streets reflect comfort. *The Handmaid's Tale* (Tom Walsh 1990) takes place in a comfortable city and its suburbs. Similarly, *The Purge* (Melanie Paizis-Jones 2014), the film that introduces the purge conceit, though it isn't the first in the series chronologically, takes place in a suburban gated community where the roads are pothole-free. The purge creates danger to people, not to the infrastructure. Slightly more down market, the dystopian suburban California in the rotoscoped *A Scanner Darkly* (Bruce Curtis 2006) shows a run down, but not destroyed street system. There may be some cracks in the bleached-out pavement, but Bob Arctor (Keanu Reeves) has no problem driving around town. *Dawn of the Dead* (2004) begins its apocalypse by showing suburbia becoming a human-vs.-zombie war zone. Ana escapes her house and infected family in her car, and carnage follows. The first stages of highways getting filled with abandoned vehicles appear at the edges of Ana's escape: crashes in intersections, car fires, and the zombies punching through windscreens and eating the people who ride the bus. The T-bone crash and the fiery explosion that follows it in *Dawn of the Dead* takes place on a smooth highway on Milwaukee's suburban fringe, showing that streets are dangerous in dystopias and in the moment the apocalypse hits, but that danger is more interpersonal than infrastructural.

FIGURE 2.1: *The Road* streetscape.

The worst-case scenario of post-apocalyptic damage in a world where people still live appears in *The Road*, where the man and the boy walk into a city where the abandoned and wrecked vehicles that clog the streets are boats and ships, rendering the damage more thoroughgoing and uncanny. *The Road* also passes through a suburb where the decaying chassis of a car, covered in a thick layer of dust, occupies the foreground as a reminder of the amount of time that has passed since the event that precipitated the end of the world (Figure 2.1). A similar suburban-decay establishing shot appears in *Warm Bodies*, showing the chaos of abandoned cars, TVs left on the front lawn, and driveways that have deteriorated into what looks like gravel rather than concrete.

Thus, the stage-setting establishing shots of dystopian movies often locate their narratives where the concrete is still in good shape, whereas post-apocalyptic movies represent a concrete world ground into gravel. For car-based cultures like the United States, Australia, and Aotearoa New Zealand (and to a lesser extent the United Kingdom), highways and streets form the basis for everyday interactions with the rest of the world. The state of the streets makes the state of dystopia or post-apocalypse visible, tangible, and legible.

Urban streets

In a dystopia, fascists tend to encourage cleanliness and often maintain their transportation well, as roads allow not only the circulation of people and goods, but also of repressive police and military. The London streets in *Children of Men* are in pretty good shape for a massive city. The street near the coffee shop where Theo

(Clive Owen) learns of Baby Diego's death registers the world's decline by what is *on* the roads – piles of trash, soot-covered buses, smoke-spewing three-wheeled taxis – rather than the roads themselves, which show some wear and tear, but no major potholes or road-patching construction sites. The coffee shop is bombed, causing havoc on the street, but no street damage. Soon after the bombing Theo visits his cousin at Battersea, where the road is very well maintained. However, at the bus stop near a council housing estate, the wavy streets show the effects of years of heavy trucks on neglected roads, and by the end of the film, near Pierpont Tower, large sections of the road are no longer paved, with sections repurposed for urban agriculture. The signs on the buses say, 'Only Britain Soldiers On', but the fascists running *Children of Men*'s Britain know the world is ending and neglect the streets that 'undesirables' use. The fascists in *V for Vendetta* seem to have a greater investment in maintaining London's streets. When the Guy-Fawkes masked and cloaked thousands march on Parliament, the streets are all impeccably paved. A few overhead shots show uniformly coloured street spaces, an indication of the attention the government pays to keeping the streets smooth near the power centre.

The fascists in *Soylent Green* somehow manage to keep the streets well looked after even as 40 million New Yorkers use them. At the Tuesday markets, the sidewalks and street look well paved. There's litter, but not a lot of potholes. When the people riot, every closeup of the riot control vehicle scoop dropping shows nary a pothole in the street. A similarly well-maintained street system appears in *The Purge*, perhaps unsurprisingly, as the film takes place not only in a fascist nation, but also in a gated community. The purpose of a gated community, in a fascist country or a nominally democratic one, would be to enjoy what the lesser sorts cannot, including well-maintained and functioning infrastructure. Subsequent *Purge* films expand the New Founding Fathers of America's United States to show more of Los Angeles, Staten Island, and Washington DC. In the film's opening multi-split-screen montage, shots of streets show plenty of property damage and garbage on the street, but not the streets themselves are not falling apart. Staten Island is supposed to be quite economically distressed, but their transportation infrastructure is in decent shape. Multiple overhead shots of Staten Island show well-maintained streets, with an equal or greater amount of space dedicated to non-car use. For instance, in an overhead establishing shot of the Park Hill towers public housing project shows mostly pedestrian and parking areas. In moments when Dmitri, the powerful local drug dealer with a heart of gold, cruises the neighbourhood to protect residents, overhead shots show a few tar patches, but overall Staten Island's roads are in pretty good nick.

On the other coast, the streets of downtown Los Angeles in *The Purge: Anarchy* do not have potholes or major physical damage. Despite the massive firepower used by Purgers, the roads hold up well, even against a trailer-mounted rotary machine gun.

Streets in *1984* evoke Blitz London; here Winston walks down a street more bomb site than street, there Winston walks along a street more puddles and holes than paving. But the street maintenance of a minimally competent fascist state appears in almost equal measure to the historically present benign neglect approach favoured by anglophone governments since at least the years leading up to *1984*'s release.

Non-fascist dystopian streets do not differ much from their fascist cousins; they're pretty well maintained, with the odd rough patch that could do with some fixing. The noir conventions in *Blade Runner* contribute to the sense of a decaying Los Angeles: near-constant rain makes the roads full of standing water, especially near the gutters, and some streets show a clear need for mending, evident in depressions filled with water and potholes. Thirty years in the future, Los Angeles' 'streets' have migrated further up into the smog-choked sky, and *Blade Runner 2049* also shows that the highway between Los Angeles and Las Vegas has been abandoned, but the desert climate means that the road remains in good shape. Though crime and debauchery take place on what seems to be every street corner in *Strange Days*, the streets themselves do not look particularly dangerous. The slick future of *The Island* shows a greater degree of street damage, with some establishing shots showing significant damage to the street, with asphalt not quite covering the entire parking lane on the edge of a street. *Elysium* shows an even greater level of decay; Los Angeles' streets range from damaged to barely paved to unpaved, depending on the level of privation the street residents live under. This kind of set as embellishment creates a clear distinction 'where Earth is characterized by smoke, filth and crumbling infrastructure, [and] Elysium is sleek, sumptuous, and tranquil' (Frame 2019: 386). The Chicago streets in *I, Robot* show few cracks, perhaps the result of robot workers. Similarly, the maglev-served Washington DC of *Minority Report* features pothole-free streets for old-fashioned cars. Dystopias here resemble their moments of creation, in which the more affluent enjoy a well-maintained street system.

Two of the most thoroughly damaged street systems appear in post-apocalyptic films set in major urban centres: London in *The Girl with All the Gifts* and New York in *I Am Legend*. The London streets in *The Girl with All the Gifts* are almost impossible see beneath all the plants, and as I noted in the introduction, a quasi-prairie set as punctuation of Times Square shows how quickly the natural world can overcome the asphalt and concrete of the transportation infrastructure. The streets of Manhattan are in better shape when the island is a prison. Though the streets feature several holes and divots, a car with chandelier hood ornaments can still navigate the streets in *Escape from New York*. Similarly, even with Los Angeles cut off from the continent thanks to a major earthquake, the roads of the offshore Los Angeles prison seem not to have suffered from the natural disaster, save for rubble piled up at the roadside (leaving aside the highways that fell into the ocean, of course). In *The Omega Man* Neville drives around an empty post-apocalyptic Los Angeles, where garbage and sawhorses and, as in *The Quiet Earth*, abandoned cars on the street present dangers, not the quality of the roads. The extreme overhead long shots of the streets of Pittsburgh in *Land of the Dead* show the city's streets in good repair. At the ground level, the spaces near and beneath overpasses are used as checkpoints, and remain paved. The roads in the hinterlands given over to zombies show some deterioration but are still usable for heavy machinery like the up-armoured Dead Reckoning.

Earlier in the zombie apocalypse, the south Florida streets of *Day of the Dead* are only litter-strewn, not destroyed. Similarly, as the apocalypse kicks off in Philadelphia, in both *12 Monkeys* (Jeffrey Beecroft 1995) and *World War Z*, the transportation infrastructure remains useful, if overcrowded. The same is true in *Blindness*, where the nameless city's streets are buried under piles of garbage, but entirely undamaged. Left alone on the streets around Auckland and Hamilton, *The Quiet Earth*'s Zac has no worries about road safety except for the hazards other, stationary, vehicles pose to him, especially coming around curves. The streets near the airport in *Warm Bodies* show some deterioration, with weeds beginning to take hold at the curbs and some holes beginning to appear. A similar kind of damage appears inside the walled city, with the market area dotted with water-filled potholes. However, the residential area where Julie lives has well-maintained streets, and the highway beyond the wall, though crowded with abandoned cars, does not appear to need repairs. Overall, the post-apocalypse often appears as empty urban streets where the accumulation of material of times past, not street damage like potholes, signals the end of civilization.

City squares, street life, and life made possible by streets

The paved and sealed roads remain in the small quasi-urban human settlements of *War for the Planet of the Apes* and *The Postman*, mostly owing to the recentness of the apocalypse. But later in the post-apocalypse, dirt-packed streets and squares form the post-apocalyptic streetscape in both the 1968 and 2001 *Planet of the Apes*. In the earlier *Planet of the Apes*, the city's 'caveman chic' (Wallender 2017: n.pag.) of adobe, stone construction, and dirt paths returns to older forms to create a set as embellishment. More than an additional level with which to stage a chase sequence, the pedestrian flyovers make literal a vertical leap in the apes' world written onto the transportation infrastructure (Long 2016b: 235–51).

The quality of street life – the provision of a public square or plaza – in dystopian and post-apocalyptic movies tends to offer a world in which there too much or not enough. To note one facet of public spaces, the presence of advertising offers an uncanny echo of the society lost to the apocalypse. Times Square retains its Broadway show and movie billboards as well as corporate chain logos (Sbarro, Hyatt, Blockbuster) in *I Am Legend*. In dystopian movies, advertising intensifies or recedes, and in both cases makes its world unfamiliar. *Ready Player One*'s Stacks feature shipping containers converted to business use, with chairs out front like cafes and billboards looming over it all, a trailer park Time Square vision of the future. As noted above, an even more pervasive form of advertising, a familiar sight and experience to late twentieth- and twenty-first-century filmgoers, appears in the interactive marketing that permeates *Minority Report*'s 2054 Washington DC. By contrast, both the unpaved District 12 market square and the massive public square in the *Hunger Games* series are free of advertising. The Hunger Games has no corporate sponsor. Capitol City residents enjoy the consumer comfort afforded by the production of other districts – haute couture, tech toys, gourmandise – but without any of the public advertising that would be familiar to a 2010s audience. Post-communist Minsk seems to offer the best analogue to Capitol City. Minsk is few people's idea of a utopian city, but its cleanliness and lack of advertising, as well as its white-haired president for what appears to be life Alexander Lukashenko, bear a strong resemblance to Capitol City and President Snow. As the architecture and cultural critic Owen Hatherley notes, 'whether hostile or complimentary, all accounts of Belarus will mention the extreme Sovietness of its capital [Minsk], and the equally extreme cleanliness and lack of commercial pollution and/or vibrancy' (2018: 253–54). The monumental squares of Capitol City are all stone and square edges, as strong a contrast as possible from the unpaved roads and puddle-pocked town square in Katniss' home district. What could be an exciting world away from endless consumption and/or extreme privation instead stifles a vibrant public square and public life. *Demolition Man* locates some of the sterility of the megalopolis of San Angeles in its lack of consumer choice: one restaurant and none of the billboard advertising common to southern California of its 1990s; a decade previous *They Live* (Daniel Lomino and William J. Durrell Jr AD 1988) satirized ubiquitous billboards as alien propaganda.

In all these cases, the contrast between urban and non-urban streetscapes within the film world not only creates a coherent fictional world, but also highlights how the invisible background of streets marks residents. Agatha and the precogs leave Washington DC for a cabin next to a lake. This replaces the high-tech maglev advertising-drenched city, a marketing equivalent to pre-crime investigations, with a tyre-rutted dirt road, a refusal of Washington DC's techno solutionism written onto the infrastructure. *I Am Legend* sees Anna and Ethan's escape from New York to rural Vermont in a similar fashion. The town in New Serbia where *Babylon AD* begins has a similar quasi-public square, a narrow street next to a brutalist apartment block, with most of the green space taken up with small-scale market stalls for guns and game. This frequent contrast in public spaces finds promise in turning away from slick, mass consumer spaces to smaller communal spaces not tied to consumption. But this bargain is predicated on someone ensuring that some type of connection stays in place so that the occasional interaction between the two modes might still happen.

Bridges and overpasses

The ground level streets, highways, and squares tend to represent social decline via relative litter distribution; the vertical components of dystopian and post-apocalyptic transportation infrastructure, bridges and overpasses, more clearly and consistently show destruction and failure. *Code 46* and its establishing shot of the Shanghai Nanpu Bridge and its massive spiral interchange on the Puxi side of the Huangpu River, stands out by showing the transportation infrastructure achieving its purpose. However, the way in which human mobility on this marvel is limited by health history medical documents, 'papeles', undercuts the engineering achievement of the bridge. Access is similarly limited, more along race and class lines, when the Verrazzano-Narrows Bridge closes in advance of nightfall and the start of the Purge in *The First Purge* (Sharon Lomofsky 2018). Highway overpasses cease to function when an earthquake hits Los Angeles, as a low-angle shot of what looks like the four-level interchange in downtown LA shows in the opening of *Escape from LA*. A bridge that does not connect seems to have no function, but can nevertheless be repurposed, both in the film narrative, as in *Johnny Mnemonic*, where the hacker space Heaven is a broken bridge *Johnny Mnemonic*, as well as in the film's message, as in *Death Race 2000*, which closes on a rudimentary drawing of a broken overpass as a closing statement on the meaning and potential for the highway as a bloodsport space.

Post-apocalyptic films use destroyed overpasses and bridges in establishing shots to make clear the social disconnection of their world. *Tank Girl*, *Escape from LA*, *Insurgent*, *Zombieland*, *Zombieland Double Tap*, *28 Days Later*, and *The Book of Eli* all use denotative images of destroyed bridges and overpasses to place their narratives in a broken world. Recognizable, famous bridges frequently appear in post-apocalyptic films, their destruction a shorthand to the end of civilization as we know it. The escape at the end of *Mad Max Beyond Thunderdome* takes Jedediah, Savannah, and the other children to Sydney, where the broken span of the Harbour Bridge makes clear that the city is not inhabited. The Mavens Gate Bridge, according to *Resident Evil: Apocalypse*'s titles, is the 'Main Entrance to Raccoon City', limiting escape routes and making Raccoon City a good place to experiment with a viral weapon. The Chicago River has dried up in the

Divergent series of films, so the bridges over the riverbed remain raised, making the faction-based segregation of the city easier. A different part of Chicago appears *I, Robot*, with a broken in half bridge that borders on the landfill where robots are discarded. Finally, the Manhattan Bridge and Brooklyn Bridge, destroyed to quarantine Manhattan Island, offer Neville nice views and a platform from which to practice his golf swing in the opening quarter of *I Am Legend*. The Golden Gate Bridge appears at the end of *The Book of Eli*, an ironic reminder of the past while the future in fact resides in Alcatraz prison.

The Golden Gate Bridge also plays a significant role in the second series of *Planet of the Apes* films, with the continuity between films centred on the bridge and relationship it creates between the city (humans) and the John Muir Woods (apes). In *Rise of the Planet of the Apes*, after Caesar and Koba lead a mission to liberate the apes being held and experimented on at the GenSys headquarters, the apes rampage through San Francisco, heading towards what Caesar understands as their home, the John Muir Woods. To reach the woods, the apes must cross the Golden Gate Bridge. Between GenSys headquarters and the bridge, the ape use of the transportation infrastructure differs from its standard use: an ape uses a parking meter as a weapon, chimpanzees use the electric cables that power streetcars as ersatz vines. When the apes engage with a streetcar, a sequence of shots makes clear the Golden Gate Bridge's function as a link and a boundary between city and 'wilderness'. The apes board the streetcar, and as it crests a hill, a shot of the apes facing the camera is cut against a second shot from behind the apes, creating a POV shot of the ape view of the bridge in the distance. The subsequent reverse shot finds the streetcar advancing at the camera, and the image zooms in on Caesar's eye, to create a sense that the streetcar can take the apes to the bridge which can take the apes to the wilderness. The film's climactic battle takes place on the bridge, and the apes' ability to use the bridge as more than a single horizontal space – the way the cops perceive it, more or less – allows them to win the battle. When Caesar sees that the cops have set up a roadblock on the north/wilderness end of the bridge, he calls the apes to a halt and most of them leave the roadway deck of the bridge, taking to the vertical cables and to the secondary horizontal level under the street. Such a reorientation of the bridge space pays off the frequent overhead shots of the apes moving through the city. The second stage of the battle plays against the predominantly horizontal shots of the first stage of the battle on the bridge by following the apes as they jump from their fog cover down onto the cops. The rest of the battle alternates the horizontal – the gun battle with cops – with the vertical – disposing of the evil GenSys executive in the helicopter above. The apes win the battle and reach the John Muir Woods, what Caesar calls their home. The last sequence of the film follows the apes as they climb the tress and Caesar reaches the top of one of the tallest trees to look out at the bridge they just crossed, now offering a buffer zone between the ape home and humans.

FIGURE 2.2: *Dawn of the Planet of the Apes* broken pavement.

I dwell on this battle because it returns in a mirror in the opening of the sequel, *Dawn of the Planet of the Apes*. In *Dawn*, humans searching for a hydro dam, as discussed in the previous chapter, encounter the Muir Woods apes, and one man accidentally shoots an ape. The apes allow the humans to leave, and the humans flee back into the city over the Golden Gate Bridge. The human trip over the bridge is shot in extreme long shots from above the bridge, and the last shot of the bridge appears as a high angle shot of apes watching from one of the bridge towers, creating an ape POV. Then the shot shifts to an interior, with the film's widescreen composition squeezed by a doorway, the double frame creating a sense of waiting for them to return. The street level of the bridge features a massive unfilled gap, with rusted-out cars resting in huge weed clumps, a sign of the destruction caused by the battle in *Rise of the Planet of the Apes*. A human figure walks out of this double-framed image of the street, the camera movement from inside a building to the exterior creates a POV shot for the human settlement leader Dreyfus, not the people arriving (Figure 2.2). In the next set of shots, the humans drive from the base of the Golden Gate Bridge to a settlement along a street with unused streetcar tracks in the middle, a reverse of the apes' streetcar ride from the first movie. Now the bridge offers some protection, but also a significant boundary to the perpetuation of human settlement, represented not only by the lack of electrical power, but also by the transportation infrastructure: the apes control the bridge from its towers and at the ground level the street is broken and in need of repair.

The destruction of both everyday transportation sights like overpasses as well as recognizable monuments shows that great engineering achievements, the stuff of civilization, can still crumble. Whether half reclaimed or unusable and unused in the background, these pieces of the transportation infrastructure remain as reminders of what once was and what could be regained with an escape from dystopia or a return to civilization after the apocalypse.

Fixing streets and bridges

The unpaved crack at the base of the Golden Gate Bridge in *Dawn of the Planet of the Apes* stands out as a rarity in most Hollywood films. To overstate the question slightly, how is it that the roads in movies are always in such good shape, even after the apocalypse? Lifespan can vary given climate and level of use and original road materials composition, but the majority of the US Interstate Highway System met or exceeded its lifespan by the end of the twentieth century. A TRIP report compared the US Interstate Highway System to a person, describing it as

> sixty-four years old, an age at which many Americans are approaching Medicare eligibility and reduced workloads, the Interstate Highway System is deteriorating, its traffic load of cars and trucks continues to increase, and the system lacks an adequate long-term care plan.
>
> (2020: 1)

Roads exposed to extreme weather can last up to 40 years, but even under the best of circumstances at some point the road will need fixing (Orange City Council 2016: n.pag.). Control of movement (dystopia) and/or population reduction (post-apocalypse), might reduce road use, but nevertheless roads and overpasses and bridges will still need maintenance. As the 2017 American Society of Civil Engineers Infrastructure Report Card notes, ‘the average bridge in the U.S. is 43 years old. Most of the country’s bridges were designed for a lifespan of 50 years, so an increasing number of bridges will soon need major rehabilitation or retirement’ (2017: n.pag.). As if to illustrate the point of the infrastructure’s lifespan and the need for maintenance, in early 2022, the 50-year-old Frick Bridge in Pittsburgh collapsed on the same day President Joe Biden visited town to spruik his infrastructure investment package, something Biden did not fail to note when he delivered his speech (Maher and Lucey 2022: n.pag.). Most bridges are reaching the end of their original lifespan because much of the US transportation infrastructure was built in the post-Second World War era as part of the construction of the US Interstate Highway System, and has been poorly maintained since. Russell and Vinsel critique the US approach to infrastructure as both a political and moral failure:

> The best of these conversations about infrastructure move away from narrow technical matters to engage deeper moral implications. Infrastructure failures – train crashes, bridge failures, urban flooding, and so on – are manifestations of and allegories for America's dysfunctional political system, its frayed social safety net, and its enduring fascination with flashy, shiny, trivial things.
>
> (2016: n.pag.)

Faced with the 2008 Global Financial Crisis (GFC), the Australian government undertook a large 'Nation Building' works programme to finance critical areas of infrastructure, including transportation projects as part of the Building Australia Fund. In doing so, they not only found a way to cushion the blow of the GFC, but also to cushion future blows caused by infrastructure failures, fending off (the logic goes) an onrushing potential dystopia.

Like every rose has its thorn, every street has its pothole. When the apocalypse comes, maintenance schedules disappear. In the post-apocalyptic streetscape, the importance of maintenance appears in a still recognizable but much less usable street system. The streets-turned urban prairie in *I Am Legend*, as covered in the introduction, show the precarious nature of streets; 4–12 inches of concrete and/or asphalt need frequent maintenance to remain passable streets. The driving sequences in *Zombieland Double Tap* show highways with weed patches at the edges of the road, encroaching on the outside lane. The plant-covered London streets in *The Girl with All the Gifts* show a further iteration of plants breaking through the thin crust of the street to retake the city. No one fixing or maintaining the streets defines the apocalypse; fixing and then maintaining streets creates the potential for civilization. The *post*-apocalypse needs a transportation infrastructure.

A dystopian civilization, on the other hand, fixes its potholes. The Australia of *Mad Max* still has a road maintenance budget, making it dystopian, not post-apocalyptic. During Max's revenge-fuelled pursuit of Toecutter and Bubba Zanetti, his police cruiser gets stuck behind a truck transporting a dozer, the sort of heavy machinery used in road construction and maintenance, an ironic vehicle type to be stuck behind while chasing murderous hoons. Adrian Martin's reading of *Mad Max* sees the film's formal connection to the western genre, but not to its more mundane literal settings: 'give Miller a clear sky and a flat plain stretching to infinity, and he's perfectly content. Geography is an abstraction in these films – as it rarely is in the American Westerns that inspired him' (2003: 68). Russell and Vinsel make the case for

> the absolute centrality of the work that goes into keeping the entire world going. Despite recurring fantasies about the end of work or the automation of everything, the central fact of our industrial civilization is *labour*, and most of this work falls far outside the realm of innovation. Inventors and innovators are a small slice – perhaps somewhere around one per cent – of this workforce.
>
> (2016: n.pag.)

Inventors and innovators represent the Great Man in late twentieth- and twenty-first-century culture in the anglosphere. Without the labour of people who repave sections of the 'flat plain stretching to infinity', no wheel on Max's V8 Interceptor will move. Great Man visions for post-apocalypse make less sense than collaborative communities. Max always has to leave because he's a catalyst rather than a saviour.

The presence of a road construction and maintenance vehicle in a chase sequence might pass invisibly, as it does in Martin's reading, but the heavy machinery shows that the roads on which Max and the Toecutter battle are not abstractions, but real and dangerous places that require maintenance by regular labourers, even if it slows righteous drivers down from time to time. A less physically violent vision of street maintenance as metaphor appears in *Never Let Me Go*. Kathy (Carey Mulligan) and Tommy (Andrew Garfield) go to the seaside town to make their case to Madame and Miss Emily that they are eligible for deferral, a temporary pause of their enforced organ donation. Tommy's art, like Kathy's before it, offers proof they are something more than what Madame calls 'poor creatures'. But there are no deferrals. The street takes on painful metaphorical power on their departure, when Kathy thanks Madame (Nathalie Richard) for talking to them, and walks back to the car. A long shot shows Kathy walking over a large patch in the street, a scar in the asphalt not unlike the scars on Tommy's organ donation-marked torso (Figure 2.3). The world of *Never Let Me*

FIGURE 2.3: *Never Let Me Go* patched road.

Go won't 'return to darkness, the days of lung cancer, breast cancer, motoneuron disease', as Miss Emily (Charlotte Rampling) puts it, and the road, the product of a visible variety of patches, affirms it. Maintaining the transportation infrastructure must continue for Kathy and Tommy to reach the seaside town; likewise, and painfully, medical patching must continue.

But is the only option to keep the road system as the primary transportation mode? What kind of transportation infrastructure will help those who rebuild after a dystopia or apocalypse?

How can we get to the future from here?

The denouement of dystopian and post-apocalyptic movies offers an access point to how the transportation infrastructure – broken and turned upside down by catastrophes – might help to construct a happy ending after the resolution of the plot's main conflict. Two issues run next to each other in such a critical approach: the state of the transportation infrastructure and where it takes or might take the people. In a number of dystopian films, the transportation infrastructure looks more or less like its contemporary moment. Road and rail and even flight continue to offer mobility. In dystopian films with happy endings, such as *Minority Report*, city streets and public transit – both the Metro and the fantastic maglev system – continue as if nothing happened. However, the precogs' happy ending entails moving away from the hyper technological world of Washington DC and leads instead to their refuge secreted away on a dirt road. *Isle of Dogs* exaggerates slightly the Japanese transportation system, but the system continues to work, only now in greater harmony with dogs. While *Minority Report* and *Isle of Dogs* have fairly unambiguous happy endings, *Strange Days* and the *Purge* films show slightly more ambivalence in their narrative resolutions, keeping questions of racial oppression and a successful fascist regime in play. However, the transportation infrastructure continues to function in these worlds. *Johnny Mnemonic* and *Ready Player One* both imagine a transportation system much like the historical moment of their release, with political questions not entirely resolved, moving some questions of mobility into the virtual realm while the slow decay of the streets continues. In the post-apocalyptic *28 Weeks Later*, the trains are back up and running to create more connections across London, but some parts of the city are left alone, turned into biowaste dumps (more on that in a future chapter). Streets left unused and unmaintained, as I have repeated throughout this chapter, tend to be reclaimed by plants in short order. *28 Weeks Later* shows the lesson of the COVID-19 pandemic *avant la lettre*: Tammy (Imogen Poots) and Andy (Mackintosh Muggleton) survive the firebombing of London's district one and make it to Wembley, where they board a helicopter that takes them past the Cliffs of Dover and into France where, a title card tells us, 28 days later zombies emerge from Le Métro and run across the Champ de Mars, towards the Eiffel Tower. The opening of air travel, first back into England and then back out of England, moves the virus via the asymptomatic carrier Andy. A more hopeful vision appears in the earlier *28 Days Later*, in which Selena, Hannah, and Jim hole up in a cabin to wait for help. In their case, flight brings help into England, where it was still possible to drive on empty highways, although filling the tank could be a bit of a difficulty. Missing from *28 Days Later*'s imagination of the future is the Underground from the film's opening. However, all is not lost. The rage virus certainly would have killed the train conductors and maintenance staff, but the train lines themselves remain in good repair, waiting for new workers to operate them. In fact, across most post-apocalyptic films, the more significant losses are human labour and expertise, not the transportation infrastructure itself, which may be broken down, but is not entirely unsalvageable because the disappearance of humans means that what remains does not suffer from overuse or human error-caused breakdown.

Water and space travel create the potential to traverse even longer distances than streets and rail lines, putting distance between dystopian societies and possible worlds. *The Island* sees a two-tier system of the international organ donor-using jetset and the rest. After Lincoln Six Echo (Ewan McGregor) and Jordan Two Delta (Scarlett Johansson) liberate the clones held in Dr Merrick's 'island', the white-clad clones emerge into a waste expanse, shielding their eyes from the sun, needing to walk to civilization. In contrast to the wilderness pedestrians, Lincoln Six Echo and Jordan Two Delta appear in the last shot of the film on a yacht. In other words, *The Island* imagines an escape from dystopia as made possible by water travel and extreme wealth. *Children of Men* finds a path out of dystopia on the water, but Theo and Kee don't take a yacht out of England. Rather, Kee escapes England by a roundabout path that uses not just roads, but also a rowboat and the ship *Tomorrow*, bound for who knows where. The ocean plays the role of space for much of *Gattaca*, as the space where Vincent (Ethan Hawke) can prove himself and retain some sliver of belief in a meritocracy amidst the genetic supremacy model under which he lives. Vincent's final triumph takes him into space under the terms he explains to his brother in their climactic ocean swim. Genetically inferior, Vincent can swim further because he 'never saved anything for the swim back'. Vincent boards the spaceship bound for Titan, with no swim back. But the cost of this triumph comes at the cost of the death of the identity he assumed, Jerome (Jude Law). In the film-closing voice-over, Vincent identifies a second cost: 'for someone who was never meant for this world, I must confess I'm suddenly having a hard time leaving it [...] Maybe I'm not leaving, maybe I'm going home'. Space travel is possible, but Vincent cannot return from Titan; there's no fixing the broken world. The same lesson applies in *Elysium,* which shows that space travel can help to fix broken people, but not the broken world. Shuttles bring the sick of Earth up to Elysium for health care. As the shuttles land on Earth, people run over unpaved streets, with mounds of trash on the shoulders and puddles in the roadway to reach them. Both *Gattaca* and *Elysium* go the furthest not just literally, by space travel, but also abstractly, starting anew in space and drawing a line under the dystopian Earth.

Space and water travel in post-apocalyptic settings offer a similar potential to start anew, but with slightly less success. *Waterworld* has a similar ending to *Children of Men*, adjusted for a watery world. After a long and winding water route, air travel carries Enola (Tina Majorino), Helena (Jeanne Tripplehorn), Old Gregor, Elder, and the Mariner to the one patch of land left on the globe. The possibility of air travel makes the better world reachable, and there are horses to ride around the island, but the Mariner, like every other person on the Earth except the airship passengers, will continue to sail the ocean blue. More sailing will be necessary after the events of *World War Z*. Though the camouflage vaccine buys the world some time, vaccine distribution and zombie destruction remain necessary. The montage that closes the film features not just air drops from planes, but a great deal of water transport, from the small boat that returns Gerry (Brad Pitt) to his family, to flotillas of displaced persons, to landing crafts boarding. These count as happy post-apocalyptic endings. Less cheerful is the world that Leo Davidson (Mark Wahlberg) faces at the end of *Planet of the Apes* (2001), where it is possible to travel by foot, or on horseback, but space offers no escape; Leo's only consolation is that at least the ape-ruled Earth is habitable. Perhaps the least optimistic ending of post-apocalyptic films comes in the Zack Snyder version of *Dawn of the Dead*. The five survivors board a boat and sail away, with the sound of the bitten-and-doomed Michael's gunshot to his own head causing a cut to black. As the credits run, video camera footage shows the boat's trip. They run out of gas. They have an engine fire. They arrive at an island, where a horde of zombies overrun the dock. What at first appears to be an escape – the videocam footage begins with a topless woman to hint at the pleasures this waterborne escape offers – merely delays the end slightly. The distance that space and water travel enable, in most cases, offers hope; *Dawn of the Dead* stands out in that it sees putting distance between survivors and the immediate post-apocalyptic danger as a false hope: survivors travel to arrive at a different place to die.

Somewhere between the local street level and space and global travel we find the transportation infrastructure required to link disparate city-states and small enclaves. In such cases, the necessity of long-distance cooperation between distant settlements to create a transportation *system* appears in the frequency of fascist regimes that control the links. *The Postman*'s first mail deliveries help to create a sense that a restored United States may in fact exist: how else would there be a postal service? *The Postman* sees a great role for the post in the post-apocalypse, with written communication travelling the roadways left over from before the nuclear war to knit the nation back together. At the film's closing statue unveiling, the Postman rides a horse, and only the eight sailboats in the small harbour near St Rose offer any sense of how people came to the unveiling if not on foot. In other words, the more abstract idea of communication prevails over its literal.

The importance of the propaganda clips Katniss makes for the rebellion in the *Hunger Games* films offers some sense of the rarity of inter-district communication, both literal and figurative. When Katniss travels to the Capitol, she travels on a high-speed passenger rail system, but all travel throughout the nation goes through the Capitol to prevent the separate districts from forging connections. Whoever runs for president in the first post-fascist Panem election would need to develop an infrastructure bill to link the districts to each other as well, creating cohesion with more than media. Rather than connection, *Aeon Flux*'s city-state of Bregna has spent the last 400 years in hermetic suspension, using cloning to solve the infertility caused by the vaccine that allowed them to survive a twenty-first-century plague. Aeon (Charlize Theron) ends the cycle of top-down control of the city by destroying the Relical, the blimp that holds all the DNA for cloning. As the people of Bregna gather near the blimp crash site, Aeon's voice-over says, 'now we can move forward', but the next cut goes backward, to a flashback of a Berlin city street. On the twenty-first-century street, Trevor asks her, 'will I see you again?' As Aeon looks back, her voice-over continues, 'to live only once, but with hope'. The hope the film closes with exists not in twenty-fifth-century Bregna, but rather in twenty-first-century Berlin, in a city that changed its enclave status only twenty years earlier. The heavy pedestrian traffic, the pleasant chaos of the street, locates the hope in the film's present human-scaled moment rather than in any techno-fix. The *Divergent* films have a similar interest in cloning and genetic experimentation in a post-apocalyptic city-state, with slightly more confidence in technology's utility. At the end of the trilogy, flight creates the potential to rebuild (an airborne bomb blows up the cloak wall), and the same surface transportation – the streets and working El – will allow Chicago to rebuild as an egalitarian space, what Tris (Shailene Woodley) describes as 'not [...] five factions, but one city'. Tris's brother Caleb, one of the Erudite faction, and his mastery of the world's technology show that the path out of the apocalypse can be found with many of the same tools that created and maintained it. The quasi-nationalism of Tris's speech claiming Chicago defers the key goal and role of the transportation infrastructure in escaping dystopian or apocalyptic settings: forging connections more broadly.

To return to roads and highways, 'the road' registers as a symbol of this potential to go elsewhere, as the history of the road movie attests (Hark and Cohan

1997; Laderman 2002; Archer 2016). In a number of cases, an ambivalently happy ending goes hand in hand with the open road as the film ends. *Mad Max* establishes its dystopian world with a shot of a battered road sign that says, 'Highway 9 Sector 26 high fatality road – deaths this year: 57' (Figure 2.4). The shot continues, moving away from the sign to show first the paved highway and then an unpaved road. Violent vehicular mayhem begins and does not let up. Both *Mad Max* and its sequel *The Road Warrior* end with chases that include multiple often fatal car crashes. Once the chases end, Max returns to the open road, driving in *Mad Max* and standing next to a car in *The Road Warrior*. There is more road on which to drive, but as the major conflict of the films shows, there is also an ever-reducing supply of fuel.

The great northern tribe of *The Road Warrior* stashes all their fuel in a few buses, and supply gets no steadier in the sequels. *I Am Legend* sees some measure of hope in the road, as it offers a pathway to the safe Vermont enclave. But the cost of the enclave is isolation not just in the form of the walls that surround it, but also in the form of the roads that will fall into disrepair after a few frost heaves. Both *Mad Max Beyond Thunderdome* and *Mad Max: Fury Road* take a slightly more pessimistic view than the previous films in the series. Vehicular mobility disappears. Max does not drive but rather walks away from the world he helped to make safe for civilization, making him more vulnerable to the next resource-hoarding warlord. The turn away from roads and toward pedestrianism tends to accompany more pessimistic visions of the post-apocalypse. For instance, *The Quiet Earth* ends with Zac on foot on another planet entirely, taking one of the last people alive on Earth off the Earth. In an example that continues to hold a place in the American cultural imagination, *Planet of the Apes* (1968) ends with George Taylor (Charlton Heston) and Nova leaving the ape city behind. They ride

FIGURE 2.4: *Mad Max* highway safety.

a horse on a beach, where upon seeing the wreck of the Statue of Liberty, George climbs off the horse to take a few uncertain steps before collapsing on the beach to yell, 'You maniacs! You blew it up! Oh damn you! God damn you all to hell!' Taylor kneels on the beach, his powerlessness accentuated by the waves that crash over him and Nova looks on, holding onto the horse's reins. Outside of the ape city's rudimentary road system, George and Nova still have the means to escape, but they cannot escape the fact that the Earth as they knew it was destroyed. Taylor visited not an ape planet, which is to say a dystopian world, but his own planet, which is to say a post-apocalyptic world. *WALL-E* inverts part of *Planet of the Apes*' ending, with its spaceship-dwelling humans returning to a destroyed Earth as a kind of happy ending. However, the people who return to Earth seem destined not to travel, and this end to their interstellar wandering represents something desirable. The sedentary lives of the spaceship make the humans barely able to walk, accentuating the strangeness of the new world to them. The spaceship Barcaloungers could create a new version of car culture, but the film's credit sequence indicates that the new earthlings have come to the end of their travels to arrive back where they started. Rather than the fully automated luxury of the spaceship, they will encounter a world of toil and pedestrian travel and experience it as a triumph, returning to a pastoral-agricultural world in which, as the ship captain puts it, '[y]ou kids are going to grow all kinds of plants. Vegetable plants. Pizza plants.' The spaceship that returns the people to walk the Earth at the end of *WALL-E* disappears, no longer needed once the regreening of the Earth is possible. At the end of *Snowpiercer* no train remains, nor does the potential for regreening the world. After Yona (Ko Asung) detonates the kronole to blow up the train, she and Timmy survive the derailment and avalanche, finding themselves on foot in the snow.

In the post-apocalypse, the danger of getting in the car is gone; the new danger is bare life. Will *WALL-E*'s rubber legged toddler-like space people raised on Big Gulps create a thriving society? The film's end credits carry the returned earthlings through the (re)development of agriculture on Earth. Bare life represents a brief step en route to a happy ending, a recreation of an inhabited Earth. Will Yona and Timmy, two young humans walking in a sub-zero landscape repopulate the world? Or will they get too near the polar bear and die in the open air? Bare life here represents a preferable end to the oppression of the train. *The Road* bridges these two sensibilities. After The Man dies, The Boy is left alone on the beach, where he encounters a man who gives him some advice, 'if you stay here you need to keep off the road'. The Boy joins the man and his family. Together they can continue to carry the fire, but carrying the fire must entail maintaining the roads that remain if there is to be more than bare life at the end of that road.

3

Water: Privatization against Public Good

Friedrich Engels writes in *The Condition of the Working Class in England* that the poor who live in 1840s Manchester are

> deprived of all means of cleanliness, of water itself, since pipes are laid only when paid for, and the rivers so polluted that they are useless for such purposes; they are obliged to throw all offal and garbage, all dirty water, often all disgusting, drainage and excrement into the streets, being without other means of disposing them; they are thus compelled to infect the region of their own dwellings.
>
> (1999: 108)

About one hundred years after *The Condition of the Working Class in England* appeared in English, the comic *Tank Girl*, drawn by Jamie Hewlett and written by Alan Martin, appeared. Like Engels, Hewlett and Martin had an interest in water and water politics. Tank Girl lives in the post-apocalyptic Australian desert, and in the film adaptation of the comic directed by Rachel Talalay, production design by Catherine Hardwicke, Tank Girl (Lori Petty) fights Kesslee (Malcolm McDowell), CEO of the aptly named Water and Power Corporation. As *Tank Girl* puts it, '[t]hey control most of the water and got all the power'. Desert-dwellers coming into conflict with a person in control of water has a logic to it, and that logic takes on added significance in the context of the end of the Thatcher years, which brought about the privatization of water to England and Wales. The main concern in dystopias and especially in post-apocalyptic narratives is getting a drink. A person can only live about three days without water. But that's not the only thing that water does. As Engels notes, water is necessary for washing, and it is also necessary for growing plants, since after three weeks or so, a person could starve. Water also plays a role in power production and industry. If, as the *Dawn of the Planet of the Apes* showed, energy is power, water is also power. Water, we might say, is life.

The film *Tank Girl* places this understanding of water in its *mise en scène*. A heart monitor represents heart rhythms as a wave. The Liquid Silver Club represents conspicuous consumption in terms of water, and water appears as a monetary unit. Water forms the basis for forced labour: Tank Girl works in the laundry and in a water mine. Water even appears as a means of torture. All these appearances show water's importance, and in almost every case, the top-down control of water oppresses. *Tank Girl*'s happy ending, and dystopian and post-apocalyptic films more broadly, hinges on water for everyone rather than just for the elite. In water's wake comes a share of power. In this way, dystopian and post-apocalyptic films like *Tank Girl* consistently figure water as the quintessential *public* good. And while governments have been doing their best to privatize the provision of water since the 1970s, directly and indirectly, dystopian and post-apocalyptic films register that the privatization of water offers a sure route to tyranny. Faced with the looming death of the planet and/or the death of humanity, the intensification of water control narratives in the real world makes their fictional representations instructive. In the midst of a sociocultural moment coming to terms with water scarcity, in which water privatization was happening in both the developing world and in the metropole, dystopian and post-apocalyptic films show that a free society worth living in, one with a future, begins with the public provision of water.

Water H_2O

Large-scale systemic water provision is a hallmark of modernization and urbanization, two things that nearly disappear in the post-apocalypse but retain a place in dystopias. In *Water and Wastewater Treatment: A Guide for the Nonengineering Professional*, Joanne Drinan and Frank Spellman write that '[w]ater is the most important (next to air) life-sustaining product on earth. There is nothing new, exaggerated, or hidden about this statement. Yet, its service delivery (and all that it entails) remains a "hidden function" of local government' (2013: 15). There is nothing new, exaggerated, or hidden about how infrastructure remains invisible until it breaks. When the water system breaks down, parasites like cryptosporidium can generate unpleasant and deadly results. Thus, historically, 'the purpose of water supply systems has been to provide pleasant drinking water that is free of disease organisms and toxic substances. In addition, the purpose of wastewater treatment has been to protect the health and well-being of our communities' (Drinan and Spellman 2013: 3). These two purposes frequently appear in dystopian and post-apocalyptic movies; here, I will concentrate on drinking water, its provision, and its importance, with wastewater covered in the chapter on waste. If you want to live a pleasant and healthy life, you would like to have a daily supply of about 5 litres of water for drinking and cooking and at least another 25–45 litres for washing yourself and cleaning your clothes and surroundings (Tansey and Worsley 1997: 11), to say nothing of the water you would want for agricultural and industrial use. However, fresh water is a scarce resource: 'If all of the earth's water fit in a quart jug, available freshwater would not equal a teaspoon' (Drinan and Spellman 2013: 4). Providing pleasant drinking water, at its base, presents a technical problem: can we provide clean water? However, beyond technical concerns, providing water also presents social problems: Who gets water, and how?

Providing access to clean drinking water is a full-time job, but often nearly invisible and non-glamourous. In an otherwise perceptive analysis of the Pat Frank's 1959 novel *Alas, Babylon*, Claire Sponsler reads clean water as a luxury, writing that 'the residents of Fort Repose [...] are more worried about how to cope with the loss of electricity, clean drinking water, and other comforts of middle-class existence' (1993: 255). Clean water isn't a middle-class comfort; clean water is a baseline for survival. Humankind lived for millennia without electricity, but all that time they had access to clean drinking water. The people of Fort Repose survive the aftermath of a nuclear blast not because a generator or windmill provides electricity but because an artesian spring on Randy Bragg's property provides water. Even if they had the greatest of survivalist skills, food stocks, and weapons, without that safe water source, they would be doomed. The immediate aftermath of a cataclysmic event, such as *World War Z*'s zombie outbreak, makes clear how doomed people are without water. The UN Deputy Secretary General updates Gerry Lane on the global situation, putting water and its importance up front: 'Malnutrition, dirty water, no gas for the winter or transportation'. Not much to eat and nothing clean to drink; the apocalypse has arrived. In *The Book of Eli*, Eli repeatedly proves his abilities as a fighter, and those fighting skills act in the service of a search for water. Early in the film, he searches an abandoned cabin, where he first establishes the building's safety, and then immediately after tries the taps on a sink to fill his canteen. Later, after killing six hijackers with relative ease, Eli arrives in a town. At the Orpheum, the western genre-conventional rough bar, he buys water. To get his water, Eli has to buy out of the Orpheum bartender's ration; the bartender's ration card allows 'barmaid' Solara (Mila Kunis) to cut in line to fill Eli's canteen, showing the relative prestige of the bartender and the manner in which the town manages water access. As tends to happen in rough bars in westerns, Eli gets into a fight with a rustler and runs afoul of the local oligarch, a man who controls access to water to the degree that he can send Eli water for washing from the town's 'special reserve, compliments of the house'. In this way, the dusty streets of a desert town familiar to the western genre replace nineteenth-century mining with a different underground bonanza, a hidden spring that allows for the invisible and more easily defended provision of drinking water and the power it affords.

Like many post-apocalyptic films, *The Book of Eli* identifies a quotidian problem – finding and providing safe water – and uses the newly risen ruling elites to show the importance of an infrastructure to solve this problem to create a *post*-apocalyptic society. Water provision poses three interlocking sets of problems: the two technical problems of finding it and making sure it is potable, and the social problem of distributing it (Melosi 2008: 299). In this way, post-apocalyptic movies like *The Book of Eli*, *Mad Max Beyond Thunderdome*, *Mad Max: Fury Road*, *Waterworld*, and *Tank Girl* reflect the problems that post-Second World War Australia and the United States faced. Environmental historian Martin Melosi provides an overview of the state of water infrastructure during the period of great economic expansion in the United States:

> The years 1945 to 1970 represented a period of unease in confronting mounting problems with the nation's water supply. The droughts and local shortages raised concerns about a pending water crisis characterized by wide-spread depletion of the precious resource. A shifting focus to chemical pollutants in almost every important inland watercourse marked a new phase in the controversy over the extent and severity of water pollution, and how it affected the quality of the water supply. In the early years of the era of the New Ecology, confidence in the ability to deliver pure and plentiful water to all Americans was being questioned seriously for the first time since the nineteenth century.
>
> (2008: 319)

The already difficult task of finding (enough) water was made more difficult by matters out of human control, such as drought, as well as under human control, such as the effects of industrial pollution. The Cuyahoga River catching on fire multiple times in 1969 presents a too-perfect metaphor for the damage done to the American water system by industrialization. Post-apocalyptic films often replace industry with nuclear fallout as the cause for non-potable water, as in *The Book of Eli*, *The Postman*, and *Mad Max Beyond Thunderdome*. Nonetheless, sometimes post-apocalyptic survivors find a source of plentiful potable water, as when *Beneath the Planet of the Apes*'s Brent discovers the ruins of a subway station and drinks from the still-flowing fountain there (Figure 3.1). Such a scenario would be very unlikely, to say the least. Water treatment plants have an extensive maintenance schedule, with at least a dozen daily, four weekly, and a further half dozen monthly tasks that ensure water remains not just available, but also safe to drink (Environmental Protection Administration n.d.b: 1–3). Without trained personnel to perform these tasks, to say nothing of the electric and material requirements to perform them, water provision would be one of the first infrastructures to cease working adequately.

FIGURE 3.1: *Beneath the Planet of the Apes* running water.

This is not to say that water would be uniformly undrinkable after the apocalypse. Brian Fagan's history of water, *Elixir: A History of Water and Humankind*, notes that in ancient Rome

> [a]queducts carried large volumes of water, so filtration was rapid at best. Some drinking water from cisterns passed through a circle of amphorae (storage jars) packed with charcoal and sand; grilles and even filtration barriers may have been used to filter aqueduct water on occasion, but they rarely survive.
>
> (2011: 186)

B. A. Brooks's 2009 prepper guide *Surviving the NWO*, perhaps unwittingly, creates continuity from ancient Rome to the present-day United States via the same kind of water filtration: 'The first thing you should do is purchase a water filtration/purification system. Berkey sells the best systems in my opinion' (2009: 1). In just the first page of the book, Brooks makes a number of recommendations that share one trait that highlights prepper foresight: 'You can purchase a rain barrel or make your own fairly easily [...] You will want to start purchasing solar and hand crank electronic items' (2009: 1). This advice registers that, in prepper lingo, when the shit hits the fan (TSHTF) we face the failure of infrastructure. Don't put off getting the materials to create potable water; start preparations now while the infrastructure still works. In the absence of working infrastructural systems, the man in *The Road* has to improvise. Though he claims in voice-over '[m]ostly I worry about food, always food. Food and the cold and our shoes', the everyday chore of finding and creating potable water appears as a nightly chore. Seated next to a river, the man pushes a piece of cloth into a plastic water bottle with the bottom cut out. The bottle is placed spout end to spout end with another bottle.

He picks up a hubcap filled with boiling water, then pours the water over the rag. In this way the water is filtered on its way down into the second bottle, creating something close to potable water for tomorrow.

Finding and then filtering/cleaning water is a technical problem. For instance, in *Interstellar* the universe-traversing astronauts bring distillery equipment down to the planet Mann falsely claimed could support life. But solving technical problems does not necessarily solve underlying sociocultural problems. In the case of Bolivia's Cochabomba Water War,

> although Cochabomba's water was returned to the people after the protracted water wars, longstanding class differentiations and a culture of political corruption meant poor residents still struggled for reliable and safe access to water. In addition to issues of class, there are also endemic gender biases that inform the water debate the world over.
>
> (Parr 2013: 69)

The water distribution in *The Book of Eli* offers a window into the class differentiations of privatized water (about which more later): Carnegie controls the water and his goons enforce the rationing and purchase of water in the town, a practice which results in long lines. Most of the people waiting in line are women, which shouldn't surprise anyone, as '[w]ater is not gender neutral, especially in low- and middle-income countries. Accessing water for subsistence agriculture, basic health and sanitation needs, and domestic consumption is primarily the role of women in these regions' (Parr 2013: 69). Dystopian and post-apocalyptic settings offer audiences in imperial and settler-colonial nations like the United Kingdom, the United States, Australia, and Aotearoa New Zealand the means to imagine in safety and comfort the same destruction they have historically inflicted on low- and middle-income countries, and the imagination of access to safe water stratified along lines of class and gender reveals the importance of water to social reproduction (Roberts 2008: 545). Social reproduction is highly gendered, which makes *Tank Girl* an apposite selection, as at its centre we find a woman fighting to bring freedom and universal access to water to the wasteland. Clearly, water is essential for survival and a key pillar to social reproduction. How do dystopian and post-apocalyptic movies imagine the infrastructure that allows people access to it?

Water provision

My main interest for this chapter falls under what we can call a municipal water system, a network that includes water treatment facilities, water storage facilities such as a reservoir or water tower, and a pipe network that distributes the treated water to customers in residential, industrial, commercial and/or institutional settings. I will touch on water for agricultural use, including irrigation, in the chapter on food. Outside of a few mentions of cooling in the chapter on energy production and distribution, I will leave water used for industry, thermoelectric cooling included, for another day.

The appearance of water in dystopian domestic settings calls attention to the 'infra' part of infrastructure, its belowness and hiddenness; water simply appears from a faucet or spigot from an unseen source somewhere else. Brian Hayes offers an overview of the water provision system parts in *Infrastructure: A Field Guide to the Industrial Landscape*: 'A typical municipal water system has four main components: a source of supply, a pipeline or aqueduct to carry the water from the source to the city, a facility for treatment and purification, and a distribution network' (2005: 75). A few films show the first part, a lake or river from which people might drink. *After Earth* (Tom Sanders 2013) shows the most likely situation in which the water would be safe to drink: humans haven't been on Earth for centuries, making the rivers and lakes safe to drink. Most films show the last stop in water's trip from original source – lake, reservoir, aquifer – to emergence at the end of the distribution network. The sprinklers watering Anderton's lawn in *Minority Report*, or the luxury showers in *Babylon AD* and *The Hunger Games* (Phillip Messina 2012). Less extravagant shower facilities appear in the shared spaces of *The Handmaid's Tale*, *Fortress*, and *Robocop* (William Sandell 1987), as well as *Rollerball*'s (John Box 1975) locker room. The post-apocalyptic *Resident Evil: Apocalypse* opens with a pre-collapse world where people can water their lawns. A scene of suburban domestic bliss shows a paperboy fling a newspaper onto a lawn, directly in front of a running sprinkler. After a short close-up of the newspaper on the ground, the sprinkler in the background, the shot dives down from ground level to an underground Umbrella Corporation facility, The Hive. But the move downwards passes through black in a masked edit, rather than through a literalized stretch of land with pipes that feed the sprinklers. These uses of water presume a functioning water provision system that remains invisible until the water comes out of the pipe. It just works. Against the smooth functioning of water provision where the relatively powerful live, the lower end of dystopias experience less certainty. Leaky pipes abound in *THX 1138*, *1984*, and *The First Purge*, appearing as denotative ambient reminders of inequality and the generally shit life most people experience in dystopian and post-apocalyptic worlds. In all of these cases, water provides both a practical measure of the pressures of survival and an index of relative deprivation. Water might remain, but how much, for what tasks beyond drinking, and under whose control?

Drinking

With throats unslaked, with black lips baked / Agape they heard me call: / Gramercy! they for joy did grin, / And all at once their breath drew in. / As they were drinking all.
(Coleridge 1834: n.pag.)

According to the Australian government's Healthdirect website, adults need about ten cups of fluids a day, which can include water as well as coffee, tea, juice, and soft drinks (Healthdirect 2021: n.pag.). Those of us who live in subtropical Meanjin Brisbane or tropical far north Queensland probably need more to keep from dehydrating. In the post-apocalyptic world of *Mad Max Beyond Thunderdome* (not Queensland but arid New South Wales and South Australia) Bartertown has water. Master Blaster's power, discussed earlier, comes from pig shit energy; much of Auntie Entity's power comes from the water spigot. It is hard to see how everyone in Bartertown can get ten cups to drink out of the one tap shown on screen. Similarly, in addition to the arsenal and goons he commands, *The Book of Eli*'s Carnegie controls access to water through a ticketing/coupon system. The front of the train limits access to drinking water in *Snowpiercer*, and the corporate elites dole out dippers of water to their prisoners in *Fortress*. The not particularly welcoming bar in *Waterworld* serves privatized water, and sells its stores dearly. By contrast, when Eli and Solara reach Alcatraz at the conclusion to *The Book of Eli*, its water tower and ready access to water with no strings attached mark it as the starting point for a *post*-apocalyptic civilization. In all these cases, the simplest matter of survival, of water to drink, poses danger both in terms of health and in terms of interpersonal conflict. The social problem remains. As Balinisteau reads the film,

> [i]f we were to imagine the setting of *Tank Girl* stories as the space of Bakhtinian carnival, Booga would represent anthropomorphized nature, that is, nature 'dressed' in human form and mocking the human claim to government of nature, made in the official voice of the body politic.
>
> (2012: 20)

A literal reading of *Tank Girl* shows that Balinisteau needs neither Bakhtin nor Kantorowicz to show how Booga – a mutant kangaroo – mocks the human claim to govern nature (in other words, survive). Like *Mad Max Beyond Thunderdome*, *Tank Girl* takes place in post-apocalyptic Australia. Kangaroos today, without mutation, can live in places where there is very little water, and only need about six cups of water per day, much less than a human (New South Wales Department of Primary Industries 2009: n.pag.). Booga would enjoy the part of his kangaroo genetics that would allow him to live where there is very little water.

Post-apocalyptic films are survival narratives, and Marq DeVillers proposes four water survival strategies in *Water: The Fate of Our Most Precious Resource*, all of which appear in post-apocalyptic films with varying degrees of success. Two strategies go hand in hand:

> **Water survival strategy 2:** If you can't get more water, use less of it. Reduce demand and **Water survival strategy 3:** By definition, water use will go down if there are *fewer people. But is this likely to happen? Was Thomas Malthus, the doomsayer who forecast worldwide famines because populations were growing faster than the food supply, right after all?*
>
> (2000: 293, 306, original emphasis)

In post-apocalyptic worlds, fewer people means a reduced demand, but the reduced availability of safe drinking water often means water provision remains a key problem. A near eco-fascist use of water as a weapon to reduce demand – and thereby population – appears in the opening of *Mad Max: Fury Road*. To celebrate Imperator Furiosa's mission to obtain more guzzeline, Immortan Joe briefly showers his people with water. The scene begins with Immortan Joe approaching a balcony to deliver a speech in the traditional dictator-on-a-balcony style, an expressive, punctuative set. The people gather below, banging pots together as they cheer. One of the old men says: 'It's coming. Get ready'. They inch forward, pots in their hands, looking up, marching past the camera for a seven second long shot that shows the scale of the crowd. Immortan Joe opens the spigots and the people surge forward, pots aloft. After a few moments of the water flowing, a cut to an extreme high angle shot of Joe looking down on the people surging towards the water, followed by a medium shot of Joe pulling the taps shut. Immortan Joe then warns the people: 'Do not my friends become addicted to water. It will take hold of you and you will resent its absence!' Immortan Joe enforces reduced demand in two ways: by demonstrating his total control of water availability (more on privatization soon) and through a public miseducation campaign against water addiction (Figure 3.2). In other words, Immortan Joe uses water to control the population both politically and numerically.

If restricting access offers one form of control, '**Water survival strategy 4:** *Steal water from others*' offers a mirror version of that control (DeVillers 2000: 309, original emphasis). The man's constant fear of losing his cart in *The Road* has a great deal to do with the water containers the cart holds. The desert-set post-apocalyptic films all feature a version of tenuous control of water, reduced demand, and depopulation. The post-apocalyptic politics of violence means fighting over resources, starting with water. Every warlord and villain – Auntie Entity in *Mad Max Beyond Thunderdome*, Carnegie in *The Book of Eli*, the prison-industrial

FIGURE 3.2: *Mad Max: Fury Road* water to the people.

complex in *Fortress*, the front of the train in *Snowpiercer*, Water and Power in *Tank Girl*, the cannibals in *The Road* – knows it.

Some post-apocalyptic worlds are not quite as violent in their resource access. DeVillers also notes that 'technological invention' or 'imaginative technologies' can provide access to water: '**Water survival strategy 1:** *If you need more water, get more water. That means either you import water from someplace where there is a surplus, or you make more fresh water yourself*' (2000: 284, original emphasis). Absent a ready source of fresh water – a river where they fill their canteens in *The Girl with All the Gifts*, rivers in the *Planet of the Apes* series, rainwater collected on rooftops in *28 Days Later* and *The Omega Man* – technological solutions tend to take an improvised form, as with the man's water filtering in *The Road* and The Postman's camping supply store test in *The Postman*. Imaginative human technology in a post-apocalyptic film appears in the opening sequence of *Waterworld*, in which the Mariner uses a distillation process to make drinking water from his urine. The people of Zion recycle their water supply in *The Matrix Reloaded*, though the means by which this is achieved remain mysterious. While it may appear strange that the set as denotation mall fountains continue to bubble in *Dawn of the Dead*, this could offer a source of drinking water to the survivors. To avoid anoxia, the depletion of oxygen in stored water that leads to the growth of anaerobic bacteria and the sulphur smell that accompanies them, 'for a long time the favored method of aerating drinking water was to build a fountain, and so many reservoirs have impressive jets and ornamental cascades' (Hayes 2005: 76). Alien overlords provision Jack with water pouches in *Oblivion*, but otherwise very few technological fixes for water, whether in the form of purification tablets or desalinization plants appear on screen. A drink of water proves less elusive in dystopian worlds, as the technology for municipal water provision inheres in fictional worlds that are recognizably 'our own', but extrapolated into the future. Thus, for example, clean drinking water simply appears in from the kitchen faucet in *Minority Report.* When water access proves more difficult, dystopian films make note of it, as in the 'potable water' sign Katniss sees during her walk around the underground District 13 in *The Hunger Games: Mockingjay, Part 1*, the line-up for water in *Soylent Green*, and the rainwater collected in *Blindness* to name a few. Whether it entails storing water for potential cut-offs, being ready to test what is on offer, or improvising solutions for self-provision, finding ways to manage water scarcity to ensure survival occupies a significant place in the dystopian and post-apocalyptic everyday. The sometimes-ramshackle infrastructure around drinking water builds the foundation for life, and further refinements of it open up further water use and the social complexity and comforts those uses enable.

Bathing and washing

Beyond drinking water, water provision allows for water to wash, and not just clothes. People – almost exclusively women – still do laundry in dystopian worlds, such as the prison laundry in *Tank Girl. Blade Runner 2049* shows a work crew power washing the city's walls and walkways. The action film generic convention of a destroyed water main appears in the showdown between John Spartan (Sylvester Stallone) and Simon Phoenix (Wesley Snipes) in *Demolition Man*'s Museum of Violence. The destruction of a water main creates a massive spout of water to soak down both Spartan and Phoenix, which is to say it shows off Stallone and Snipes' physiques. More traditional forms of bathing, showers and baths, happen with great frequency in dystopian and post-apocalyptic films, usually as a measure of societal decay or as a moment of regained 'normalcy'. In *The Book of Eli*, Carnegie tries to bring Eli into the fold with a wash basin of water, as Eli normally washes with KFC wet wipes. An even more important instance of washing appears when a medic tries to remove shrapnel stuck in Carnegie's leg. Carnegie stops him, asking, 'did you wash your hands?' Pleasingly, by the end of the film Carnegie has an infection. A similar mapping of privilege appears in *Soylent Green*, where the rich enjoy high pressure showers while Thorn, a member of the underclass, washes with a handful of water out of a cooler. In *The Road* bathing happens out in the open, under a cold waterfall, but a lucky discovery of a bomb shelter means a bath in a tub. *Brazil*'s Sam soaks in a tub filled with dirty grey water, perhaps expressing the ink of his bureaucratic society. In *A Boy and His Dog* (Ray Boyle 1975), Vic pays a tin of sardines and a tin of beets to enter a walled settlement where they not only show movies but also offer a shower. People fallen nearly to the state of beasts wash in the falling rain in *Blindness*, while the genetically superior

Valids of *Gattaca* wash in high-tech sealed tubes, a piece of elaborate set design that expresses the luxury Valids enjoy. Bathing can indicate love and caring, as when Neville, the lone survivor in *I Am Legend*'s Manhattan, finds time to give his dog a bath and when *Children of Men*'s Theo brings water into the stable in anticipation of Kee delivering the first baby on earth in more than eighteen years. Contrariwise, enforced bathing and delousing, as in *12 Monkeys*, *Allegiant* (Alec Hammond 2016), *V for Vendetta*, and *Fortress* disempower people treated as prisoners. And in the famous 'it's a madhouse!' sequence in the 1968 *Planet of the Apes*, the apes use hoses to violently pacify their human prisoners, drawing on the news photos of American police using water cannons against Black Americans and Civil Rights activists throughout the 1960s. The one time enforced bathing does not feature water appears in the desert-set *Tank Girl*, in which Tank Girl's prison-intake shower is set up as a soak-the-star moment of eroticism, like the broken water main scene in *Demolition Man*, but then shows Tank Girl covered in delousing powder, rather than water. Across dystopian and post-apocalyptic films, water infrastructure controlled from the top down can be used violently to place people outside of community belonging, whereas moments of bathing like the man's waterfall show the bracing freedom that water for all can offer.

Water as a signifier

Substituting powder for water in the shower presents one of many examples of the shifting signification of water in *Tank Girl*. At various points in the film water acts as not only drink for humans, mutated kangaroos, and plants, and as washing medium, but also as currency, decoration, script, and weapon. As in the late twentieth- and early twenty-first century, a swimming pool signifies wealth; an Olympic-sized swimming pool holds more than two million litres of water, so any world with swimming pools has enough water. But who gets to enjoy this wealth measured in water matters. A pair of Tom Cruise examples illustrate two versions of wealth that a pool makes concrete. *Minority Report*'s Anderton takes his son to the public pool, showing he's a man of the people. *Oblivion* places Jack in a house that floats above earth, complete with infinity pool. Such an engineering feat, a set as punctuation and embellishment, demonstrates his importance as one of the last people remaining, a form of wealth. The ceilings in Niander Wallace's building feature wave-like shimmering lights, distinguishing the elite's space of aesthetic wonder from the functional spaces K occupies in *Blade Runner 2049*. Fountains such as those in both *Dawn of the Dead* films and *The Matrix Reloaded* decorate otherwise uninspiring locations (a mall and toilet, respectively). Sometimes water serves a simple utilitarian function, such as fire defence in *Resident Evil* or engine cooling in *Mad Max: Fury Road*. In all of these cases, water makes social life visible and legible, as 'both publics and their states are brought into being *with* the discrete, partial, and compromised pipes and liquid materials of water infrastructures that form the city' (Anand 2017: 158). In *Hydraulic City: Water and the Infrastructures of Citizenship in Mumbai*, Nikhil Anand identifies the utopian promise of a working water infrastructure:

> When very wealthy and very poor residents live in neighborhoods served by the same water line, as they often do in Mumbai, they constitute publics that are often surprisingly heterogeneous [...] Residents in Mumbai's settlements correctly recognize in mundane water pipes the promise of a durable form of urban belonging at some point in the future.
>
> (2017: 156, 168)

The belonging belongs to the future, but nevertheless a utopian potential appears in water provision. The dystopian potential for water appears in *Blindness*, where the strong control resources with personalized violence, making it necessary for people to collect rainwater. *Isle of Dogs*'s Trash Island may separate its trash types quite rigidly, but the water collected in its cistern is dangerous to drink. The weakest faction in *Insurgent*, Amity, seem to get their water from a cistern as well, but rather than danger the cistern represents something positive. The water independence afforded by the cistern gives Amity one way to assert themselves against the more powerful and violent factions. In the *Hunger Games* series, the pump in District 12 shows that while the Capitol grips the district with top-down policing, water remains under local control. Frank's method for collecting rainwater in *28 Days Later* – hundreds of yellow, green, red, and blue buckets on a rooftop – creates a half-joyful splash of colour in London's grey cityscape, a fitting expression of Frank and Hannah as survivors who have retained their humanity. Outside of cities, streams offer water that no longer carries the danger of pollution, as the apocalypse has eliminated industry, as in *The Girl with All the Gifts* and *Oblivion*. The relative scarcity of water and who accesses it registers not just the practical matters of survival, but also the human experience of building and living in a world that manages scarcity, either for limited privilege or common use, to create a specific form of community.

Wastewater

In this section I return briefly to the purpose of water supply systems described by Drinan and Spellman, to focus on the second part, 'to protect the health and well-being of our communities' (2013: 6). In addition to bringing safe drinking water into buildings and public places like parks, the water infrastructure also goes the other way, with water carrying waste products away. The water that goes down the tub drain, the oil and food scraps from dish washing, and the urine, faeces, and vomit from the toilet all go into the sewer and to a water treatment plant. These plants clean the water. Getting the olive oil and soap residue out of the water is important, but more important is getting the human waste products out. As Rose George notes, waterborne illnesses such as typhoid, cholera, giardia, and E. coli are in fact shit-borne illnesses (2008: 2). Protecting health and well-being makes the primary mission of a wastewater treatment plant 'to treat the waste stream to a level of purity acceptable to return it to the environment or for immediate re-use' (Drinan and Spellman 2013: 15). You flush the toilet and the waste goes away, but then the waste has to go somewhere and the water will return, reused in some form. The problem with such a system, as environmentalist Wendell Berry noted, is that it involves an already scarce resource. In his foreword to *The Toilet Papers: Recycling Waste and Conserving Water*, Berry writes that

> [i]f I urinated and defecated into a pitcher of drinking water and then proceeded to quench my thirst from the pitcher, I would undoubtedly be considered crazy. If I invented an expensive technology to put my urine and feces into my drinking water, and then invented another expensive (and undependable) technology to make the same water fit to drink, I might be thought even crazier.
>
> (1999: 1)

Berry argues here against the techno-solutionist approaches favoured by wastewater treatment engineer types like Drinan and Spellman, who claim that the time of 'pipe to pipe (toilet to treatment plant to drinking water tap) is quickly approaching' (2013: 4). Like self-driving cars, drinking water from poop, crossing the streams of wastewater and drinking water, has always been just around the corner. Bill Gates, a big believer in pipe to pipe, wrote a 2015 blogpost that begins,

> I watched the piles of feces go up the conveyer belt and drop into a large bin. They made their way through the machine, getting boiled and treated. A few minutes later I took a long taste of the end result: a glass of delicious drinking water.
>
> (2015: n.pag.)

In other words, Bill Gates raises a toast to a future in which the world's poor will eat/drink shit to survive. If that's the future coming down the pipe, the wastewater system needs to be top-notch.

Waterworld sees a slightly less grim post-apocalyptic future. The Mariner only has to treat his own urine. After voice-over narration explains that the world is now covered entirely by water, the camera descends from the clouds, slowly approaching a catamaran, a human figure on one of its hulls. A cut from the long shot of the boat is followed by a close-up of a plastic bottle cut in half to create a larger opening. A stream of urine enters from the top of the frame with a gurgling sound effect. The camera pulls away from the close-up of the bottle to show two feet, then moves up to show a rear end and the herky-jerky motions of a person zipping up. The camera tilts back down to follow the figure reaching down to pick up the bottle, following the bottle as the person pours the bottle's contents into a funnel. The camera moves back downwards, catching sight of a hand turning a crank to put the mechanical contraption of tubes and coils and receptacles into action. As the sound of the crank continues, the camera moves down to a faucet, moving into a tighter close-up of the spigot as a hand turns it open, a weak stream of clear water emerging into a cup. The camera follows the cup up until it comes up to the mouth of a man, backlit by the sun, who drinks from the cup. With this almost continuous shot, one of the most incredible introductions to an action hero in Hollywood cinema history, *Waterworld* shows not just the Mariner's ability to survive, but also that pipe to pipe is indeed the future.

Unlike *Waterworld*, *The Matrix Reloaded* keeps its water treatment at a distance, in the background of the image during Counselor Hamann and Neo's conversation. At one point Hamann gestures towards the rear of the image, asking '[y]ou see that machine? It has something to do with recycling our water supply. And I have absolutely no idea how it works. But I do understand the reason for it to work.' As I have already noted in the case of the man filtering water in *The Road*, the technology to create potable drinking water is not particularly complicated, the workings of the device a matter of simple chemistry. In the prepper zine *The Survivor*, Kurt Saxon emphasizes the importance of kitchen chemistry:

> The lay chemist, the amateur with imagination and idealism, will give the others the reasons for bearing up under the struggle. The chemist will not need to be armed, nor will he or she need to be physically strong or even physically whole. The only qualification will be a good mind and the motivation to create something good out of practically nothing. Such a one will be treasured by any survival community.
> (1976: 24)

The continuous shot in *Waterworld* underlines the ingenuity and improvisation needed to create the filtration device as well as the simple 'kitchen chemistry' of the filtration process. A simple filtration process based on kitchen chemistry knowledge could, like kung fu, be downloaded as needed from the matrix.

Fancy technological fixes to water treatment do not appear in dystopian and post-apocalyptic films to the degree that broadly applicable claims about future better worlds are possible, but the space between use and treatment – sewers – does appear. I analyse sewers in depth in the waste chapter; here I will only touch lightly on them. In their introduction to *The Promise of Infrastructure*, Hanna Appel, Nikhil Anand, and Akhil Gupta echo Susan Leigh Star's claim that

> to study a city and neglect its sewers and power supplies, you miss not only essential aspects of distributional justice and planning power, but also dreams and aspirations, breakdowns and suspensions, and the intimate rhythms of how we wash or go to the bathroom, how we see in the dark or cool our food, and how we travel across space. (2018: 11)

One of the clearest cases of the sewer revealing how power operates over space appears in the mildly dystopian *The Third Man* (Lyndon-Haynes production manager 1949); the kiosk-entry sewers make Vienna's four occupation zones more permeable. That the exploitation of sewer-borne mobility also leads to needless deaths further underlines the role of the sewer in public health. The connection of social cleansing appears in the alternative uses sewers are put to the poorest and most disadvantaged reside in sewers in *Mimic* (Carol Spier 1997), *It* (Paré 2017), the documentary *Dark Days* (Singer 2000), and low-budget horror films like *Alligator* (Michael Erier AD 1980) and *C.H.U.D.* (William Bilowit 1984). The use of sewer spaces as, for example, a hideaway in *Escape from New York*, or as an escape route in *Children of Men*, *Dawn of the Dead*, *Escape from LA*, *Isle of Dogs*, *Resident Evil: Afterlife* (Arvinder Greywal 2010), and *WALL-E* reveals that the microscopic danger sewers carry, waterborne diseases, can be displaced onto larger dangers: monsters that must be dispatched with fists or fire or firearms rather than flocculation, sedimentation, filtration, and disinfection.

Privatization

Both *28 Days Later* and *The Girl with All the Gifts* show London water not working after the apocalypse, while in *World War Z* the Welsh WHO facility seems to have water provision. On the one hand, this is a matter of accurately reflecting the chaotic state of post-apocalyptic life – a WHO medical research facility would have its own power generators to pump water and the survivors could make do and repair as needed. On the other hand, the UK government, at the end of the 1980s, was one of the first to move towards water privatization, and the track record since privatization has been mixed (Water UK 2019a: n.pag., 2019b: n.pag.). Alan Moore's comic book *V for Vendetta* (David Lloyd and Tony Weare, artists) was, like *Tank Girl*, published during the United Kingdom's Thatcherite move toward water privatization in England and Wales, from its first proposal as a Conservative Party policy in 1984 until the institution of privatized water in 1989. Thus, the attack on the water treatment plant in the film version of *V for Vendetta*, from a world of in-place private water, bears analysis. The water treatment plant, for its part, receives comparatively little attention or screen time in the film, making it the least-engaged-with part of the fascist state's origin, revealed through Finch's investigations into V's killings. Through these investigations, Finch learns about the St Mary's virus and the Larkhill detention centre. Then an internet (or interlink, as the film calls it) archival search reveals a series of newspaper headlines which trace the virus' path: 'at least 230 killed in tube station', 'St. Mary's virus kills 178', 'Three waters infected. Drinking water contaminated by unknown virus', and finally 'Epidemic'. Finch's investigations lead him to ask, correctly,

> [w]hat if the worst, the most horrifying biological attack in this country's history was not the work of religious extremists? [...] But I see this chain of events, these coincidences, and I have to ask: What if that isn't what happened? What if someone else unleashed that virus?

V, posing as William Rookwood, confirms Finch's suspicions, telling him that '[t]hree targets [were] chosen to maximize the effect of the attack: a school, a Tube station, and a water treatment plant. Several hundred died within the first few weeks.' Thus, while the closed-down Tube is central to the film's imagination of creating a better post-dystopian world by blowing up Parliament, a functioning water infrastructure offered the best way to create a dystopia by spreading the virus. As Delia Surridge, the scientist in charge, puts it, '[n]uclear power is meaningless in a world where a virus can kill an entire population and leave its wealth intact'. Practically speaking,

> [s]ignificant damage to the nation's wastewater facilities or collection systems would result in loss of life, catastrophic environmental damage to rivers, lakes, and wetlands, contamination of drinking water supplies, long-term public health impacts, destruction of fish and shellfish production, and disruption to commerce, the economy, and our normal way of life.
>
> (Drinan and Spellman 2013: 39)

Our normal way of life is particularly vulnerable because the water infrastructure is vulnerable and almost ubiquitous. The length of water pipes, which are often under the road, exceeds the length of roads in England; 215,000 miles of pipes carry water while 189,700 miles carry people and vehicles (and cause runoff)

(Rotherham 2020: n.pag.; UK Department of Transport 2020: n.pag.). But while the Tube line appears at the end of *V for Vendetta* and the masked thousands take to the streets, the water infrastructure never appears. It functions quietly and invisibly in the background.

The virus attack demonstrates that who controls a well-functioning water infrastructure matters a great deal. The water infrastructure in England has proven to be quite profitable, if not well functioning, with nearly £60 billion in dividends paid out since privatization began (Laville 2020: n.pag.). Even though water is not yet privatized in the United States or Australia, the logic and historical-contextual fact of privatization flows through their dystopian and post-apocalyptic films. Water privatization and commodification as the opposing forces to water as a public good reveal the significance of water and water provision in dystopian and post-apocalyptic films and what it means to the horizon of imagination for anglophone culture in the late twentieth- and early twenty-first century. While the dystopian and post-apocalyptic movies I analyse in this chapter do not, for the most part, show the infrastructure of private ownership of water beyond the faucet/spigot, they do offer a more legible representation of 'privatization': the commodity of bottled water or an explicit cash exchange for water in a wasteland. Enemies sell you water or at least expect something valuable in return. Friends share water. It's not that water privatization is happening *everywhere* in the late twentieth- and early twenty-first century, but neo-liberal governments, such as Thatcher-and-later United Kingdom, and those under the pressure of structural readjustment such Chile, and to a degree Mexico and Argentina, show water privatization as an increasingly likely solution imposed from the top down, placing a public good under private/corporate control (Their 2022: 156).

Margaret Thatcher didn't do anything new in pushing for the privatization of water in England and Wales. As Karen Bakker notes in 'A political ecology of water privatization', '[t]he first companies to supply London with water were privately owned; after a period of state (municipal and then national) ownership in the twentieth century, the English water supply utilities were privatized by asset sale in 1989' (2003: 37). This return to an early nineteenth-century approach to water provision places England and Wales outside of the norm, as 'England and Wales remain one of the few territories in the world to have a fully privatised water and sewage disposal system' (Choudri 2020: n.pag.). The logic of privatization was quite simple: compared to the bloated public sector, the private sector could do the same job cheaper and more efficiently. As Andrea Muelebach notes,

> [s]ince their wholesale sell-off by Margaret Thatcher, three decades ago, English water companies have funneled a total of £57 billion to shareholders while failing to

> carry out significant national infrastructure improvements. Publicly owned Scottish Water has, in contrast, invested nearly 35 percent more per household into infrastructure in the past 18 years and charges households 14 percent less for its services.
>
> (2020: n.pag.)

During the 1980s, the water and sewer of my hometown of Carpentersville, Illinois, population 23,000, was run by the village. It still is. Meanwhile, when it came to water provision outside of the country, the United States-driven Washington Consensus pushed for 'the privatization of state assets, particularly those that subsidize[d] users and fail to operate along the lines of full cost recovery, an approach that clearly characterized the majority of water services during the post-war era' (Roberts 2008: 539). In other words, even if water was treated as a public good in almost every town in the United States (Food & Water Watch 2018: 3), the rest of world would need to move towards privatizing, or at least public–private partnerships, if they wanted financial support. Granted, what I am calling privatization is more complex:

> The British case is frequently cited as an example of water privatization [...] More careful analyses distinguish between full privatization (divestiture – the sale of assets to the private sector), and what are (in Canada) termed 'public-private partnerships' [PPP] [...] The majority of water supply 'privatizations' to date are, in fact, PPPs, many of them in urban areas of developing countries.
>
> (Bakker 2003: 38)

But while my use of privatization may simplify matters, it offers the clarity of the prioritization of profit over public provision/service.

The push for privatization led to a situation in developing nations not unlike the transportation systems I described in the transportation chapter, in which water infrastructure was put in place during the nineteenth century to serve colonial elites, not the people whose land it was and is. Then, soon after former colonies gained their independence, the energy crisis of the 1970s squeezed governments, leading to increasing debts. Thus,

> [d]uring the lost decade for development associated with the debt crisis of the 1980s some governments started to reduce their investment in water and sanitation infrastructure and by the 1990s a reduction in government spending had become a conditionality of multilateral loans. The gap in water management that a withdrawing state left became filled through increased participation from a diverse range of water user groups including, in some cases, transnational private-sector interests.
>
> (Laurie 2011: 174)

In other words, water privatization offers the potential for large profits for elites and the creation of a near-dystopian world for the poor who have no choice but to pay for a necessity of life.

But as I noted above, dystopian and post-apocalyptic movies tend not to feature representations of the privatization of water in terms of the control of the literal pipes and contracts for provision. Something else takes the place of the concept of privatized water: not water from the tap, the product of an invisibly functioning infrastructure, but rather bottled water paid for at point of purchase, rather than in a monthly bill or as part of your rates. In *Privatizing Water: Governance Failure and the World's Urban Water Crisis*, Bakker argues that privatization and commercialization must be understood as distinct processes: 'Privatization can occur without full commercialization [and] […] Commercialization can be initiated prior to privatization, or while ownership is retained in the public sector' (2010: 103). Local water boards in Aotearoa New Zealand, for example, are government-run but have also let private companies tap aquafers for bottled water (Wellington Higher Courts Reporter 2021: n.pag.). A further short step moves from commercialization to commodification. In the introduction to a special issue of the geography journal *Antipode*, Becky Mansfield writes that

> [s]carcity, as created by privatization, leads not only to the capitalist labor relation, but also to capitalist commodities and markets. What makes privatization more than just an institutional shift from public to private management is that it creates new objects of property that can be bought and sold; privatization is a key moment for creating commodified things.
>
> (2017: 398)

At the end of the 1990s, '[a]t the same time that international forums were promoting water commercialization, newly emerging transnational companies were searching for new investments' (Laurie 2011: 175). One of those major new investments took the form of bottled water. Right as the continued lack of maintenance meant that municipal water treatment showed some strain, soft drink companies decided to diversify their portfolios. Bottled water offered something better, something worth a premium cost; it was unlike and better than the municipal water from the tap. Alleged sources formed part of the appeal – words like mountain and spring abound in brand names – as well as special filtration process. In the United States, the success of Reaganism meant that government services had a bad rap. Other people might have to depend on municipal water, but those who could afford it could indulge in bottled water, first with mineral waters like Perrier or San Pellegrino, and then dozens of water brands. Dystopian films like *Strange Days* offer a peek into this shift in the form of Lenny Nero's in-home water cooler. A twenty-first-century version of commodified water appears in the background of Tallahassee's initial appearance on screen in *Zombieland*. After driving his up-armoured SUV across a highway divider, Tallahassee stops upon seeing Columbus in the road. They have a stare down, pointing their guns at each other. The background of the image behind Tallahassee features a multiple-car pileup. Slightly closer to Tallahassee are dozens of Dasani water bottles, no doubt ejected from the vehicles in the crash. Bottled water offers personalized access to water, feeding the lone wolf survivalist dream; Tallahassee and Columbus push against that sensibility, teaming up for a better chance to survive.

Water associated with the profit motive, or with dictatorial control, and sometimes both together appears in dystopian and post-apocalyptic movies as a signal of the relative welcoming nature of a settlement and as an index of how far civilization has regressed. The more water is a scarce and expensive resource, the more physical danger the majority of survivors face. Conversely, publicly available water controlled by a larger percentage of the population usually augurs well for the peacefulness and life expectancy of the settlement. Post-apocalyptic survivors alternate between purchasing commodified water and discovering settlements based around privatized water. For instance, in addition to his self-provisioning via urine filtration, *Waterworld*'s Mariner keeps a number of one-gallon glass jars (wrapped in rope to make them less vulnerable to breakage) and plastic bags to store water. When he arrives at the peaceful atoll, he stocks up on water by trading from his personal stores of plants and other useful objects. Similarly, in *Mad Max Beyond Thunderdome*, Max wanders the wasteland with his own limited store of water in skins. Upon arriving in Bartertown, he meets a man selling nuclear-poisoned water out of an old boiler mounted on a cart and then obtains safe water at the cost of working on Auntie Entity's behalf to kill Master Blaster. Whereas the warlord Auntie Entity uses access to drinkable water to assert and maintain power, both Pig Killer – an outcast in Bartertown – and the children who live in a desert oasis outside of Bartertown's control share water with Max. Pig Killer sends a monkey into the desert with a skin full of water as a lifeline to Max; the children pile their waterskins together so Max and the search party for Savannah can survive the desert. In all of these cases, the personal water container remains a constant, but who fills it, where the water comes from – and at what cost – and whether that water is shared all signal the relative level of civilization. Those who sell water, and especially those who control people by restricting access to water, put a brake on the development of a liveable post-apocalyptic world. After the apocalypse, even a Pig Killer can redeem himself if he shares water.

A petty dictator like Auntie Entity, empowered by exclusive access to privatized and commodified water, appears in *The Book of Eli*. The importance of water to Carnegie's rule becomes evident when he loses the majority of his personal army: the people once under his foot loot his headquarters, carrying away his water bottles. Water bottles are portable, and a single pump not the most efficient way to provide water to even a small town. Carnegie can only aspire to regional power; the limits of the hand pump keep his town and power base small. However, the basis for Carnegie's control of the town and possible expanded power becomes clearer when Solara shows Eli the underground springs Carnegie had seen before the apocalypse. 'Carnegie knows about two more springs up north', she tells him. 'He says he's going to build more towns.' That is to say, Carnegie *thinks about* expanding. But to build new towns, he'll need to depend on both guard labour and water infrastructure.

The power water infrastructure makes possible to a post-apocalyptic warlord appears quite forcefully in *Mad Max: Fury Road*. The story begins as Imperator Furiosa leaves the Citadel to haul the brand-name-like 'Aqua Cola' to Gas Town to trade for guzzeline. Water is the main natural resource of the Citadel, where it is both privatized and commodified (as are women). Immortan Joe is a low-rent version of an extraction-economy resource dictator. His domain is larger than Carnegie's not just because he has a massive army of guard labour in the War Boys, but also because he controls a far more extensive water infrastructure. For instance, in the space behind Joe's 'throne' area, a pool of water sits in the middle of the frame, with pumps to both sides, punctuating his power and importance. Interestingly, even though somebody killed the world, they didn't kill the technology to pump water up from aquafers. David Feldman argues in *Water Politics: Governing Our Most Precious Resource* that

> the provision and management of water are not merely technical problems whose resolution hinges on hydrological principle, economic cost, or engineering feasibility. They are and have always been products of decisions made by institutions that exercise control over access to water, that determine who gets it as well as prescribing the condition people receive it, and that define the goals for its use.
>
> (2017: ix)

Just like all infrastructural problems, water provision is both a technical and social problem. In Mexico, Kurt Hackbarth notes, the NAFTA-driven *Ley de aguas nacionales* transferred public resources like water into private control:

> With public water fountains virtually nonexistent, and with six out of ten rivers suffering from serious levels of contamination, the stark fact in Mexico is that, if you don't have money for a *garrafón* or fuel to boil your water, what you wind up drinking will almost certainly be unsafe. It should surprise no one, then, that Mexicans are the largest consumers of bottled water in the world, while at the same time the country is ranked number four in the world in the amount of water extracted.
>
> (2022: n.pag.)

Water for public use is taken out, sold to the agricultural and mining sectors, and whatever is left is sold as bottled water to those who can afford it. In the post-apocalyptic Citadel, the same technical solutions – and social damage – remain in place. The Citadel could have public provision of water, it enjoys water pipes fed by pumps we see Joe briefly open when he salutes Imperator Furiosa's mission to Gastown. Early in the film, during his attempted escape from the War Boys, Max sees water and the plant-covered tops of the table mountains. At about the film's halfway point, after Furiosa leads the escape from Immortan Joe's original pursuit, faced with the empty salt desert in front of them, Max proposes a return to the Citadel. When one of the Vuvalini incredulously asks, 'what's there to find at the Citadel?' Max answers 'Green'. Toast, who has lived in the fully provisioned part of the Citadel with the other Brides, adds a clear description of privatization: 'And water. There's a ridiculous amount of clear water [...] [Immortan Joe] pumps it up from deep in the earth. Calls it Aqua Cola and claims it all for himself'. Dag then notes the broader commodification in play, '[a]nd because he owns it he owns all of us'. Toast and Dag sum up the problem – the danger – water privatization poses. Immortan Joe can withhold water, and so holds power. Making the water available to all would take away Joe's dictatorial power. As Bakker puts it in *Privatizing Water*, '[i]n practical terms [...] (in many cases) access to water is a problem of distribution rather than absolute availability. This perception should give us hope. It suggests that scarcity is socially constructed' (2010: 217–18). The gender equality inherent in *Mad Max: Fury Road*'s frequently noted feminist stance includes access to water. Technical solutions may appear neutral insofar as anyone can operate a pump, but the conditions under which people receive water and which people have access shows that the mere presence of water provision represents only one step towards the re-establishment of civilization.

Tank Girl imagines re-establishing civilization as the joyous freedom of water and power for all, and this joy looks even more desirable after seeing the misery privatized water inflicts on people and mutant kangaroos. Before getting to this better world, *Tank Girl* offers extensive evidence to the importance of water as both a means to survival and a means to control populations. In the film's opening, Tank Girl finds a dead body in the desert and takes a water bottle, branded Water & Power bottled water, off the corpse. Soon after, she explains the relationship she and her friends have with Water & Power: 'Yeah we steal water. But as long as they don't find out, who gives a shit?' Water & Power soon finds out, and Tank Girl gets arrested and imprisoned. The commandments that Water & Power post for prisoners to follow create a world of apparent scarcity: 'Failure to recycle body fluids is a violation. Hoarding water rations is a violation. Siphoning body fluids from another prisoner is a violation.' However, the interior of the Water & Power building contains what looks like more than 100 pumps, which would be unnecessary if there were no water. Scarcity is, if not fake, manufactured so that Water & Power can retain control of water and power. With its own private prison extracting free labour to extract more water, Water & Power consolidates its monopoly on an essential resource for life, expanding its access and profit margins, and thereby its power. All that stands between Water & Power and total control of the region's water is the 3 million litres of water underneath the Blue Dunes. (To demonstrate how scarce water is in *Tank Girl* the Kirkwood-Cohansey Aquifer in New Jersey has more than 15 trillion gallons in it.). In other words, *Tank Girl* is a film about a privatizing monopolistic corporation that functions as a de facto state against an insurgency. A resource war.

The insurgency is at first led by the Rippers, kangaroo–human hybrids, who operate as 'a committee' and vote on decisions. The Rippers were made by Johnny Prophet, who in addition to making hybrids also dabbles in hydrology, having left Australia to go 'to New Zealand for a little while to help some scientist guy who was making seawater so you could drink it'. The Rippers continue Prophet's work, as painted on a mural Booga narrates to *Tank Girl*: 'It's one of Johnny Prophet's dreams. See how the people are all free and the water just comes down from the sky and it don't cost nothin'. With flowers and rainbows.' Tank Girl agrees: 'It's beautiful.' Tank Girl and Jet join the insurgency to provide the necessary force and courage to make the Rippers' democratic and free-to-all vision for water in the post-comet-strike world come true. After infiltrating Water & Power's headquarters, Tank Girl kills Water & Power's head Kesslee, and Jet dispatches his second in command Sergeant Small. The film closes in an animated sequence that celebrates water not as power, but as freedom and joy. Animated Tank Girl shoots the Water & Power logo, which explodes, water pouring everywhere, taking up the entire frame both in photographic shots of churning water and in animated images of columns of rushing water. Water splashes on a close-up of Animated Tank Girl's upturned smiling face, and then Animated Tank Girl and Animated Booga embrace each other underwater. Finally, Animated Tank Girl pulls a water-skiing Animated Booga toward a waterfall, and they fly over the top of the waterfall, defying gravity as the credits roll. The triumphant collaboration of the anarchic Tank Girl, the technologically savvy Jet, and the democratic Rippers takes water away from the exclusive control of Water & Power and repositions it as the resource that does more than make life possible. Jet solves the technological problems, the Rippers ensure democratic control, and Tank Girl ensures pleasure. Pairing the explosions of water with the Cole Porter ode to sexuality, 'Let's Do It', not only creates a none-too-subtle ejaculatory joke amidst all the streaming water (Figures 3.3 and 3.4), but also shows technical solutions feeding social development. The pleasure of returning water *to* everyone generates pleasure *for* everyone.

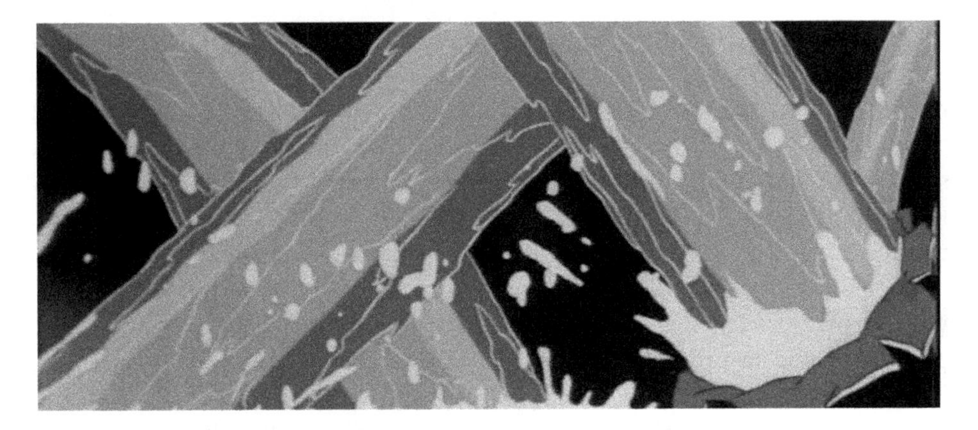

FIGURE 3.3: *Tank Girl* waterlogged ending 1.

FIGURE 3.4: *Tank Girl* waterlogged ending 2.

Water privatization happened in a rich anglophone country, Thatcher's England, but not in Australia, or Aotearoa New Zealand. While it has happened in a few US locations, a recent National Infrastructure Advisory Council report recommended revisiting public–private partnerships (Conley 2023: n.pag.; NIAC 2023: 10). Privatization *did* happen in the developing world, and our anglophone world film-derived vocabulary appears in descriptions of it. To sketch a region sucked dry by drinks bottlers, Kurt Hackbarth writes, '[t]his is not an exercise in dystopian imagination or some Mad Max spin-off: this is Monterrey, Mexico, today' (2022: n.pag.). In 1990s South America, to name a few examples: Chile sold off its water system on the advice of the Chicago Boys; Argentina privatized its water system as part of the neo-liberal turn; Bolivia's water privatization led to the Cochabomba Water War at the end of the decade (Their 2022: 156–57). And so while water privatization was not actually happening throughout the rich anglophone world where this chapter's films were produced, privatization of infrastructure was, forgive the metaphor, the water in which political discussions swam. The privatization and marketization of everything looked (and looks) increasingly likely as a solution for any problem. As a non-substitutable resource, privatized water has historically been shown to exacerbate inequality, as in the case of Cochabomba. As a non-substitutable resource in dystopian and post-apocalyptic worlds, privatized water similarly functions as not just a way to control the population and secure power but also to immiserate any rivals. Thus water, and in particular privatized water, functions in dystopian and post-apocalyptic movies as a catalyst to confront the importance of a non-privatized, perhaps democratic, water provision system to securing a life worth living in a post-dystopian and/or post-apocalyptic world, even though water privatization hasn't yet happened in their specific cultural setting.

Conclusion

Restricted access to water can make a bad situation worse. The person or institution that controls access to water enjoys the power of life and death over those who live in that area. In a dystopia, the top-down control of life includes water. The fascist state both uses the water supply system to spread a virus to cement its regime and then retains control of the water supply, providing safe drinking water for those who remain in *V for Vendetta*. Water might as well be privatized in *V for Vendetta*, as it expands the oppression toolkit to include a daily necessity that can disappear with a loss of favour. Lewis Prothero's extravagant shower not only reveals his masturbatory self-regard, but also offers a window into the luxury available to favourites, as is also seen in *Soylent Green*. Control of water after the apocalypse is not just a licence to print money but also a means to control what little recovered civilization available. *The Book of Eli*, *Mad Max Beyond Thunderdome*, and *Waterworld* all feature moments in which their heroes encounter a less than salubrious person selling water of dubious quality, showing that the necessary bonds of trust to create a stable society are tenuous. This commodification of water outside of public provision appears in situations similar to the western's generic conventions, with the wandering hero looking for a drink upon arriving in town. At a scale one step above the wandering hero entering town, in *Mad Max: Fury Road*, Immortan Joe controls access to the Citadel's water, affording him control over not just the Wretched, but also the War Boys, Mill Rats, Milk Mothers and, until they rebel, the Five Wives. Kesslee from *Tank Girl*'s Water & Power represents a suit-wearing corporate version of Immortan Joe, the executive who oversees the violent control of a desert wasteland's water.

Whether controlled by fascists or in the hands of the people, water is power. Not to indulge in the worst version of anti-fluoridation thinking, but *V for Vendetta* sees clearly that closed private control rather than open public oversight, imperfect though it may be, makes it more likely that a virus might be introduced into the water supply to eliminate large swathes of the population without the damage to buildings and infrastructure that a bomb would create. Privatization introduces the logic of competition and individualism rather than cooperation and community into the provision of something literally no one can do without. Public rather than private access to and control of water can make a bad situation somewhat better by prioritizing access to the basis for human (and kangaroo) life, providing a baseline for survival. In *The Matrix Reloaded* the people of Zion recycle their water, making it possible to have water to drink and grow their own food. In the *Hunger Games* movies, Katniss shows bravery by sneaking outside the fence to hunt, but in addition to food, District 12's water source offers a small political victory. The water pump in District 12's town square creates a sense of community for the *Hunger Games*'s oppressed. The residents of District 12 may not have universal access to water like in the Capitol, but the communal water pump represents one less thing controlled by the fascist government in the Capitol. Similarly, Imperator Furiosa cements her triumphant return to the Citadel in *Mad Max: Fury Road* by opening the water taps to everyone; making the water public offers the Wretched something like hope. Finally, the explosion of joy after *Tank Girl* breaks the hold of Water & Power generates a happy ending overflowing with rain-driven/ironically ejaculatory imagery. *Tank Girl* wrests water and power away from Water & Power and redirects it to *everyone* rather than the elite. Water creates a better post-dystopian, post-apocalyptic life when it goes to the people, for the people, by the people.

4

Food: Dystopian and Post-apocalyptic Food Systems

It's hard to start a discussion of food in dystopian and post-apocalyptic film worlds without mentioning *Soylent Green*. *Soylent Green*'s dystopian New Yorkers eat processed food in the form of the vegetable concentrates Soylent Red and Soylent Yellow, which provide them with quick energy and nutrition. On Tuesdays, they can have 'new delicious Soylent Green, the miracle food of high energy plankton gathered from the oceans of the world'. The mystery of *Soylent Green*'s plot concerns a murder. But, as E Anne Kaplan notes,

> Thorn's investigation of the murder masks the real purpose of the movie, which is not only to expose the corruption and seizure of power by the few, which is central to all the dystopian political thrillers, but to show what happens to humans and social life when resources for food, water, and power run out.
>
> (2016: 63)

To be precise, in dystopian 2022 New York/America, resources have not in fact run out, they have been made artificially scarce. The rich still have their 'hoarded food, water, and electricity resources' (Kaplan 2016: 61). The poor, on the other hand, have to generate their own electricity, queue up for water, and eat Soylent. As Thorn (Charlton Heston) discovers when he follows Sol to the suicide centre, *Soylent Green* isn't plankton. It is, I am sure you know, people.

This fear of inadvertent cannibalism shows that concerns over food remain at the heart of many dystopian and post-apocalyptic films, with food shortages, ways of addressing those shortages, and political unrest going hand in hand. In *Soylent Green* the elite produce cannibalistic foodstuffs; in *The Running Man* (Jack T. Collis 1987) the elites produce something else: culture. Though *The Running Man* has no cannibalism like *Soylent Green*, food remains a salient factor in everyday life, appearing on the edges of the frame, as finger food in the television studios. Food's appearances at the beginning and end of the film offer not hints but clear statements about food's centrality to control and resistance in everyday dystopian life.

The Running Man opens with scrolling white text on a red background that grows progressively darker as the text rolls up the screen:

> By 2017 the world economy has collapsed. Food, natural resources and oil are in short supply. A police state, divided into paramilitary zones, rules with an iron hand. Television is controlled by the state and a sadistic game show called 'The Running Man' has become the most popular program in history. All art, music and communications are censored. No dissent is tolerated and yet a small resistance movement has managed to survive underground.

As the background loses its last red tinges the final lines read, '[w]hen high-tech gladiators are not enough to suppress the people's yearning for freedom' and finally, over full black, 'more direct methods become necessary'. From the black screen there is a cut to a low angle shot of a helicopter flying past. Inside the helicopter, pilot Ben Richards (Arnold Schwarzenegger) tells control tower in a blasé manner, '[f]ood riot in progress. Approximately fifteen hundred civilians. No weapons evident'. The appearance of a food riot signals how far gone the United States is.

> Food riots in North America are all the more terrifying a prospect because they are not felt to 'belong' here; they 'belong' in countries like Indonesia, where scarcity is seen as a natural result of the land's carrying capacity or as part of some Malthusian check that limits overpopulation.
>
> (Ross 1996: 195)

When control replies, '[p]roceed with plan alpha', there is a cut to close up of Richards looking shocked, and the control tower elaborates: 'Eliminate anything moving'. Richards gets agitated. 'I said the crowd is unarmed! There are lots of women and children down there all they want is food for God's sake!' Control tower remains adamant: 'As you were Richards. Proceed with plan alpha. All rioters must be eliminated'. In a tight closeup in profile to accentuate his moral outrage, Richards says: 'To hell with you. I will not fire on helpless people'. A fight breaks out in the helicopter and in the end, Richards is overwhelmed. The turn to a black background and the invocation of 'more direct methods' calls attention not just to the violence done to the people in a dystopia, but also the root causes of what the more direct methods address: food shortages are a cause and an effect of dystopian life.

Two scenes of eating, one in *Soylent Green* and one in *The Running Man*, highlight how food operates as a shorthand for pleasure and potential escape in the dystopian imagination. In *Soylent Green*, Thorn returns home with a haul of food taken from a rich man's apartment. In their dingy dining room, a denotative set, Thorn and Sol feast on a beef and onion stew, a lettuce salad, and, for dessert, an apple (that Thorn eats in its entirety, leaving only the stem). Sol, an old man, returns to real food, and Thorn, a younger man, eats it for the first time; both can't stop smiling and laughing so great is their pleasure. In *The Running Man*, as powerful game show host Killian (real-life game show host Richard Dawson) and his producer Tony discuss what criminals to cast on the show, Killian's bodyguard Sven (Sven-Ole Thorn), napkin tucked into the collar of his tunic, eagerly eats the finger food on plates throughout the conference room, at one point pulling one more piece off the plate as the catering staff walks towards another person to serve them (Figure 4.1). While the napkin is a bit of a broad stroke, Sven's dedication to getting as much to eat as possible shows not only the boredom of being a bodyguard in a locked building, but also the importance of staying fed. That is to say, in a dystopian world, a bodyguard would not be likely to have come from the powerful class, and would know the value of a good meal. Food makes clear that Sven is, when all is said and done, one of the people. After Richards leads the resistance to a bloody victory, Killian demands that Sven fight Richards. Sven walks away rather than fight. Limited access to finger food can only buy so much loyalty.

Agricultural workers – agronomists, crop and livestock farmers, and field labourers, to name a few – undergird dystopian worlds. Food doesn't come from nowhere after all. While it is easy to imagine farms somewhere in a dystopian world, it is a little harder to imagine farms after the apocalypse, especially on

FIGURE 4.1: *The Running Man* bodyguard grabbing finger food.

the industrial scale familiar to the anglophone audience of the Hollywood, UK, Australian, and Aotearoa New Zealand films I analyse here. However, in this chapter I will show that while agricultural work occupies a key background or mediated position in dystopian films, often as an index of top-down control, in post-apocalyptic films, agriculture itself is central to creating a future, to creating a desirable, functioning civilization from the bottom up, on a more local scale. To do so, I will consider how people in dystopian and post-apocalyptic societies get their food, what constitutes food, and how the food system is organized. After a short analysis of the prevalence of agriculture in the *Divergent* series' imagination of post-apocalyptic Chicago, I will analyse the how diet, shopping and scavenging, hunting, and agriculture place food at the heart of dystopian and post-apocalyptic world-making. Such an analysis will show how food links energy, transportation, and water, and also generates waste to create a synthetic vision of how to imagine a better world in the face of dystopian oppression and/or post-apocalyptic destruction. In particular, the frequently imagined future in which urban agriculture creates the potential for settlements that draw people together, using proximity to build self-sustaining communities.

Food in sci-fi and post-apocalyptic films

Food on film is often analysed metaphorically, as a means to critique consumption, as the site where technology and the body intersect, and as the source of bodily and social pleasures. In 'Futuristic foodways: The metaphorical meaning of food in science fiction film' Laurel Forster establishes a baseline for food on film analysis, seeing 'the metaphorical meaning of food as part of the political and cultural comment made by science fiction regarding both futuristic messages and reflections on contemporary society' (2005: 253). One particular futuristic message that reflects contemporary society is that disasters are piling up on the horizon; the apocalypse in zombie movies gives us an access point to think about our own 'food apocalypse' (Newbury 2012: 91–97). The industrialized slaughter of the agribusiness-driven meat-heavy diet meets its match in the zombie apocalypse, which dispatches with the redemptive possibility of 'pastoral landscapes, farmer's markets, and organic alternatives' to extinguish with 'brutal enthusiasm all aspirations to retrieving the pastoral, the natural, or alternatives to the industrial food chain' (Newbury 2012: 97; Sublette 2016: 168). This sort of reading understands the consumption of food as the result of a series of institutional structures that stock grocery stores' shelves. On the one hand, people eat to survive, making food consumption slightly different than the conspicuous consumption of McMansions, SUVs, and haute couture. On the other, food consumption can still 'reek[] of excess or extravagance' (Sublette 2016: 168). The rich who orbit the Earth in *Elysium*, for instance, not only enjoy exclusive access to miracle-cure health care, but also to food unavailable to the poor who toil on Earth.

The oversimplified schematic of orbit-comfort terrestrial-toil in *Elysium* proves useful to think about how food on film operates as a metaphor as well as how food on film shows how technology and the body intersect. In Jean Retzinger's account, '[f]ood at once serves as our most fundamental connection to the environment (as all food represents in one form or another sun, soil, water, and seeds transformed into sustenance) and, simultaneously, illustrates our indebtedness to science and technology' (2008: 371). *Elysium* again provides a clear instance of this: those who live on Elysium live in an artificial environment that transforms pieces taken from Earth – soil, water, seeds – into their sustenance. They play at being gods from their orbit, remotely managing the Earth as a factory to maintain their station. Their debt to technology is so great that they are less 'human' than those on Earth, who have less food, but a more direct connection to its creation. In this way, the distinction between classes shows a specific instance of what Forster sees across sci-fi films: 'In both the cases of mass industrialized food production and of a society dominated by computers and technology, we can see how the grand narratives of normalcy, natural morals, and human compassion have gone awry' (2005: 253). Starting with *Elysium* and broadening to post-apocalyptic movies in general, the disappearance of technology necessitates new relationships with food, both in its consumption as well as in its production, which can mean a less technologically dependent combination of hunting, scavenging, and farming on a smaller scale.

In addition to the metaphorical meaning of food and its consumption, studies of food on film also investigate the pleasure that food can generate. In an article that takes seriously Tallahassee's obsessive quest for a Twinkie in *Zombieland*, Cammie Sublette argues that 'availability and nutrition aside, sometimes this junk-food subsistence is about more than eating to live. Sometimes, the consumption of junk-food is also about hedonistic pleasure and nostalgia' (2016: 170). For Sublette, the ideal meal – it could be a pile of Twinkies – in a zombie post-apocalypse 'is about culinary pleasure, not survival' (2016: 166). Retzinger also sees a socially informed kind of pleasure in play, noting that familiar foods can 'serve as an anchor in an altered world' and assuage anxieties (2008: 370, 374). In these moments of pleasure, nostalgia, and anxiety reduction, food itself recedes slightly. For instance, Forster notes that in the gloop-food moments in *Brazil*, *Blade Runner*, and *The Matrix*, 'food metaphorically demonstrates our loss of meaningful connections with society, and our loss of stable identities' (2005: 264). However, metaphorical readings take for granted the physicality of food as an actual thing in the film's world. At a number of points in 'The last twinkie in the universe: Culinary hedonism and nostalgia in zombie films'. Sublette offers more prosaic readings which, in their rareness and contrast to metaphorical readings, prove quite useful in reminding us how food functions in the post-apocalyptic imagination. For instance, even though Tallahassee spends *Zombieland* search for a Twinkie, Sublette notes that 'our four survivors consume so little food that it's difficult to fathom how they are, in fact, surviving' (2016: 174). Sublette offers three possible explanations for Jim's headache and distaste for the junk-food at hand at the beginning of *28 Days Later*, none of them metaphorical: too much sugar (in-film), a half-starving person would want protein-rich and fatty foods (food psychologist), and, finally, '[p]erhaps a better explanation for Jim's headache and food avoidance, though, is that he has just awakened from one trauma, a month-long coma, into an arguably worse trauma – his discovery that London has been decimated by some unknown cause' (Sublette 2016: 170–71). The presence of food and meals and foodways can reveal the metaphorical and ideological contours of post-apocalyptic films and the cultures that produce them, as Retzinger, Baron, Forster, Cawley, and dozens of others ably show. Even before we consider food consumption, the literal presence of food generated by its production can provide access to a mundane but fruitful understanding of post-apocalyptic films' vision for what a liveable future might look and behave.

Such a literal-minded approach to food on film has to get the facts right, reading the corners of the frame carefully to see how food gets into bellies. It's hard to write about food in a world gone to hell without mentioning *Soylent Green*, an instructive case for how critics read the literal fact of Soylent Green. Diarmuid Cawley writes that in post-apocalyptic films, '[p]erhaps most famously of all, *Soylent Green*, a film far ahead of its time, depicts a world in which an overpopulated planet mainly survives on a dubious plankton-based high-energy supplement produced and controlled by the Soylent Corporation' (2017: n.pag.). Retzinger's foundational article makes much the same claim, noting '[t]he mass of humanity subsists on a mysterious diet of soylent green' (2008: 373). This is incorrect; the 40 million people of New York are not surviving on Soylent Green. For the most part they have been eating soylent red and yellow, the 'high-energy vegetable concentrate'. When Thorn turns on the TV at the beginning of the film, the newscaster reads an ad on air, and red and yellow are the first things mentioned. Soylent Green is *new*, 'the miracle food of high energy plankton gathered from the oceans of the world […] Remember, Tuesday is Soylent Green day'. Soylent Green comes once a week, a perverse version of fish on Friday. I nit-pick here because the *other* colours of Soylent are the everyday food in the background that deserves attention to understand the world in greater detail.

To be literal-minded in my analyses of food as it appears in dystopian and post-apocalyptic movies will provide a clearer vision of the quotidian in those worlds as imagined and navigated on film. 'From farm to table' is an ideology; literally going from farm to table entails a practical system operating in the background, the film's production design functioning like decoration, designed and maintained by people.

The political economy of post-apocalyptic Chicago

The *Divergent* series imagines a dystopian post-apocalyptic world in which nearly every resident of Chicago is sorted into one of five groups: Dauntless, Amity, Erudite, Abnegation and Candor. The unlucky few belong to a caste of untouchables – the Factionless – and a still-smaller group combines the features of those five groups – the titular Divergent. These groups form the basis for a society that provides full employment based on group membership. For the most part, Abnegation run the government. Dauntless are cops and military. Candor form the judicial system. Erudite appear to ensure the technological society continues (including, one hopes the planning and maintenance of the city's infrastructure). The Factionless are small in number and represented as untouchable, so they couldn't make up a working class to service the city or a lumpenproletariat. The faction that does the most – that actually *produces* – is Amity. This more detailed vision of agriculture shows how practically useless white-collar office-worker skills would be in the post-apocalypse than most other films. However, the villains in many post-apocalyptic films come from white-collar work: General Bethlehem (*The Postman*) was a Xerox salesman; Carnegie (*The Book of Eli*) was a white-collar worker. In dystopian and post-apocalyptic movies, meritocratic professional managerial class types are the villains of their fictional worlds because they're the villains of our world *now*. While Abnegation appears to do some artisanal food processing, they depend on Amity's labour in an agricultural sector that includes large-scale grain farms, market farms, and something like a clothes production industry that services the entire city of Chicago.

Perhaps *Divergent*'s Erudites are agronomists in a rigidly maintained system, similar to those who worked Eastern Bloc countries during the twentieth century, or planners in the mould of Leonid Vitalevich Kantorovich in Francis Spufford's *Red Plenty*. In *Red Hangover: Legacies of Twentieth-Century Communism*, Kristen Ghodsee tells the story of finding evidence of utopian planning in communist-era archival folders in a quasi-dystopian Sofia. Passing a public park trash bin, she sees a collection of files which turn out to be the personnel file of Andrei Andreev. The files provide a picture of Andreev's work in the Bulgarian Ministry of Agriculture and Food Production:

> During the time of the creation of the vegetable belt around Sofia city, I was appointed as a specialist in vegetable production in the agricultural cooperative in the village of

> Kostinbrod. In 1963, I was appointed as the chief agronomist in the same cooperative [...] I have been actively involved in politics as an agricultural specialist working for twenty-three years, of which thirteen years were spent working with Polish vegetable crop production and ten years were spent in the production of greenhouse vegetables. As a specialist I have worked faithfully, using all my knowledge and skills to increase agricultural production.
>
> (Ghodsee 2017: 16)

As Ghodsee summarizes the context for Andreev's work,

> Under communism, Bulgaria was a planned economy, meaning that the state owned and operated a vast majority of the agricultural sector. The Ministry of Agriculture and Food Production coordinated with central planners to feed the Bulgarian population; no private farmers sold produce at prices determined by the fluctuations of supply and demand. The government built huge greenhouses to keep the vegetable supply constant throughout the year, and sold domestically produced vegetables at fixed and subsidized prices. Mr. Andreev oversaw the daily operation of these massive, indoor vegetable farms.
>
> (2017: 17)

The first images of agriculture in *Divergent* do not greatly resemble the intensive greenhouse production of Andreev's autobiography. Rather, in one long shot huge grain fields stretch out to the horizon and beyond; it is Illinois, after all (Figure 4.2). In another image a labour-intensive work crew seems to be harvesting some kind of cabbage or kale. In *Insurgent*, the second film in the series, Tris hides out on a smaller-scale farm which produces fruit and vegetables. We see about twenty farm workers among a few rows of shoulder-high plants, weeding and picking (Figure 4.3). Whereas the workers in *Divergent* loaded their cabbages next to a mechanical tractor to transport them, the smaller *Insurgent* farm uses horse-drawn carts to carry goods to a train for shipping into the city. In one of the last images of the farm in *Insurgent*, an overhead shot follows Tris and her comrades as they flee their pursuers. On the edge of the image, a few polytunnels appear. Not quite Bulgarian greenhouses, but more controlled climate spaces for special vegetables and fruit, the sort of thing an Erudite could design and monitor from afar, leaving its tending to an Amity (*Insurgent* and *Allegiant*, the third film in the series, do not return to Amity-as-farmers for generic reasons: Dauntless are action heroes. The key to resolving an action movie trilogy is fighting, not farming.). Colin Tudge could well be describing the agricultural world of *Divergent* in *So Shall We Reap: What's Gone Wrong with the World's Food – And How to Fix It* when he writes,

FIGURE 4.2: *Divergent* Amity farm labour.

FIGURE 4.3: *Insurgent* agriculture.

> [t]he world could do with a great deal more horticulture. In general horticulture focuses on high-value crops that are nutritionally highly desirable (like tomatoes and capsicums) yet are not 'staples': that is, they are not key suppliers of energy and protein, as cereals and pulses are.
>
> (2004: 71)

Seen in terms of its imagination of collectivized agriculture, the *Divergent* series remains post-apocalyptic, but less dystopian. This connection of the *Divergent* series' vision of agriculture and the Eastern Bloc is less fanciful when we consider that the farms in *Divergent* are next to an electrified border wall that surrounds post-apocalyptic Chicago, and that the wall is played by the former Soviet Duga radar fence in Ukraine. The *Divergent* series, it seems, goes back to the future by fusing Russia's preindustrial serfs with the Soviet Union's mechanized collective farms to imagine a self-sustaining post-apocalyptic outpost.

Divergent and *Insurgent* stand out in their foregrounding of agriculture and agricultural workers as significant to world-building a dystopian post-apocalyptic world. Most other dystopian and post-apocalyptic movies engage not with agriculture and agricultural workers, but with food itself. After analysing how people in dystopian and post-apocalyptic societies get their food, what constitutes food, and how the food system is organized, I will turn back to agricultural work as it appears on the edges of the frame to show how food helps to plot a way back to civilization.

From farm to table: The dystopian diet

Part of a dystopia is not only lack of food, but also control over and restrictions on food. Sometimes food is available, but at a severe social cost. *Blade Runner 2049* goes back to the future, both in the form of an automat that offers what looks like an incredible range of choices, as well as in its predecessor's Orientalist vision of east Asian culture. Then again, most of California is a desiccated landscape, which takes the shine off of a nice bowl of ramen. The dinners in *The Purge: Anarchy* show comforting family meals in humble dining rooms, but under the threat of a state-sanctioned night of murderous mayhem. A similar threat of violence hangs over the home-cooked meal the mercenary Toorop cooks for himself in the opening scenes of *Babylon AD*. More often in a dystopia, you are likely to have greatly limited options or to go hungry most of the time; in the post-apocalypse you are starving most of the time and when there is something to eat, it's usually not something you would have plucked off the shelf in the beforetimes. Lack of food and dietary restrictions are often represented as communal dining in cafeteria-style mess halls. Winston wakes up one morning to hear the news that 'improved diet has been responsible for a dramatic decrease in rickets', but Oceania's diet in *1984* is a gross grey glop ladled out in an equally drab cafeteria setting. In *The Handmaid's Tale*, an expressive set design shows the handmaids housed in a dormitory prison setting where they take their meals and are issued their medication in a cafeteria. Similarly, the donors in *Never Let Me Go* are fed a controlled diet to keep them healthy enough to donate good organs over multiple surgeries. *Fortress* features a location-appropriate chow line in its underground prison. Tris and her comrades join their Amity hosts in an ersatz cafeteria line in *Insurgent*. And when Tris and Four leave Chicago in *Allegiant*, they are taken in at the Genetic Department and given no special treatment: they eat in a military mess hall-like setting.

In the immediate aftermath of *World War Z*'s zombie explosion (when the world is not quite *post*-apocalyptic) survivors eat in a chow line on the *USS Argus*, ceding civilian life to the logistical knowhow and firepower of the military. Finally, in *The Island* meals are controlled via an internet of things – represented as a toilet that provides instant urine tests – that monitors the residents and relays the results to the island's cafeteria workers

For the residents of *The Island*, food options are restricted according to current health status. The choices come out of standard American breakfast options. Because of his test results one morning, Lincoln Six Echo can have 'fruit, oatmeal, or any type of bran', according to cafeteria worker, but 'no bacon, no eggs over easy, no sausage'. On the other hand, Jordan Two Delta who is already cleared for 'powdered eggs, dried fruit and yogurt', sweet-talks the cafeteria worker into some bacon. In *The Island*'s world, a greying and highly unequal population makes America dystopian, not the food. In *Never Let Me Go* the donor children have standard cafeteria food, with fruit and veg and milk and medications, although when the donors leave for their brief pre-donation lives in the real world, their diets change drastically. Kathy, Tommy, and Ruth tuck into the much less healthy sausage, eggs, and chips with Chrissie and Rodney soon after starting their lives away from Hailsham. In the *Divergent* movies, food is bountiful at the Amity farm where Tris and friends hide out, but choice is restricted along the lines of what their agriculture can provide. The most utilitarian approach to food and control appears in *Judge Dredd*, during an early visit to a mega-tower block. A machine/robot that looks like a repurposed streetsweeper rolls down the hall, a recorded voice repeating 'recycled food. Good for the environment. OK for you'. To add to the scene's ironic punch, a bit of product placement – a Coors sign – appears on the top of the recycled food machine. The recycled food won't kill you. That's good enough, right? Throughout these films, food mediates ideas of social control and a dystopian concern over public health through a healthy, regimented diet.

Regardless of how healthy it is, most dystopian movies feature moments in which characters eat something from the food pyramid choices of meat, fruit and vegetables, starches, and fat, oil, and sugar. The distance between late twentieth- and early twenty-first-century versions and availability of those foods and how they appear on screen often indicates just how far gone the dystopian/post-apocalyptic world is. Some movie dystopias are close to the worlds from which they emerge. *The First Purge* shows a family breakfast with eggs; *Isle of Dogs* shows people making and eating sushi. Often food offers an index of decline. For instance, in *1984* Winston has a naked lunch moment while staring at a pink glob on his spoon. His lunchmate, the convinced Ingsoc member Parsons says, 'do you know, I don't think there is a single piece of meat in this stew. Looks like meat. Tastes like meat. Isn't meat at all'. Unlike Winston, who sees the pink glob as the poverty of his situation, Parsons appears to be quite satisfied with the illusion of meat/freedom. A similar kind of illusory meat appears at the restaurant where Sam Lowry (Jonathan Pryce) has lunch with his mother in *Brazil*. In an overhead shot, we see Sam look down a plate covered in pink goo; another plate holds a pile of green glop. The pink is steak and the green veal; meat is available, but only as an artificial and alienating experience. That is to say, *1984* and *Brazil* show broken-down versions of their contemporary culture in their set design and use the finer-grained details of their food to show the impoverishment of those worlds' sensory experience. Neither society can muster something so satisfying as a beef-steak, something that an English person would be used to as standard-issue food, as the United Kingdom was in the 1980s one of the meat-eatingest countries in the world (Ritchie 2019: n.pag.). In fact, it is often easy to tell who has it good in a dystopia by who eats meat. For example, *Elysium*'s mercenary killer Kurgan enjoys a rooftop BBQ while he awaits orders from the elites on Elysium, cooking up what looks like an entire side of beef for himself. One thing that makes life in the *Hunger Games* series' District 12 bearable and survivable for Katniss and the Everdeen family is the game fowl that Katniss hunts to supplement otherwise meagre diet. In *Minority Report*, cop John Anderton fries eight burgers without any evidence there are eight people present in his. This resembles eating habits near the film's 2002 American release (US Department of Agriculture 1999). The availability of a meat-heavy diet under an all-encompassing surveillance regime in *Minority Report* shows that the material conditions of dietary scarcity are not the only thing that can create dystopias. But food is a sure route to the control of the populace's everyday life and ability to resist their conditions.

Living in a dystopia makes it a little harder to get five servings a day of fruit and vegetable, and the appearance of vegetables often signifies along lines similar to the appearance of meat. For instance, in *Never Let Me Go* a man delivers a crate of fruit and veg to the recently graduated donors living on The Farm. Delivering fruit and veg to a farm hints at a low-grade surveillance that signals the donors' lives and health remain important to the extent that someone else needs them to stay healthy. Is the deliveryman *only* a deliveryman? Later on, after one of Ruth's surgeries, Kathy keeps an orange aside as something Ruth can look forward to after another organ is harvested. Sam keeps a large jar of pickled something or other in his fridge in *Brazil*, and like much of the food in the film, it is hard to say exactly what it is – onions? eggs? In the *Divergent* series, a vegetarian diet predominates; the Abnegation faction are avowedly ethical vegans. A domestic scene in *Divergent* sees Beatrice cutting up cabbage, onion, celery, parsnip, and carrot as the family prepares dinner. It appears that Amity are also vegans. Their potluck family-style meal in *Insurgent* has lots of fruit and veg in evidence: corn cobs, lettuce, carrots, onions, tomatoes, apples, drying herbs, and bottles of juice.

Johanna (Octavia Spencer) does not decorate her barn-office with pictures but rather stores jars of dried spices. In *The Handmaid's Tale*, when the Commander (Robert Duvall) tries to show Kate (Natasha Richardson) some affection early after her arrival, he shares strawberries with her. While Volker Schlöndorff uses close-ups of the strawberries to draw attention to the fruit's symbolism and their mediation of Commander and Kate's relationship – a red fruit with all those seeds – *Rollerball* art director Robert Laing places a bowl of apples on the edge of the frame of a long shot of Jonathan's (James Caan) television room. The imbalance of the shot – on the left side three smaller screens in a line above a large one, in the middle Jonathan looking at the screens, to the right a window and the bowl of fruit – directs attention to the corporate mediation of *Rollerball*'s world, but leaves the window and fruit visible, a latent bit of potential. A similar opposition appears in *Silent Running* (Francisco Lombardo 1972) in two opposing shots, one of the processed packaged food the crew eats and one of Freeman Lowell with lettuce and other vegetables he's grown himself. These examples indicate how, in dystopic films, fruit and vegetables represent not the power of meat, but instead something optimistic and connected to a better world by virtue of their status as 'real food' connected to the land.

The appearance of bread and sweets in dystopian movies also often carries positive associations. In *1984* Julia brings the almost unbearably decadent bread and jam to one of her illicit meetings with Winston. When the young donors graduate from Hailsham in *Never Let Me Go*, their first tastes of freedom are accompanied by frequent toast and jam sandwiches. Evie (Natalie Portman), in *V for Vendetta*, breakfasts on egg in toast thanks to both V (Hugo Weaving) and Dietrich (Stephen Fry). The Commander's kitchen in *The Handmaid's Tale* shows a group of women making bread, the large workforce testament to his importance and the breadmaking a testament to the bread it takes to keep Gilead's population at least fed (neither bread and roses nor bread and circuses, but rather bread and public executions keep the population quiescent). Sweets are consistently connected to brief moments of joy and excitement in dystopian life. In addition to oranges, Kathy also finds some dark chocolate for Ruth (Keira Knightley) for after her surgery. Winston fondly recalls stealing chocolate as a young boy and Julia brings not only jam to their meetings, but also real sugar. The pleasure jam brings to *Soylent Green*'s Martha (Paula Kelly) is so great that she forgets to hide her spoon covered in it when Thorn shows up to search her apartment. Even in the simulated world of *The Matrix*, the Oracle (Gloria Foster) bakes cookies, a treat and a comfort before the inevitable battle with Mr Smith (Hugo Weaving) that Neo must have.

Dystopian diets hold together body, if not spirit; moments of indulgence accompany pleasure and possibility. If chow lines restrict food choice to the point of rendering people mere cogs in the dystopian machine, then the search for food that can combine taste and nutrition and offer a moment of pleasure and control that may not topple the dystopian order, but at least offer a respite. In this way, the happy ending of a square meal at a family picnic at the end of *The Hunger Games: Mockingjay, Part 2* not only reifies the heteronormative family and the marriage plot, but also signals that Katniss most enjoys her personal victories over President Snow and President Coin at mealtime.

The post-apocalyptic diet

Rather than the dystopian world's relative closeness to the traditional food pyramid of farmed meat, fresh fruit and vegetables, starch, and sweets and oil, the post-apocalyptic world offers preserved or hunted meat; preserved, processed, or picked by luck fruit and vegetables. Sometimes the options are worse. It can be hard to find a good meal in the post-apocalypse, so much so that diet in the post-apocalypse can often look like non-food. Even when food is plentiful, as in the endlessly regenerative buffet in *WALL-E*, it's not good for you. And if too much food and soda doesn't kill you, sometimes people just starve, as they do in *Oblivion* after the aliens arrive. In the jumbled timeline of *The Terminator*, Kyle Reese (Michael Biehn) tells Sarah Connor (Linda Hamilton) that in the future the remaining humans are starving. A flashforward then shows the remaining humans eating some kind of runny, greasy glop. Because *Robocop* is a satirical dystopia, the paste that fuels Robocop is not an unpalatable greasy sludge as it is in *The Terminator*, but rather something closer to baby food, which Omni Consumer Products executive Morton (Miguel Ferrer) notes when he sneaks a taste. The soft and gloppy prison chow that the band of survivors has to eat in *Resident Evil: Afterlife* makes the radio broadcast of New Arcadia's promise of 'safety and security, food and shelter' more difficult to pass up, leading them to literally sail into the unknown in search of that promise. The apes conscripted for labour in *War for the Planet of the Apes* strike to demand food and water. The Colonel (Woody Harrelson) meets their demand, but offers only a trough of grain, with buckets for the apes to carry it away. This management decision to treat food as a weapon against its conscripted workers leads to a violent uprising. That is to say, food is very serious business in post-apocalyptic worlds.

In *The Matrix*, the motivation behind Cypher selling out his fellow *Nebuchadnezzar* shipmates to the machines is that he is tired 'of being cold, of eating the same goop every day'. Even though he knows it is imaginary, Cypher prefers the illusory steak and wine the machines reward him with to the goop that looks like runny oatmeal. The goop is the visual opposite of the kung fu dojo Neo and

Morpheus train in. Whereas the dojo is a shared illusion that allows Neo to learn at a frightening cyborg pace, the food goop – 'a single-cell protein combined with synthetic aminos, vitamins, and minerals. Everything the body needs' – is the dirty material world in which their bodies still require sustenance. The idea of a preference for illusory food returns in a more aestheticized form in *The Matrix Reloaded*, in which a piece of cake is not only a computer program, but also described as poetry, although Zion has plentiful and diverse food available when Neo arrives. The more widespread non-food in the *Matrix* series appears as the amniotic sac the battery people are kept in. The same artificial womb imagery also appears in *Resident Evil: Extinction*'s warehouse of Alice clones and the dystopian *The Island*, all elaborately embellished sets that show an insidiously instrumental production of people on an industrial scale.

Meat remains an important part of the post-apocalyptic diet, even after we look beyond the amount of human meat that zombies consume and the one vegan in the post-apocalypse, *Zombieland Double Tap*'s Madison. Post-apocalyptic meat frequently takes the form of something not found in the familiar western meat choices of beef, chicken, fish, lamb, pork, and veal. These more familiar meats do appear. For instance, in the 1978 *Dawn of the Dead* the survivors eat preserved, salty meats like SPAM and salami, in *I Am Legend* Neville has bacon in his kitchen, and in *Waterworld* the Mariner catches and grills a massive fish (he eats the eyeballs raw). There are train cars dedicated to fish – a beautifully constructed piece of artifice – as well as beef and chicken in *Snowpiercer*. In terms of less common meats, some residents of an atoll in *Waterworld* have a shark butchery. In *The Road Warrior*, Max (Mel Gibson) eats dog food, and later on Gyroman fights with Max's dog over a snake they both want to eat. Max (Tom Hardy) eats a live two-headed lizard in *Mad Max: Fury Road*. The Mad Max series avoids the Australian bush tucker like kangaroo, bunya nuts, and grubs, perhaps as a way to show the continued ignorance of Indigenous people or, perhaps, their total disappearance (I will pick up this thread in the book's conclusion). And while *Dawn of the Dead* and *The Quiet Earth*'s survivors also find a tin of caviar as a token of the beforetimes plenty, Eli resorts to the less frequently eaten cat meat in *The Book of Eli*. Rather than human flesh, *The Girl with All the Gifts* Melanie (Sennia Nanua) is fed a ration of maggots. Perhaps most famously in recent post-apocalyptic movies, the lower-class residents of *Snowpiercer*'s train eat protein bars made out of bugs. In the United States, the Food and Drug Administration allows an 'average of 60 or more aphids and/or thrips and/or mites per 100 grams' (2018: n.pag.), and eating bugs is not exactly unheard of in the world. Chapulines – roasted grasshoppers – are part of Mexican cooking, and the Hokitika Wildfoods Festival has frequently included bugs in its offerings. All the same, it seems that the processed-bug protein bar, like dog food and cat meat, is intended to generate queasiness in the audience, a visceral reaction to the lengths post-apocalyptic survivors must go to eat.

While the necessities of post-apocalypse lead to a greater variety in survivors' meat consumption diet, fruit and vegetable choices seem to be slightly more limited. The various *Planet of the Apes* films, from *Planet of the Apes* (1968) through *War for the Planet of the Apes* (2017), find room for fruit and vegetables, both for their human and ape characters. In the first *Planet of the Apes*, as the soldiers explore the planet they have crash-landed on, they find some melons, leading one to quip, 'blessed are the vegetarians'. In the sequel, *Beneath the Planet of the Apes*, Brent eats an apple during a conversation with the human-friendly Cornelius. In the most recent series, the Colonel eats an apple during his negotiations with Caesar. While apples would probably still be plentiful in the Pacific Northwest, the lack of food available for the ape slaves indicates that food is in limited supply, making an apple proof of the Colonel's power and importance. Apes aligned with the more conciliatory Caesar are shown eating fruit and vegetable during a scene at the ape settlement in *Dawn of the Planet of the Apes*. At a party in *Aeon Flux*'s post-apocalyptic planned city of Bregna, people carry around boxes of fruit that they take from large bowls placed throughout the room, including pears, grapes, and more exotic fruit like persimmon and dragon fruit. The apocalypse is only a few days old when Zac Hobson eats fresh fruit in *The Quiet Earth*, but the apocalypse is much further in the rear view mirror for Neville in *I Am Legend* and he still enjoys fresh fruit – he has a bowl of pears in his kitchen, likely picked from backyards or Central Park – and fresh corn. The city of Zion in *The Matrix Reloaded* has fruit when Neo and his friends arrive. Finally, because the world is almost entirely covered in water, *Waterworld*'s Mariner knows the danger scurvy poses to sailors; he carries a miniature lime tree and tomato plant on his catamaran for vitamin C. The limes are a valuable commodity – the Mariner kills a man in revenge for stealing his limes. *The Postman* was widely criticized for its old-fashioned mawkishness, and one token of its old-fashioned nature is the presence of canning and preserving as a way for the people of post-apocalyptic Oregon to have fruit and vegetables through the winter. The post-apocalyptic problem of finding edible fruit and vegetables – something essential to surviving, staying healthy, and even having some mealtime pleasure – makes a comic appearance in the self-aware *Zombieland Double Tap*, which makes Madison, a vegan, a figure of mockery, treating her continued survival somewhat contemptuously.

Finally, whereas bread and jam and sugar and oil appear with some regularity in dystopian movies, they are much less common in post-apocalyptic ones. The menu in *Dawn of the Dead* features some bread, cheese fondue, spices, coffee, and candy, all thanks to how recently the zombies had appeared. When Neo visits the Oracle's kitchen, she has just baked some cookies, but this kitchen is part of the matrix, and the cookies are not, strictly speaking, real. A visceral instance of a small part of the food pyramid taking on added importance appears in *The Book of Eli* when Eli uses the fat he renders off a cat not only as a food oil, but also as a moisturizer. While Eli may have learned to process the resources at hand to survive, the frustrations and pain of post-apocalyptic life are exacerbated by the unprocessed nature of the food on offer. On these terms, the Twinkies that Tallahassee seeks throughout *Zombieland* form the constitutive absence of post-apocalyptic life. A gloriously sweet and empty Twinkie, with its almost infinite shelf life, represents the American Dream that the apocalypse proved false.

Grocery shopping in a dystopia and grocery shopping after the apocalypse

Now that I have outlined what people eat in dystopian and post-apocalyptic movies, let's look at how they get their food. In a dystopia there are still shops. They may be restricted in what they have, but there's food on the shelves. For now. The fascist England of *V for Vendetta* has shops, and Ruth, whose story V uses to convert Evie to his cause, is to have been taken away when she was buying food. Gilead in *The Handmaid's Tale*, another fascist nation, also has shops, which use scanner tokens for what appears to be a restricted but familiar set of choices: signage points to fruit and vegetable, grains, and milk; eggs, apples, oranges, and lemons appear in shots of the handmaids shopping; and a roll of butcher paper indicates that there is some meat available as well. Food coupons also appear in *Soylent Green*, as an alternative to cash. Much like getting more in trade than in cash when reselling a book at a second-hand shop, a woman is given the option of 200 cash or 250 in food coupons. A different form of shop – the open-air market – appears in *Babylon AD*, establishing the film's grimy, used future aesthetic. And while a shop never appears in the films, the frequent appearance of a logistics system in *Divergent* and *Insurgent* seems to point to shops or at least distribution centres. For instance, the Amity farmers load crops onto a train, implying a central processing centre in the city.

To get something good to eat, scavenging for food is one of the key generic conventions of post-apocalyptic and zombie films. As I have noted elsewhere, finding food is one of the three main occupations of most post-apocalyptic zombie movies (Long 2016a). Scavenging is played joyously in *28 Days Later*, and as an everyday job in *Land of the Dead*. *Zombieland* takes place early in the apocalypse, so the Blaine's grocery is still well stocked, making it an ideal location for a joyous stocking-up scene. Also taking place early in the apocalypse, Romero's *Dawn of the Dead* first treats scavenging as joyous, then as the days pass an everyday experience, and finally as something stultifying. Going 'shopping' has become just another chore for Neville in *The Omega Man*; his shock at meeting Lisa (Rosalind Cash) in the shop shows how habituated he has become to total access. Three years into post-apocalyptic life, *I Am Legend* finds Neville past the period of joyful scavenging; but unlike his *The Omega Man* predecessor, he meticulously plans his excursions to former residences, marking off places on his map of the city to ensure his continued survival. In the first rush of the zombie apocalypse, people in *World War Z* stock up at grocery stores and also load up at pharmacies, as they also do in *Warm Bodies*. This broader vision of scavenging for both food and medicine comes up in the dialogue in *Resident Evil: Extinction*, in which 'hitting a big city' to resupply means looking for anything that may improve survival odds, in particular food and medicine as well as fuel for vehicles. Away from the city, the ship stranded offshore at the end of *The Road* shows that the last vestiges of pre-apocalypse global shipping are still available, but dangerous to reach. Billy J. Stratton argues that

> Our collective inability to make sense of the gravity of the situation defines the reality in which the man and the boy find themselves entrapped – mere scavengers dependent on the detritus of a lost world of excess and waste – guided by a map severed from its moorings and leading them along a road to nowhere.
>
> (2014: 102)

The variety of things shipped together in the age of container shipping mean that the ship could have *Cast Away*'s (Rick Carter 2000) inedible VHS tapes, divorce papers, black and leopard print dress, ice skates and volleyball, or it could have imported foods like cured meats (we never see what the man brought back from the ship in *The Road*). The cast away bits of that 'lost world of excess and waste' are all that keep them in the condition of bare life, fending off starvation.

Scavenging comes with its own set of dangers, as post-apocalyptic shops are not only appealing to other survivors, who may not value other human lives too dearly, but also they are dark and likely to hide non-human predators. Zombies have learned, in *The Girl with All the Gifts*, that scavenging humans can be baited into shops where narrow aisles make them easy prey. In the opening montage to *The Road Warrior*, voice-over narration establishes that 'only those mobile enough to scavenge' survived. Mobility and scavenging as the keys to survival go hand in hand. The on-foot scavenging that takes up the entirety of *The Road* shows that once the man is no longer mobile – an arrow wound significantly restricts his mobility – he dies. Scavenging in *The Road* shows them scraping subsistence of what remains from a dead world. All that remains is carrion and once the corpse is picked clean what can remain when everything is already dead? But sometimes scavenging of a sort offers evidence of the possible return of civilization. The food drop in the post-apocalyptic prison of *Escape from New York* shows an orderly group of people waiting for whatever pallet of food awaits them. Similarly, in *28 Weeks Later*, the presence of pallets of aid – much of it likely to be food – shows that the Green Zone is reclaiming London from the zombie hordes.

All of this scavenging leads to a common image across such movies: SPAM and military ready-to-eat rations (MREs). Both *Land of the Dead* and *Waterworld* have multiple shots in which SPAM tins offer evidence of the limited diet for survivors (SPAM gets changed into the fictional brand SMEAT in *Waterworld*). SPAM tins and MREs appear across Romero's *Dawn of the Dead* and *Day of the Dead*, as well as in *War for the Planet of the Apes*. Beyond SPAM and MREs, the post-apocalyptic pantry often appears as almost entirely composed of food tins. Neville's lavishly appointed house in *The Omega Man* not only has a well-stocked wine cellar, but also a pantry stocked floor to ceiling with tins. The 2007 Neville of *I Am Legend* also stocks up, with at least three tin-stocked pantries in his Manhattan home-lab. The bomb shelter the man and boy find in *The Road* makes good on the Cold War promise of a redoubt against the end of the world fuelled by tinned food, if only for a short, gorging period. Julie lives on the stockpile of airline snacks and food court fruit cocktail tins available at the airport she briefly lives in with R in *Warm Bodies*. The most realistically stocked post-apocalyptic pantry appears in *Zombieland*. Bill Murray's pantry is stocked with a hodgepodge of olive oil, hot sauce, honey, mustard, and flour. He does, however, retain a supply of popcorn for his home theatre.

In all of their scavenging, post-apocalyptic survivors tend to depend on tinned food. So much dumpster diving would seem to pose some health dangers, as dented tins are often reputed to be susceptible to botulism. John Hoffman, the author of *The Art & Science of Dumpster Diving*, dismisses such fear mongering. 'So long as the can isn't punctured, it is safe'. He elaborates:

> Think about this: many cans are made with invisible imperfections. Why aren't people dropping dead left and right? What is the difference between one large dent and the *hundreds* of microdents inflicted on the innocent can as it travels? And what about the 'flexible cans' in army MREs? Those things are treated brutally before soldiers eat them months or years later. They *should* be deadly, but they're not. The whole 'dented can' theory is bull.
>
> (Hoffman 1993: 79)

Hoffman may be onto something, because post-apocalyptic survivors base their diet on scavenged, often unlabelled tins of uncertain vintage and yet their main worries are zombies and infection, not food poisoning. Max shares a tin of

Dinki-Di dog food with his dog in *The Road Warrior*. In *The Book of Eli*, breakfast comes out of tins. In *A Boy and His Dog*, Vic relies on tins of food to feed himself and his telepathic dog Blood. *Resident Evil: Extinction* has fun with the generic convention of the mysterious food tin, with Otto predicting the contents of unlabelled tins. He tells one kid, '[c]at food. Just kidding. It's pork and beans', and correctly identifies a tin not just as soup, but as cream of mushroom soup. 'Just one of my skills', he says, adding that, 'it's a dying art, unfortunately. This is the last of it' as he hands out the last tin. That is to say, to adapt what someone once sort of said, the problem with scavenging after the apocalypse is that while it may be safe to eat food well past the expiration date stamped on the tin, eventually you run out of other people's groceries.

The hunted becomes a hunter

In the options of shop and scavenge, the food is already there. Shopping in a dystopian world sacrifices control; elites can elect to starve you, as in *The Running Man*, or make you become an accidental cannibal, as in *Soylent Green*. And scavenging will at some point exhaust the available resources. Hunting, on the other hand, exists in a world of greater plenty, one of self-sufficiency familiar in survivalist and prepper rhetoric. The importance of control to dystopian regimes may explain why hunting rarely appears in dystopian movies. In *The Hunger Games*, Katniss is effectively a poacher when she goes out hunting. Later on, the authorities look the other way when she goes hunting, thanks to her position as a Hunger Games winner, and she can feel a modicum of control and normalcy by bringing game fowl home for dinner in *The Hunger Games: Mockingjay, Part 2*.

After the apocalypse, going about armed at all times functions not only as self-defence, but also as readiness for food-gathering. The *I Am Legend* Neville keeps a rifle in his Mustang so that when he sees a herd of deer during his drive through Manhattan he can leap out and supplement his pantry full of tins with venison. Amongst all of the traps around his home in *The Road Warrior*, Gyro-man has a snare that catches a snake, which must be good eating, as Max's dog is willing to fight for it. A later version of Max in *Mad Max: Fury Road* shows how well-adapted he is to his environment. He catches and eats a small – and quick – two-headed lizard. And Eli is introduced in *The Book of Eli* in mid-hunt. He ends up bagging a cat as food, and he uses some of the cat meat as a lure for mice he hopes to catch in a repurposed food tin, showing the intertwined survival skills needed in the wasteland. Cannibals hunt people, either by ambush or by subterfuge in *The Road* and *The Book of Eli*. Humans are not the only creatures struggling for survival. Zombies must hunt people to eat them, usually their brains.

Though he has some success at scavenging, at the end of *A Boy and His Dog* Vic kills the woman who saved him, Quilla June Holmes, so his dog Blood can eat and survive. The zombies in *The Girl with All the Gifts* use tins outside of a shop as a kind of lure for their human prey. Even apes get into hunting – the gorillas go human hunting in *Planet of the Apes* (1968), but they don't eat the humans; their approach resembles English fox hunts, right down to the trophy pictures. And with the establishment of their forest city, the apes in *Dawn of the Planet of the Apes* hunt elk and go spear fishing. In all of these cases of hunting, the hunters feed themselves, hone their skill with planning and weapons, and retain their position high on the food chain, all of which are essential to survival.

Return to agriculture

Getting by on scavenged food will only take survivors so far. Hunting, even when successful, requires a great deal of effort and time. If a dystopian society is to change and post-apocalyptic survivors are to rebuild society, where will the food come from once the tins run out? Dystopian movies offer momentary visions of agriculture. Sometimes agriculture is not for food production. The mass cultivation in *A Scanner Darkly* is for the drugs that are destroying society, not food. A District 11 cotton field – rather than a field of grain, for instance – appears in *The Hunger Games: Catching Fire*, but the potential for rebirth growing crops represents appears in *The Hunger Games: Mockingjay, Part 2* when Katniss starts a garden (Districts 9, 10, and 11 are the agricultural districts. That District 11, identified with its African American tribute Rue, would be represented by cotton fields rather than food crops seems in bad taste). Two England-set films, *Never Let Me Go* and *Children of Men*, both use farms as settings. In *Never Let Me Go* Tommy, Ruth, and Kathy leave Hailsham school for Cottage Farm, though we never see any cultivation; Kathy later stops by a farm field that has just started to grow, though her access to the field is prevented by a barbed wire fence dotted with torn and decaying plastic bags, showing that life and growth remain off limits to her and other donors. In *Children of Men* Theo and Kee flee London for a small-scale dairy farm, a reminder that some animals can still reproduce. Farming also shows that even the likely end of human civilization cannot dislodge capitalism; *Children of Men*'s shots of burning cow carcasses call to mind the food that goes uneaten as spoilage at the best of times, in the expected 30–40 per cent of wastage in the United States and the United Kingdom, and in the unexpected case of millions of pounds of potatoes thrown out at the start of the COVID-19 pandemic when fast food chains stopped buying potatoes for French fries (US Department of Agriculture n.d.: n.pag.; Narishkin et al. 2020: n.pag.). Though not entirely agricultural,

The Handmaid's Tale contrasts the oppressive city with the open country. Kate escapes Gilead and goes off the grid, spending the winter in an Airstream trailer. *Brazil* contrasts a small rural cabin, surrounded by grass and trees, a few sheep penned up and cow grazing nearby, with the duct-riddled, grey city. Away from the control that the concentration of people a city affords, a return to the land, with hints of self-directed and self-sustaining farm work, can offer a vision of hope in dystopian movies.

Post-apocalyptic films show farming and cultivation in action (rather than by implication) with greater frequency, as farming offers an index of the relative lack of or return to civilization. For instance, *Planet of the Apes* (1968) finds the just-landed astronauts Taylor, Dodge, and Landon fleeing through rows of crops, evidence of an ape society that has mastered large-scale agriculture. *Zombieland* passes by a farm with no crops planted, but at some point a little farming must have returned, because Dave Sanderman wins zombie kill of the week for his use of a thresher to kill and bale a zombie in Riverside, Iowa in *Zombieland Double Tap*. *Oblivion*'s Jack and Victoria have their food provided for them, but Jack still surreptitiously grows tomatoes on some of the remaining arable land on Earth. *Waterworld*'s Mariner also grows a tomato plant and goes to some trouble to keep it in his possession during his escape from a Smoker attack; Mariner also has a lime tree, essential to prevent the scurvy that a literal life at sea would threaten. In *The Quiet Earth*, almost immediately after the event that erases almost every human on Earth, or at least all the people on Te Ika-a-Māui, Zac goes to the garden supply for a shovel, some garden hose, and two large bags of seed potatoes. Julie's happy flashback memories in *Warm Bodies* take place in an apple orchard, and Lowell Freeman's job on *Silent Running*'s spaceship is to look after the orchard that would regreen the world, a plan that is foolishly abandoned. In hiding from murderous drilling machines, residents of Zion have kitchen gardens in *The Matrix Reloaded*. One train car is dedicated to horticulture in *Snowpiercer*; Tanya grabs an apple and eats it as she walks through the car. Whatever his other faults, Immortan Joe brings a real skill for supervising innovative agriculture in *Mad Max: Fury Road*'s wasteland. Inside the citadel, a hydroponic garden produces greens. In addition, a mothers' milk dairy farm operates on a small industrial scale. Though Immortan Joe mainly operates through exploitation and violence, the food production in the fortress shows that Immortan Joe's austerity regime maintains control of food supply as a measure of his power. The brides' escape from their broodmare lives turns to a different sort of reproduction when The Dag takes on the responsibility of carrying on the 'seeds, trees, flowers, fruit' given to her by the Vuvalini. In this regard the Vuvalini, residents of the Green Place that was swallowed by a dead swamp, appear as seed collectors. Perhaps the most famous seed collection is in Svalbard, in the Seed Vault, but

> Seed collecting did not begin with the Seed Vault. In fact, the Vault has never been involved with gathering seeds directly from the field. In the 1970s agricultural scientists sounded the alarm that the wave of modern seed varieties sweeping across the world was massively displacing traditional varieties and driving them into extinction. Today there are 1,700 collections of crop diversity. In total, these genebanks house more than 7 million samples, up to 1.5 million of which are thought to be distinct. (Fowler 2016: 304)

The film's last image of the citadel shows the water flowing down onto the people, the tops of the mesas already green. The Dag's return with the seeds and release of the water to all promises a habitable and more equal city rather than an unequal and barely survivable citadel. *Mad Max: Fury Road* isn't subtle about its vision for rebirth, but it is important to note that in addition to the human forms of the pregnant brides returning and ascending, the preserved seeds hold out the promise of feeding the next generations in a less violent and exploitative manner. The film's promise appears to be steps towards equity: the tops of the mesas will stay green and, with the ascent of Furiosa and the return of water to the people, the ground level will soon become green. A similar greening of the world appears in *WALL-E*. The space-exiled descendants of earthlings return to Earth, intent on turning the plant that Eve brings to the *Axiom* into the basis for farming. However, the agriculture the ship's captain so eagerly introduces, even if he conceives of it as growing vegetables and pizza, is a monoculture. Eve found only one plant, after all. A similar monocultural approach appears in *No Blade of Grass* (Elliot Scott AD 1970) and *Interstellar*. During a television newscast, a newscaster says, '[t]his graph shows the decline in grain surfaces in the United States'. The newscaster describes 'the nerve gas bombings of the Chinese air force of major population areas. The Chinese government justified this horrendous action as necessary for survival'. The newscaster then introduces an ecologist, who admits the action 'appears rather barbarous on the surface. But, logically, they were acting to ensure the continuance of the Chinese nation'. This leads to a heated argument, and the station goes to a strange version of a test image: the graph of world wheat storage shown a minute earlier, creating a second chance to see the importance of a grain grown on an industrial scale. The first line of dialog in *Interstellar* describes one version of farming:

> My dad was a farmer. Like everybody else back then. Course he didn't start that way [...] The wheat had died the blight came and we had to burn it. And we still had corn. We had acres of corn. But mostly we had dust.

The film's first third establishes a dystopian world in which farming is failing, crop by crop. More precisely, large-scale industrial farming with lots of mechanical/chemical inputs is failing. There's no sense that there's another way to farm. In 'caretaker' mode for the world, there's no scaling back; there's no evidence of an urbanized world trying something different. When Cooper (Matthew McConaughey) visits the research centre, NASA is doing all kinds of agricultural experiments in pylo-huts. But rather than turn to some other form of agriculture on and in the Earth *Interstellar* heads to space. In this light, both *WALL-E* and *Interstellar* see not the far-off future of *WALL-E*'s ostensible setting, but the contemporary production that created the problems as the movie identifies them: most obviously high fructose corn syrup and the Big Gulps the people enjoy on their space cruise ship, as well as the invisible, far-away labour required to produce food elsewhere, represented as magically appearing treats on the *Axiom*.

With this vision of a planet reclaimed from hyper consumerist trash by agriculture, we can return to the *Divergent* series and Kristen Ghodsee's discovery of Andrei Andreev, the agronomist responsible for Sofia's cucumber supply, and start to look at the edges of the frame in dystopian and post-apocalyptic movies. At the edges of the frame we can start to see the importance of new approaches to agriculture, or more precisely smaller-scale and less/non-mechanized agriculture, to a vision of possible liveable futures. In the first halves of both *Divergent* and its sequel *Insurgent*, images of farming, as massive fields of grain, grain silos, smaller allotment-like vegetable gardens, livestock trailers used to ship food into the city, and a Garden City-like settlement beyond the wall, aid in the film series' world building. As I noted above, the films do not return to agriculture in their conclusions because generic action heroes solve problems physically though violence, not through growing crops. However, the *Divergent* world's division of labour hints at agriculture's importance. Jobs are determined by faction, and the population is divided more or less evenly across the five factions – the auditorium where young people choose their faction shows an equal distribution in its seating. *Divergent*'s workforce is 20 per cent Dauntless, who are the police and military. The US Department of Defense employs a total of 3.2 million people, including civilian non-combat workers, or about 2 per cent of the total workforce. Even if we treated every one of the approximately 21.5 million government workers as police, we would still only reach 16 per cent of the workforce as police and military. Fascism and ethnic cleansing are easier to achieve in such a society (and the revelation that the cities are open-air laboratories makes this job distribution logical). However, it also bears noting that the workforce is also 20 per cent Amity agricultural workers. This distribution is even more out of line with workforce participation in twenty-first-century developed nations. The number of agricultural workers in the United States decreased throughout the twentieth century, mostly owing to mechanization and industrialization. Agricultural workers as a percentage of the total workforce peaked at 31 per cent in 1910 (Bureau of Labor

Statistics 2016: n.pag.), and by 2020, '[h]ired farmworkers [made] up less than 1 percent of all U.S. wage and salary workers' (USDA 2022: n.pag.). By way of comparison, in 2019, more than 40 per cent of India's labour force worked in agriculture (World Bank 2021a: n.pag.). Like a great deal of India's agriculture, the post-apocalyptic world is not highly mechanized (although Amity has the odd tractor); post-apocalyptic agriculture will need many hands, working manually, to feed those who remain. The development of agriculture in the West over the twentieth century meant that

> [t]raction power, for example, is no longer provided by locally bred animals but by factory-produced machines. Cultivation practices requiring few purchased inputs but a great deal of labour have been replaced by practices requiring specialized machinery and chemical treatments produced in factories and bought-in seeds.
>
> (Tansey and Worsley 1997: 86)

The *Divergent* series reverses this sequence to show us limited traction power, specialized machinery and chemical treatments, and bought-in seeds and a great deal more labour. Starting with a vanguard of Erudite agronomists directing production and rusticated youths being sent into the countryside after choosing the Amity faction, post-apocalyptic Chicago turns to a labour-intensive quasi-collectivization of agriculture as a means to build a society after the apocalypse.

Different forms of post-apocalyptic agriculture appear in *Blade Runner 2049*, one that both recalls a fleeting moment in the original *Blade Runner* and imagines a future for protein production rather than grain, fruit and vegetables. During the film's opening titles, we learn that the 'collapse of ecosystems in the 2020s led to the rise of industrialist Niander Wallace, whose mastery of synthetic farming averted famine'. In the sequence that follows, an extreme closeup of an eye is followed by a series of overhead extreme long shots and high-angle shots that show the landscape of southern California as a near-abstract set of patterns, dozens of solar arrays and desiccated blocks of land that resemble circuit boards. After a high-angle travelling shot of a flying car over a near-lunar landscape, a cut takes us to a viscous pool, where a red-gloved hand reaches in and pulls out a handful of grub-like creatures. This is Sapper Morton's (Dave Bautista) Wallace-designed protein farm, and when the person driving the flying car, the Blade Runner K lands, he emerges out of a fog, walking past a dead tree held in place with guy wires. The grubs look not unlike Sago grubs, something people in Southeast Asia already cultivate and eat, and the farmland looks not unlike the moon, the dead tree part of a desolate grey landscape with modular buildings and polytunnels. The unearthly feeling of the farm also appears in the labour itself; Sapper

FIGURE 4.4: *Blade Runner 2049* protein farm.

wears something resembling a space suit as he wades in a shallow pool flanked by liquid-filled tanks on either side, and he has to decontaminate before disengaging the air supply of the suit and returning to the farmhouse. This unearthly setting and its 'artificial farming' of grubs fed by tanks of some yellow liquid recalls the 'farming the moon' newspaper headline in *Blade Runner*, except the 'moon' is a dying Earth (Figure 4.4). The Earth's death is tinted silver grey in California, and orange in the Las Vegas, where Rick Deckerd (Harrison Ford) has beehives and protein tanks in his penthouse. While these small-scale farms occupy a great deal of the film's elaborate set design (as do the energy production and recycling mentioned in other chapters), traditional western agriculture – large-scale wheat or corn, dairy farming, livestock farming of cows or even chickens – does not. The protein farm is a version of the agriculture that not only plays a narrative function in these dystopian worlds, but points to a way forward in the contemporary moment, toward an agriculture that can provide food security for survivors on a budget.

Food security in dystopian and post-apocalyptic worlds

Dystopian and post-apocalyptic movies show people trying to find or make a place where food is available not just for a moment but over time. That is to say, dystopian and post-apocalyptic movies are interested in food security (EC FAO Food Security 2008: n.pag.). As Adrian Parr writes, '[t]he four dimensions of food security are: (1) food availability, (2) food accessibility, (3) food utilization, and (4) food system stability' (2013: 77). In other words, control over food creates room for oppressive structures to be 'necessary' to survival. As I noted above, dystopian elites who control food can elect to starve you, as the affinity for cafeteria-style food distribution shows. In such a set-up food is available, accessible, usable, and stable, but beyond the people's control. Leaving such a system means forgoing food security. The creation of food deserts, in fiction as in real life, is a political choice. Julian Cribb takes on a dystopian tone in placing food at the centre of upheaval:

> In past history, rulers understood that food security was the bedrock of all subsequent governmental stability, economic growth, equity, and social progress. Without it, poverty, upheaval, and crisis are almost inevitable. Without food there is no stability, and without stability no government, education, health care, or civil society. Why so many nations have lost sight of this simple truth in recent times is hard to fathom.
>
> (2010: 196)

Many of those who wish to upend their dystopian worlds – the heroes of dystopian movies – combat the top-down control of food in favour of something more durable, long-lasting, and locally controlled, much like the electricity production analysed earlier.

Food security has a spatial component, its reach expanding and contracting depending on infrastructural variables. In 'Supply chain response to terrorism: Creating resilient and secure supply chains – Interim report of progress and learnings', Rice and Caniato note that

> a terrorist attack could destroy the transportation infrastructure (highways, railroads, airports) in a specific location. If all of the suppliers were located in the general area such that they were all somewhat dependent on the same highways and railways, then the firm would still be at risk of complete supply loss due to one disruption.
>
> (2003: 34)

In the case of Great Britain, its island status means that one disruption, sea shipping, could cause a great many problems. Geoff Tansey and Tony Worsley's note that in Great Britain

> Food self-sufficiency before the [second world] war was only about 30 per cent – ie, Britain produced less than one-third of the food consumed by its people. As much food as possible had to be grown in the country during the war and it had to be well distributed if the population was to be adequately nourished. Unprecedented

> measures were taken to ensure that a basic, nutritionally sound diet was available to all in the population – itself a splendid achievement.
>
> (1997: 45)

Reduced safety in shipping meant that less food could arrive, necessitating increased local production. This lesson appeared to be lost 75 years after the Second World War with Brexit, with many vegetables predicted to become significantly more difficult to find and afford. Or, to put it less kindly, a lack of food security showed the United Kingdom what happens to an imperial power that takes from its colonies and depends on safe long-distance trade and shipping when unfavourable exogenous factors come into play.

In addition to the international and national scale of the example of the Second World War Great Britain, food security had a local scale. Some parts of England had – and have – greater difficulty in providing food for all. A poor district in Blitz-era London or Liverpool would be more likely to have hungry people than a poor area of an agricultural region, where at least there would be hens for eggs and perhaps a subsistence-level garden plot. Areas without access to nutritious food are now called food deserts, 'tracts in which a substantial number or proportion of the population has low access to supermarkets or large grocery stores' (Dutko et al. 2012: 5). If we take supermarkets and grocery stores to mean food availability and storage more generally, dystopian movies tend to take place in food deserts that heroes try to escape or irrigate into something better. Post-apocalyptic movies, for their part, tend to take place in food wastelands and introduce ways of producing food as a first step towards the re-establishment of civilization. Theodore Martin, in his analysis of the post-apocalyptic novel, describes them as giving us

> the atavism of apocalypse: the end of the earth as back-to-the-land. The point of the pre-capitalist nostalgia of the post-apocalyptic novel is that all the work it describes isn't actually work because it is something less alienated and more fulfilling: it is survival.
>
> (2017: 167)

But dystopian and post-apocalyptic movies, for the most part, do more than show survival. They offer a glimmer of hope, a path back to civilization similar to what striking coal miners' families could achieve in rural Appalachia: 'Because they had all those gardens, and they canned so much, and they killed that hog, they could go on strike. They could go out for two months; they were stocked and ready' (Stoll 2017: 225). Such autarkic outposts, both real and imagined, are more than back-to-the-land subsistence agricultural settlements, they are in fact places where people not only survive but also forge a future which offers more than the minimum of bare life on a small, local scale.

Urban agriculture

In addition to the rural settings of the Second World War England and coal mining Appalachia, dystopian and post-apocalyptic urban and quasi-urban spaces make room for agriculture. In fact, agriculture abounds in brief cutaway moments and at the edges of the frame in many dystopian and post-apocalyptic movies. For instance, the troops living in an underground bunker and cave complex in *Day of the Dead* still return topside, where they have a small garden of what look like cannabis plants. In the previous film in the series, the mall where the survivors live has an indoor 'forest' that also acts as an impromptu burial site. A New York City like *Soylent Green*'s, with 40 million people, doesn't have much room for greenery, but there is a small tree sanctuary in an empty lot that Thorn visits. Babette Tischleder claims that '*Soylent Green* (1973), set in 2022, presents Earth as a planet depleted of all its natural resources and ravaged by greenhouse gases and overpopulation' (2016: 442), but the only location shown in the film is New York. A small sample size really. The Commander's wife in *The Handmaid's Tale* has a room full of plants that are green but, perhaps as might be expected, do not have the reproductive evidence of fruit or flowers. There are plenty of flowers in the *Hunger Games* series President Snow's greenhouse, as he needs the roses to cover the smell of poison. *Aeon Flux*'s Bregna looks like it has no agriculture, but it does have a large greenhouse for decorative plants. Such examples of non-food horticulture show that growing things can be helpful to relax, to see something of the past destroyed world, to grow something, and even to perfume and decorate yourself. Perhaps unsurprisingly, all of these examples come from dystopian movies except for the weed in the post-apocalyptic *Day of the Dead*; growing cannabis seems to signal that the bunker-dwellers plan to enjoy themselves before the end they know is coming finally arrives.

But dystopian and post-apocalyptic survivors want more than to play out the string; they want to make a world worth living in and worth passing on. Cut off from imported food and freed from the demands of the market, dystopian and especially post-apocalyptic survivors can turn their attention to different approaches to agriculture. Cuba was faced with a dystopian situation in the 1990s, losing 75 per cent of their import/export capacity when the Eastern Bloc fell and still facing an embargo from what might otherwise be a large trading partner, the neighbouring United States. In 'Urban agriculture in Havana: Opportunities for the future', Jorge Peña Diaz and Phil Harris note that Cuba had to identify 'what strategy would serve to meet the food demands of a predominantly urban population heavily dependent on the produce of a depressed countryside?' (2005: 137). One key step was a turn to urban agriculture.

> By 2011 there were nearly 400,000 urban farms [in Cuba], supplying 70% of the vegetables eaten in cities like Havana and as a result of this (and land redistribution supporting peasant agriculture), Cuba could boast the best food production in Latin America. It is a particularly noteworthy store because this is a sustainable agriculture, carried out perforce without organophosphate fertilizers, oil-dependent mechanization, or long supply chains.
>
> (Graham-Leigh 2015: 166)

A number of dystopian and post-apocalyptic movies have urban (*I Am Legend*, *Ready Player One*, *Resident Evil: The Final Chapter*, *The Book of Eli*, *Warm Bodies*, *Children of Men*) and quasi-urban (*Snowpiercer*, *The Road Warrior*) settings that, while they do not occupy the centre of the frame or the heart of the plot-driven narrative, appear to round out the setting and to show how civilization survives and endures.

When people grow crops, the crops appear not so much as the amber waves of grain that once represented freedom and plenty but as small-scale urban gardens. The post-apocalyptic *I Am Legend* represents a large-scale space of urban agriculture, with Neville growing corn in Central Park repurposed as a farm. The dystopian *Ready Player One* features a rooftop container garden full of tomato plants and vegetables (Figure 4.5). The rooftop garden, as Wade observes, makes time go 'so much slower', perhaps because urban agriculture offers a healthier solution to the corn syrup drought mentioned in the opening narration. *Resident Evil: The Final Chapter* also has a rooftop garden of a few rows of grain (with water tanks next to the plants). Finally, the Rippers' hideout in *Tank Girl* has an indoor kitchen garden and greenhouse, where they grow chilis, greens, succulents, and even decorative plants.

FIGURE 4.5: *Ready Player One* rooftop garden.

The sorts of livestock that appear reveal a change to meat-eaters' diets. People don't eat a lot of beef in dystopian and post-apocalyptic worlds, at least if the livestock on screen is any indication (although *Warm Bodies* shows some cows grazing in the green spaces of the walled city). Some meat choices remain from the beforetimes. Chickens, which can provide eggs and meat, appear in the small oil-pumping fortress in *The Road Warrior* and in Carnegie's town in *The Book of Eli*. Pigs are also present in *The Road Warrior* and *Elysium*. A flock of sheep takes over an entire street in *Children of Men*. Some less common livestock also appear: camels and rabbits in *The Road Warrior* and cockroaches in *Snowpiercer*'s quasi-urban food processing factory car. Camels are particularly suited to the dry climate of Australia, rabbits are a famously successful invasive species, and maintaining a cockroach feedstock makes sense in the cramped confines of a train-city. In their description of the future of global food systems, Godfray et al. argue that

> [s]witching from ruminants [cows, sheep, goats, water buffalo] to monogastric livestock [horses, rabbits, gerbils, hamsters] may help, as will technological advances in how intensively maintained animals are reared [...] Maintaining viable livestock production will be critical in climate change adaptation, especially for very many poor smallholders whose animals are central to their livelihoods.
>
> (2010: 2772)

The one kind of meat production that does not appear in the films I analyse here, not even in *Waterworld*, is aquaculture, even though it is often bruited as a protein source of the future: 'Looking ahead, we can expect to see a marked increase in aquaculture and product development involving lower-cost species, especially in low- and mid-income countries' (Godfray et al. 2010: 2772). That is to say, even though most movies don't engage with the pets-or-meat problem, the switch from cows as the most common signifier of livestock to another group animals signals a representational change to 'livestock' and a different vision for dystopian and post-apocalyptic urban agriculture.

Conclusion

To return to Andrei Andreev, the Sofia greenbelt greenhouses full of Andrei's cucumbers and other agronomists' vegetables were part of Bulgaria's self-sufficiency in food production, a way to build a new socialist future separate from the exploitation of capitalism. Such an ability to feed everyone offered Bulgaria food security. Producing for the people's consumption, rather than for profit, placed the Bulgarian model closer to what is now called food sovereignty, which, as the international farmer's collective Via Campesina defines it, means 'solidarity, not competition, and building a fairer world from the bottom up' (2018: 1). Food sovereignty, environmental activist Walden Bello argues, 'challenges at every point the pillars of capitalist industrial agriculture' (2009: 148). Much as centrally coordinated agriculture monitored by agronomists outside of the capitalist system as a utopian alternative to market-driven agriculture, food sovereignty imagines another kind of

> systemic change – about human beings having direct, democratic control over the most important elements of their society – how we feed and nourish ourselves, how we use and maintain the land, water and other resources around us for the benefit of current and future generations, and how we interact with other groups, peoples and cultures.
>
> (Via Campesina 2018: 2)

In response to the question, 'what we would eat in Utopia', Elaine Graham-Leigh answers, '[w]e can't know for sure how easy it would be to feed the world without the current capitalist system in the way, but we don't have to assume that it would need to start from a position of scarcity' (2015: 191). The dystopian and post-apocalyptic diet as imagined by the agriculture visible both at the centre and the edges of the frame has less grain and starch, and depends more heavily on unconventional (to western tastes) meat, fruit and vegetables. The pleasure of food in a lot of dystopian and post-apocalyptic movies appears in the form of fresh fruit and vegetables. Growing your food takes time and safety (trees, bushes, plants are pretty sedentary), which are at a premium. But it is possible to grow food, to make a horticultural turn, in urban settings, which seems more plausible in the post-apocalypse, when people band together in small communities, often barricaded against an external threat like zombies, and produce food with and for each other.

5

Waste: The Social Relations of Trash and Recycling

In *Screening Space: The American Science Fiction Film* Vivian Sobchack describes a scene so common that it is possible to imagine dozens of films for which it applies:

> Cars eternally stalled on a bridge, newspapers blowing down the street as if to mock animate existence – these are the recurring images in the postholocaust cities of science fiction [...] Different than the visual impact of the photographed action of disaster, this is the still and silent 'garbage of disaster'.
>
> (1990: 119)

The concept of social breakdown finds its most economical concrete expression in an establishing shot with visible garbage in most post-apocalyptic and many dystopian movies. In the ellipses I created for this quote, Sobchack qualifies the images as 'from the fifties through the seventies', but, as I will show in this chapter, the 'garbage of disaster' persists through the 2010s. Annette Kuhn characterizes Sobchack's analysis of sci-fi films as mapping a social relationship in which, 'with their rubbish-strewn ruined cityscapes, these films take for granted, even eroticize, the effects of disaster' (1990: 4). One of the effects of disaster, the end of civilization as we know it, reveals itself in and with the presence of garbage. Waste disposal holds disaster at bay; waste disposal might rebuild social bonds.

The ending to the franchise-opening *Resident Evil* shows the durability of the role garbage plays in the imagination of disaster. Alice emerges from the Raccoon City hospital onto a city street without any people. A shot of a newspaper reading 'THE DEAD WALK' is followed by an overhead shot of Alice looking through the windows of two police cars. Alice pulls a shotgun out of a police car, followed by a close-up of Alice's face. The close-up of Alice holds for five seconds, and then the camera begins to pull away from her. Once her upper body is in the frame, she pumps the shotgun. The camera continues to pull back, revealing a street filled with knocked-over police barricades and motorcycles as well as burning cars and police cruisers covered in blood. Paper waste nearly covers the street. Within *Resident Evil*, this shot sequence moves from Alice's micro-level experience of the effects of the T-virus (emerging from defeating the final boss) to the elaborate macro-level view (the wider world). Within the *Resident Evil* series of films, the sequence operates like a statement of purpose: the T-virus is in the world, the world has been wrecked, and Alice must fight everywhere. *Warm Bodies* features a second generic establishing shot: the untidy suburban neighbourhood. During R and Julie's journey from the airport to the walled city, they take refuge in a suburban neighbourhood filled with the garbage of disaster: paper waste, broken televisions, wrecked cars. Paper waste, when paired with larger-scale garbage like a television or a burned-out car chassis clogging street spaces, offers a shorthand for the disappearance of a functioning society. *World War Z* shows the importance of sanitation workers: they clear a path through traffic at the start of the zombie outbreak, and WHO aid worker Gerry Lane follows. It's not the police but sanitation workers and waste disposal that represent the thin line between a desirable civilization and a world not worth living in.

In this chapter I consider the forms waste and waste disposal take, both in the foreground as well as the background and edges of the frame, in narratively significant and world-building moments. On the one hand, dystopian and post-apocalyptic films show that to emerge out of the wreckage of the old, to create a better world, it is necessary to overcome the garbage of disaster to reassert order on a broken world. However, these films frequently show an eroticized or aestheticized garbage rather than the workings of waste disposal. Similarly, dystopian and post-apocalyptic films often have showy examples of recycling without any consistent vision of a functional *bricolage* of the old order. To re-engineer the world outside of the consume and discard formula seems beyond most films' imaginary horizon.

Three sections will lay the groundwork: first I will define a cluster of key terms, then I will consider how literal waste and ideas of waste can be used as a means of exclusion, as a way to draw a public–private distinction. To finish this groundwork, I describe briefly what I want to call the trash aesthetic in dystopian and post-apocalyptic film. Then I will begin my analysis of the appearance of solid waste, sewers and wastewater, and recycling and the infrastructures designed and/or improvised to undertake e-waste disposal. Considering the mechanics and demands of waste and waste disposal will open up space to see how waste helps to define social relations in dystopian and post-apocalyptic films. As I have throughout the book, I will offer an overview of tendencies and then turn my attention to in-depth readings of key examples. The definition of waste and the control of its disposal registers power. The powerful can draw boundaries between what belongs/can be seen/retains value and the discarded/rendered invisible/unvalued. The waste disposal systems of *WALL-E*, *Isle of Dogs*, *Ready Player One*, *Demolition Man*, and *Blade Runner 2049* dispose of some things but reuse, recycle, and treasure others, revealing the parts of contemporary society perceived to hold the greatest potential in creating liveable futures. Waste and waste disposal create and maintain conceptual and physical boundaries, revealing the spatial character of social relations in dystopian and post-apocalyptic worlds. The workings of waste disposal not only register the expended value of trash buried in a landfill or burned in an incinerator, but also the potential future value of a reused or recycled item. In other words, waste is more than the past, but also the present and a possible future. The sites of waste disposal in dystopian and post-apocalyptic worlds thus identify what functions have ceased to work, locate where those functions have been sent as waste, and in some cases how those functions and spaces might be made to work once again through recycling/reuse to escape a dystopia or secure a *post*-apocalyptic life.

Trash aesthetic

Trash plays a clear role in the creation of the dystopian and post-apocalyptic aesthetic. In dystopian settings, trash comes to the fore of the denotative frame. For instance, the time travel in *The Terminator* happens next to dumpsters denotative of the fringes of urban life, with the electrical charges and wind whipped up by the process swirling paper waste about. *The First Purge* appears to have been scheduled for bin night, with trash on the street offering both an ongoing commentary on the Purge's social cleansing purpose and convenient hiding places. Even though Los Angeles was mostly destroyed by earthquakes, *Escape from LA*'s streets are well kept, with the rubble of destroyed buildings piled up on the side, creating berms that both create a sense of enclosure on the street and hide whatever is beyond them (a canny low-budget solution to set decoration). Drawing connections across a number of examples of 'visionary cities', including those in *Blade Runner* and *Brazil*, Janet Staiger notes that 'they are entropic, characterized by debris, decay, and abandonment. Thus, these dystopias' city architectures comment on a potential post-industrial age-of-communication society. The forecast is not favorable' (1999: 100). A future full of waste holds less appeal; too much debris and you have a dystopia. The production design of *Blade Runner* testifies to how much work some judicious waste placement can do. Giuliana Bruno describes the Los Angeles of *Blade Runner* as

> not an orderly layout of skyscrapers and ultra-comfortable, hyper-mechanized interiors. Rather, it creates an aesthetic of decay, exposing the dark side of technology, the process of disintegration [...] Next to the high-tech, its waste. It is into garbage that the characters constantly step, by garbage that Pris awaits J. F. Sebastian.
>
> (1990: 239)

The dark side of technology is not disintegration, but rather non-integration: waste. As Matt Hanson explains in *The Science Behind the Fiction: Building Sci-Fi Moviescapes*, the first step to creating *Blade Runner*'s aesthetic of waste was retrofitting Warner Bros. Old New York City Street set; the second step was 'layering it with pipes, tubing, neon signs – the flotsam and jetsam of the future – to fast forward it into the world of 2019' (2004: 19). Writing at the time of the film's production, Bart Mills predicted that 'no filmgoer next summer will recognize these buildings, which appeared in *Funny Lady*, *The Way We Were*, and half the pictures Cagney and Bogart made for Warner Bros' because

> present-day buildings will still be in place, grimier than ever. Filthy pollution-control devices will sprout on every structure. Enormous garbage trucks the color of sick will stalk the streets spewing vile steam. Cars will be ugly and cramped. Streets will be heaped with rubbish, and surplus people will set up housekeeping in the gutters.
> (1982: 45)

Mills uses a stream of words related to waste – grimier, filthy, pollution, garbage, sick (vomit), spewing, rubbish, surplus, gutters – to describe what makes it easy both not to recognize the sets used and to understand the dystopian future on display in *Blade Runner*.

Waste does not render London unrecognizable in *Children of Men*, but rather makes the future London a logical extension of its moment of production and, in doing so, recognizably (more) dystopian. Even in happy moments, such as when Jasper and Theo get high together, Theo finds himself amidst a reminder of the leftovers of the time before, in an expressive set that registers 'the accumulation of debris that testifies to life' (Cubitt 2016: 59). But more frequently, and more pessimistically, as Sean Cubitt argues,

> In *Children of Men*, the abundance of waste operates as a constant reminder of the audience's present, and as a midden where the history of our present is carried forward into the past of the diegesis. Rather than an emblem of lassitude, the rubbish piles in *Children* work against the principle, so central to advanced economies, that waste is the shabby secret underbelly of consumerism.
> (2016: 55–56)

From the film's first scene, in which the camera follows Theo as he walks past a massive pile of garbage bags on the sidewalk, and then throws his coffee cup onto the street as he flinches in fright at the sound of an explosion, and as the camera reverses course, back towards the pile of garbage bags (and the people sitting amidst them), waste is inescapable in the cityscape. As noted in the earlier chapter on the transportation infrastructure, the too-clean streets of the Capitol in the *Hunger Games* series create a sense of the uncanny, a city too perfectly maintained. While *Children of Men* dives onto the street level in handheld shots, *Hunger Games* films deploy long shots that provide a sense of the Capitol's physical scale and the scale of control required to keep the city so spotless, even in the absence of rubbish bins.

The trash aesthetic of post-apocalyptic films appears in further sedimentation of waste, as the end of days means the end of trash day. The near-monochromatic extreme long shots throughout *The Book of Eli* feature not just cars, but knocked-over trailers, tankers, shopping trolleys, and rusted barrels along long stretches of highway. Similarly, *The Road*'s 'protagonists encounter the ghostly remains of the world we know – roads littered with wrecked and abandoned cars' (Kaplan 2016: 84). *The Road* establishing shots show a large variety of everyday locations as the man and the boy carry the flame across the country, with more than just dead cars: in an extreme long shot of a city, for instance, something almost unimaginably large is both out of place and broken, turned to trash: two rusted ships on a highway. Other establishing shots, long shots of the industrial part of a city, an office park, a mall, a boardwalk, a beach, an overpass, a farm, a suburban neighbourhood, and an urban residential area, all feature waste – a rusted car, a bulging plastic bag, and so on. Waste is everywhere; the devastation is total. In addition to the streets filled with rusting car chassis and the accumulation of added layers of dust on surfaces, another image common to post-apocalyptic films sees money scattered on the street or the floor, now simply paper waste. When the man and the boy walk through an abandoned mall in *The Road*, they walk over piles of dollar bills without pausing. In *Day of the Dead*'s opening credits, 'money blows about the abandoned city streets, so much meaningless paper' (Wood 2003: 289). Paper money acts not as legal tender but as something frivolous and disposable in *Zombieland*: in the same scene US$ 100 bills act as the 'play money' in a game of Monopoly, Tallahassee uses bills as Kleenex to wipe away tears. Once-useful objects like car bodies and shopping trolleys, and smaller once-valuable objects like paper money and pearls no longer perform their original function, leaving only their physical form, which can be reused by imaginative hands.

We can broadly classify dystopian and post-apocalyptic movies' vision of waste and waste disposal according to a Goldilocks approach. The omnipresence and proximity of waste common to the post-apocalypse and some lower-functioning dystopias is too hot, signalling the mountain of work that must be done to return to civilization. Excessively scrubbed, waste-free spaces are too cold, indicating a tight social control preventing a return to an open, free society. The option for just right would resemble something like the used universe of the *Star Wars* movies: battered, a bit of surface grime, but still functioning. The used universe depends in part on the development and maintenance of a waste disposal system. Locating moments of waste – papers blowing down the street, rusted barrels, crashed and abandoned cars – and the spatial dimensions of waste disposal and management, in the centre and at the edge of the frame, brings the importance of waste infrastructure to rebuilding a liveable world into clearer focus.

Waste terminology

Waste takes many forms: municipal solid waste, industrial waste, commercial waste, toxic waste, to name a few. Though we might recognize waste when we see it, identifying the type of waste under discussion can sharpen what we might do in an analysis of it. Waste generates its own varied and often overlapping terminology. Starting with a very broad term, solid waste constitutes

> any solid, semi-solid, liquid, or contained gaseous materials discarded from industrial, commercial, mining, or agricultural operations, and from community activities. Solid waste includes garbage, construction debris, commercial refuse, sludge from water supply or waste treatment plants, or air pollution control facilities, and other discarded materials.
>
> (US EPA n.d.a: n.pag.)

A more precise term used in the waste management industry and government,

> Municipal Solid Waste (MSW) – more commonly known as trash or garbage – consists of everyday items we use and then throw away, such as product packaging, grass clippings, furniture, clothing, bottles, food scraps, newspapers, appliances, paint, and batteries. This comes from our homes, schools, hospitals, and businesses.
>
> (US EPA 2016: n.pag.)

John Scanlon moves past the merely descriptive aspect of this definition in *On Garbage*, defining garbage as 'what remains when the good, fruitful, valuable, nourishing and useful has been taken' and has its origins in 'the privatization of human wastes' (2005: 13, 124). One of the forms of waste that humans create, trash, 'is created by sorting' (Strasser 2014: 5). Sometimes the sorting reaches a level of detail the average person may not imagine. For instance, in Europe there are 66 total types of paper that one might dispose of, classified under five different grades: ordinary, medium, high, kraft, and special (Waste Paper Trade n.d.: n.pag.). Draft report on bond paper or apple core, 'trash is the visible interface between everyday life and the deep, often abstract horrors of ecological crisis'

(Rogers 2013: 3). With this very brief overview of the use of garbage and trash in mind, I will use 'garbage' and 'waste' to refer to larger, category-level examples; I will use trash to refer to specific instances of an everyday object that no longer retains its usefulness in the film narrative and/or *mise en scène*.

Readers of this book will be producers of MSW and have a familiarity with it from bin night. Another form of waste that readers of this book will produce and know intimately is sewage, also referred to as wastewater, which is produced and disposed of both at home and in workplace settings through the sewer systems of urban regions. To complete this brief waste lexicon, the term e-waste is

> loosely applied to consumer and business electronic equipment that is near or at the end of its useful life. There is no clear definition for e-waste; for instance whether or not items like microwave ovens and other similar 'appliances' should be grouped into the category has not been established.
>
> (CalRecycle n.d.: n.pag.)

No longer used electronics and home appliances do not represent a cut and dry case of e-waste because they can be 'reused, refurbished or recycled to minimize the actual waste that might end up in a landfill or improperly disposed in an unprotected dump site' (US EPA 2022a: n.pag.). In this way, unlike a dinner plate broken into six pieces can no longer function as a dinner plate, e-waste offers an option for disposal that sits on the border of recycling, 'reusing materials and objects in original or changed forms rather than discarding them as wastes' (US EPA n.d.a: n.pag.). In this chapter I will use these definitions as a rough guide to my engagements with waste and/in infrastructure in dystopian and post-apocalyptic films.

Waste is a social relation

The office where I work has one red bin for trash and one yellow bin for recycling next to each other near the desk area. A small green box for food scraps sits next to the sink in the tearoom. As in many offices, someone has added handwritten signs to clarify what goes where: Takeaway coffee cups go in the red bin; their lids go in the yellow; teabags can go in the green. These containers are, in turn, emptied into larger red, yellow, and green bins that large trucks take away. The people who perform waste disposal work for the office where I work perform a 3D – dirty, dangerous, and demeaning – job, and 'as with so much other waste management, the handling of materials bring with it particular ideas of class and status' (Scanlon 2005: 41–42; Jørgensen 2019: 78). A waste disposal worker does not enjoy a great deal of relative prestige based on their job title, falling above farm workers and shoe salespeople, but below fellow labourers like welders, stevedores, and bus drivers as well as most white-collar professions like my bureaucrat position (Colorado Adoption Project 2007: n.pag.). Pay can take some of the sting out of the relative lack of prestige. In the United States, the annual mean wage for a worker in waste collection in 2020 was $40,990, which sits comfortably alongside other traditionally solid working-class job like auto workers with a $38,890 annual mean wage (Bureau of Labor Statistics 2022: n.pag.). But while an auto worker makes a vehicle that people see and use frequently, a waste collector adds Ds to dirty, dangerous, and demeaning. A waste collector does not produce an object but rather makes waste disappear; a waste worker creates distance between waste producer and waste. The public nature of a waste worker's job might inform the relative lack of regard for the job. In his anthropological account of the workings of a midwestern US landfill, Joshua Reno notes that

> [n]ot many will work directly with or live close to mass waste in their lifetimes, but waste subtraction can and does break down. Occasionally sewer pipes burst and basements flood with effluent, or garbage collection halts and Dumpsters overfull; there are garbage strikes, neglectful municipal governments, and unregulated or criminal monopolies. In these moments, bodies are exposed and forced to mix, however temporarily, with untransferred transience. Waste management can no longer be forgotten, and we become surrounded by what our hands have flushed and tossed, by garbage that keeps coming. But such exceptional circumstances merely lend support to the general rule: for many North Americans, transience, ends up elsewhere.
> (2016: 57)

The waste disposal infrastructure becomes visible in its breakdown, when waste does not safely disappear. When the private waste of houses and workplaces doesn't disappear, and remains visible in public space, waste becomes a problem.

> As Dominique Laporte has pointed out, the privy made the act of wasting private, while the creation of municipal infrastructures cast cleaning as public. The upshot of this was that wasting – whether bodily excretions, the flow of castoffs from a household, or the effluent of industry – was hidden from view and public consciousness.
> (Rogers 2013: 74)

Waste elsewhere is the solution. Red, yellow, and green bin waste may disappear from view, but not from the world. It goes elsewhere: to a dump, or a landfill.

Three films, *Gattaca*, *Land of the Dead*, and *WALL-E* use waste to show social relations in three distinct manners: waste undergirds a caste-like system in *Gattaca*; waste makes class conflict concrete in *Land of the Dead*; and waste gives form to ideological commitments in *WALL-E*. First, *Gattaca* imagines a future eugenic dystopia, where Valid citizens are designed in vitro. Vincent is an Invalid, made the old-fashioned way. Valids wield the power, and only Valids can enjoy space travel. Vincent explains in a voice-over how he was able to travel into space by making a deal with Jerome:

> Each day I would dispose of as much loose skin, fingernails, and hair as possible. To limit how much of my Invalid self I would leave in the Valid world. At the same time Jerome prepared samples of his own superior body matter so that I might pass for him. Customized urine pouches for the frequent substance tests. Fingertip blood sachets for security checks. And vials filled with other traces. While Jerome supplied me with a new identity, I paid the rent and kept him the style to which he'd become accustomed.

In *Gattaca*, social control creates a very ordered world, in which waste is invisible. *Gattaca*'s exteriors – such as the Marin County Civic Center and the Sepulveda Dam – are large-scale, symmetrical (or close to it), and modernist in style. Filming at the Marin County Civic Center creates continuity with another dystopian film, *THX 1138*, which also kept waste off screen for the most part. But for as much as MSW is kept off screen, *Gattaca* creates a world in which the commodification of *bio*-waste undergirds the relationship between Invalid Vincent and Valid Jerome, who live together symbiotically. Vincent pays Jerome for his blood and hair, which is sort of a normal exchange, as blood and hair are 'useful' in a sense beyond this fictional one (although Vincent isn't making a wig with Jerome's hair). But Vincent also buys Jerome's urine. Jerome's wastes signal Valid. Conversely, as Vincent discovers when his eyelash appears at a murder scene, he must constantly monitor his own bodily wastes, lest they expose him, either as a murderer or worse, as Invalid, lesser in the social hierarchy. That Vincent can go into space on the back of impersonating Jerome via waste products demonstrates the social relation that waste has in *Gattaca*'s dystopia: if you are of the elect, even your waste is worth more than your lessers'.

Second, in *Land of the Dead*, Cholo (John Leguizamo) frames his social relation with Kaufman (Dennis Hopper) and the social relations within Fiddler's Green, an exclusive enclave, in terms of garbage. When Kaufman dismisses Cholo's hope of moving into Fiddler's Green, Cholo angrily reminds Kaufman that he has spent three years 'takin' out your garbage, cleaning up after you. And then you're gonna say I'm not good enough [to live in Fiddler's Green]? Let me tell you something. You're gonna let me in. 'Cause I know what goes on around here. Do your committee members know what the fuck is going on with the garbage? So you're gonna let me in, you hear me?' Kaufman summons a security guard to escort Cholo out, and Kaufman describes Cholo to the security man as a kind of waste product: 'I won't be needing this man anymore.' Cholo sees himself as a useful worker whose profession informs him in socially useful ways, and thus worthy of a place in the enclave. Kaufman sees him as a tool to dispose of whenever maintenance becomes too onerous.

Third, *WALL-E* puts the main social relation in place when it comes to waste as part of Pixar's overall corporate signature. James Douglas's analysis covers not just *WALL-E*, but other Pixar films *Toy Story 2*, *Toy Story 3*, and *Inside Out*. I quote Douglas at length to show how he places *WALL-E* in Pixar's broader project, which can be summed up in one word: work. 'In *WALL-E*' he writes,

> the close of the second acts finds the film's robotic protagonist tossed down into a garbage disposal vault in the bowels of the spaceship *Axiom*, where larger-model robots collect the waste to be released into space. *Toy Story 3* reaches an emotional peak at a suburban landfill, where Woody, Buzz and their fellows toys face down a violent death by incinerator. In *Inside Out*, right on cue at the close of act two, Joy is temporarily stuck in a Memory Dump – a pit of discarded memories, jettisoned as Riley grew up. Pixar conceptualizes death not as the end of existence per se, but as the state of becoming waste. Waste does not work. Waste does not have a function. Waste is obsolete. Waste is undifferentiated. For Pixar, the model individual represents usefulness in their own unique way. A virtuous accountant can't just be like all the other accountants – they have to be their own special kind, they have to be the lead in their own story.
>
> (Douglas 2015: n.pag.)

The toys' (unfounded) fear – that their job, their function, no longer exists, as Andy has put away childish things – comes true in the landfill. Finding themselves at the landfill places Woody and Buzz outside their workplace, unable to perform their required function. Woody is a cowboy and Buzz Lightyear an astronaut; but the first *Toy Story* makes clear that the Woody and Buzz in the film have a different job: Andy's toys. Once Woody and Buzz are accidentally set out for curbside collection, the social relation changes from 'Andy's toy' to 'no longer Andy's toy'. The goal the toys share is to get back to work. The landfill – in particular the incinerator – threatens to make unemployment as a toy permanent. Without the *Deus ex machina* of The Claw, Woody and Buzz (and the other toys) would be incinerated just the same as the MSW and household waste because they *are* household waste once they're in the landfill. This situation resembles Sosna and Brunclikova's contention that '[t]he indeterminacy of waste emerges when one moves beyond the functional paradigm where waste (or refuse) comes into being when artefacts are discarded because they cannot perform their functions' (2016: 4). You cannot perform the function of toy, even one in the reserve army of storage, if you are a pile of ashes. Similarly, you cannot perform the function of waste allocation load lifter if you are crushed by a spaceship's industrial-strength compactors. At that point, you're waste. *Gattaca* and *Land of the Dead* use waste to show institutionalized social inequalities, and *WALL-E* uses waste to show what undergirds the Pixar films, Hollywood films in general, and anglophone culture more broadly: an ideological attachment to work, in particular to industrial production for obsolescence and the waste that is sure to follow it. This attachment to work, to productivity above all, leads to one frequent and terrifying destination within the waste disposal system: the landfill.

Waste and landfills

As with any infrastructural system, waste disposal represents a technical challenge and a social challenge. Martin Melosi's massive history *The Sanitary City: Environmental Services in Urban America from Colonial Times to the Present* argues that the technologies of sanitation, '[t]aken as a group – water, supply, wastewater, and solid-waste collection and disposal – are basic and fundamental to the urban experience. To function effectively the American city has to be a sanitary city' (2008: 426). For a city to function it must meet the technical challenges. The placement of landfills, to name one example, represents one part of the social challenge of waste collection and disposal. The waste I generate at home and at work travels less than 20 km to the local landfill, which is close to a parkland set aside for koalas, an endangered species. The extinction of koalas collides with the need to dispose of takeaway coffee cups. This juxtaposition offers one layer of meaning embedded in a landfill. Daniel Sosna compares landfills to libraries and computer servers, in that 'they conserve an immense amount of information' (Sosna 2016: 173). However, Sosna notes, the content of landfills defies easy classification, as they are

> extremely heterogenous, with an inconspicuous internal structure. Diverse categories of things are intermixed in a way that ignores classification of things [...] in libraries texts, maps, audio and video files carry signs, language represents the primary vehicle for semiosis, and sings are ordered and catalogued to facilitate recalling of memory. Servers unify all signs under the umbrella of digital code. Landfills, in contrast, are composed of incredibly heterogenous carriers of meaning accumulated in an unintentional manner. Not only texts, clothing, nappies, furniture, food, construction material, or garden waste but also specific smells provide potential for signification. (2016: 173)

Information abounds in a landfill, but no easy schema to discern its patterns and meanings presents itself. And this presumes the information holds value. In some cases, landfills, unlike cemeteries, 'are perceived as places of forgetting. Once waste is disposed and buried, it should disappear from the mind of most humans' (Sosna 2016: 175). For instance *Isle of Dogs*' flu-bearing dogs are not killed but exiled to the landfill. When Rex explains the presence of the young boy Atari in the landfill he tells fellow dogs King, Duke, and Boss,

> let's look at the pros. That boy flew here, all alone and crash-landed onto this island for one reason; one reason only: to find his dog. To the best of my knowledge, no other master, not one single human master, has made any effort to do that. They've forgotten all about us.

Rex knows that the main result of going to the landfill, whether you're a dog or a plastic bottle, is being forgotten. But in such cases as Atari's, when someone digs into the landfill and its contents, landfills can represent not forgetting but rather access to buried and sometimes unexpected memories. In film terms, the contents of a landfill tells a story characters cannot, both about themselves and their worlds. In other words, landfills are dense accumulations of social relations (Sosna 2016: 175), both to discarded material objects and the relations they make concrete.

As the dogs exiled to Trash Island show, landfills offer a location that signals wilful forgetting, a psychological exile. For instance, Neill Blomkamp associates the dispossessed and waste sites in *District 9* (Philip Ivey 2009), in which the sociologist Sarah Livingstone explains, 'the derogatory term "prawn" is used for the alien and obviously it implies something that is a bottom feeder, that scavenges the leftovers'. Livingstone's interview moves from a talking head in university office to quasi-voice-over of a street scene, as a cut after 'bottom feeder' creates a voice-over narration of a shot of an alien picking through trash (Figure 5.1). During one vox-pop street interview, an alien appears in the background, rummaging through a dumpster while a woman answers the question in the foreground. *I, Robot* turns a Chicago-area landfill into slum housing. The equation of landfills and slum housing in proximity to the city in *Isle of Dogs*, *Chappie*, *District 9*, and *I, Robot* echoes Janet Staiger's argument about *Blade Runner*, *Brazil*, and *Max Headroom* in 'Future noir: Contemporary representations of visionary cities' that '[i]ntegral to all these dystopias is a bleak criticism of utopian version of high modernist architecture and modern cityscapes, structures which harbour corrupt economic and social institutions' (1999: 120). In such places, '[t]he omnipresence of waste serves as a sign that the digestive tract of advanced capital's body politic must still be working, indeed working "overtime" and at full capacity' (Sobchack 1990: 135). These landfill spaces collect their societies' material waste. They also maintain corrupt economic

FIGURE 5.1: *District 9* prawn rooting through trash during vox-pop.

and social institutions by collecting the waste products of those institutions – the humans-canines-aliens-robots who are no longer necessary.

In addition to landfills as slum-residence, landfills as work sites make clear the continued utility of waste disposal to the maintenance of society. In the scene from *Land of the Dead* I analysed earlier, Cholo provides Kaufman with luxury goods and food, and also provides him with waste disposal services. In the film's opening sequence, Cholo and his friend Foxy dump boxes into a landfill. Foxy notes, '[w]hole lotta trash this week' and Cholo sagely replies, '[t]hat's life bro, whole lot of trash. The trick is not to get in with it', which, unfortunately, he does. As Cholo and Foxy flip the box over, a close-up of the box reveals blood leaking out. Cholo's disposes of inconveniently dead people for Kaufman. Knowing the contents of the garbage provides valuable information, the key to life in the city, as 'a functioning city is but a collage of such unacknowledged, unglamorous services like trash collection, made possible by the tireless grunt labor of individuals' (Marty 2021: n.pag.). Waste disposal is a dangerous job under ideal circumstances, and the addition of zombies makes it more dangerous. The necessity of this unglamourous, dangerous but necessary labour informs Cholo's belief that Kaufman will create a space in the safe, comfortable gated community Fiddler's Green for him as a reward for grunt services rendered. Kaufman does not. Cholo is, after all, a working-class Latino, making him undesirable to the board of directors who police Fiddler's Green's restrictive housing, as disposable as the bodies he dumps in the landfill for them. The various forms of waste that accumulate in the landfills of dystopian and post-apocalyptic worlds reveal a social relationship that displaces 'undesirables' outside of the liveable centres and, failing that, buries them altogether.

Incinerators and disposal chutes

An even more forceful – and permanent – displacement takes the form of burning, whether in an open fire or an incinerator. In a literal sense, burning waste eliminates danger. Zombie movies like *28 Weeks Later* offer the strongest version of burning as the quickest path to eliminate waste and the dangers it presents. In addition to the buildings burning and the flamethrower fight sequences, the conclusion of *World War Z* shows bodies in amongst the MSW in landfills set afire, eliminating the never-understood cause for the zombie apocalypse with its hosts. More abstractly, the memory hole in *1984* offers the clearest articulation of how fire can eliminate the evidence of wrongthink, maintaining the purity of a dystopian world's discursive boundaries. Incinerators can dispose of evidence of the world's faults, as when *The Island*'s evil Dr Merrick orders the clones be destroyed, leading, in a tasteless scene, to them being herded into a large incinerator. Tris incinerates her clothes, full of 'the toxins which plague our world', as part of the decontamination process upon arriving at the Bureau of Genetic Welfare in *Allegiant*. But dystopian and post-apocalyptic people do not always use incinerators as intended. They also repurpose incinerators, as in *Soylent Green*, where Martha Philips uses her apartment's incinerator to hide an illicit jar of jelly. In a more complicated repurposing, in *Judge Dredd* Judge Dredd and his sidekick Fergie seek to infiltrate Mega City One. Dredd explains,

> [t]here is a way in. Six years ago, two refugees figured it out. It's a vent to the city's incinerator. There's a burst twice a minute. That means somebody could run through that tube and have thirty seconds before it flames again.

Dredd admits that the refugees 'were roasted. But the theory is sound'. The massive vent and tunnels act as visual embellishment to Dredd's infiltration of Mega City One based on inside Judge knowledge.

Such a playful repurposing of the waste disposal infrastructure, only in the 'correct' direction, appears in Alice's parkour escape through a garbage disposal chute in *Resident Evil: Apocalypse*. Fleeing from the mutant supersoldier Nemesis, Alice runs down an office building hallway. A zooming POV shot shows a close-up of a metal door labelled 'Garbage Disposal', and Alice shoots the wall beneath the door as she continues running. She then slides along the floor, through the hole she made in the wall, tumbling down the garbage chute into a large skip and relative safety. Incinerators and waste disposal chutes, though they appear as unidirectional and irreversible, nevertheless frequently appear as testaments to possibility, moments where life in a dystopia needn't be so terrible, or where life after the apocalypse can begin making space for something better.

The trash aesthetic and social relations in landfills

Paper waste blowing along the street signifies differently than toxic waste seeping up from the ground, though both are waste. As John Scanlon argues,

> the meaning of 'waste' carries force because of the way in which it symbolizes an idea of improper use, and therefore operates within a more or less moral economy of the right, the good, the proper, their opposites and all values in between.
>
> (2005: 22)

Nick Pinkerton's review of *Ready Player One* identifies the film with waste, from its title – 'Le Cinéma du Glut' – to its almost-constant references to – 'a glut of accumulated pop *effluvia* […] the medium is the *mess* […] 30-odd years of accumulated popular-culture iconography can be seen *cluttering* the screen […] hotchpotch accumulation of the *detritus* of recognizable pop iconography' (2018: n.pag., emphasis added). Pinkerton links form and content, arguing that '[l]ike few feature films before it, Spielberg's movie exemplifies an aesthetic of […] the junk-pile jumble of accumulated mass-manufactured character properties at the end of pop history – the aesthetic of glut' (2018: n.pag.). This aesthetic finds its most powerful expression in The Stacks, an elaborate multilevel trailer park slum where Wade lives and games. As Pinkerton describes them, The Stacks are 'a habitable junkyard of sorts – among the great landfills of recent cinema, along with those of *WALL-E* (2008) and *Isle of Dogs* – neglected by a population in thrall to the virtual' (2018: n.pag.). Pinkerton mixes his metaphors, moving from favela to landfill, from cultural productions to trash. The key social relation is between residents and pop culture, not the MSW on the street, making The Stacks a vertical slum not a landfill. Wes Anderson's compositions in *Isle of Dogs* – fussy symmetrical shots showing discarded objects arranged neatly by colour, by shape, by texture, and so on, into trash hills – visualize the key social relation on Trash Island, closely matching the concerns of the landfill: who belongs where. Somewhere between these two we can find *WALL-E*. Its cutesy used-universe LEGO-block vision of landfill Earth contrasts with the bright shiny curves and fat phobia of outer space. On Earth trash is everywhere whereas in space trash simply disappears down chutes hidden in the *Axiom*'s walls. When the exiles aboard the *Axiom* return to Earth, they terraform it into a green globe that can once again support human life. In this happy ending 'we are made to believe that garbage, discarded objects, and obsolete media can be repurposed in meaningful ways' (Tischleder 2016: 457). To be overly literal, we are made to believe that the landfill humans have made of the Earth can be redeemed, both physically/ecologically and, for lack of a better word, spiritually. In a sense this is true. The Fresh Kills landfill on Staten Island changed from the largest landfill in the world into a 2,200 acre park at the turn of the twenty-first century (Freshkillspark n.d.: n.pag.). But the happy ending depends on a trick of filmmaking *Ready Player One*, *Isle of Dogs*, and *WALL-E* share. The Stacks of *Ready Player One*, Trash Island of Isle of Dogs, and the landfill earth of *WALL-E* and were not shot on location. These three films spend a great deal of screen time in landfill-like spaces, and find great potential for hope there, but those spaces do not exist in the world, but rather as digital and/or miniaturized models. Freed from the constraints of location shooting, the physical forms of the landfills carry no leftover meaning from their actual sites, instead registering in *Isle of Dogs* and *WALL-E* the freedom of action made possible by the total isolation of islands and abandoned planets and, in *Ready Player One*, registering the potential for cultural rediscovery and remixing that living amongst the detritus of the past offers.

Sewers

The breakdown of civilization is not quite complete at the beginning of *Zombieland*, as Columbus can still find a working public toilet. Ten years later, with the ersatz family of Columbus, Wichita, Tallahassee, and Little Rock ensconced in the White House, Columbus changes his advice for the audience of *Zombieland Double Tap*: '[T]he world is your bathroom'. The power may still be on, but the sewer system no longer works. Two practical factors explain the non-functioning sewer system of many post-apocalyptic worlds: no water to (waste on a) flush and no technology and expertise to perform treatment. In terms of intended use, dystopian and post-apocalyptic sewers usually don't transport waste to a treatment plant, but they still maintain boundaries. Heather Rogers builds on Dominique Laporte's *History of Shit*, writing that

> the privy made the act of wasting private, while the creation of municipal infrastructures cast cleaning as public. The upshot of this was that wasting – whether bodily excretions, the flow of castoffs from a household, or the effluent of industry – was hidden from view and public consciousness.
>
> (2013: 74)

As Slavoj Žižek loves to point out, a toilet offers an opportunity for someone like Columbus to contemplate excremental excess; it also, when in working order, is part of a system that disposes of that excess (1997: 5–6, 2004: n.pag.). The path that disposal takes, the physical sewer that remains – underground, difficult to access, full of forking paths, and dark – often plays a significant role in dystopian and post-apocalyptic worlds because of the privacy it offers those who would use it for a different sort of waste transport.

Sometimes a sewer is just a sewer. In post-apocalyptic worlds, as civilization has already been lost, sewers feature far less frequently. In *The Matrix* the sewer is all that remains of human cities. *Waterworld* features a form of human waste disposal in The Atoll, not a sewer but a septic 'tank' at the base of the large tree around which the settlement is built. In dystopian worlds, sewers continue to function, and the control of their function provides an index of who wields power. One of the propaganda messages broadcast to the people in *1984* crows about improved sewerage, an empty boast when Winston later only has a bucket as a toilet during his imprisonment. The radically stratified and genetically monitored world of *Code 46* shows that in a world of seamless global travel for some, the presence of open sewers in impoverished parts of cities offers a clear indication of who enjoys fewer rights. But overall dystopian worlds present a clean image of sewers in cities, if they appear at all, with the major exception of *Brazil*. Saw Lowrey returns home to find the Central Services maintenance workers Spoor and Dowser fixing a problem with his flat's thermostat. They issue him an H22O6 form, taking away his flat for making unnecessary repairs. Luckily, the freelance engineer Harry Tuttle waits outside, and he redirects the flat's sewage outflow into the air tubes feeding Spoor and Dowser's climate control suits. With waste swapped for air, the climate control suits soon fill to the point of explosion. Turning sewer-bound waste into a weapon shows the undercurrent of danger that waste disposal represents: misdirected, it can be deadly.

But by far the most common role that sewers perform in dystopian and post-apocalyptic movies is that of the improvised escape route or hideaway home. Sewers as an alternative to street travel echo Steve Graham and Simon Marvin's characterization of the city:

> To Haussmann the road network was the city's circulatory system; the rationally engineered sewer and cemetery systems were the waste disposal 'organs' of the metropolis; and green spaces were the city's 'respiratory' system. The street system, in fact, was the physical framework for the 'bundling' of buried water networks, lighting, drains and sewers – a situation so familiar today that we take it for granted.
> (2001: 55)

The circulation of people, for Haussmann, takes place on the streets, while the circulation of waste takes place in the sewer and cemetery. But the bundling of other networks beneath the city streets brings with it latent potential for reuse, especially for those familiar with the city and its layout. Zack Snyder's *Dawn of the Dead*, in addition to being a remake of George Romero's 1978 film, features an attempted escape through the sewers similar to the one attempted in John Carpenter's dystopian *Assault on Precinct 13* (Tommy Lee Wallace AD 1976). The escape, like many sewer escapes, depends on the sewer connecting spaces underground, rather than above ground, where the post-apocalyptic dangers await. Thus rather than chance the dangers above ground, Snake Plissken twice uses the sewer to *Escape from LA*; similarly, Alice uses sewers as tunnels that offer alternative access/escape routes in *Resident Evil: Afterlife*. Atari, Chief, and Spots find themselves in a sewer that functions both as a boundary and an escape route in *Isle of Dogs*. Sewers offer a space for second-hand escape as well: in *The Island* Lincoln Six Echo pisses out the tracking sensors Dr Merrick put in him, using the sewers to send his enemies the wrong way. Finally, in the *Hunger Games* series the Capitol's sewers double as tunnels that offer alternative access routes into the city like the exhaust vents in *Judge Dredd*.

The sewer only appears by implication in *Escape from New York*, but soon after Snake Plissken arrives in New York, the Crazies emerge from the sewers. They come above ground, the woman Snake meets in Chock Full O'Nuts explains, when they run out of food. In other words, they live in the sewers. The sewer as home appears with great in a number of other dystopian and post-apocalyptic movies. The most extensive domesticated sewer appears in *Demolition Man*, where the revolutionary Edgar Friendly and his Scraps live. It seems that the three seashells found in every bathroom have rendered sewers superfluous. The underground sewer spaces that allow them to access the megacity of San Angeles via manholes also provide substantial living space. On the one hand, if Victor Hugo is right and the sewer is the conscience of the city, then San Angeles' conscience is clean – witness the near-zero crime rate. On the other hand, San Angeles' world without sewers seems to have cleaned up sexual expression to an extreme degree, as Spartan discovers when Huxley (Sandra Bullock) is not familiar with kissing. Similarly, even carnality, imagined as violence, exists as an abstraction, as Spartan discovers when only he knows how to deal with the violence Simon Phoenix brings to the future. In this way *Demolition Man* shows the necessity of sewers to civilization, from their ability to take away necessary waste to their potential for alternative travel routes and even escape.

Reduce, reuse, recycle

The straitened circumstances of most dystopian and every post-apocalyptic world means that of the three R's of waste management – reduce, reuse, recycle – *reducing* waste tends to be easy. The Blitz-like world of *1984* makes a bag of tea or coffee a precious treasure. *The Hunger Games*' District 12 does not seem to have a single plastic bottle; the people seem to have but a few sets of clothes; children do not have large collections of toys and dolls. Similarly, the underground District 13 maintains quasi-military discipline in its austere approach to personal possessions. The brief glimpses at the agricultural and forestry districts show a similar reduction in personal effects. The people in the extractive districts of the *Hunger Games* series' Panem share with the people of *1984*'s Airstrip One a very limited wardrobe, their clothing options reduced to functional worker clothing like coveralls. In post-apocalyptic films, the reduction in the amount of all resources used appears in the familiar form of wearing the same clothes every day, as in *The Matrix* and the *Resident Evil* series, and in the ability to put every single possession into a single small container, sometimes a ship's hull, as in *Waterworld*, a shopping cart, as in *The Road*, or even a bag, as in *The Book of Eli* and *Mad Max Beyond Thunderdome*. Evan Calder Williams reads this reuse as part of what he calls 'salvagepunk', noting that

> the world of zombie hordes is a radical contraction of what is desirable to possess: if it can't kill, heal, feed, help escape, burn, or barricade, then it only slows you down. Exchange value rots even faster than the bodies, leaving behind objects in their naked utility and hardness.
>
> (2011: 84–85)

Reducing consumption and thereby reducing waste registers the baseline of naked utility, the bare minimum for dystopian despots to ensure for their oppressed people and for post-apocalyptic survivors to achieve on their own or in concert with a small group of allies.

When naked utility takes precedence, reuse takes on added urgency, especially in post-apocalyptic worlds where industrial production no longer occurs. Post-apocalyptic survivors almost uniformly reuse important means of transport, weapons, and tools. *WALL-E*, for example, uses broken down *WALL-E* units for replacement parts. The taken-for-granted importance of reuse after the apocalypse appears when reuse doesn't occur, as when Neville simply walks away from his car after the tyre comes off the rim in *The Omega Man*. Rather than put on the spare, Neville goes to a car dealership and drives a new car off the lot. Some of the most visually arresting approaches to dystopian and post-apocalyptic recycling appear when objects get reused in new but critical fashions. The dogs in *Isle of Dogs* reuse materials from Trash Island to create a medical prosthesis for a dog missing a leg. The bright teal of the attachment to the dog's foreleg, centred and bright against an otherwise dark image creates a visual distinctiveness that signals possibility amidst the sad detritus of the island. The Mariner in *Waterworld* dives to underwater cities not only to dig up dirt for trade, but also for other possibly useful items such as the car bumpers that form the frame of his catamaran's mesh platform. The Mariner is not alone in this dedication to reuse. A fellow wandering trader wears a jacket made of plastic six-pack rings linked together, and the people who live under the Deacon's command on the Exxon Valdez reuse sardine tins as cups. In such examples, waste products show the potential in repurposing objects in meaningful ways to create a new civilization and culture out of the wreckage of the past.

Dystopian worlds address their own limits by finding a use – or better yet reuse – for materials like old six-pack rings. Those hoping to reuse components and materials in building design can use one or more of the approaches Bill Addis describes in *Building with Reclaimed Components and Materials*, such as reusing in situ, reusing salvaged or reconditioned products and reclaimed materials, using recycled materials (2006: 14–15). Matt Hanson notes that trash in *Johnny Mnemonic* reappears as building materials (2004: 58). The hacker site Heaven in *Johnny Mnemonic* reuses in situ (the bridge changes from transportation to residence), salvages old metal and furniture (file cabinets form a sort of deck), and recycles old circuit boards. The world of *Johnny Mnemonic* and other reuse-heavy dystopian and post-apocalyptic worlds resembles less the high-end housing that Addis's book inspired and more the approach taken by community groups like the building supplier Buffalo ReUse, which became Reuse Action, and the eco arts and reuse co-op Reverse Garbage Queensland. Both groups accentuate the reuse of materials and their affordability, essential to *Johnny Mnemonic*'s hacker-anarchist Heaven, as well as for the steam engine-equipped (and chandelier-decorated) cars prisoners drive in *Escape from New York* and the Dauntless training centre in a former quarry in *Divergent*, all of which accentuate the essential nature of naked utility and reuse's ability to deliver utility as a step toward a liveable future.

Recycle

Some instances of dystopian and post-apocalyptic recycling look quite similar to in-place technology. In *The Hunger Games: Mockingjay, Part 1*, Katniss walks through a military installation in District 8, she passes a stack of cubes, their compressed form a familiar denotative image of recycling. The same recycling cube imagery pervades *WALL-E*, and forms the basis for mountains and skyscrapers on the depopulated Earth (The cubes are less recyclables than the kind of general waste 'ecobales' that led to the 'Italian Chernobyl' of criminally mismanaged waste disposal in the Campania region) (Dickie 2013: 437–43). However, neither film imagines a recycling system but rather reuse: in *The Hunger Games: Mockingjay,*

Part 1 the cube offers another option for cover should the installation be overrun; in *WALL-E* the cubes form post-human ziggurats. The Matrix includes both energy production and waste disposal in its infrastructure. In much the same way Neo encounters a power plant in the Matrix/*The Matrix*, he later encounters Rama Khandra, 'power plant systems manager for recycling operations' in the Matrix in the opening of *The Matrix Revolutions* (Owen Paterson 2003). However, Rama, who is himself a computer program, speaks not of recycling but something like landfilling when he tells Neo

> I love my daughter very much. I find her to be the most beautiful thing I've ever seen. But where we are from that is not enough. Every program that is created must have a purpose. If it does not, it is deleted.

One of the most innovative appearances of recycling comes out of the *Waterworld* Atoll's criminal justice system. The ultimate penalty they mete out is not the death penalty but rather the recycling penalty, which entails drowning in The Atoll's septic tank-like waste into fertilizer patch. *Soylent Green*, *Judge Dredd*, and *Dredd* all take a more direct route to recycling dead bodies. *Soylent Green* recycles bodies which once provided labour power into food to fuel the still-living labour power. In *Judge Dredd* a robot wanders an apartment building offering recycled food. The hapless Fergie hides in the robot and repeats its mantra, 'eat recycled food, for a happier, healthier life. Be kind and peaceful to each other. Eat recycled food. Recycled food. It's good for the environment and OK for you'. This recycling of bodies offers a reduction of another type of consumption, meat. The queasiness *Soylent Green* invites at its conclusion

> They're making our food out of people. Next thing they'll be breeding us like cattle for food. You gotta tell 'em. You gotta tell 'em. You tell everybody. Listen to me Hatcher, you gotta tell 'em: Soylent Green is people! We've gotta stop 'em somehow!

accentuates the fear of cannibalism that dystopian and post-apocalyptic worlds bring with them. The more humorous sense of recycled food in *Judge Dredd* resembles the recurrent hoax of poop burgers. In 1993, a short time before *Judge Dredd*'s release, stories about food made from recycled human excrement appeared numerous English-language newspapers in the United States, Canada, the United Kingdom, and Australia; the same story appeared a couple decades later, with Fox News reporting on it (Elliot 2011: n.pag.). In an early chase sequence in *Dredd*, Dredd summons RECYK, a municipal service for murder scene clean up (Figure 5.2). As the RECYK machine cleans the food court through which Dredd chased a criminal, the voice on the loudspeaker declares 'the level one food court will reopen in 30 minutes. Thank you for your patience' over shots of dead bodies stacked

FIGURE 5.2: *Dredd* recycling bodies.

in the RECYK's wagon. The scene is played for laughs and offers an ambiguous future for the dead bodies – burial or recycling? As Baron Haussmann knew, cemeteries act as a disposal system; but the limited space of future dystopian worlds – overcrowded New York City, the walled Mega City One – makes cemeteries less likely, and creates the need for a more extensive recycling system, up to and including human bodies.

E-waste and the spatial fix

E-waste disposal in *Blade Runner 2049* shows how waste and waste disposal can reveal the importance of what David Harvey calls the spatial fix of capitalism, and its importance to the imagination of what can improve a dystopian world and can ensure the post- of a post-apocalyptic world. While MSW and many other forms of waste remain close to home, in landfills or dispersed into the ground/air/water as pollution, e-waste and the ships that carry global trade do not stay close to home for the United States, the United Kingdom, Australia, and Aotearoa New Zealand residents. That waste goes elsewhere, usually to Asia or Africa, as do the effects of that waste, and the effects of e-waste are considerable. More than the presence of waste, the presence of waste disposal – specific kinds of waste disposal most especially – offers an index of dystopianism. Rich countries export e-waste disposal and ships for breaking; poor countries perform the e-waste disposal. While some security-conscious military shipbreaking happens in the Global North, the overwhelming majority of shipbreaking occurs in the Global South: Bangladesh, China, India, and Pakistan. Dystopian and post-apocalyptic worlds stage the return of e-waste disposal and shipbreaking to the rich world. The massive sets as embellishment in

Blade Runner 2049 show that waste makes comfortable civilization at the cost of damaging disposal elsewhere.

Blade Runner 2049 shows a continuation of the status quo of its 2017 release: People in rich countries generate most of the globe's waste and e-waste. Durable goods like televisions, dishwashers, refrigerators, clothes washers and dryers, stoves, and air conditioners may last a little longer than planned obsolescence exemplars like desktops, laptops, tablets, and mobile phones, but all eventually end their useful life as e-waste. Broadly speaking, rich countries export their waste, and not just e-waste. For instance, some EU trash stays within Europe, but leaves the immediate vicinity of where it was produced. Roberto Saviano's Camorra exposé *Gomorrah* details the importance of waste disposal within Italy. Expanding the circle slightly, Jana Tsoneva writes of how Bulgaria functions as a dumping ground for EU member states:

> [T]he European directive regulating waste shipments has had a paradoxical effect: the rise of literal trash markets that transfer waste to Eastern Europe. If in the past the problem of trash was an outsourcing to China – the largest recipient of trash from the EU – this changed in 2018 when it enforced draconian restrictions on waste imports. With China abruptly shutting down the trade, the pollution outflow that began choking affluent European nations had to find alternative outlets. The trash, and the pollution associated with burning it, continues to be shipped eastward – but now it's citizens of other EU member states who must deal with the effects.
>
> (2020: n.pag.).

Though China shut down much of its waste importation, countries outside of the EU and North America continue to take in waste, including e-waste, and 'in 2019, American exporters shipped almost 1.5 billion pounds of plastic waste to 95 countries' including Mexico, Thailand, Malaysia, Ghana, Uganda, Tanzania, South Africa, Ethiopia, Senegal, and Kenya (Lerner 2020: n.pag.). Within this exported waste, the 'majority of the E-waste from [the] developed world, i.e. the USA, Britain and Europe, is transferred to developing nations' (Vaish et al. 2020: 222).

K. Grace Pavirtha et al. describe one common e-waste management and disposal system, the 'collection outside the take-back system':

> In a developed waste management system, Electronic-waste which is collected by the individual dealers is accounted, and the Electronic-waste end[s] up [in] locations such as metal recycling; plastic recycling is explored, and the information is not reported to the official take-back system to avoid double counting. In undeveloped countries [...] local dumping, export, and recovery of value-added substance is done.
>
> (2020: 206–07)

Some parts of e-waste can be *recycled*, but other parts need to be *recovered*. The location of these processes makes clear that some parts of waste disposal entail more danger than others. Recycling metal and plastic occurs in rich countries. The 'recovery of value-added substance' happens in poorer countries. And given that a person in a rich country, for instance an EU country, generates 15 kg of e-waste per year – a cell phone, a Blu-ray player, a hair dryer, it adds up – the recovery of value-added substances represents no small task (Pavithra et al. 2020: 205). This exported e-waste creates 'fields of dead motherboards [...] left to be stripped for usable bits', as shown in Jennifer Baichwal's 2006 documentary *Manufactured Landscapes*, which explores the environmental devastation of the industrial and waste disposal locations Edward Burtynsky photographed in his 2003 collection of the same name.

Proximity to waste disposal sites carries with it environmental and health impacts. Sharon Lerner writes that

> [a] 75-foot tall heap of mixed plastic and organic garbage known as Mount Pirana has risen near a school in the western [Indian] city of Ahmedabad. Every day, 4,000 tons of new waste are added to the landfill, and children who live near it suffer from headaches, nerve pain, respiratory problems, and cancers.
>
> (2020: n.pag.)

Proximity to e-waste disposal sites presents similar, and heightened dangers. In Ghana,

> Agbogbloshie is the final destination for much of the estimated 40 million tons of electronic waste the world produces every year [...] [E]ggs laid by chickens that forage nearby contained the second-highest level of brominated dioxins ever measured, according to the International Pollution Elimination Network, which performed the tests last year. The chemicals can harm developing fetuses, disrupt the functioning the immune and endocrine systems, and cause cancer.
>
> (Lerner 2020: n.pag.)

E-waste disposal and value-added recovery is dangerous and highly polluting, but also presents an advantage: it reclaims aluminium, copper, gold and silver. But the reclamation comes with a significant environmental and human (health) costs. Finn Arne Jørgensen observes that 'waste processing of industrial waste has steadily been moved to developing countries in Asia and Africa, where labor is cheaper and environmental regulation less strict' (2019: 136–37). In addition, the people shipping their e-waste elsewhere can hold the lives of the people in Asia and Africa cheaply, distant and othered as they are. When K enters the massive space where hundreds and hundreds of children hunch over small tables, disassembling chip boards, Mister Cotton, the adult in charge, is in the middle of a shouted threat that explains their exploitation in no uncertain terms: 'Work! Every little piece! I'll put you outside where the sky is raining. Where it's raining fire. You're in here to work, and if you're not working, I don't need you'. Upon misrecognizing K as a potential buyer, he stops shouting. A cut brings a long travelling shot from table height, gliding past the ramshackle tables stacked with circuit boards that the dirty, poorly clothed children pull apart. Mister Cotton explains the work to K, 'the nickel is for the colonial ships, the closest any of them, or any of us, is gonna get that grand life offworld'. The waste disposal K sees – by hand, by child labour – appears to take him into the past, into a poorer country. The e-waste disposal also performs a kind of extractive labour, providing the raw materials for colonization and the further marginalization and immiseration of both the Los Angeles region and the people and replicants who labour there.

In his advocacy research, David Naguib Pellow describes his approach to situating and historicizing environmental justice:

> I explore the ways in which our garbage is imposed upon vulnerable populations and how it impacts those of us who are forced to live on or near it and those of us whose job it is to dispose of it.
>
> (2004: 2)

The previously 'more human than human' replicants are now the less-than-human waste workers, engaged in the 3D labour of e-waste disposal and recycling. The massive scale of e-waste recovery in *Blade Runner 2049*, performed by child labour no less, shows that the United States has become poor to the degree that it performs 3D jobs previously offshored (Figure 5.3). Not the clean, green services-based knowledge economy of previous dreams of the future, but a system that further exploits its dehumanized population, Earth-bound humans and replicants alike. The piles of e-waste in *Blade Runner 2049* do not show the charming symmetry and near-architectural status of the compacted trash of *WALL-E*. Babette Tischleder observes that

> the creators of *WALL-E* made sure that their depiction of trash does not resemble e-waste in any way. A salvaged iPod is the only obsolete digital gadget we see in the film, and it is, magically, still working after 700 years. *WALL-E* thus obfuscates the close connection between the pleasures that digital technologies afford and the e-waste that is sure to follow in their wake. Keeping its diegetic trash free from unsettling associations and foregrounding its own aesthetic style, the Pixar movie celebrates digital design while disavowing its implication in wasteful economies.
>
> (2016: 458)

FIGURE 5.3: *Blade Runner 2049* recycling and child labour.

The waste disposal systems that K sees show not just the effects of wasteful economies in the present of the film's release, but also the diegetic present of 2049. The view of the waste disposal system shows the degree of dystopian future *Blade Runner 2049* imagines: that shipbreaking and e-waste disposal systems have relocated to southern California places the United States as the recipient of waste, placing it lower on the world hierarchy. The presence of e-waste and shipbreaking waste disposal systems makes clear the United States is now a poor country with a very rich resident, Niander Wallace. Where once the United States could displace its trash elsewhere, now the trash and its dangerous disposal stays on shore, where its polluting effects appear to have rendered the land barren.

In this manner, *Blade Runner 2049* and *WALL-E* both reveal the way the social relations that waste disposal creates and maintains have an essentially spatial character in dystopian and post-apocalyptic movies. While *Blade Runner 2049* operates by implication, *WALL-E* takes a more didactic approach, showing an advertisement that says 'Too much garbage in your face? There is plenty of space out in space. BNL Starliners leaving each day. We'll clean up the mess while you are away'. Earth becomes the landfill, the *Axiom* the means to put distance between human life and the waste it produced. Interstellar travel presents an even grander vision of the geographical expansion of globalization. As David Harvey writes,

> [c]apitalism, we might say, is addicted to geographical expansion much as it is addicted to technological change and endless expansion through economic growth. Globalization is the contemporary version of capitalism's long-standing and never-ending search for a spatial fix to its crisis tendencies.
>
> (2001: 24–25)

The spatial fix, as Harvey argues, is one of the central contradictions of capital:

> [I]t has to build a fixed space (or 'landscape') necessary for its own functioning at a certain point in its history only to have to destroy that space (and devalue much of the capital invested therein) at a later point in order to make way for a new 'spatial fix' (openings for fresh accumulation in new spaces and territories) at a later point in its history.
>
> (2001: 25)

In the social relations inherent in the examples throughout this chapter, the spatial fix boomerangs. The space has been destroyed through dystopian control or apocalyptic event, but the residents – survivors – remain.

In the Goldilocks sense, the too hot world suffers from proximity to trash and the too cold world displaces its trash too far away. In between, the waste disposal infrastructure does its work. In an abstract sense, waste and waste disposal create conceptual boundaries between belonging and exile, as in *Gattaca* and *Land of the Dead*, boundaries between the powerful and the vulnerable as in *Blade Runner 2049*, and boundaries between the known and the forgotten in *1984*. More concretely, waste and waste disposal create physical boundaries between the seen and the unseen as in *Soylent Green*, the liveable and the uninhabitable as in *Ready Player One*, *Demolition Man*, and *WALL-E*, and the safe and the unsafe as in *28 Weeks Later* and *Allegiant*. When used for something other than waste disposal, the infrastructure creates airlocks between civilization and wasteland, as in *Judge Dredd*, *Escape from New York*, and *Children of Men*. And the in moments of alternative use, the waste disposal infrastructure can bend time and space, providing escape routes and alternate paths as in *Resident Evil: Apocalypse*, *Escape from LA*, and the *Hunger Games* series.

In this chapter's examples, some locations, their people, and/or their descendants are almost entirely missing: the continents outside of North America, Europe, and Australia. The waste disposal infrastructure reveals a sense that mass entertainment Hollywood-UK-Australian films register that the United States or, in a pinch, the anglophone world losing its spot at the top of the trash pile would be synonymous with dystopia at best, apocalypse at worst. Having to recycle and make do with old products, sometimes putting them to markedly different uses out of necessary, from six-pack ring jackets to landfills turned tenements, shows that the world has fallen out of joint. To be at the bottom of the trash pile indeed means living in a dystopian at best world. And the trash has to go somewhere. The apocalypse is already now for a lot of places in the world. The rich countries like the United States, the United Kingdom, and Australia are simply catching up. Living in a dystopia, in the ongoing apocalypse, is what the next chapter will analyse.

Conclusion

> *The earth, our home, is beginning to look more and more like an immense pile of filth.*
>
> (Pope Francis 2020: 20)

> *In the late twentieth century the unimaginable, the unspeakable, has already happened, and continues to happen. And, paradoxically, while unimaginable, it is at the same time quite visible.*
>
> (James Berger 1999: 42)

Some of the close to one hundred films analysed in this book so far take place in what is now, for us, the past. Some films made predictions that came true. The panic buying in *World War Z* looks familiar after the COVID-19 runs on toilet paper. The police's violent removal of the unhoused makes *They Live* an accurate representation of American life before, during, and since its release in 1988. The precarious existence of poor and working class people appears in the park encampments of *They Live* and *12 Monkeys* as well as the substandard housing in the *Hunger Games* series and *Dredd*, to name a few. *Escape from New York* and *Escape from LA* offer a window into the increasingly carceral state of US culture. *The Running Man* thought it would be game shows offering the circuses, not a combination of reality TV, twenty-four-hour news, and Prestige TV, but the usefulness of television and film (and literature and video games) to manufacture consent and apathy is clear. Dystopian and post-apocalyptic movies expand on current circumstances; the *Purge* films (2013–21) capture the years in which they were released: a society of ever increasing spectacle, religiously informed reactionaries accumulating power, and pervasive racialized violence.

Dystopian and post-apocalyptic infrastructure on film are shaped by different questions, many of which are generated by historical conjunctures. For this reason, I have included dystopian and post-apocalyptic films from other rich anglophone countries – Aotearoa New Zealand, Australia, the United Kingdom – for the comparative approach they make possible and for the relationship with the post-war United States they reveal. Historical conjunctures include *The Quiet Earth* (1985) and Aotearoa New Zealand's Think Big policy agenda in energy production and its nuclear free stance. *Mad Max* (1979) and Australia's highway death toll, which persisted well into the 1970s, much later than in the similarly wide-open highways of the United States. *Tank Girl* (1995), water privatization in the United Kingdom, and the privatization agenda Washington pushed for the developing world, but not at home. *WALL-E* (2008) and the hyperconsumerist culture of the twenty-first-century industrialized world and *Blade Runner 2049* (2017) by the tech-driven e-waste disaster. *Zombieland* (2009) and the wages of processed food; *Snowpiercer* (2012) and *Warm Bodies* (2013) and the increases in beef consumption that are destroying forests worldwide. We're already living in versions of such dystopian/apocalyptic worlds.

I begin this conclusion by considering the apocalypse of twentieth and early twenty-first-century life in the United States through an examination of two movies that propose specific actions to reverse the slide into apocalypse and root those actions in a particular infrastructural form. *First Reformed* identifies the toxic waste site as key, and proposes to destroy the executives of polluting corporations and to forge deeper human and religious connections as an alternative to the physical and spiritual pollution of twenty-first-century life. However, this solution loses its footing in the infrastructure that supports the decaying world. And so I turn to *Sorry to Bother You*, which presents a vision that argues for democracy to infuse and inform our lives and shows how the sidewalk can offer a key infrastructural site for change. The sidewalk, understood as a public space under democratic control, can offer a path to a better world, starting not with a post-apocalyptic desert or dystopian city-state, but with the infrastructure that links our homes, neighbourhoods, workplaces, and cultural sites and makes room for shared public action.

Rebuilding from the post-apocalyptic happens on a smaller practical scale compared to the global scale of devastation of the apocalypse. Hollywood films face a problem here; infrastructure, post-apocalyptic or not, offers the baseline foundation of everyday life in technological society. Just getting by is what infrastructure promises, but just getting by is not much of a happy ending. A happy ending – *flourishing* – is a social project. As lower-budget pictures with formal-financial constraints that open up different paths to infrastructural solutions to the social project of generating a liveable world for people already living through the current apocalypse *First Reformed* and *Sorry to Bother You* enable a shift in focus towards a smaller scale: the local. Local *control* of infrastructure can matter just as much the infrastructure itself. Local control creates the potential to flourish in different ways, for different groups of people. Writing about the covid pandemic, Srećko Horvat argues that

> what really happened in 2020 was not just a sudden and unexpected 'Apocalypse': it was a process that had been boiling beneath the surface of so-called 'normality' for decades. Whether the current situation will lead to a planetary revolution, or to a new form of destructive and authoritarian capitalism (or postcapitalism) and consequently to mass extinction, still remains uncertain.
>
> (2021: 2)

Taking the second option first, *First Reformed* imagines what happens when, as Reverend Ernst Toller (Ethan Hawke) puts it, 'somebody has to do something' because a few thousand dollars can wash away the sin of polluting the earth, and all that is sacred is profaned. I will then consider the possibility of workers reclaiming workplace and civic power in an examination of *Sorry to Bother You*. I draw the book to a close by considering the world beyond Hollywood and rich anglophone countries with a reading of the narrative, images, diegetic sound, and dialog of the US-Rwandan co-production *Neptune Frost*. I end with *Neptune Frost* to make clear how it presents a vision for the present and the future distinct from mass audience movies, in no small part because of its cultural provenance, and also as a result of its formal construction outside the constraints of mass audience conventions.

First Reformed: *Can God forgive us for what we've done?*

First Reformed makes clear that the people who currently control the world should not. However, who might replace them remains unclear. While a didactic movie like *Don't Look Up* (Clayton Hartley 2021) devotes much of its attention to media criticism and the importance of awareness of the problem, *First Reformed* provides a recipe for action: kill CEOs. *First Reformed* begins with Mary (Amanda Seyfried) asking her pastor Reverend Ernst Toller to speak to her husband Michael (Philip Ettinger), who has just been released from prison. Michael wonders if it is possible to 'sanction' bringing children into the world, given the effects of climate change that will no doubt make the world nearly uninhabitable. Michael is not alone in his wondering. In 'We broke the world', Roy Scranton asks much the same thing:

> Without the belief in future generations who might build on our work, benefit from it, celebrate it, or remember it, that work itself loses much of its meaning [...] Why devote yourself to cancer research if you know for a fact that humanity is soon going to be wiped out by an asteroid? Why have a child? Why write books? Why work for labor rights or racial justice? Why do anything?
>
> (2019: 91)

The subheading to Scranton's article, 'Facing the fact of extinction', resembles Hayes Brown's encapsulation of the reckoning we face: 'The weight of knowing, this time *really* knowing, our future is taking its toll' (2019: n.pag.). After starting the discussion with the usual form of futurity, a child, Michael turns his attention to what bothers him even more: the unsolvable and impersonal problem of climate change. Toller counsels that the unforgivable sin is to give in to the sickness unto death, despair. While much of their discussion takes place in real time, Toller interjects with a voice-over, creating the sense of an even longer discussion that the film does not show. Toller describes this longer implied discussion as makes him feel like Jacob wrestling with the angel. Michael's voice intrudes on the soundtrack, ending the voice-over, to ask Toller about martyrdom. He asks the question that guides the rest of the film: '[C]an God forgive us? For what we've done to this world?' Toller, flustered, can only whisper, 'I don't know'.

Tatiana Prorokova argues that '*First Reformed* does not offer eco-terrorism as an appropriate response. Human death that the viewer can witness against the background of much more horrifying images of already dead nature is an inevitable ramification of environmental degradation' (Prorokova 2020: 172). But after admitting he does not know if God can forgive us for the environmental degradation for which we are responsible, Toller does not whisper but rather states clearly, though he looks down and away, 'who can know the mind of God? But we can choose a righteous life'. Later, Michael dies by suicide and Mary discovers a vest rigged with explosives among his possessions. Seeing the vest, Toller endorses the righteousness of eco-terrorism, advising Mary not to tell the police about what she found: 'Michael was troubled but his cause was just. There's no reason to bring disrepute on that cause'. The form a righteous life can take takes up much of the space in Paul Schrader's films. In a recent analysis of *The Card Counter* (Ashley Fenton 2021), Katherine Krueger describes the righteous life in recent films Schrader has written and directed:

> Schrader is depicting solitary men each on a kind of ideological suicide mission. He also seems to suggest that, in a twisted way, an act of violent self-negation is almost a logical response to the broad, unsolvable structural evils they're each railing against. A pastor donning an explosives vest will effectively do nothing to curb the worldwide effects of climate change, just as a dishonorably discharged former soldier's willingness to suffer greatly or even give up his life won't meaningfully challenge America's war machine. But if you internalize and individualize the soul-crushing enormity of sins like killing our planet or torturing Iraqi taxi drivers to death, you shove out any room for your own soul to remain.
>
> (2021: n.pag.)

The ambiguous ending of *First Reformed* leaves the question of whether God can forgive us for killing a mass-polluting executive open (He can). Though this takes us closer to what we might do to make the world a better place in the short term, it does not address how the infrastructure of upstate New York functions in *First Reformed*'s vision of despair, sin, and righteousness.

Toller goes through a variety of everyday interactions with infrastructure that show a quiet life, cloistered as he is in a gift shop with an extra room where he gives communion. Schrader's directorial style, the 1:1.33 aspect ratio, and the film's production design all work to create an austere world that includes Toller's experience of infrastructure. For instance, in Toller's everyday life at the rectory, he uses as little electricity as possible; usually only one light is on. When he brushes his teeth, a single uncovered bulb lights the bathroom. When he uses a laptop to research climate change, he sits in the dark, the sparse, undecorated rectory interior and his face illuminated by the screen. At some points Toller eschews electricity altogether, working in candlelight. When others use energy around him, excess is the rule. When the police linger at the scene of Michael's death, they leave their cruisers idling. When the sheriff leaves, he revs the engine and emits a huge plume of exhaust, a final indignity thrown onto Michael. By contrast, one of Toller's few moments of happiness occurs when he rides a non-polluting means of transport, a bicycle. The bicycle ride, one of the few scenes shot with a mobile camera in the film, features Toller and Mary smiling and laughing. Toller in voice-over says, 'it's amazing the simple curative power of exercise'; cycling offers exercise less weighty than wrestling with an angel. Toller spends more time in the film doing tasks such as trying to fix the rectory's plumbing and cleaning up the church and cemetery grounds, than in delivering sermons, showing that even a pastor's everyday life has degraded and strayed from the light (Prorokova 2020: 179). Waste disposal presents evidence for a church elder to show concern for Toller, as the rectory's garbage can is filled with the empty liquor bottles Toller drinks to dull the spiritual and physical pain he endures. Toller treats himself to sushi at one point, but the imbalance of his life registers in his diet, more bread-and-water and whiskey-and-Pepto than meat and veg.

When Ed Balq, the industrialist sponsoring First Reformed's 250th anniversary reconsecration event arrives at a planning meeting at Millie's Pancake House, he orders apple pie. 'The apple pie, I know, is a cliché, but they make it right here. It's organic. It's local'. Balq uses food miles rhetoric to forgive himself, a perfect smokescreen for an industrial polluter. Robin McKie writes about how the over-simplification of 'food miles' creates the illusion of reducing waste and doing good with the example of apples in the United Kingdom. The UK apple harvest happens in September and October. In September, October, and November, you would have nice fresh locally grown apples with minimal food miles. So far so good.

> But by August those Coxs and Braeburns will have been in store for ten months. The amount of energy used to keep them fresh for that length of time will then overtake the carbon cost of shipping them from New Zealand.
>
> (McKie 2008: n.pag.)

Careful attention to food miles offers Balq the same thing his donations to the church offer: forgiveness. However, the sin for which Balq seeks to buy indulgences isn't gluttony or excess food miles, but toxic waste production. Low food miles for the apples help to greenwash Balq's diner order like sponsoring the 250th event washes clean his company in the eyes of the people in upstate New York. But can Toller, acting on behalf of Michael, forgive Balq for what he's done to the world? Toller asks Balq, 'can God forgive us for what we've done to His creation' and on the heels of the apple pie greenwashing, Balq dismisses Toller's concerns over pollution in their immediate vicinity: '[T]he Hanstown site by the way isn't even polluted. It was cleaned up with EPA Super Funds.' As Reverend Jeffers tries to intercede on behalf of Toller, Balq cuts him off, 'gimme some credit, alright? I'm in the energy business. It's my business to stay informed'.

Two locations intersect with this diner booth conversation as the key sites of the creation, deposition, and afterlife of pollution. The first is the Hanstown Superfund site, where Michael asked his ashes to be spread; the second is the BALQ Industries factory. Formally, Hanstown Kills and First Reformed are both introduced via a fact-based sign. At Hanstown Kill a rusted rectangular sign reads, 'WARNING: Due to water pollution this area of the Hanstown Kill is unsafe for swimming or fishing. Fish caught in this area may be contaminated and unsafe to eat'. A red triangular sign immediately below has an image of a gas mask and the single word 'Pollution' (Figure C.1). This location introduction aligns with the First Reformed Church: a blue State Education Department sign reads, 'First Reformed Church of Snowbridge, New York. Organized 1767, built 1801 by settlers from West Friesland led by Dominie Gideon Wortendyk. Oldest continually in operation church in Albany County. An Abundant Life historical church'. The sign introduction escalates closer to the film's conclusion, as the reconsecration is a BALQ Industries-branded event on the sign that hangs over the entry of First Reformed. BALQ Industries pollutes both Hanstown Kills and poisons First Reformed. The funeral at the Kills site, in Prorokova's compelling reading, invites viewers to consider not the small crowd gathered, but rather 'the surroundings, which display the devastating effects of human activity on the environment [where] [...] As the scene ends, Mary scatters the ashes into polluted water, thus only adding to the already existing grave' (2020: 176, 177). The BALQ Industries factory creates the pollution and fills the Hanstown Kill grave with effluent as well as destroyed human lives/ashes. During his online research, Toller searches 'World Top Polluters', and only has to

FIGURE C.1: *First Reformed* Hanstown Kill.

scroll down a little bit to find BALQ Industries at number five. BALQ Industries seeks absolution through donations to charity. Toller finds their contributions are insultingly small: $13,215, $10,500, $6,500, $4,200, $5,500. BALQ's largest contribution of $85,000 goes to Abundant Life Church of Christ and Christian Fellowship. And so Toller visits the factory, where the tour guide explains that BALQ Industries was '[a]mong the first companies to realize the need to address environmental concerns [...] this unit makes recyclable plastic markers'. In a country where less than 10 per cent of plastic is recycled, recycl*able* plastic markers achieve nothing but greenwashing (US EPA 2022b: n.pag.).

The futility of the current reduce-reuse-recycle approach in the face of a company like BALQ Industries, which makes not just recyclable markers but also paper goods and fertilizers in eighteen countries, creates the ambient dread that informs Toller's experience of The Magical Mystery Tour he shares with Mary:

> [P]eaceful images slip away as Toller can't help but think about the waste and destruction. Instead, his vision transforms into a wasteland of tires and factories. It is too late.

> Toller glides past the site of Michael's memorial service. The dead man stands on the deck of a rusting ship, haunting him.
>
> (Ribera 2020: 202)

The least austere moment in an otherwise formally restrained film sees the contemporary world as apocalyptically drowned in toxic waste.

The effects of the trash-drowned world register not only in Michael's questions, but also in Toller's cancer diagnosis. Jean-Thomas Tremblay and Steven Swarbick's multifaceted and powerful analysis of *First Reformed* bears extended quotation, as when they analyse the centring of Ernst Toller,

> a white character as the paradigmatic victim, actual or potential, of a toxicity it attributes to the joint actions of a white oil magnate and a Black megachurch pastor. *First Reformed* covers up toxic inequality by having Toller internalize it. His martyred internalization of planetary destruction indeed entails the internalization of racist geographies of toxic exposure. Insofar as Toller's planned suicide is meant to spectacularize extinction, it encompasses all deaths by environmental causes including the deaths of people of color, who are here made invisible despite their statistically higher exposure to toxicity. Toller is the world; the world is (in) Toller. Toller and the film itself thus absorb toxicity while disavowing its operation as an agent of whiteness's reproduction.
>
> (2021: 18)

Toller absorbs toxicity not just in his diet as mentioned above – too much liquor, mercury-loaded fish, Drano – but also in an accelerated, narratively convenient/meaningful way through his environment, getting a cancer diagnosis based in part on a test of a waste product, brown bloody urine (Tremblay and Swarbick 2021: 15). Toller's insistence that 'someone has to do something!' leads to his planned spectacular detonation, which is personalized. Toller directs it at some*one* and by some*one*, himself as a terminal case, an eco-terrorist martyr killing a stand-in for structural ills, Ed Balq. If Tremblay and Swarbick are right, and I think they are, and Toller's actions show the shortcomings of any propaganda of the deed, what actions should he take?

Here the film introducing – and then never returning to – Toller's speech about the church's place in the Underground Railroad plays a key role. Rather than the spectacular killing of one white CEO and dozens of people of colour, a return to the role of the Underground Railroad would seem, if not a narratively pleasing conclusion, then at least a more apt metaphorical close to what Tremblay and Swarbick call the film's 'framing dispositif: abundant life' (2021: 17). A young teacher, Miss Suriya, brings a group of five children to First Reformed, where they sit in the first row of pews. Miss Suriya tells them, 'so last week we read *The Patchwork Path*, and the Underground Railroad, which was not a railroad but?' Rosa raises her hand and answers, '[i]t was a slave trail'. Suriya elaborates, 'it was an escape route from the south to the north. And this church, First Reformed, was one of the stops on that route. Reverend Toller?' While Suriya talks to the children, Toller's face makes him look a million miles away, consumed with his own pain. When Suriya invites him to speak, Toller begins what sounds like a well-rehearsed speech:

> [S]laves fleeing north to Canada were often helped, fed, hidden by homes and churches along this route. Calvin Verlander was the domine, the minister here at First Reformed, and he was very active in the abolitionist movement. He assisted in, Miss Suriya let me try this.

For the next 45 seconds Toller comes alive, interacting with the children and giving them a sense of both the mechanics of the Underground Railroad, and its emotional contours. Schrader's shot selection changes as well. Rather than frontal shots of Suriya and Toller cut against the children lined up in a pew in a reverse, the shot changes to Suriya on the left, the children on the right, and Toller between them (Figure C.2), ending their separation with the visual arrival of a trap door:

FIGURE C.2: *First Reformed* underground railroad 1.

TOLLER: Why don't you all stand up for a second and take a look right here. Do you see one part of wood that seems different than the other part? You all see that, don't you? Does it seem a little bit like a secret door? Yeah. What's your name?

BENNY: Benny.

TOLLER: Benny, will you give me a hand? Come on over here. You see there used to be a pew over this. And they would move it, and then they would lift this up. Can you do it? Help me. Yes. Come around everybody. Slaves would hide in here, sometimes whole families. Be really careful, alright? Can you imagine that?

When he asks the children to imagine, the scene cuts to a shot looking through the trap door onto the dirt floor. Toller continues, in what amounts to a voice-over point of view shot: 'In the dark. The air hot. Shaking with fear'. Here two of the key cuts in the film arrive. After seeing the hiding place, we see a medium shot of all five children with Toller. All five children's faces are in the frame, but we do not see Toller's face, only his body, his arm on Benny's shoulder (Figure C.3). Toller keeps describing the

FIGURE C.3: *First Reformed* underground railroad 2.

moment, 'the sound of the slave hunters' horses outside'. Another cut shows Toller's face in a low-angle medium close-up, and his description turns inward, describing the Underground Railroad and himself: '[O]n their knees, holding each other's hands, praying for God to save them.' The potential in the Underground Railroad as an infrastructure emerges in the first cut, the older generation offering what little hope they can from the past. The second cut, in revealing Toller in a low-angle shot steps back from the nihilism of the previous shot, showing that enduring the pain and struggle was made possible by people like Toller, working with like-minded people, to save people.

The two best critical engagements with *First Reformed*, Prorokova's and Tremblay and Swarbick's, both see the insufficiency of Toller's individual action as the starting point for understanding how the film offers a vision for not giving in to despair. For Tremblay and Swarbick, '[i]nstead of folding the ego's destruction into a realm of intrapsychic, nonnormative preservation, queer ecocide in *First Reformed* calls for an irrecuperable abolition of the individual – its subtraction from the act of thinking sociality' (2021: 11). For Prorokova, '[t]he deaths of Michael and Toller – in the case of the latter, if not a physical then a spiritual one – symbolize the futility of individual, random fights against environmental degradation, and call for a collective action' (2020: 185). In both arguments, Toller errs in acting alone, in not heeding the lessons that were under his feet at the First Reformed Church. The infrastructure of waste disposal failed the upstate New York community. But the First Reformed Church's history as a stop in the Underground Railroad testifies to its ability to undertake a collaborative effort to address an apocalyptic situation. When Toller speaks of people in flight, hiding under the church's pews, he imagines the potential in the Underground Railroad to liberate. The church's purpose is communion. In lay terminology, community or union.

Sorry to Bother You

The potential for union in *First Reformed* takes an explicitly religious form through the infrastructure of the Underground Railroad, something Toller and the children experience together. But unlike Toller, *Sorry to Bother You*'s Cassius Green is not one of God's lonely men. He has Detroit, Squeeze, Sal, Langston, and his Regal View co-workers. *Sorry to Bother You* is more didactic than *First Reformed* in its call to think beyond the individual; it's about unionizing the workplace, after all. This agenda comes to its climax when the telemarketers' union takes ownership of the infrastructure to assert control over the workplace. The sidewalk in *Sorry to Bother You* provides the key location where Detroit (Tessa Thompson), Sal (Jermaine Fowler), Squeeze (Steven Yeun), and the rest of Oakland, even Power Caller Cash (LaKeith Stanfield), can start to reclaim power in the dystopian tech/gig workplace to make a better place to work, live, and thrive.

If the Regal View call centre where Cash, Detroit, Sal, Langston, and Squeeze work represents a form of alienated labour – they must stick to the script, they have nothing to do with the final product of their labour – Cash's ability to use his white voice, once Langston (Danny Glover) teaches him, creates a further layer of psychological and social alienation. Cash's journey to work at Regal View shows how Oakland's transportation infrastructure physically alienates working class residents from their surroundings. Writing at the same time *Sorry to Bother You* was released in cinemas, Christina Nichol writes that in 'California, the only people who own houses are people who bought them in the 1970s, work for tech companies, or were on the receiving end of a miracle' (2018: n.pag.). The miracle appears to be running out for Cash's uncle Sergio, who tries to keep up with his mortgage payments by renting the garage to Cash. Long exterior shots of the street show well-tended houses on a hill, which creates a canted shot. Cash emerging into this angled world makes him slightly off-balance, not quite on the square, as he heads to work. But the street teems with vibrant life: when Cash's 'front door' (Segio's garage door) opens, people walk along the sidewalk and ride BMX bikes on the street. Rather than a bleak or anonymous place, Cash's home street retains a sense of a living community through the presence of pedestrians and cyclists on the sidewalks and streets.

That changes when Cash drives to work. After the complicated but human world of his garage apartment and a street with pedestrian and bicycle life, a cut carries us to an empty street, as Cash turns into a gas station. Getting out of the car, Cash walks in a long shot, the only human figure in an image filled with cars passing, and the BART whizzing from right to left. Mari Crabtree writes that *Sorry to Bother You*

> unfolds against a backdrop of sprawling homeless encampments under highway overpasses and on sidewalks, everyday scenes of poverty that, for many, are both familiar and unremarkable. Yet, not until Riley's satirical critique comes to the surface through his leaps into the absurd and the comical do we really see the suffering (and the shadow world behind the suffering) we live amid.
>
> (2021: n.pag.)

Cash is working poor: telling a gas station worker '40 on 2' matched with a shot of a quarter, a nickel, and a dime, shows as much. However, when the scene shifts to a high-angle overhead shot of Cash driving parallel to the freeway, along a trash-strewn street, greater poverty appears on the sidewalks. Cash drives past a line of tents along a sidewalk, one of many small encampments that appear throughout the movie. All the while, Cash remains alone in his car, isolated from his surroundings and disconnected from other people.

But this does not mean that the transportation infrastructure only alienates. For example, a shared car rides tends to offer something better, even something as simple as the sociality of meeting new people, sharing in-jokes, and even the exercise of pushing the car the last block, as when Cash drives Detroit, Sal, and Squeeze to a bar. En route to the bar with Detroit, Sal, and Squeeze, Cash disparages the football players who never gave up their former glory. 'Look at our high school football team', he says. 'Literally. Look at 'em'. Cash's dialog directs the action to a cut to a shot of a scrum of football players on a sidewalk. Back in the car, Cash argues that 'all they do is work at the home furniture store and play football. All day. It's like they're stuck or something'. Sal asks, 'what the hell you talking 'bout? I mean, they're friends'. Sal's suspicious question undercuts the alienation and cynicism the car makes possible. Cash as a driver wants to float past the group of friends physically connected with each other on the sidewalk. Sal, as a passenger in the shared ride, won't allow it. Further, the transportation infrastructure is more than the street or the mass transit line; it includes the sidewalk. When Cash picks up Detroit to go to the bar, she's just finishing a shift twirling an advertising sign on the sidewalk. Later, Squeeze meets up with Detroit at her sign-spinning spot and shows off the moves he learned from his time organizing sign twirlers. Shots of groups of people on the sidewalk, overflowing onto the street, proliferate throughout the movie, creating an equation between the sidewalk space and the importance of joining together to fight for a better world (Figure C.4). In 'Alienated labor's hybrid subjects: *Sorry to Bother You* and the tradition of the economic rights film', Leshu Torchin engages with the problem of placing the film generically by placing it in conversation with the tradition of economic rights films. In the article's section 'Mobility's confinements', Torchin writes about the laborscape present in both *Sorry to Bother You* and a group of economic rights

FIGURE C.4: *Sorry to Bother You* Royal View on strike on the sidewalk.

FIGURE C.5: *Sorry to Bother You* Cassius walks to work after promotion.

films. Torchin argues that 'the aspirations and fantasies of capitalism, the upward mobility and the desired rewards, mask the real lack – of mobility, of access, and of resources – felt by its inhabitants' (2019: 33). I want to step back from the (accurate) structural critique to take mobility literally. Cash's trip to work on his first day after promotion to power caller demonstrates the difference between the status quo and a possible future. All we see of Power Caller Cash's trip to work is the last stage, the final block on an empty sidewalk, a Power Caller alone (Figure C.5). On that same sidewalk, Squeeze readies the low-level Regal View callers who have gone on strike. Whereas Cash walks in a medium close-up on his own, the striking workers share the frame, with three, four, or more people all occupying the frame together. Taking over the public space of the sidewalk in such groups plainly shows the Regal View workers' power when they stand together: the striking workers are so numerous they block access to the building and even overflow the sidewalk; armed guards must brutally clear a path for high-level management and Power Callers to enter the building. In the office the Regal View telemarketers experience their power as workers when they stage their 'phones down' protest at prime calling time. Outside the office experience their own power by staking a claim to the sidewalk.

And people need not be present to reclaim the sidewalk. While Detroit's art opening for the 'fake-ass bougie gallery world' features an extended engagement with waste products, her brief and interrupted vandalism of a WorryFree billboard and erection of a statue seem to create a more immediate social effect. Franco 'Bifo' Berardi writes in *Futurability: The Age of Importance and the Horizon of Possibility* that 'dystopia has taken centre stage in show business: Hollywood blockbusters bring us a perception of the future which is simultaneously violent and depressing' (2017: 44). Berardi singles out the *Hunger Games* series as an exemplary case of this combination of violence and depression, unleavened by even the potential for solidarity.

> Acts of solidarity may occur in the *Hunger Games*. For instance, the protagonist, Katniss Everdeen, enters the violent contest in order to save her sister from a near-certain death. But this is the solidarity of despair, the solidarity of people who cannot even imagine a life of peace, let alone one of happiness.
>
> (Berardi 2017: 45)

In addition to the solidarity of despair, Hollywood films can offer 'what Robert Pfaller has called "interpassivity": the film performs our anti-capitalism for us, allowing us to continue to consume with impunity' (Fisher 2009: 12). As shown in previous chapters, dystopian and post-apocalyptic Hollywood films do not lack for violence in its many forms, and many show a depressing vision of the future. But without the large budget of a tentpole piece of IP, a movie like *Sorry to Bother You* can afford to squeeze in joyous solidarity through an exhortation to activity rather than passivity or interpassivity. Cash ends the film not as the lone triumphant hero but part of a collective that has a long fight ahead of it, telling Salvador: '[I]f the new and glorious telemarketers union will have me. We got to start fighting somewhere'. The where takes two forms: the call centre, which is to say the workplace, and public space. The Brazilian geographer Milton Santos describes the lives of workers like those at Regal View when he writes,

> [t]he house, the place of work, meeting points, and the routes that unite these locations are passive elements that condition the activity of men [*sic*] and order their social practice. Praxis, the fundamental ingredient in the transformation of human nature, is a socioeconomic fact, but it is also a tributary of spatial conditions.
>
> (2021: 103)

While the streets and freeways place people in cars that alienate them, the sidewalk offers a location where workers can join to resist the alienation work and other parts of the transportation infrastructure impose or directly to act on their social world. In other words, a better life for the people must include the sidewalk.

A better end of the world is possible

In a 1980 *New Left Review* article about Rudolf Bahro's *The Alternative in Eastern Europe*, Raymond Williams writes,

> [t]he fact is that either in Eastern or Western Europe, of course under different local conditions, the challenge which Bahro is making must immediately encounter and engage – for that is its whole purpose – the fixed institutional and ideological habits of 'actually existing socialism'.
>
> (1980: n.pag.)

Hollywood movies aimed at a mass audience may tinker with small changes, but hew closely to the fixed institutional and ideological habits of their historical moment. In other words, the films in this book encounter and engage the actually existing dystopianism of their time. *A Scanner Darkly* comically illustrates the downward trajectory of everyday life in a dystopia. Sitting in a diner with his Substance-D-tweaking friend Charles Freck (Rory Cochrane), James Barris (Robert Downey, Jr.) blithely observes, 'this is a world getting progressively worse, can we not agree on that?' Barris then nonchalantly turns to the waitress, pushes his glasses back up his nose, and asks, 'what's on the dessert menu?' before imagining her taking off her top while she lists the options. A world getting progressively worse comes across as the most commonsensical observation possible, the material conditions that drive Charles's logical retreat to drugs and Barris's to fantasy. New Optimists like Steven Pinker insist that lower levels of violence and disease represent indicators of an uninterrupted upward trajectory towards utopia fuelled by technology. Dystopian films like *A Scanner Darkly* see something else entirely: the things that seem like they improve the world for some make it worse for more. Post-apocalyptic films start once the world has already gotten much, much worse.

If actually existing dystopianism offers a pessimistic echo of Raymond Williams, an optimistic echo would begin with Williams's sense of the possibility of communism: 'It has, after all, been widely believed before. It has, nevertheless, been widely believed' (1980: n.pag.). That belief brings with it a particular vocabulary and set of metaphors related to infrastructure: build, support, plan, share. For instance, in the preface *Another End of the World Is Possible*, Dominique Bourg writes that the book does not aim

> to convince us of a probable collapse – an exercise which has already been accomplished – but to prepare us internally to face it, and in a way to go beyond it, by preparing from now on for the world that is to come, the world that we would choose to rebuild, on new principles, among the other worlds that might take shape.
>
> (2021: xv)

Early in the book the authors state that they have

> no desire to see the continued existence of a violent society that selects for the most aggressive individuals. Wanting to live beyond the shocks, and not just survive them, is already to start our preparation with a different attitude, one that looks toward joy, sharing and fraternity.
>
> (Servigne et al. 2021: 9)

This echo of the French national motto equates liberty with joy, sharing with equality, and keeps the fraternity. In the actually existing dystopias analysed in this book, the only thing most people share is joylessness, which tends to preclude fraternity/solidarity. Moments such as Reverend Toller's description of the Underground Railroad and the Regal View workers on strike move beyond shocks and toward a more equally shared (joyful) communion. Infrastructure enables such a situation. Laleh Khalili's 'Apocalyptic infrastructures' begins with the proposition, '[f]or infrastructure to serve the public and steward the world's air, water and soil for future generations, it has to be planned through more open, egalitarian and environmentally militant processes' (2021: n.pag.). Beyond Michael and Toller's environmentally militant actions, a less violent glimmer of hope appears in places people can gather together – the walking trail where Toller finds Michael's dead body and begins his process of radicalization, the bike path where he finds a moment of joy, and the historical precedent of a transportation and food system that provided safety and a path to freedom to the most exploited and endangered people. Open and egalitarian processes find a home on the sidewalks where the Regal View telemarketers union recognizes that together they have greater power. In these cases in particular and also more generally, the distance between infrastructure components is not great. While Squeeze and Detroit and Sal stand the sidewalk, the power lines are a couple storeys overhead, the sewer and water pipes a few feet below ground, a rubbish bin nearby, and food across the street. One step takes you from the sidewalk to the street. And such a step not in close-up but in a multi-person shot shows a belief rooted in the material, in pushing ahead to rebuild on the ruins or, more hopefully, the still-working infrastructural remains of the present.

Combined and uneven apocalypse

I want to conclude by acknowledging the some of this book's blind spots. The horizon of expectations that my analyses sketches is only that, a sketch. I want to consider briefly that ways in which two forms of dystopia and apocalypse I do not engage in this book, colonialism and climate change, demand critical attention if we are to draw an infrastructurally informed picture of the future. I offer this book not as a final, definitive statement on dystopian and post-apocalyptic film and infrastructure, but rather as a first step that will likely be superseded by subsequent engagements with the same films and their imagination of the infrastructure of the future as well as with work that analyses non-Hollywood, generically non-dystopian/post-apocalyptic films. Thus I offer only the most tentative of steps towards how a consideration of colonialism and climate change intersect with and inform imaginations of infrastructure – in dystopian and post-apocalyptic films in particular – to imagine the work that will soon present a more detailed and developed picture of better future worlds we might create from the examples films offer.

The cyberpunk novelist William Gibson is usually credited with the saying 'the future is already here – it's just not very evenly distributed'. Similarly, in the face of rapidly advancing climate change and rapidly increasing inequality, the apocalypse has already happened; we already live in a dystopian post-apocalypse. But some people – those in the Global South, the poor in general – are experiencing it more frequently and intensively. Walter Rodney offers an extended analysis of the way in which dystopia was enforced on Africa and African people in *How Europe Underdeveloped Africa*. Entertaining the notion that perhaps there is a positive to take from colonialism, Rodney writes, '[w]hat did colonial governments do in the interest of Africans? Supposedly, they build railroads, schools, hospitals, and the like. The sum total of these services was amazingly small' (2018: 246). As Rodney works through the sum total of these services, he notes a consistency in the form they take: infrastructure.

> The high proportion of [post-WWII] 'development' funds went into the colonies in the form of loans for ports, railways, electric power plants, water works, engineering workshops, and warehouses, which were necessary for more efficient exploitation in the long run.
>
> (Rodney 2018: 257–58)

The result of colonial presence is an infrastructural form that enables the transport of raw materials from the interior to a port. As Khalili describes the effects of colonialism's infrastructural work,

> [t]he British built railways in their colonies in Africa and Asia. But especially in Africa, the rails lead to the sea from inland mines, sometimes entirely avoiding population centers, and when they were not used to extract raw resources, they were conduits for the movement of troops.
>
> (2021: n.pag.)

In other words, infrastructure serves not the people in Africa, but those who build and control the infrastructure; 'the roads in Africa led to the seaports and the sea lanes led to Western Europe and North America. That kind of lopsidedness is today part of the pattern of underdevelopment and dependence' (Rodney 2018: 280). In 2021, according to the World Bank, in the Democratic Republic of the Congo '73% of the Congolese population, equaling 60 million people, live[s] on less than $1.90 a day (the international poverty rate)' and 43 per cent of children are malnourished (World Bank April 2021b: n.pag.). Such a situation seems dystopian.

In *Noir Urbanisms: Dystopic Images of the Modern City*, Jennifer Robinson writes that

> [f]or current-day dystopic urban writers, it is once again Africa that carries the burden of imaginative spatial and temporal projection. But now this involves casting (mostly African) poorer cities as the future of all cities. What this means is that according to some of the most prominent urbanists of our time, many millions of people are already living in dystopia.
>
> (2010: 218)

But is the situation more than dystopian? In a *Tribune* piece titled 'Notes from an apocalypse', Mark O'Connell argues that 'I don't think the apocalypse is a thing that can really happen. Of course, it can happen, but this is just history. This is human life. This is business as usual' (2020: n.pag.). Business as usual places rich anglophone nations and the Global North at the centre of global history; the wages of settler colonialism and imperialism continue to affect the people of the Global South, who lack the financial power to develop otherwise and suffer in the wake of whatever 'solutions' the rich Global North finds to facilitate the search for profits. O'Connell's book on the apocalypse, *Notes from an Apocalypse: A Personal Journey to the End of the World and Back*, ranges across the globe – including Ireland, the United States, Ukraine, and Aotearoa New Zealand – but it doesn't touch down in Africa or South America or Central America, where business as usual looks different and might trouble the sense that the apocalypse hasn't really happened.

The Hollywood and Anglophone films in this book, like mass audience films in general, don't show contemporary life anywhere on almost the entire continent of Africa. *Mad Max: Fury Road* was *filmed* in Namibia but is not *set* in Namibia; the three previous entries in the series establish that Mad Max lives in post-apocalyptic Australia. UK-produced films are likely to stay in Great Britain or perhaps wander into western Europe. But rarely further. South America appears only as the nameless city in *Blindness* – Montevideo, Uruguay – and as somewhere spoken of – *Children of Men*'s Baby Diego in Argentina. Of the films I analyse in this book, only two have a clear African setting: *Chappie* and *District 9* (both written and directed by the South African filmmaker Neill Blomkamp), both of which take place in Johannesburg, South Africa, and show an impossible to miss engagement with a dystopian world where poverty, inequality, and bigotry present challenges not just to space alien-prawns and sentient robots, but also to the city's underclass, almost all of whom are Black.

In this book I have been interested in American, British, Australian, and Aotearoa New Zealand films that imagine *future* dystopias and apocalypses. What about films set in their current moment outside of the rich countries? What kind of chaos and upheaval, written on the infrastructure, can we see and analyse? What form does business as usual take? Colonialism and its continuing effects represents a form of apocalypse, destroying civilizations, and this apocalypse appears across the globe and within countries. One form of apocalyptic business as usual occurred and occurs in rich countries: the dispossession of Indigenous and Māori and Native American people, which began centuries ago and continues to this day. In the United States, Australia, and Aotearoa New Zealand, spatial exclusion has marked the settler-colonial project, pushing Indigenous, Māori, and Native American people away from the metropole and power: boundary streets in Australia, the Foreshore and Seabed Act in Aotearoa New Zealand, and reservations in the United States to name but three examples. In addition to literal spatial exclusion, those people and their cultures and stories have been enclosed inside new national discursive frameworks while remaining excluded from them, and have only recently begun to receive long-overdue critical attention.

If you were to take your cues from Hollywood movies, including dystopian and post-apocalyptic ones, you would think that the hinterlands were peopled almost exclusively by white people struggling to return to heteronormative families. There are no Native Americans in, to name a few examples, the dystopian *The Hunger Games*, the tentatively post-apocalyptic *Interstellar*, or the post-apocalyptic *The Book of Eli*. Beyond Hollywood, there is a Māori man in *The Quiet Earth*, but the narrative quickly pits Māori and pākehā against each other over artificially scarce resources. Indigenous people do not appear in the post-apocalyptic Australia of *Mad Max* movies, and figures like the Feral Kid and his razor-edged boomerang make a mockery of them in their absence. The total absence of Indigenous people from any significant role in the *Mad Max* films is a symptom of the thorough-going whiteness of imagined futures (and pasts), not just in Australian films, but also in Hollywood and British films. In 'The lost races of science fiction' Octavia Butler writes:

> Back when *Star Wars* was new, a familiar excuse for ignoring minorities went something like this: 'Science fiction is escapist literature. Its readers/viewers don't want to

> be weighted down with real problems.' War, okay. Planet-wide destruction, okay. Kidnapping, okay. But the sight of a minority person? Too heavy. Too real.
> (2016: 283)

More than 40 years later, science fiction and science fiction-adjacent dystopian and post-apocalyptic films have their wars and kidnappings and planet-wide destruction and are still populated by mostly white people from the rich countries of the Global North. The planned violence of imperial and colonial infrastructure makes these worlds' visions for the future sorely lacking, and the absence of any significant characters who might have experienced that violence first hand further weakens that vision as remaining exclusionary.

Climate crisis

I have also not dealt directly with climate change, in part because of the boundaries I set for the project and in part because the source of the dystopian and post-apocalyptic worlds was less often climate change-driven. However, climate change and environmental crisis – and the clifi narratives they generate – have, as Frederick Buell notes, 'become more and more a place in which people dwell, a context in reference to which they represent themselves' (2005: 250). In March 2021, the climatologist Michael Mann wrote in a *Guardian* op-ed that 'Australians can't seem to catch a break. But it's not too late to forestall a dystopian future that alternates between Mad Max and Waterworld' (2021: n.pag.). I live in Australia, Meanjin Brisbane, Queensland more precisely. In 2011, Meanjin Brisbane and southeast Queensland experienced extensive flooding, with flood waters reaching almost 4.5 m (14.75 ft). Then almost two-thirds of Queensland – a state two and a half times as big as Texas, seven times as big as the island of Great Britain – suffered through drought from 2013 to 2021. Queensland had bush fires in 2019, as did New South Wales and Victoria. In 2021 *and* 2022 floods returned, with the Brisbane River reaching a maximum of 3.8 m (12.5 ft) in 2022. In other words, Queensland *already* alternates between *Mad Max* and *Waterworld*.

The same situation appears in the United States. In 'The end of the world will be a non-event', Jacob Bacharach observes that

> [c]limate change lends itself to a full-on apocalyptic vision of a scorched and uninhabitable earth, but in reality, plenty of places will remain habitable, and the political crises regarding access to higher land and better drinking water are already with us.
> (2019: n.pag.)

The cities of Houston, New Orleans, Miami, and their surrounding regions are sinking and may disappear (by sinkhole, by rising water levels, by flight) during the twenty-first century, rendering almost 15 million people climate refugees. The people of Flint, Michigan haven't had clean drinking water since 2014. Along these lines, Bacharach argues,

> [t]his is not meant to be callous, or to wave away the magnitude of potential coming crises – we don't need to imagine a post-apocalypse of walled enclaves and tens of millions of migratory climate refugees to grasp the direct effect of a human-altered biosphere on our own little lives right now. If anything, conjuring up an End Times becomes a *comforting* kind of fantasy, because so long as the crack of thunder and flash of divine judgment doesn't arrive, the emergency is *always in the future*.
>
> (2019: n.pag.)

A movie like *Oblivion* offers a comforting view of a future planet earth squeezed dry because aliens, not people, did it; *Dredd* imagines a post-nuclear war mega-slum, fascism at a safe distance, in a dystopian future. Rather than what films imagine, such as aliens arriving or nuclear war kicking off,

> [t]he collapse of our civilization will not be a single event or catastrophe, but a series of disastrous events (cyclones, industrial accidents, attacks, pandemics, droughts, etc.), taking place against a backdrop of equally destabilizing gradual changes (desertification, the disruption of the seasons, persistent pollution, the extinctions of species and of animal populations, and so on).
>
> (Servigne et al. 2021: 2)

Infrastructure can play a significant role in preparing for the worst so that the climate change-altered future might be merely dystopian rather than apocalyptic. The 2009 financial stimulus package put forward by President Barack Obama sought to use 'shovel-ready' projects both to help to rebuild the post-GFC economy and also to inoculate against climate change's worst effects. However, the stimulus

> ultimately failed to bring about a strong, sustainable recovery. Money was spread far and wide rather than dedicated to programs with the most bang for the buck. 'Shovel-ready' projects, those that would put people to work right away, took too long to break ground. Investments in worthwhile long-term projects, on the other hand, were often rushed to meet arbitrary deadlines, and the resulting shoddy outcomes tarnished the projects' image.
>
> (Grabell 2012: n.pag.)

This is not to say that infrastructural work was not completed:

> First and foremost, the Recovery Act – the largest public works project since the Eisenhower Interstate System – showed a quantifiable relationship between transportation investment and outcomes. Investments improved more than 42,000 miles of roads and almost 2,700 bridges; they paid for 850 new transit facilities, nearly 12,000 new buses, and nearly 700 new rail cars; and they repaired about 800 airport facilities.
>
> (Lew and Porcani 2017: n.pag.)

Even Alberto Mingardi, a conservative economist writing for the Cato Institute, understands that infrastructure is broadly held to be the key to improving life; the difference comes in who drives and profits from such development (2018: n.pag.). Along techno-utopian lines, Annalee Newitz writes of IBM's

> Smarter Cities program, which is essentially a suite of software and services that the company sells to cities whose governments want to predict everything from traffic and crime patterns to the best exit strategy in a flood. The goal is to create cities whose traffic, food systems, energy grids, water management, and even health care are managed in a 'smart' way, based on real-time data that reveals what's needed where.
>
> (2013: 177)

Given IBM's corporate history, entrusting them to create a data-driven approach to disaster science, to manage potential climate refugees from above, both before disaster and after, may best be avoided (Black 2002).

Matthew Wolf-Meyer offers a different, qualitative, anthropological approach to coming to grips with and addressing the problems posed by the ongoing apocalypse:

> [W]ho knows what will happen next and what the ramifications will be? What can possibly be done to prepare for the unexpected? Speculative fiction and social theory both ask us to consider these questions, and in finding answers we make new futures possible.
>
> (2019: 3)

Infrastructure in speculative fiction, such as the 'ecodystopian' genre (Buell 2005: 230), as well as dystopian and post-apocalyptic films, leaves traces both of technical possibility – massive hydrorigs! grub-protein farming! – and their effects on everyday human life. The people most likely to bear the burden of infrastructural violence in everyday life and the people most likely to bear the brunt of climate change are the same: marginalized, disempowered groups such as Indigenous, Māori, and Native Americans. Their everyday life is already post-apocalyptic. Where is their cinematic post-apocalypse? Coming to terms with and surviving the world that imperial, settler-colonial powers like the United States, the United Kingdom, Australia, and Aotearoa New Zealand created will require coordination in and across communities rather than individual choice, and millions of actions from below rather than diktats from above. Collaboration, community mindedness, and a sense that we're all in this together are concepts that mass audience and Hollywood pictures are not great at. In better case scenarios a reformist perspective reigns. But this does not mean that moments of bottom-up community coordination never appear on film.

Neptune Frost

I'd like to step away from mass audience movies and their preference for Global North settings to consider *Neptune Frost*, which confronts the dystopian and post-apocalyptic nature of everyday life in Africa.[1] To begin with the overall visual experience of the film: co-director (with Saul Williams) and cinematographer Anisia Uzeyman gives *Neptune Frost* a vibrant colour palette rather than the dour grey-blue-brown grim palette so common to mass audience dystopian and post-apocalyptic movies that need to signal bad news. From large to small *Neptune Frost* shows vast deep green valleys and fields of crops; blacklit rooms with glowing bicycle wheels and scenes bathed in hot pink lighting; red dresses, royal purple shirts, bright pink police uniforms; orange cyborg limbs; and red, orange, and yellow makeup. Further, the visualization of information overload when the film explodes into digital imagery of code and words and human forms retains the pinks, oranges, and greens that give the film a sense of vitality and life. The film's vibrancy thus creates an undercurrent of latent potential, of colourful joyful life there for the taking, while also showing everyday life permeated by the exploitation and extraction that creates infrastructure that conspires against the people of Rwanda.

To summarize the events of *Neptune Frost*, when the overseers at a Rwandan coltan mine murder the miner Tekno, his brother and fellow miner Matalusa leaves the mine and his home. As he walks across the country, the need to build a new world that refuses the world given them comes to Matalusa in a dream. The need to

> hack into land rights and ownership. Hack into business law, proprietorship. Hack into the history of the bank. Hack and question the business of slavery, of free

> labor, its relation to today's world. Hack into ambition, into greed. Into suffering and sufferance

takes concrete form in Matalusa's waking life in the lack of functioning water infrastructure for the people in his position, those who have no land rights or ownership or proprietorship. As Matalusa walks across the country, he passes through non-permanent housing with open sewers and encounters running water in the form of runoff from a pile of plastic pipes, showing that a functioning hydraulic system has yet to be universally established across the country. The waste infrastructure reveals Rwanda's position as an exporter of valuable materials and an importer of non-valuable waste. When Matalusa walks into town, there are piles upon piles of empty plastic containers, large yellow containers which reappear, repurposed, throughout the film, including as backpacks that protesting students wear.

Matalusa eventually arrives at a village where the architecture is made up of discarded/recycled plastic and computer parts, e-waste taken from a dump in Rwanda (Haddick 2022: n.pag.) (Figure C.6). The village turns e-waste into building products, making a virtue of the necessity that e-waste processing offshoring creates. There he meets Elohel, a sound designer who came to the village first (also because of a dream) and Memory, who acts something like the central point of gravity for the village. Later the dissident student Psychology arrives in the village,

FIGURE C.6: *Neptune Frost* e-waste materials as building materials.

as do the coltan miners who witnessed Tekno's murder. As everyone arrives on foot, the transportation infrastructure and food systems appear to be in useable condition. Neptune first walks, then takes a boat, then once again walks on mostly unpaved streets that nevertheless connect disparate locations across Rwanda. In the city, the students briefly retake the street space in front of the university during their protest. As in the countryside, the street is unpaved but given the relative invisibility of cars compared to bicycles and pedestrians, the lack of concrete and bitumen is not a significant deficit. When Neptune walks across the country, they walk past large farms and stop off at a smaller-scale farm where women harvest by hand. When Matalusa passes through towns, kitchen gardens and urban agriculture appear in the background and corners of the frame. At the same time, Neptune takes a similar path across the country, encountering the not only the gender-based violence and heavy police presence that motivates the young peoples' rebellion, but also pockets of support and peace on the way to the village. The union of miners and students and intellectuals begins to hack infrastructure away from their exploiters, taking control of the internet and discovering the power, both literal and figurative, they can make in the Matalusa/Martyr Loser Kingdom.

Rwanda is one of the main nations where coltan is mined, and Tekno's murder happens at a mine that belongs not to the people of Rwanda but, as Psychology points out, to a company headquartered in Toronto. Coltan, an essential element for mobile phones and computers, makes possible the global communications infrastructure and creates the basis for the continued exploitation of colonized Africa. The communications system that rich countries mourn the loss of in dystopian and post-apocalyptic movies – and that the village hacks in its contemporary moment – constitutes 'all that you pay not to see' in *Neptune Frost*'s Rwanda. Or as Neptune puts it when meeting Matalusa: 'Unanimous Goldmine is the greeting of the resource rich who face a world beholden to the currency of our depletion'. The multivalence of currency and depletion appears in the song 'The noise came from here':

> The bullets in your guns / You know we paid for it all / Your scriptures severing tongues / You know we paid for it all / With oil and our blood / You know we paid for it all / We won't be silenced, no / You know we paid for it all.

The miners pay coming and going. The raw materials make the very things that come back to kill them either quickly like a bullet or a rock to Tekno's head, or more slowly like the violence of imperialism and neocolonialism. For one more piece of coltan. This is not a new phenomenon, as Mark Dery asked when seeking to define Afrofuturism, '[c]an a community whose past has been deliberately rubbed out, and whose energies have subsequently been consumed by the search for legible traces of its history, imagine possible futures?' (1994: 180). To cite one example, Matalusa Kingdom offers a starting place for a possible future that does not lose sight of the depletion and disappearance of dead Black bodies across the centuries. When Psychology says, 'recognise the pattern in the coding. The Black bodies floating in space, in the Mediterranean, the bottom of the Atlantic, and beneath us. They're the same Black bodies, mined and mining', Elohel responds with a play on words: '[M]ined and mining. What is mine?' Taken as a whole *Neptune Frost* sees 'a future that though deeply burdened by the past, nonetheless, holds infinite possibilities of transformation, liberation, and being otherwise' (Hart 2021: 197). And this includes the physical foundations, such as the energy infrastructure, of the world and the social relations they make possible.

The presence and creation of energy pervades *Neptune Frost*, from its coltan mine setting, to the mysteriously rotating chunk of coltan in the sky in the last third of the film, from the village starting with no power but gradually accumulating more people and, in time, electrical power to match its social and political power. Thus, when Matalusa first arrives at the village, Memory offers him a warm beer, admitting 'I haven't figured out how to get power yet'. In another of Matalusa's prophetic dreams, he says, 'we power the system' with a rotating chunk of coltan floating behind him. Finally, the very presence of the intersex and digital-cyborg Neptune – whom Memory calls the Motherboard – creates power, both literal and infrastructural. Neptune's arrival to the village activates their communications and their belief in the village offering an alternative world beyond their current one. Once their village has electric power and they begin to reach out into the world, Matalusa reminds his fellow miners and the other people in the village, 'they use our blood and sweat to communicate with each other but have never heard our voice. Until now. We are miners. We do the work that is hidden behind their screens. Coltan distributes power through the motherboard. Our power!' *Neptune Frost* translates power literally through the coltan – the miners repeat the phrase 'The miner is the power source! dig!' in the song 'Cukura' – and through the collaborative action of the people. Psychology assesses what they can do with the power Neptune brought which, as a first step, disrupted global communications. Having already gained some visibility in this disruption, might the Matalusa Kingdom take some other actions? Psychology proposes they 'Crash the market. Erase debt. Transfer the colonial debt d'independence', a counter to 'the usual calls for sacrifice and austerity – calls which usually fall on the victims of the crisis rather than those who caused it' (Noys 2014: 64). The energy that Neptune, Matalusa and the miners, and intellectuals like Psychology bring/create can be turned away from false solutions (which is to say control) imposed from without, such as the colonial debt d'independence and the Washington Consensus that put Rwanda in its current position, in favour of the self-determination local conditions clearly make possible. *Neptune Frost* shows the power of bottom-up coordination in the face of crisis in creating not a perfect world, but a struggle that takes individual problems seriously and sees coordination and collaboration as better avenues to working towards a better, liveable post-dystopian or post-apocalyptic world. In contrast to the current competitive order which barely functions for the people who live there while extravagantly rewarding far-off mining companies and corporations, this greater sense of coordination and collaboration imagines *public* utility as its end, in infrastructural and social forms.

The end is here. What will we do after?

In the face of a rapidly approaching end of the world, will we ever build castles in the sky, finding it possible to be a hunter, fisher, herder, violinist, and critic all in one day? What would it look like? Would mass audience movies like those out of Hollywood give us any positive examples – in their narratives and their production design – to pursue, or would we be best served to look past the products of the system's winners? Most of the mass audience films in this book and *Neptune Frost* take a sceptical approach to the internal combustion engine, turning the transportation infrastructure to non-motorized transport like walking. Similarly, the mass audience films in this book and *Neptune Frost* envision food systems that turn away from mechanized large-scale industrial farming and towards smaller-scale farming and horticulture as a path to a liveable future. The infrastructure in, for example, a rich country like the United States represents an incredible technical and, it bears noting, social achievement. Considering the role of scale, Khalili writes that

> [w]hile we sometimes stand in awe of gargantuan infrastructures like ports and bridges, we hardly ever appreciate the aesthetics of water and sewer systems whose subterranean routes make them invisible, or even electricity lines, telecommunication masts and satellite dishes, which are visible but unremarkable because of their ubiquity. These basic utilities constitute the furniture of our everyday lives.
>
> (2021: n.pag.)

The things we pass by every day on the way to work, the structures and systems that go unnoted but undergird everyday life would disappear with the apocalypse. The ubiquity of *working* infrastructure is slowly becoming less ubiquitous, as the water systems of Flint, Michigan and Jackson, Mississippi show. The awe of the technological sublime giving way to the awe of beautiful ruins can happen in movies as an aesthetic experience. It's less desirable in an everyday life sense.

The first *Mad Max* movie shows not a post-apocalyptic Australia, but a dystopian one, only a few years in the future. Which is not to say that the tipping over into post-apocalypse in time for *The Road Warrior* comes as much of a surprise. Jim Poe observes that in *Mad Max*

> [a]midst a general sense of lawlessness and dystopia, characters do jarringly ordinary things, like go to cafés or the beach. This may seem strange for fans of the bleaker later entries in the series. But rewatching the original *Mad Max* now, it brilliantly evokes a sense of social breakdown occurring alongside normal life.
>
> (2021: n.pag.)

To use another Australian example, in the novel *On the Beach*, and its 1959 film adaptation, a deadly cloud of nuclear fallout approaches the southern hemisphere as the people of Melbourne continue to go to work. On the one hand, such a dedication to clocking in looks ridiculous. On the other, I keep going to my office job every day, processing candidature interruption requests and updating stipend expiry dates while climate change continues unabated. Or, more precisely, I continue to work while a pandemic hits peaks and troughs and the city where I work floods. Poe concludes that 'the future will probably resemble *Children of Men* more than *Mad Max* or *The Road*. It's hardly a comforting thought' (2021: n.pag.). Perhaps the future will resemble *Children of Men* taking place inside *Mad Max*, with a grim *The Road*-like ending. After all, the pandemic barely made a dent in fossil fuel use, and the global temperature looks sure to increase by more than 2 degrees Celsius in the next 25 years.

In the face of the current world's rulers' inability to take any action to improve the lives of the billions, what Bradley Garrett calls 'this sluggish apocalypse' (2021: 268), I have been looking at filmic background details, still-working or re-worked infrastructure, as part of a project to register how dystopian and post-apocalyptic movies help us to understand the absolute centrality of the work that goes into keeping the entire world going.

> Despite recurring fantasies about the end of work or the automation of everything, the central fact of our industrial civilisation is *labour*, and most of this work falls far outside the realm of innovation. Inventors and innovators are a small slice – perhaps somewhere around one per cent – of this workforce.
>
> (Russell and Vinsel 2016: n.pag.)

Part of the poverty of imagination on view in mass audience films is their inability to imagine a world other than the one we currently inhabit, a fossil fuel industrial consumer world and the infrastructure that comes with it. Another shortcoming of mass audience films' imagination of dystopian and post-apocalyptic worlds is that those films, though they seek to imagine a world after the dystopia or apocalypse tend to avoid the post-world. They destroy a tremendous amount of infrastructure and face down villains but don't show much getting built after the great confrontation. For instance, in the *Mad Max* series Max encounters a community in danger, kills and blows up a lot of stuff, and then always has to leave. He's a catalyst rather than a saviour, lurching from crisis to crisis. What happens to the people who fled for the Sunshine Coast in *The Road Warrior*? The life made possible by Max's heroic deeds – and Furiosa's in *Mad Max: Fury Road* – remains offscreen; the life survivors build on the Sunshine Coast or the water-rich table mountains remains a promise rather than a reality. I am not asking for a Mad Max extended universe of films that show small outposts developing new agricultural solutions to life in nuclear fallout Queensland. Instead I am interested in how, as Russell and Vinsel argue, '[w]e can think of labour that goes into maintenance and repair as the work of *the maintainers*, those individuals whose work keeps ordinary existence going rather than introducing novel things' (2016: n.pag.). Maintainers sit at the heart of *Neptune Frost*, repurposing waste that has been piled onto their lives and homes, creating their own electric power to convert e-waste into tools that unsettle the rich and take steps towards political power and self-determination for the hyper-exploited poor. Speaking of people in rich countries who are convinced the world is coming to an end, Garrett writes,

> [o]ften, I came away from my encounters with doomsday preppers, survivalists, scholars, bunker builders and the devoutly religious with a sense of latent hope – hope of rebirth from disaster. All prepping is about hope for a better future, even if that hope casts a dark shadow.
>
> (2021: 15)

Neptune Frost's musical number 'The Noise Came from Here' features the refrain 'you'll never touch my love', a rebuke of the exploiters that finds hope in their current disaster. Elohel has a hopeful part in the song: '[Y]our never ending war will not be waged from here'. Later, Elohel again finds a measure of hope in the face of disaster, linking the Rwandan genocide to the threat of retaliatory drone strikes on the village: With their village is under the threat of annihilation, she says, 'when they cut off my arm, they left me for dead. A woman and little man healed me and pointed me in this direction. I'm not running anymore. If it's over, it's over. We harm nobody here'. Elohel delivers this speech wearing jewellery made from old transistors, and copper wire running from one transistor up to her head, where her hair, also wrapped in copper wire, makes her a cyborg of recycled parts, even without the orange and yellow plastic prosthetic arm in the frame. Elohel gives the ultimatum in the village she was one of the first to build from waste parts and temporarily non-functional components brought to life by the presence of the people and the power, both literal and figurative, they generated together. Elohel and Memory and Matalusa and Neptune and Psychology and their fellows invent possible liveable futures by rescuing a significant physical manifestation of the past, infrastructure, and reinventing more abstract social relations to guide life within those settings. That is to say, events and dialog placed amidst such production design creates a setting which imaginatively prepares the film audience for a better future.

Confronting the fixed institutional and ideological habits of actually existing dystopianism and apocalypse are the necessary precondition for imagining our way out of doom. In closing with the case of *Neptune Frost*, a film made outside of the Hollywood mass audience system, I hope to provide a useful contrast and path forward to develop my main point: that movies, made under the local conditions of the rich anglophone core, offer a form of visual vocabulary and mental framework for the role of infrastructure in creating the baseline for a particular kind of everyday life before, during, and after dystopian life and the apocalypse. The imagination that generated the momentum taking the world from dystopia to apocalypse, even in the rich countries, may not be sufficient to imagine a way out of apocalypse. It may be that a *post*-apocalyptic world would need an imagination rooted in something else entirely, perhaps something closer to the Afrofuturist vision of *Neptune Frost*.

Between 1968 and 2021 the dystopian nature of everyday life in an increasingly unequal global order has made it all but inevitable that 2.5 degrees Celsius of warming will occur before 2100, with climate, environmental, and social apocalypses sure to follow. They don't appear in post-apocalyptic movies, but Pacific Island nations will disappear under rising seas; Mexico, most of South America, and much of India, Pakistan, and southeast Asia will be uninhabitable or underwater. Some optimists with a tech bent envision high density smart cities in the remaining habitable places like Aotearoa New Zealand and Tasmania; reforestation in places like Antarctica; massive solar energy production across Australia, Africa, and the Middle East; and agriculture across what is now the tundra of Canada and Russia (Jacobs 2017: n.pag.). This future presumes a level of cooperation and coordination emerging from the same system that is producing and exacerbating the problem.

In the forward to *Another End of the World Is Possible* Dominique Bourg summarizes the goal of the book as

> preparing from now on for the world that is to come, the world that we would choose to rebuild, on new principles, among the other worlds that might take shape [...] to

> remain upright in the coming storm and to rebuild a shared, open house in which we can all live.
>
> (2021: xv, xvi–xvii)

In an early declaration of principles, the book's authors write,

> [w]e have no desire to see the continued existence of a violent society that selects for the most aggressive individuals. Wanting to live beyond the shocks, and not just survive them, is already to start our preparation with a different attitude, one that looks toward joy, sharing and fraternity.
>
> (Servigne et al. 2021: 9)

Joy, sharing, and fraternity can look like something as simple as the fairy lights that line the town square in *The Postman*, small joyful moments that infrastructure makes possible. In the face of exploitation and repression, *Neptune Frost* foregrounds this kind of joy, sharing, and fraternity in the world the village's confluence of people and skills makes possible, what Elohel calls the Matalusa Kingdom, showing what Kyle Whyte calls the 'epistemology of coordination' (2020: 53). The provisional creation of quasi-utopian spaces in dystopian and post-apocalyptic narratives, in places such as a small village in *Neptune Frost*, a mall in *Dawn of the Dead*, or an encampment in *They Live*, offer the first steps towards the sorts of collaborative works take up what Srećko Horvat calls

> our Herculian [*sic*] task [...] not only to understand the Apocalypse, but to imagine a future that comes after the Apocalypse, to embark onto a relentless fight for the very possibility of a future in the ruins of our present [...] us[ing] our general intellect and imagination, a strong sense of transnational justice and intergenerational solidarity in order to go beyond the Apocalypse.
>
> (2021: 34, 41)

The boundaries of our collective imagination, as imagined in dystopian and post-apocalyptic movies, and the practical concrete foundation of such worlds and lives as we can imagine might take many forms. Building on top of the ruins of our current infrastructure means that someday in the future, someone – many someones I hope – might cycle along a path of what used to be the M3 Motorway near where I am typing this, perhaps delivering a replacement part or visiting a friend for lunch and philosophical discussion. They might then stop at the community park garden and put in a shift under the guidance of a horticulturalist. They might then head over to the train/underground station, perhaps heading north on a high-speed train to a revitalized Great Barrier Reef, or perhaps the station will have been repurposed in some way I lack the imagination to predict. This vision resembles what we have now, but I hope that it would at least be different enough to be better. From crowd-pleasing mass audience dystopian and post-apocalyptic films we can take big budget dreams and the frequently espoused belief in the importance of local democratic control to begin imagining. But as this conclusion makes clear, trusting mass audience films to encompass the full horizon of possibilities reveals itself to be a narrow vision. The future is too big for those limits.

NOTE

1. The songs in *Neptune Frost* were written by Saul Williams, many of them for the 2016 album *MartyrLoserKing* and translated for the film by many of the actors who performed them, including Eric '1key' Ngangare, Cécile Kayirebwa, Kivumbi King, Bertrand 'Kaya Free' Ninteretse, and Trésor Niyongabo. I use the English subtitles for the translated song lyrics and film dialog.

References

Addis, Bill (2006), *Building with Reclaimed Components and Materials: A Design Handbook for Reuse and Recycling*, London: Earthscan.

Affron, Charles and Affron, Mirella Jona (1995), *Sets in Motion: Art Direction and Film Narrative*, New Brunswick: Rutgers University Press.

American Society of Civil Engineers (2017), 'Report card for America's infrastructure', *infrastructurereportcard.org*. Accessed 11 February 2023.

Anand, Nikhil (2017), *Hydraulic City: Water and the Infrastructures of Citizenship in Mumbai*, Durham: Duke University Press.

Anderson, Paul W. S. (2002), *Resident Evil,* DVD, USA: Sony Pictures.

Anderson, Paul W. S. (2010), *Resident Evil: Afterlife,* DVD, USA: Sony Pictures.

Anderson, Paul W. S. (2016), *Resident Evil: The Final Chapter*, USA: Sony Pictures.

Anderson, Wes (2018), *Isle of Dogs,* DVD, USA: Fox Searchlight.

Anonymous (2017), 'Preparing for an EMP', Survival beyond the 21st Century, 1 January, https://www.survival.ark.net.au/emp.php. Accessed 3 January 2021.

Appel, Hanna, Anand, Nikhil and Gupta, Akhil (2018), 'Temporality, politics, and the promise of infrastructure', in H. Appel, N. Anand and Akhil Gupta (eds), *The Promise of Infrastructure*, Durham: Duke University Press, pp. 1–40.

Archer, Neil (2016), *The Road Movie: In Search of Meaning*, New York: Wallflower/Columbia University Press.

Arrighi, Giovanni (2010), *The Long Twentieth Century: Money, Power and the Origins of Our Times*, New and Updated Edition, New York/London: Verso.

Australian Institute of Health and Welfare (2006), *Mortality over the Twentieth Century in Australia: Trends and Patterns in Major Causes of Death*. Mortality Surveillance Series no. 4. AIHW cat. no. PHE73, Canberra: Australian Institute of Health and Welfare.

Baccolini, Rafaella and Moylan, Tom (2003), 'Introduction. Dystopia and histories', in R. Baccolini and T. Moylan (eds), *Dark Horizons: Science Fiction and the Dystopian Imagination*, Abingdon: Routledge, pp. 1–12.

Bacharach, Jacob (2019), 'The end of the world will be a non-event', *The Outline*, 3 June, https://theoutline.com/post/7522/the-end-of-the-world-will-be-a-non-event. Accessed 7 February 2023.

Baker, Erik (2023), 'It is happening again', N+1, 17 February, Nplusonemag.com/online-only/online-only/it-is-happening-again/. Accessed 18 February 2023.

Bakker, Karen (2003), 'A political ecology of water privatization', *Studies in Political Economy: A Socialist Review*, 70:1, pp. 35–58, https://doi:10.1080/07078552.2003.11827129.

Bakker, Karen (2010), *Privatizing Water: Governance Failure and the World's Urban Water Crisis*, Ithaca: Cornell University Press.

Baldick, Chris (2015), *Oxford Dictionary of Literary Terms*, Oxford: Oxford University Press.

Balinisteau, Tudor (2012), 'Goddess cults in techno-worlds: Tank Girl and the Borg Queen', *Journal of Feminist Studies in Religion*, 28:1, pp. 5–24.

Bartel, Paul (1975), *Death Race 2000*, DVD, USA: Universal Pictures.

Bay, Michael (2005), *The Island*, DVD, USA: DreamWorks Pictures.

Beal, Sophia (2013), *Brazil under Construction: Fiction and Public Works*, New York: Palgrave MacMillan.

Belanger, Pierre (2016), *Landscape as Architecture: A Base Primer*, London: Routledge.

Bello, Walden (2009), *The Food Wars*, London: Verso.

Berardi, Franco (2017), *Futurability: The Age of Impotence and the Horizon of Possibility*, London: Verso.

Berger, James (1999), *After the End: Representations of Post-Apocalypse*, Minneapolis: University of Minnesota Press.

Berry, Wendell (1999), 'Foreword' in S. Van der Ryn (ed.), *The Toilet Papers: Recycling Waste and Conserving Water*, White River Junction: Ecological Design Press/Chelsea Green, p. 1.

Bertetti, Paolo (2017), 'Building science-fiction worlds', in M. Boni (ed.), *World Building, Transmedia, Fans, Industries*, Amsterdam: Amsterdam University Press, pp. 47–61, https://doi:10.5117/9789089647566/CH02.

Bevan, Alex (2019), *The Aesthetics of Nostalgia TV: Production Design and the Boomer Era*, London: Bloomsbury Academic.

Bigelow, Katherine (1995), *Strange Days*, DVD, USA: 20th Century Fox.

Black, Edwin (2002), *IBM and the Holocaust: The Strategic Alliance between Nazi Germany and America's Most Powerful Corporation*, New York: Three Rivers Press.

Bliss, Laura (2020), 'How Trump's $1 trillion infrastructure pledge added up', *Bloomberg CityLab*, 17 November, https://www.bloomberg.com/news/articles/2020-11-16/what-did-all-those-infrastructure-weeks-add-up-to. Accessed 30 January 2021.

Blomkamp, Neill (2009), *District 9*, DVD, USA: Sony Pictures.

Blomkamp, Neill (2013), *Elysium*, DVD, USA: Sony Pictures.

Blomkamp, Neill (2015), *Chappie*, DVD, USA: Sony Pictures.

Bong, Joon-ho (2013), *Snowpiercer*, DVD, Republic of Korea: CJ Entertainment.

Bourg, Dominique (2021), 'Foreword', *Another End of the World Is Possible. Living the Collapse (and Not Merely Surviving It)* (eds P. Servigne, R. Stevens and G. Chapelle, trans. G. Samuel), Cambridge: Polity, pp. xiv–xvii.

Boyle, Danny (2002), *28 Days Later*, DVD, USA: Fox Searchlight.

Brambilla, Marco (1993), *Demolition Man*, DVD, USA: Warner Bros. Pictures.

Bridges, James (1979), *The China Syndrome*, DVD, USA: Columbia Pictures.

Brooks, B. A. (2009), *Surviving the NWO*, 2009, https://archive.org/details/SurvivingTheNewWorldOrder. Accessed 28 February 2023.

Brown, Hayes (2019), 'The end times are here, and I am at target', *The Outline*, 6 August, https://theoutline.com/post/7754/climate-change-doomsday-cults-prophecy?zd=2&zi=x-lmr7bav. Accessed 28 February 2023.

Bruno, Giuliana (1990), 'Ramble city: Postmodernism and *Blade Runner*', in A. Kuhn (ed.), *Alien Zone: Cultural Theory and Contemporary Science Fiction Cinema*, London: Verso, pp. 183–95.

Buell, Frederick (2005), *From Apocalypse to Way of Life: Environmental Crisis in the American Century*, London/New York: Routledge.

Burger, Neil (2015), *Divergent*, DVD, USA: Lionsgate.

Burton, Tim (2001), *Planet of the Apes*, DVD, USA: 20th Century Fox.

Butler, Octavia (2016), 'The lost races of science fiction', in G. Canavan, *Octavia Butler*, Urbana: University of Illinois Press, pp. 181–86.

CalRecycle (2023) 'What is e-waste?' https://www.calrecycle.ca.gov/electronics/whatisewaste. Accessed 28 February 2023.

Cameron, James (1984), *The Terminator*, DVD, USA: Orion Pictures.

Cannon, Danny (1995), *Judge Dredd*, DVD, USA: Buena Vista Pictures.

Carpenter, John (1981), *Escape from New York*, DVD, USA: AVCO Embassy Pictures.

Carpenter, John (1988), *They Live*, DVD, USA: Universal Pictures.

Carpenter, John (1996), *Escape from LA*, DVD, USA: Paramount Pictures.

Cawley, Diarmuid (2017), *The Future of Food in Blade Runner 2049*, Technological University Dublin Agricultural Education Commons, https://arrow.tudublin.ie/cgi/viewcontent.cgi?article=1031&context=tfschafoth. Accessed 27 February 2023.

Cheek, Douglas (1984), *C.H.U.D.*, DVD, USA: New World Pictures.

Choudri, Aniqah (2020), 'Water privatisation has been a disaster – it's time to take it back into public hands', *Tribune*, 12 October, https://tribunemag.co.uk/2020/10/water-privatisation-has-been-a-disaster-its-time-to-take-it-back-into-public-hands. Accessed 28 February 2023.

Clover, Joshua (2008), *The Matrix*, London: Palgrave Macmillan/bfi.

Coleridge, Samuel Taylor (1834), 'The Rime of the Ancient Mariner (text of 1834)', *Poetry Foundation*, https://www.poetryfoundation.org/poems/43997/the-rime-of-the-ancient-mariner-text-of-1834. Accessed 2 October 2021.

Colorado Adoption Project (2007), 'National Opinion Research Center (NORC). Prestige scores for all detailed categories in the 1980 census occupational classification', 13 April, Ibg www.colorado.edu/~agross/NNSD/prestige%20scores.html. Accessed 11 February 2023.

Conley, Julia (2023), 'Biden infrastructure report pushes "disastrous water privatization schemes" watchdog says', Commondreams, commondreams.org/news/biden-water-privatization. Accessed 2 September 2023.

Connor, J. D. (2015a), 'The New Hollywood, 1981–1999', in L. Fischer (ed.), *Art Direction and Production Design*, London: IB Tauris, pp. 118–138.

Connor, J. D. (2015b), *The Studios after the Studios: Neoclassical Hollywood (1970–2010)*, Stanford: Stanford University Press.

Connor, J. D. (2018), *Hollywood Math and Aftermath: The Economic Image and the Digital Recession*, London: Bloomsbury.

Costner, Kevin (1997), *The Postman*, DVD, USA: Warner Bros. Pictures.

Crabtree, Mari N. (2021), 'Stick to the script?! No, stick it to the man!' *Post*45*, 22 June, https://post45.org/2021/06/stick-to-the-script-no-stick-it-to-the-man/. Accessed 28 February 2023.

Cribb, Julian (2010), *The Coming Famine: The Global Food Crisis and What We Can Do About It*, Collingwood: CSIRO.

Cubitt, Sean (2016), 'Hope in *Children of Men* and *Firefly/Serenity:* Nihilism, waste, and the dialectics of the sublime', in S. Redmond and L. Marvell (eds), *Endangering Science Fiction Film*, New York: Routledge, pp. 51–65.

Cuarón, Alfonso (2006), *Children of Men*, DVD, USA: Universal Pictures.

Cuddon, J. A. (1998), *Penguin Dictionary of Literary Terms & Literary Theory. Revised by CE Preston*, London: Penguin.

Davies, Dominic (2017), *Imperial Infrastructure and Spatial Resistance in Colonial Literature, 1880–1930, Race and Resistance across Borders in the Long Twentieth Century* 2, Oxford/New York: Peter Lang.

Del Toro, Guillermo (1997), *Mimic*, DVD, USA: Miramax.

DeMonaco, James (2013), *Purge*, DVD, USA: Universal Pictures.

DeMonaco, James (2014), *Purge: Anarchy*, DVD, USA: Universal Pictures.

DeMonaco, James (2016), *Purge: Election Year*, DVD, USA: Universal Pictures.

Dery, Mark (1994), 'Black to the future: Interviews with Samuel R. Delaney, Greg Tate, and Tricia Rose', in M. Dery (ed.), *Flame Wars: The Discourse of Cyberculture*, Durham and London: Duke University Press, pp. 179–222.

DeVillers, Marq (2001), *Water: The Fate of Our Most Precious Resource*, New York: Mariner.

De Vries, David (2009), *Life after People*, DVD, Australia: Australian Broadcasting Corporation.

Diaz, Jorge Peña and Harris, Phil (2005), 'Urban agriculture in Havana: Opportunities for the future', in A. Viljoen (ed.), *CPULS Continuous Productive Urban Landscapes: Designing Urban Agriculture for Sustainable Cities*, Amsterdam: Elsevier Agricultural Press, pp. 135–45.

Dickie, John (2013), *Mafia Republic: Cosa Nostra, 'Ndrangheta, Comorra, 1946 to the Present*, London: Sceptre.

Dobigny, Laure (2019), 'Sociotechnial morphologies of rural energy autonomy in Germany, Austria and France', in F. Lopez, M. Pellegrino and O. Coutard (eds), *Local Energy Autonomy: Spaces, Scales, Politics*, London/Hoboken: ISTE/John Wiley & Sons, pp. 185–212.

Douglas, James (2015), 'The Pixar theory of labor', *The Awl*, 15 July, https://www.theawl.com/2015/07/the-pixar-theory-of-labor/. Accessed 28 February 2023.

Drew, Elizabeth (2016), 'A country breaking down', *The New York Review of Books*, 25 February, https://www.nybooks.com/articles/2016/02/25/infrastructure-country-breaking-down/. Accessed 28 February 2023.

Drinan, Joanne and Spellman, Frank (2013), *Water and Wastewater Treatment: A Guide for the Nonengineering Professional*, second ed., Boca Raton: CRC Press/Taylor & Francis.

Dutko, Paula, Ver Ploeg, Michele and Farrigan, Tracey (2012), 'Characteristics and influential factors of food deserts', *US Department of Agriculture Economic Research Service Economic Research Report* 140.

Ede, Laurie (2010), *British Film Design: A History*, New York: IB Taurus.

Elliot, Justin (2011), 'The mystery of the Japanese "poop burger" story', Salon.com, 23 June, https://www.salon.com/2011/06/23/japan_feces_meat_viral/. Accessed 9 July 2021.

Engels, Friedrich (1999), *The Condition of the Working Class in England*, Oxford: Oxford University Press.

Fagan, Brian (2011), *Elixir: A History of Water and Humankind*, New York: Bloomsbury.

Fair, Ray (2021), 'U.S. infrastructure: 1929–2019', https://fairmodel.econ.yale.edu/rayfair/pdf/2019D.PDF. Accessed 28 February 2023.

Feldman, David (2017), *Water Politics: Governing Our Most Precious Resource*, Cambridge/Malden: Polity Press.

Fisher, Mark (2009), *Capitalist Realism: There Is No Alternative*, Winchester: Zer0 Books.

Fleischer, Richard (1973), *Soylent Green*, DVD, USA: Metro-Goldwyn-Mayer.

Fleischer, Ruben (2009), *Zombieland*, DVD, USA: Sony Pictures.

Fleischer, Ruben (2019), *Zombieland Double Tap*, DVD, USA: Sony Pictures.

Food & Water Watch. (n.d.), *America's Secret Water Crisis: National Shutoff Survey Reveals Water Affordability Emergency Affecting Millions*, https://foodandwaterwatch.org/wp-content/uploads/2021/03/rpt_1810_watershutoffs-web2.pdf. Accessed 3 September 2023.

Forster, Laurel (2005), 'Futuristic foodways: The metaphorical meaning of food in science fiction film', in A. Bower (ed.), *Reel Food: Essays on Food and Film*, New York and London: Routledge, pp. 251–66.

Forster, Marc (2013), *World War Z*, DVD, USA: Paramount Pictures.

Fowler, Cary (2016), 'Seeds on ice', *American Scientist*, 104:5, p. 304, https://doi:10.1511/2016.122.304.

Fresnadillo, Juan Carlos (2007), *28 Weeks Later*, DVD, USA: Fox Atomic.

Fresh Kills Park Alliance (2023), 'Home page', freshkillspark.org. Accessed 28 February 2023.

Garrett, Bradley (2021), *Bunker*, London: Penguin.

Gates, Bill (2015), 'This ingenious machine turns feces into drinking water', GatesNotes: The Blog of Bill Gates, 5 January, https://www.gatesnotes.com/Development/Omniprocessor-From-Poop-to-Potable. Accessed 28 February 2023.

George, Rose (2008), *The Big Necessity: The Unmentionable World of Human Waste and Why It Matters*, New York: Henry Holt.

Ghodsee, Kristen (2017), *Red Hangover: Legacies of Twentieth-Century Communism*, Durham: Duke University Press.

Gilliam, Terry (1985), *Brazil*, DVD, USA: Universal Pictures.

Gilliam, Terry (1995), *12 Monkeys*, DVD, USA: Universal Pictures.

Glaser, Paul Michael (1987), *The Running Man*, DVD, USA: TriStar Pictures.

Godfray, Hugh Charles Jonathan, Crute, Ian, Haddad, Lawrence, Lawrence, David, Muir, James, Nisbett, Nicholas, Pretty, Jules, Robinson, Sherman, Toulmin, Camilla and Whitely, Rosalind (2010), 'The future of the global food system', *Philosophical Transactions: Biological Sciences*, 365:1554, pp. 2769–77.

Gordon, Stuart (1992), *Fortress*, DVD, USA: Dimension Films.

Grabell, Michael (2012), 'How not to revive an economy', *New York Times*, 11 February, https://www.nytimes.com/2012/02/12/opinion/sunday/how-the-stimulus-fell-short.html. Accessed 28 February 2023.

Graham-Leigh, Elaine (2015), *A Diet of Austerity: Class, Food and Climate Change*, Winchester: Zer0 Books.

Graham, Steve and Marvin, Simon (2001), *Splintering Urbanism: Networked Infrastructures, Technological Mobilities and the Urban Condition*, London: Routledge.

Hackbarth, Kurt (2022), 'Multinational corporations are sucking Mexico dry', *Jacobin*, 8 July, https://jacobin.com/2022/07/mexico-water-crisis-nuevo-leon-monterrey-garcia-privatization/. Accessed 9 July 2022.

Haddick, Alicia (2022), 'Neptune Frost's radical sci-fi future', *The Verge*, 3 June, Theverge.com/2022/6/2/23059928/Neptune-frost-movie-interview-saul-williams-anisia-uzeyman. Accessed 11 February 2023.

Hambling, David (2017), 'What is an EMP and could North Korea really use one against the US?' *Popular Mechanics*, 28 September, https://www.popularmechanics.com/military/weapons/news/a28425/emp-north-korea/. Accessed 28 February 2023.

Hanson, Matt (2004), *The Science Behind the Fiction: Building Sci-Fi Moviescapes*, Mies: Rotovision.

Hark, Ina Rae and Cohan, Steven (eds) (1997), *The Road Movie Book*, London and New York: Routledge.

Hart, William David (2021), 'Afterlives of slavery: Afrofuturism and Afropessimism as parallax views', *Black Theology*, 19:3, pp. 196–206, https://doi:10.1080/14769948.2021.1990495.

Harvey, David (2001), 'Globalization and the "spatial fix"', *Geographische Revue*, 2, pp. 23–30.

Hassler-Forest, Dan (2017), 'The politics of the Planet of the Apes', *Los Angeles Review of Books*, 26 August, https://lareviewofbooks.org/article/the-politics-of-the-planet-of-the-apes/. Accessed 28 February 2023.

Hatherley, Owen (2018), *The Adventures of Owen Hatherley in the Post-Soviet Space*, London: Repeater.

Hayes, Brian (2005), *Infrastructure: A Field Guide to the Industrial Landscape*, New York: Norton.

Healthdirect (2021), 'Drinking water and your health', https://www.healthdirect.gov.au/drinking-water-and-your-health. Accessed 28 February 2023.

Hewlett, Jamie and Alan Martin (2002), *Tank Girl 1*, London: Titan Books.

Hewlett, Jamie and Alan Martin (2002), *Tank Girl 2*, London: Titan Books.

Hewlett, Jamie and Alan Martin (2002), *Tank Girl 3*, London: Titan Books.

Hillcoat, John (2009), *The Road*, DVD, USA: Dimension Films.

Hoffman, John (1993), *The Art & Science of Dumpster Diving*, Port Townsend WA: Loompanics Unlimited.

Horn, Eva (2018), *The Future as Catastrophe: Imagining Disaster in the Modern Age* (trans. V. Pakis), New York: Columbia University Press.

Horvat, Srećko (2021), *After the Apocalypse*, Cambridge: Polity.

Hughes, Allen and Albert Hughes (2010), *The Book of Eli*, Blu-ray, USA: Warner Bros. Pictures.

Jacobs, Frank (2017), 'What the world will look like 4°C warmer', *BigThink*, 22 May, https://bigthink.com/strange-maps/what-the-world-will-look-like-4degc-warmer/. Accessed 25 February 2023.

James, Colin (1992), *New Territory: The Transformation of New Zealand 1984–1992*, Wellington: Allen & Unwin.

Jewison, Norman (1975), *Rollerball*, DVD, USA: United Artists.

Johnston, Stephen (2017), 'Can President Trump make US infrastructure great again?' *Global Markets*, 7 March, https://milfordasset.com/insights/can-president-trump-make-us-infrastructure-great. Accessed 30 January 2021.

Jones, L. Q. (1975), *A Boy and His Dog*, DVD, USA: Shout! Factory.

Jørgensen, Finn Arne (2019), *Recycling*, Cambridge: MIT Press.

Kaplan, E. Ann (2016), *Climate Trauma: Foreseeing the Future in Dystopian Fiction and Film*, New Brunswick: Rutgers University Press.

Kassovitz, Mathieu (2008), *Babylon AD*, DVD, USA: 20th Century Fox.

Khalili, Laleh (2021), 'Apocalyptic infrastructures', *NOEMA*, 23 March, https://www.noemamag.com/apocalyptic-infrastructures/. Accessed 27 May 2021.

Kosinski, Joseph (2013), *Oblivion*, DVD, USA: Universal Pictures.

Krueger, Katherine (2021), '"The Card Counter' and the sins of a nation', *Defector*, 30 September, https://defector.com/the-card-counter-and-the-sins-of-a-nation/. Accessed 28 February 2023.

Kruszelnicki, Karl (2001), 'EMP – the gentle killer', *ABC Science*, 4 October, http://www.abc.net.au/science/articles/2001/10/04/380431.htm. Accessed 3 January 2021.

Kuhn, Annette (1990), 'Introduction', in A. Kuhn (ed.), *Alien Zone: Cultural Theory and Contemporary Science Fiction Cinema*, London: Verso, pp. 1–10.

Kusama, Karyn (2005), *Aeon Flux*, DVD, USA: Paramount Pictures.

Laderman, David (2002), *Driving Visions: Exploring the Road Movie*, Austin: University of Texas Press.

Larkin, Brian (2008), *Signal and Noise: Media, Infrastructure and Urban Culture in Nigeria*, Durham: Duke University Press.

Larkin, Brian (2013), 'The politics and poetics of infrastructure', *Annual Review of Anthropology*, 42:3, pp. 327–43.

Laurie, Nina (2011), 'Gender water networks: Femininity and masculinity in water politics in Bolivia', *International Journal of Urban and Regional Research*, 35:1, pp. 172–88, https://doi:10.1111/j.1468-2427.2010.00962.x.

Laville, Sandra (2020), 'England's privatised water firms paid £57bn in dividends since 1991', *The Guardian*, 2 July, https://www.theguardian.com/environment/2020/jul/01/england-privatised-water-firms-dividends-shareholders. Accessed 28 February 2023.

Lawrence, Francis (2007), *I Am Legend*, DVD, USA: Warner Bros. Pictures.

Lawrence, Francis (2013), *The Hunger Games: Catching Fire*, DVD, USA: Lionsgate.

Lawrence, Francis (2014), *The Hunger Games: Mockingjay – Part 1*, DVD, USA: Lionsgate.

Lawrence, Francis (2015), *The Hunger Games: Mockingjay – Part 2*, Blu-ray, USA: Lionsgate.

Lefebvre, Martin, (2006), 'Between setting and landscape in the cinema', in M. Lefebvre (ed.), *Landscape and Film*, New York: Routledge, pp. 19–59.

Lerner, Sharon (2020), 'Africa's exploding plastic nightmare', *The Intercept*, 19 April, https://theintercept.com/2020/04/19/africa-plastic-waste-kenya-ethiopia/. Accessed 28 February 2023.

Levine, Caroline (2015), 'The strange familiar': Structure, infrastructure, and Adichie's *Americanah*', *MFS Modern Fiction Studies*, 61:4, pp. 587–605, https://doi:10.1353/mfs.2015.0051.

Levine, Jonathan (2013), *Warm Bodies*, DVD, USA: Lionsgate/Summit.

Lew, Shoshana and Porcari, John (2017), 'Eight years later: What the Recovery Act taught us about investing in transportation', *Brookings.edu*, 22 February, https://www.brookings.edu/blog/the-avenue/2017/02/22/eight-years-later-what-the-recovery-act-taught-us/. Accessed 28 February 2023.

Linklater, Richard. (2006), *A Scanner Darkly*, DVD, USA: Warner Independent Pictures.

Long, Christian B. (2016a), 'Infrastructure after the zombie apocalypse', *Journal of Asia-Pacific Pop Culture*, 1:2, pp. 181–203.

Long, Christian B. (2016b), 'Chase sequences and transport infrastructure in global Hollywood spy films', in J. Anderson and L. Webb (eds), *Global Cinematic Cities: New Landscapes of Film and Media*, New York: Wallflower/Columbia, pp. 235–51.

Longo, Robert (1995), *Johnny Mnemonic*, DVD, USA: TriStar Pictures.

Lonthimos, Yorgos (2015), *The Lobster*, DVD, Australia: Universal Sony Pictures.

Lucas, George (1971), *THX 1138*, DVD, USA: Warner Bros. Pictures.

Luxemburg, Rosa (1951), *The Accumulation of Capital* (trans. A. Schwarzschild), New Haven: Yale University Press.

Maher, Kris and Lucey, Catherine (2022), 'After Pittsburgh bridge collapses, Biden stresses need to invest in infrastructure', *The Wall Street Journal*, 28 January, https://www.wsj.com/articles/pittsburgh-bridge-collapse-frick-park-11643379723. Accessed 28 February 2023.

Malewitz, Raymond (2015), 'Climate-change infrastructure and the volatizing of American regionalism', *MFS Modern Fiction Studies*, 61:4, pp. 715–30, https://doi:10.1353/mfs.2015.0050.

Malm, Andreas (2016), *Fossil Capital: The Rise of Steam Power and the Roots of Global Warming*, London: Verso.

Mandel, Ernest (1980), *Long Waves of Capitalist Development: The Marxist Interpretation*, Cambridge: Cambridge University Press.

Mann, Michael (2021), 'It's not too late for Australia to forestall a dystopian future that alternates between *Mad Max* and *Waterworld*', *The Guardian*, 24 March, https://www.theguardian.com/commentisfree/2021/mar/24/catastrophic-fires-and-devastating-floods-are-part-of-australias-harsh-new-climate-reality. Accessed 24 March 2021.

Manners, Gerald (1966), *The Geography of Energy*, London: Hutchinson University Library.

Mansfield, Becky (2017), 'Privatization: Property and the remaking of nature–society relations: Introduction to the special issue', Special Issue: 'Property and the remaking of nature-society relations', *Antipode*, 39:3, pp. 393–405.

Mantoan, Lindsey (2018), *War as Performance: Conflicts in Iraq and Political Theatricality*, Cham: Palgrave Macmillan/Springer.

Marshall, Kate (2013), *Corridor: Media Architectures in American Fiction*, Minneapolis: University of Minnesota Press.

Martin, Adrian (2003), *The Mad Max Movies*, Strawberry Hills/Canberra: Currency Press/Screensound Australia.

Martin, Theodore (2017), *Contemporary Drift: Genre, Historicism, and the Problem of the Present*, New York: Columbia University Press.

Marty, Jonathan (2021), 'Urban democracy's documentarian', *Public Books*, 23 April, https://www.publicbooks.org/urban-democracys-documentarian/ Accessed 24 April 2021.

Marx, Karl (1845), *The German Ideology*, Marxists Internet Archive Library, https://www.marxists.org/archive/marx/works/1845/german-ideology/ch01a.htm#a4. Accessed 11 February 2023.

McBride, James and Moss, Jessica (2020), 'The state of U.S. infrastructure', *Council on Foreign Relations*, 1 September, https://www.cfr.org/backgrounder/state-us-infrastructure. Accessed 30 January 2021.

McCarthy, Colm (2016), *The Girl with All the Gifts*, DVD, USA: Warner Bros. Pictures.

McKay, Adam (2021), *Don't Look Up*, Streaming, USA: Netflix.

McKibben, Bill (2010), *Eaarth: Making a Life on a Tough New Planet*, New York: Times Books/Henry Holt and Company.

McKie, Robin (2008), 'How the myth of food miles hurts the planet', *The Guardian*, 23 March, https://www.theguardian.com/environment/2008/mar/23/food.ethicalliving. Accessed 28 February 2023.

McMurray, Gerard (2018), *First Purge*, DVD, USA: Universal Pictures.

McNichol, Elizabeth (2019), 'It's time for states to invest in infrastructure', Center on Budget and Policy Priorities, 19 March, https://www.cbpp.org/research/state-budget-and-tax/its-time-for-states-to-invest-in-infrastructure. Accessed 30 January 2021.

McTeigue, James (2005), *V for Vendetta*, DVD, USA: Warner Bros. Pictures.

Meirelles, Fernando (2008), *Blindness*, DVD, USA: Miramax.

Melosi, Martin (2008), *The Sanitary City: Environmental Services in Urban America from Colonial Times to the Present*, Pittsburgh: University of Pittsburgh Press.

Miller, George (1979), *Mad Max*, DVD, USA: Warner Bros. Pictures.

Miller, George (1981), *The Road Warrior*, DVD, USA: Warner Bros. Pictures.

Miller, George (2015), *Mad Max: Fury Road*, DVD, USA: Warner Bros. Pictures.

Miller, George and Ogilvie, George (1985), *Mad Max Beyond Thunderdome*, DVD, USA: Warner Bros. Pictures.

Mills, Bart (1982), 'The Brave new worlds of production design', *American Film January*, 1, pp. 40–46.

Mingardi, Alberto (2018), 'P.T. Bauer and the myth of primitive accumulation', *CATO Journal*, 28 September, https://www.cato.org/cato-journal/fall-2018/p-t-bauer-myth-primitive-accumulation. Accessed 28 February 2023.

Moore, Alan, Lloyd, David, Whitaker, Steve and Dodds, Siobhan (1990), *V for Vendetta*, New York: DC Comics.

Moylan, Tom (2000), *Scraps of the Untainted Sky: Science Fiction, Utopia, Dystopia*, Boulder: Westview.

Muelebach, Andrea (2020), 'Water as right, water as future', *Public Books*, 4 December, https://www.publicbooks.org/water-as-right-water-as-future/. Accessed 28 February 2023.

Mulcahy, Russell (2007), *Resident Evil: Extinction*, DVD, USA: Sony Pictures Releasing.

Murphy, Geoff (1985), *The Quiet Earth*, DVD, New Zealand: Cinepro.

Murray, Stuart (2008), '"Precarious adulthood": Communal anxieties in 1980s film', in I. Conrich and S. Murray (eds), *Contemporary New Zealand Cinema: From New Wave to Blockbuster*, London and New York: IB Taurus, pp. 169–80.

Muschiettti, Andy (2017), *IT*, DVD, USA: New Line.

Neuman, Michael (2006), 'Infiltrating infrastructure: On the nature of networked infrastructure', *Journal of Urban Technology*, 13:1, pp. 3–31, https://doi:10.1080/10630730600752728.

Newbury, Michael (2012), 'Fast zombie / slow zombie: Food writing, horror movies, and agribusiness apocalypse', *American Literary History*, 24:1, pp. 87–114.

Newitz, Annalee (2013), *Scatter, Adapt, and Remember: How Humans Will Survive a Mass Extinction*, Collingwood: Black Inc.

NIAC The President's National Infrastructure Advisory Council (2023), *Cross-Sector Collaboration to Protect Critical Infrastructure: Barriers and Recommendations for Improvement*, https://www.cisa.gov/sites/default/files/2023-05/NIAC_Cross-Sector_Collaboration_to_Protect_Critical_Infrastructure_Report_2023_03_28.pdf. Accessed 3 September 2023.

Niccol, Andrew (1997), *Gattaca*, DVD, USA: Columbia Pictures.

Nichol, Christina (2018), 'An account of my hut', *N+1*, Spring, https://nplusonemag.com/issue-31/essays/an-account-of-my-hut/. Accessed 28 February 2023.

Nolan, Christopher (2014), *Interstellar*, DVD, USA: Paramount Pictures.

Noys, Benjamin (2014), *Malign Velocities: Accelerationism and Capitalism*, Winchester: Zer0 Books.

Nye, David (1999), *American Technological Sublime*, Cambridge: MIT Press.

O'Connell, Mark (2020), 'Notes from an apocalypse', *Tribune*, 16 April, https://tribunemag.co.uk/2020/04/notes-from-an-apocalypse. Accessed 27 February 2023.

O'Donnell, Marcus (2015), '*Children of Men*'s ambient apocalyptic visions', *Journal of Religion and Popular Culture*, 27:1, pp. 16–30.

Orange City Council (2016) 'How long do roads last?' 23 May, https://yoursay.orange.nsw.gov.au/roads/news_feed/how-long-do-roads-last?posted_first=true. Accessed 28 February 2023.

Otter, Chris (2002), 'Making liberalism durable: Vision and civility in the late Victorian city', *Social History*, 27:1, pp. 1–15, https://doi:10.1080/03071020110094174.

Parr, Adrian (2013), *The Wrath of Capital: Neoliberalism and Climate Change Politics*, New York: Columbia University Press.

Pavirtha, Kirubanandam Grace, Rajan, Panneer Selvam Sundar, Dhandapani, Balaji and Gopinath, Kannappan Panchamoorthy (2020), 'Sustainable electronic-waste management: Implications on environmental and human health', in Anish Khan, Inamuddin, and Abdullah Asiri (eds), *E-waste Recycling and Management*, Switzerland: Springer Nature, pp. 201–18.

Pawson, Eric (2010), 'Economy and the environment', TeAra.govt.nz, 11 March, https://teara.govt.nz/en/economy-and-the-environment/print?fbclid=IwAR2fMgT3drx6WdKf2azbo-zQh5_gz5fGX5aVqb5SZLcCH1RPGZ-1RtDXk8RI. Accessed 29 January 2023.

Peebles, Stacey (2017), 'On being between: Apocalypse, adaptation, McCarthy', *European Journal of American Studies*, 12:3, Open Edition, https://doi.org/10.4000/ejas.12283.

Pellow, David Naguib (2004), *Garbage Wars: The Struggle for Environmental Justice in Chicago*, Cambridge: MIT Press.

Perkins, John H. (2018), 'Sustainability and energy services: A framework for discussion', in A. Vasel and D. S-K. Ting (eds), *The Energy Mix for Sustaining Our Future Selected Papers from Proceedings of Energy and Sustainability 2018*, Cham: Springer, pp. 168–81.

Phillips, Kendall (2012), *Dark Directions: Romero, Craven. Carpenter, and the Modern Horror Film*, Carbondale: Southern Illinois University Press.

Pinkerton, Nick (2018), 'Le cinéma du glut', *Film Comment*, May–June, https://www.filmcomment.com/article/le-cinema-du-glut/. Accessed 28 February 2023.

Poe, Jim (2021), 'Today, we're all living in Mad Max's world', *Jacobin*, 9 February, https://jacobinmag.com/2021/02/mad-max-capitalism. Accessed 11 February 2021.

Pope Francis (2015), 'Laudato Si: On the care of our common home', 24 May, https://www.vatican.va/content/francesco/en/encyclicals/documents/papa-francesco_20150524_enciclica-laudato-si.html. Accessed 11 February 2023.

Pope Francis (@Pontifex) (2015), 'The earth, our home, is beginning to look more and more like an immense pile of filth', Twitter, 18 June, https://twitter.com/Pontifex/status/611518771186929664. Accessed 11 February 2023.

Post, Ted (1970), *Beneath the Planet of the Apes*, DVD, USA: 20th Century Fox.

Preston, Ward (1994), *What an Art Director Does: An Introduction to Motion Picture Production Design*, Ann Arbor: University of Michigan Press.

Prorokova, Tatiana (2020), '"Every act of preservation is an act of creation": Paul Schrader's eco-theology in *First Reformed*', in M. Moore and B. Brems (eds), *ReFocus: The Films of Paul Schrader*, Edinburgh: Edinburgh University Press, pp. 171–88.

Proyas, Alex (2004), *I, Robot*, DVD, USA: 20th Century Fox.

Rabin, Nathan (2007), 'My year of flops case file #76 *Strange Days*', *AV Club*, 16 October, https://film.avclub.com/my-year-of-flops-case-file-76-strange-days-1798212726. Accessed 28 February 2023.

Radford, Michael (1984), *1984*, DVD, USA: 20th Century Fox.

Reeves, Matt (2014), *Dawn of the Planet of the Apes*, DVD, USA: 20th Century Fox.

Reeves, Matt (2017), *War for the Planet of the Apes*, DVD, USA: 20th Century Fox.

Reilly, Katie (2016), 'Read President Obama's speech in Flint on water crisis', *TIME*, 4 May, https://time.com/4318909/barack-obama-speech-flint-michigan-transcript/. Accessed 28 February 2023.

Reno, Joshua (2016), *Waste Away: Working and Living with a North American Landfill*, Berkeley: University of California Press.

Retzinger, Jean (2008), 'Speculative visions and imaginary meals: Food and the environment in (post-apocalyptic) science fiction films', *Cultural Studies*, 22:3&4, pp. 369–90, https://doi:10.1080/09502380802012500.

Reynolds, Kevin (1995), *Waterworld*, DVD, USA: Universal Pictures.

Ribera, Robert (2020), 'Leaning on the everlasting arms: Love and silence in *First Reformed*', in M. Moore and B. Brems (eds), *ReFocus: The Films of Paul Schrader*, Edinburgh: Edinburgh University Press, pp. 189–206.

Rice, J.B. and Caniato, F. (2003), *Supply Chain Response to Terrorism: Creating Resilient and Secure Supply Chains, Interim Report of Progress and Learnings*, DSpace@MIT, http://web.mit.edu/scresponse/repository/euroma_presentation.pdf. Accessed 27 February 2023.

Riley, Boots (2018), *Sorry to Bother You*, DVD, USA: Focus Features.

Ritchie, Hannah (2019), 'Which countries eat the most meat?' BBC.com, 4 February, https://www.bbc.com/news/health-47057341. Accessed 11 February 2023.

Robbins, Bruce (2007), 'The smell of infrastructure', *Boundary 2*, 34:1, pp. 25–33.

Roberts, Adrienne (2008), 'Privatizing social reproduction: The primitive accumulation of water in an era of neoliberalism', *Antipode*, 40:4, pp. 535–60, https://doi:10.1111/j.1467-8330.2008.00623.x.

Robinson, Jennifer (2010), 'Living in dystopia: Past, present, and future in contemporary African cities', in G. Prakash (ed.), *Noir Urbanisms: Dystopic Images of the Modern City*, Princeton: Princeton University Press, pp. 218–40.

Rodney, Walter (2018), *How Europe Underdeveloped Africa*, London: Verso.

Rogers, Heather (2013), *Gone Tomorrow: The Hidden Life of Garbage*, New York: The New Press.

Romanek, Mark (2010), *Never Let Me Go*, DVD, USA: Fox Searchlight Pictures.

Romero, George (1978), *Dawn of the Dead*, DVD, USA: United Film Distribution.

Romero, George (1985), *Day of the Dead*, DVD, USA: United Film Distribution.

Romero, George (2005), *Land of the Dead*, DVD, USA: Universal Pictures.

Ross, Andrew (1996), *Strange Weather: Culture, Science and Technology in the Age of Limits*, London: Verso.

Ross, Gary (2012), *The Hunger Games*, DVD, USA: Lionsgate.

Rotherham, Scott (2020), 'Water supply in the UK – 5 facts about our water and the network behind It', Piperepair.co.uk, 9 December, https://piperepair.co.uk/2020/12/09/water-supply-in-the-uk-5-facts-about-our-water-and-the-network-behind-it/. Accessed 28 February 2023.

Rothstein, Adam (2015), 'How to see infrastructure: A guide for seven billion primates', *Rhizome*, 2 July, https://rhizome.org/editorial/2015/jul/2/how-see-infrastructure-guide-seven-billion-primate/. Accessed 28 February 2023.

Rubenstein, Michael (2010), *Public Works: Infrastructure, Irish Modernism, and the Postcolonial*, South Bend: Notre Dame University Press.

Rubenstein, Michael, Robbins, Bruce and Beal, Sophia (2015), 'Infrastructuralism: An introduction', *MFS Modern Fiction Studies*, 61:4, pp. 575–86, https://doi:10.1353/mfs.2015.0049.

Russell, Andrew and Vinsel, Lee (2016), 'Hail the maintainers', *Aeon*, 7 April, https://aeon.co/essays/innovation-is-overvalued-maintenance-often-matters-more. Accessed 27 February 2013.

Ryan, Michael and Kellner, Douglas (2004), 'Technophobia/Dystopia', in S. Raymond (ed.), *Liquid Metal: The Science Fiction Film Reader*, London: Wallflower, pp. 48–56.

Sagal, Boris (1971), *The Omega Man*, DVD, USA: Warner Bros. Pictures.

Santos, Milton (2021), *For a New Geography* (trans. A. Davies), Minneapolis: University of Minnesota Press.

Saxon, Kurt (1976), 'The Survivor. Vol. 1 (1976). Self-published zine', The Internet Archive, 26 September 2016, Archive.org/details/THESURVIVOR/mode/2up. Accessed 4 February 2023.

Scanlon, John (2005), *On Garbage*, Chicago: University of Chicago Press.

Scranton, Roy (2019), 'We broke the world', *The Baffler*, 47, pp. 86–93.

Schaffner, Franklin (1968), *Planet of the Apes*, DVD, USA: 20th Century Fox.

Schlondorff, Volker (1990), *The Handmaid's Tale*, DVD, USA: Cinecom Pictures.

Schmidt, Christopher, 'Why are dystopian films on the rise again?' *JSTOR Daily*, 19 November, https://daily.jstor.org/why-are-dystopian-films-on-the-rise-again/. Accessed 28 February 2023.

Schrader, Paul (2017), *First Reformed*, DVD, USA: A24.

Schrader, Paul (2021), *The Card Counter*, DVD, Australia: Universal Sony.

Schwentke, Robert (2014), *Insurgent*, DVD, USA: Lionsgate.

Schwentke, Robert (2016), *Allegiant*, DVD, USA: Lionsgate.

Scott, Ridley (1982), *Blade Runner*, DVD, USA: Warner Bros. Pictures.

Sergeant, Alexander (2021), *Encountering the Impossible: The Fantastic in Hollywood Fantasy Cinema*, Albany: SUNY Press.

Servigne, Pablo, Stevens, Raphaël and Chapelle, Gauthier (2021), *Another End of the World Is Possible. Living the Collapse (and Not Merely Surviving It)* (trans. G. Samuel), Cambridge: Polity.

Shyamalan, M. Night (2013), *After Earth*, DVD, USA: Sony Pictures Releasing.

Singer, Marc (2004), *Dark Days*, DVD, Australia: Madman Entertainment.

Snyder, Zack (2004), *Dawn of the Dead*, DVD, USA: Universal Pictures.

Sobchack, Vivian (1990), 'The virginity of astronauts: Sex and science fiction film', in A. Kuhn (ed.), *Alien Zone: Cultural Theory and Contemporary Science Fiction Cinema*, London: Verso, pp. 103–20.

Sosna, Daniel (2016), 'Heterotopias behind the fence: Landfills as relational emplacements', in L. Brunclikova (ed.), *Archaeologies of Waste: Encounters with the Unwanted*, Barnsley: Oxbow Books, pp. 162–78.

Sosna, Daniel and Brunclikova, Lenka (2016), 'Introduction', in L. Brunclikova (ed.), *Archaeologies of Waste: Encounters with the Unwanted*, Barnsley: Oxbow Books, pp. 1–13.

Spielberg, Steven (2002), *Minority Report*, DVD, USA: 20th Century Fox.

Spielberg, Steven (2018), *Ready Player One*, DVD, USA: Warner Bros. Pictures.

Sponsler, Claire (1993), 'Beyond the ruins: The geopolitics of decay and cybernetic play', *Science Fiction Studies*, 20:2, pp. 251–65.

Spufford, Francis (2010), *Red Plenty: Inside the Fifties' Soviet Dream*, London: Faber and faber.

Staiger, Janet (1999), 'Future noir: Contemporary representations of visionary cities', in A. Kuhn (ed.), *Alien Zone II: The Spaces of Science-Fiction Cinema*, London: Verso, pp. 97–122.

Stanton, Andrew (2008), *Wall-E*, DVD, USA: Walt Disney Studios Motion Pictures.

Starosielski, Nicole (2015), *The Undersea Network: Sign, Storage, Transmission*, Durham: Duke University Press.

Starr, Susan Leigh (1999), 'The ethnography of infrastructure', *American Behavioral Scientist*, 43:3, pp. 377–91.

Stoll, Steven (2017), *Ramp Hollow: The Ordeal of Appalachia*, New York: Hill and Wang.

Stout, James (2020), 'A brief history of the Molotov cocktail', *Huck*, 21 October, https://www.huckmag.com/perspectives/a-brief-history-of-the-molotov-cocktail/. Accessed 28 February 2023.

Strasser, Susan (2014), *Waste and Want: A Social History of Trash*, New York: Macmillan.

Stratton, Billy J. (2014), '"Everything depends on reaching the coast": Placelessness in John Hillcoat's Adaptation of *The Road*', *Arizona Quarterly*, 70:4, pp. 85–107.

Sublette, Cammie M. (2016), 'The last Twinkie in the universe: Culinary hedonism and nostalgia in zombie films', in J. Martin and C.M. Sublette (eds), *Devouring Cultures: Perspectives on Food, Power, and Identity from the Zombie Apocalypse to Downton Abbey*, Little Rock: University of Arkansas Press, pp.165–79.

Talalay, Rachel (1995), *Tank Girl*, DVD, USA: MGM/UA Distribution Company.

Tansey, Geoff and Worsley, Tony (1997), *The Food System: A Guide*, London: earthscan.

Tashiro, C. S. (1998), *Pretty Pictures: Production Design and the History of Film*, Austin: University of Texas Press.

Taylor, Charles (2004), *Modern Social Imaginaries*, Durham: Duke University Press.

Teague, Lewis (1980), *Alligator*, DVD, USA: Lionsgate.

Their, Hadas (2022), 'Capital's muddy waters' *Jacobin*, 45, pp. 153–60.

Tischleder, Babette (2016), 'Earth according to Pixar: Picturing obsolescence in the age of digital (re)animation', in C. Gersdorf and J. Braun (eds), *America After Nature: Democracy, Culture, Environment*, Heidelberg: Winter Universitätsverlag, pp. 441–60.

Torchin, Leshu (2019), 'Alienated labor's hybrid subjects: *Sorry to Both You* and the tradition of the economic rights film', *Film Quarterly*, 72:4, pp. 29–37.

Travis, Pete (2012), *Dredd*, DVD, USA: Lionsgate.

Tremblay, Jean-Thomas and Swarbick, Steven (2021), 'Destructive environmentalism: The queer impossibility of *First Reformed*', *Discourse*, 43:1, pp. 3–30.

TRIP (2020), 'Restoring the interstate highway system: Meeting America's transportation needs with a reliable, safe & well-maintained national highway network', 1 July, https://tripnet.org/wp-content/uploads/2020/07/TRIP_Interstate_Report_2020.pdf. Accessed 28 February 2023.

Trumbull, Douglas (1972), *Silent Running*, DVD, USA: Universal.

Tsoneva, Jana (2020), 'How Europe's "trash market" offloads pollution on its poorest countries', *Jacobin*, 13 June, https://jacobinmag.com/2020/06/european-union-green-new-deal-garbage-waste. Accessed 28 February 2023.

Tudge, Colin (2004), *So Shall We Reap: What's Gone Wrong with the World's Food – and How to Fix it*, London: Penguin.

UK Department of Transport (2020), 'National statistics: Road lengths in Great Britain', 4 February, https://www.gov.uk/government/statistics/road-lengths-in-great-britain-2020/road-lengths-in-great-britain-2020. Accessed 28 February 2023.

United States Department of Agriculture Economic Research Service (1999), 'Food consumption: Red meat, poultry, and fish', https://www.ers.usda.gov/webdocs/publications/47097/14802_sb965f_1_.pdf?v=0. Accessed 28 February 2023.

United States Department of Agriculture Economic Research Service (2022), 'Farm labor', 15 March, https://www.ers.usda.gov/topics/farm-economy/farm-labor/. Accessed 5 February 2023.

United States Environmental Protection Agency (2022a), 'Cleaning up electronic waste (W-Waste)', 15 November, https://www.epa.gov/international-cooperation/cleaning-electronic-waste-e-waste. Accessed 28 February 2023.

United States Environmental Protection Agency (2022b), 'Plastics: Material-specific data', 3 December, https://www.epa.gov/facts-and-figures-about-materials-waste-and-recycling/plastics-material-specific-data#:~:text=While%20overall%20the%20amount%20of,plastic%20containers%20is%20more%20significant. Accessed 28 February 2023.

United States Environmental Protection Agency (n.d.a), 'Vocabulary catalog: Environmental issues terms & acronyms', https://sor.epa.gov/sor_internet/registry/termreg/searchandretrieve/home.do. Accessed 28 February 2023.

United States Environmental Protection Agency (n.d.b), 'Examples of operation & maintenance tasks', 30 July, https://www.epa.gov/sites/production/files/documents/om_checklisttasks.pdf. Accessed 28 January 2023.

United States Geological Survey (2019), 'Irrigation water use', 1 March, https://www.usgs.gov/mission-areas/water-resources/science/irrigation-water-use?qt-science_center_objects=0#qt-science_center_objects. Accessed 13 April 2020.

US Bureau of Labor Statistics (2016), 'The life of American workers in 1915', 1 February, https://www.bls.gov/opub/mlr/2016/article/the-life-of-american-workers-in-1915.htm/. Accessed 4 February 2023.

US Census Bureau (2022a), 'Quick facts: Grosse Point city, Michigan', https://www.census.gov/quickfacts/grossepointecitymichigan. Accessed 28 February 2023.

US Census Bureau (2022b), 'Quick facts: Flint city, Michigan', https://www.census.gov/quickfacts/flintcitymichigan. Accessed 28 February 2023.

US Department of Agriculture (n.d.), 'Why should we care about food waste?' https://www.usda.gov/foodlossandwaste/why. Accessed 20 August 2023.

US Energy Information Administration (2020), 'Weekly New York midgrade reformulated retail gasoline prices', 13 April, https://www.eia.gov/dnav/pet/hist/LeafHandler.ashx?n=–PET&s=EMM_EPMMR_PTE_SNY_DPG&f=W. Accessed 30 January 2021.

US Energy Information Administration (2021), 'Frequently asked questions: How much tax do we pay on a gallon of gasoline and on a gallon of diesel fuel?' https://www.eia.gov/tools/faqs/faq.php?id=10&t=10. Accessed 30 January 2021.

US Environmental Protection Agency (2016), 'Wastes – non-hazardous waste – municipal solid Waste', https://archive.epa.gov/epawaste/nonhaz/municipal/web/html/. Accessed 28 February 2023.

US Food & Drug Administration (2018), 'Food defect level handbook', 7 September, https://www.fda.gov/food/ingredients-additives-gras-packaging-guidance-documents-regulatory-information/food-defect-levels-handbook. Accessed 28 February 2023.

Vaish, Barkha, Sharma, Bhavisha, Singh, Pooja and Singh, Rajeev Pratap (2020), 'E-waste and their implications on the environment and human health', in Anish Khan and Abdullah M. Asiri (eds), *E-waste Recycling and Management*, Switzerland: Springer Nature, pp. 219–32.

Verhoeven, Paul (1987), *Robocop*, DVD, USA: Orion Pictures.

Verhoeven, Paul (1990), *Total Recall*, DVD, USA: Carolco Pictures.

Via Campesina (2018), *Food Sovereignty Now!: A Guide to Food Sovereignty*, Brussels: ECVC.

Villeneuve, Denis (2017), *Blade Runner 2049*, DVD, USA: Warner Bros. Pictures.

Wachowski, Lana and Wachowski, Lilly (1999), *The Matrix*, DVD, USA: Warner Bros. Pictures.

Wachowski, Lana and Wachowski, Lilly (2003), *The Matrix Reloaded*, DVD, USA: Warner Bros. Pictures.

Wachowski, Lana and Wachowski, Lilly (2003), *The Matrix Revolutions*, DVD, USA: Warner Bros. Pictures.

Wallender, Lee (2017), 'Planet of the Apes (1968) set design', Invisiblethemepark.com, 10 July, https://www.invisiblethemepark.com/2017/07/planet-of-the-apes-set-design-1968/. Accessed 28 February 2023.

Waste Paper Trade (2021), 'EN643 list of European standard types of waste paper', https://www.wpt-nl.com/en/en643-list-of-waste-paper-grades/. Accessed 4 July 2021.

Water UK (2019), '30 years of progress: Cleaner, safer, better water', Water UK Blog, 5 July, https://www.water.org.uk/news-item/30-years-of-progress-cleaner-safer-better-water/. Accessed 30 October 2021.

Water UK (2019), 'Thirty years on, what has water privatisation achieved?' Water UK Blog, 18 July, https://www.water.org.uk/blog-post/thirty-years-on-what-has-water-privatisation-achieved/. Accessed 30 October 2021.

Wegner, Phillip (2003), 'Where the prospective horizon is omitted: Naturalism and dystopia in *Fight Club* and *Ghost Dog*', in R. Baccolini and T. Moylan (eds), *Dark Horizons: Science Fiction and the Dystopian Imagination*, New York and London: Routledge, pp.167–86.

Weik von Mossner, Alexa (2012), 'Afraid of the dark and the light: Visceralizing ecocide in *The Road* and *Hell*', *Ecozono*, 3:2,pp. 42–56.

Weisman, Alan (2007), *The World Without Us*, New York: Thomas Dunne/St Martin's.

Wellington Higher Courts Reporter (2021), 'Appeals against water bottling consents confront Environment Canterbury processes', *Stuff.co.nz*, 17 August, https://www.stuff.co.nz/the-press/business/126096350/appeals-against-water-bottling-consents-confront-environment-canterbury-processes. Accessed 11 February 2023.

White, Kyle (2020), 'Against crisis epistemology' in B. Hokowhitu, A. Moreton-Robinson, L. Tuhiwai-Smith, C. Andersen and S. Larkin (eds), *The Routledge Handbook of Critical Indigenous Studies*, 1st ed., New York: Routledge, pp. 52–64.

Wilde, Cornel (1970), *No Blade of Grass*, DVD, USA: Warner/Allied Vaughn.

Williams, Evan Calder (2011), *Combined and Uneven Apocalypse*, Winchester: Zer0 Books.

Williams, Raymond (1980), 'Beyond actually existing socialism', *New Left Review*, March/April, https://newleftreview-org.ezproxy.library.uq.edu.au/issues/i120/articles/raymond-williams-beyond-actually-existing-socialism. Accessed 27 May 2021.

Williams, Saul and Anisia Uzeyman (2021), *Neptune Frost*, Digital, USA: Kino Lorber.

Wills, Matthew (2021), 'The permanent crisis of infrastructure', JSTOR Daily, 12 August, https://daily.jstor.org/the-permanent-crisis-of-infrastructure/. Accessed 28 February 2023.

Wilson, Ara (2016), 'The infrastructure of intimacy', *Signs: A Journal of Women in Culture and Society*, 41:2, pp. 1–34, https://doi:0097-9740/2016/4102-0001S10.00.

Winterbottom, Michael (2003), *Code 46*, DVD, USA: MGM.

Witt, Alexander (2004), *Resident Evil: Apocalypse*, DVD, USA: Sony Pictures Releasing.

Woetzel, Jonathan, Garemo, Nicklas, Mischke, Jan, Hjerpe, Martin and Palter, Robert (2016), 'Bridging global infrastructure gaps', McKinsey Global Institute, https://www.mckinsey.com/business-functions/operations/our-insights/bridging-global-infrastructure-gaps. Accessed 28 February 2023.

Wolf, Mark J. P. (2012), *Building Imaginary Worlds: The Theory and History of Subcreation*, London: Routledge.

Wolf-Meyer, Matthew (2019), *Theory for the World to Come: Speculative Fiction and Apocalyptic Anthropology*, Minneapolis: University of Minnesota Press.

Wolfe, Gary (2011), *Evaporating Genres: Essays on Fantastic Literature*, Middletown: Wesleyan University Press.

Wood, Robin (2003), *Hollywood from Vietnam to Reagan… and Beyond*, New York: Columbia University Press.

World Bank (2021a), 'Employment in agriculture (% of total employment) (modelled ILO estimate) – India', 1 January, https://data.worldbank.org/indicator/SL.AGR.EMPL.ZS?locations=IN. Accessed 5 February 2023.

World Bank (2021b), 'The World Bank in DRC', 2 April, https://worldbank.org/en/country/drc/overview. Accessed 7 February 2023.

Wright, Edgar (2004), *Shaun of the Dead*, DVD, Australia, Universal Sony Pictures.

Wyatt, Rupert (2011), *Rise of the Planet of the Apes*, DVD, USA: 20th Century Fox.

Yaeger, Patricia (2007), 'Introduction: Dreaming of infrastructure', *PMLA*, 122:1, pp. 9–26.

Yarmuth, John (2019), 'Strong infrastructure and a healthy economy require federal investment', House Committee on the Budget, 22 October, https://budget.house.gov/publications/report/strong-infrastructure-and-healthy-economy-require-federal-investment. Accessed 30 January 2021.

Zemeckis, Robert (2000), *Cast Away*, DVD, USA: 20th Century Fox.

Žižek, Slavoj (1997), *The Plague of Fantasies*, London: Verso.

Žižek, Slavoj (2004), 'Knee-deep', *London Review of Books*, 2 September, https://www.lrb.co.uk/the-paper/v26/n17/slavoj-zizek/knee-deep. Accessed 28 February 2023.

Index

Page numbers in italics indicate images.